COUNTERFEIT
JUSTICE

COUNTERFEIT JUSTICE

THE ROGER BRINKMAN SERIES
#2

TIM W. JAMES

IRON SPIKE
PRESS

Jackson, WY

For permission requests, write to the publisher, addressed
Attention: Permissions Coordinator
Sastrugi Press, P.O. Box 1297, Jackson, WY 83001, United States.
www.sastrugipress.com

Library of Congress Cataloging-in-Publication Data available

ISBN-13: 978-1-64922-295-4 (Paperback)

Cover design Copyright © Sastrugi Press LLC.

Iron Spike Press is an imprint of Sastrugi Press LLC.

10 9 8 7 6 5 4 3

This book is dedicated to my parents, Merritt and Dorothy Linsdau.

Although Dad was skilled and Mom resourceful, we lived modestly but well. They brought us up in a Christian home filled with love for all and discipline. Not harsh discipline, but the kind that teaches and never threatens.

For most of my youth, we lived in Wyoming. Its nickname is Wonderful Wyoming, but it was more a state of wonder than wonderful. The winters are cold and the wind would blow snow up my pantlegs to the kneecaps when walking home from school.

But summers visiting Jackson Hole, the Tetons, and Yellowstone Park inspired my adventure stories of the Wild West. Had we lived during an earlier time, we could well have been the Brinkmans.

All my love,
Tim W. James

Chapter 1
A Pirate's Plot in Mexico

The distant rumble of the surf could be heard in the distance through the open door of the cantina. The air was calm and the landscape around Campeche, located on the eastern coast of Mexico's Yucatan Peninsula, was in bloom following the winter rains. A gentle breeze circulated through windows, as unprotected as the doorway.

A man in his late fifties sat at a table near the back of the establishment. He was dressed in a three-piece suit, white with gold trim on his waistcoat. His matching sombrero hung on a pegboard attached to the wall behind him. He sat sipping on a warm margarita eyeing a man across the room from his table.

"Who is that man, Enrico?" said the older man, speaking Spanish.

"You mean the one sitting below the window by the door?" Enrico asked in the same language.

"Si," said the gentleman.

"They say he is a former pirate," Enrico replied. "Visitors are intrigued by his dress. They say the patch over his eye is fake and he straps up his leg so he can wear the wooden one. The parrot on his shoulder is real, however."

"Ask him if he would like to join us," the gentleman said, continuing to gaze at the man under the window near the door.

"Si, Señor," Enrico replied, rising from his chair and approaching the customer uniquely dressed as a buccaneer.

Enrico Pasqual Peralta reached the table and leaned over to talk to the man with the eyepatch. Enrico noticed the man's uncovered eye was also trained on his companion across the room. After an exchange of words, Enrico returned to his table.

"He said he does not want to relocate," Enrico said. "But said you are welcome to join him at his table."

The elder gentleman in the white suit slowly turned to look at Enrico and nodded. He rose from his chair, retrieved his sombrero and placed it on his graying head. The two crossed the room to where the pirate's companion was positioning two chairs for the visitors.

"Welcome, mi amigos," said the man seated by the window, speaking Spanish. He swept his arm across the table in a gesture to present the seats to his visitors. "Paco has graciously set you a chair. You don't mind that he joins us, do you?"

"Not at all," the gentleman responded. "This is Enrico, my trusted companion and valet. He will be joining us too."

As the three men took a seat, the man perched under the parrot continued to speak.

"I am Captain Cutlass Baudelaire. Paco here is my first mate, though we do not spend a lot of time on the open seas these days."

"Pleased to meet you, Captain," the elder man said, removing his sombrero. "I am Victor Giles. I live in the Hacienda Real located above town."

"Then you would be King Victor. I have heard of you," Cutlass said. "I have often admired your fine estate."

"Allow me to freshen our drinks," Victor said. "Enrico, would you inform the waitress we would like drinks all around?"

"Thank you, Señor Victor," Cutlass said. "I and Paco would each have a pint of rum.

"Now, Señor Victor, you wanted to speak to me?"

"I do, Captain Cutlass. Now I assume, because of your attire, that you have some connection to pirating. Or is this just a costume?"

"Oh no, I assure you, Señor Victor, my attire is not just for show. However, I don't mind the attention it attracts, and I do like to talk about the days gone by," Cutlass said.

"I am under the impression that the art of buccaneering is still practiced," Victor said.

"Oh, indeed but I am a throwback to Jean Lafitte," Cutlass said with a broad smile. "I was just a cabin boy when he was driven from Texas. That is how I ended up here. I think Lafitte returned to France."

"So, what do you do now?" Victor said, probing for more information.

"Let's just say, working for Lafitte was quite lucrative and I did not give up the trade when Lafitte departed. Paco and I live quite comfortably now, but I could not leave the sea entirely. It is lovely here, don't you think, Señor Victor?"

"It is now my home and I, too, have given up my past trade and live comfortably," Victor said. "However, I have not lost my spirit of adventure, if you know what I mean."

The waitress served the men their drinks, and Cutlass consumed a good deal of his rum in one swallow. He wiped the back of his hand across his mouth while putting the goblet back down.

"I am not sure, Señor Victor," Cutlass started. "I too love adventure, but my fine ship, the Tiburon, has been in, how you say, 'mothballs.'"

"You still have your ship, then?" Victor continued to probe. "Do you ever feel like setting her sails and putting the Tiburon out to sea again?" Victor took a drink of his margarita, while continuing to watch Cutlass's expression.

"Awk, out to sea," the parrot chimed in.

"It looks like maybe your bird would like to set sail again, too," Enrico said, laughing.

"Ahh, Maggie, she talks too much and dreams of days long ago," Cutlass answered. "Her kind lives long, and she does love the sea."

"What would it take to make the Tiburon seaworthy again?" Victor asked, fingering the stem of his margarita glass.

"Are ya wanting to take a cruise?" Cutlass said, leaning forward on the table. "For the right price, I could get her ready to sail in less than a month."

"I'm pleased to hear you say that, Captain, but it's not a cruise I'm in search of," Victor replied, staring into Cutlass's uncovered eye.

"Really?" hesitating as he was about to take another swig of rum.

"What would you be wanting her for?"

"Let's just say I know where there is real treasure to be had, but it would require a sailing vessel," Victor offered. "An experienced captain and a few… let's just say, 'pirates'… would be needed as well."

"Treasure, you say," Cutlass said, locking his eye onto Victor after casting a glance at Paco. "I'm not much for diggin' or divin' if that's what you have in mind."

"No, this would be similar to your old line of work," Victor started, "but I've said too much already. Why don't you and your first mate join me for dinner at the hacienda sometime, and we can discuss it further."

"We would be honored to accept your invitation, King Victor. "As for raising the Jolly Roger on the Tiburon again, …" Cutlass paused to laugh, "I will have to think that one over."

"Excellent," Victor said, finishing his margarita. "How shall I get in touch with you?"

"Just leave word for me here at the cantina," Cutlass instructed. "It will reach me soon enough."

"Awk, raise the Jolly Roger," Maggie squawked.

"Oh, and bring Maggie too," Victor said. "I like her enthusiasm."

The men enjoyed a laugh, as Victor and Enrico shook the hands of the two men and left the cantina.

"What do you think, Paco?" Baudelaire said, turning to his companion and lifting his eyepatch to expose a second perfectly good eye.

"It is intriguing what Señor Victor proposes, but navies are more sophisticated than they were years ago," Enrico answered.

"I think it depends on what King Victor has in mind. If it requires sacking and pillaging, I'm afraid I'm not up to that anymore," said the former pirate, finishing his goblet of rum, and removing his finger to allow the patch to fall over his eye once again. "But I never met a naval captain I couldn't outsmart. Now let's get out of here, my leg is beginning to cramp up."

***

Victor's carriage was the finest in Campeche. Enrico took his place on the driver's seat while Kensington climbed into the back. Once they reached the hacienda, Enrico halted the horses and turned to the judge.

"Do you really think that old pirate could pull off this job?" he asked in English.

"I don't know about that. He's an old fraud, but he has a ship and rumor has it that he was quite a swashbuckler in his day, former judge Victor Giles Kensington said. "But I intend to let my boys take care of what he can't. I think that new bank in Galveston, Texas, could be in for a big surprise."

Chapter 2
Fort McRae

"I appreciate you folks looking after Brinker II while I'm gone," Pastor Roger Brinkman called out to Paul Zimmerman. Roger was giving the horse one last brushing before he departed for Fort McRae.

"It's no trouble at all, Pastor," Zimmerman called back, as he pitchforked hay into the stall that would house the animal in Roger's absence. "It's no small thing to be traveling to Galveston to baptize your brother.

"You say he would have been a slave if you're father had not rescued him?"

"More than likely, he was just a lad around ten years old and was among a number of captured Africans brought to America by slave traders. None of his relatives was among them," Roger added, as he put down the brush and grabbed Brinker II's halter. He gazed into the horse's eyes while stroking the animal's bald face.

"I'm going to miss you, boy," he murmured as he turned to lead him in the direction of the stall where Paul was standing.

"You say the U.S. Army has offered to include you in a cavalry patrol headed east?" Paul remarked as Roger passed by leading Brinker into the stall.

"It's a patrol being led by Major George Trundell, someone I met a few years back," Roger answered. "I mentioned to him I was planning a trip back to Texas, and he offered to take me as far as the Pecos River. The army is moving troops to Fort Stockton, so I'll have good company for that part of my trip." Roger removed

Brinker's halter and stepped out of the stall.

"Well, we're sure going to miss you, Pastor," Paul said. "But don't you worry. Me and the other elders will keep the circuit going until you get back."

"Paul, you've been a Godsend. Riding this circuit has been a great experience, but I could never have pulled this together without you and the others."

The two men left the barn and walked back to the house where Peter Zimmerman had the wagon waiting to transport Roger to Fort McRae.

"Peter will take you to Fort McRae. I assume the army is supplying you with a horse, and you've got all your supplies in the wagon," Paul said.

"You assume correctly," Roger replied as he approached the wagon. "I'll have use of the military horse until we reach Fort Stockton."

"Sally packed a basket of food to eat along the way," Paul said. "There's one thing we don't do around here and that's to go hungry. "There's a slice of berry pie in there as well."

"It's a good thing I'm on the road most of the time," Roger said, chuckling. "If I hung around here for long I'd weigh too much for Brinker to carry."

Sally, Andrew, and Matthew came out of the house to bid Roger goodbye.

"Sally, I swear, nobody takes better care of me than you folks every time I visit," Roger said with a broad smile.

"That's because you acquaint 'care' with my cookin'," Sally said, returning Roger's laugh. Roger gave Sally a hug and then shook the hands of Paul and his two boys. Roger climbed into the wagon and soon he and Peter were on their way to Fort McRae.

Roger had grown to love the open country of New Mexico's high desert, but he did miss the rolling, tree-lined hills of Missouri. The soil in New Mexico could not match the fertility of Missouri's, but the skills of Mexican farmers turned these seeming wastelands into fields of bountiful crops.

Roger marveled at the fare Sally prepared, as he picked his way through her basket of food. He spotted the pieces of pie but put aside the temptation in favor of a venison sandwich.

Game animals were plentiful in New Mexico and for good reason – hunters were few and far between. Cattle ranching was on the rise, but supplementing the dinner entre with wild meat was common. There were also a few buffalo herds that crisscrossed the southern border separating Mexico from the New Mexico Territory.

"Can I get you something from this goodie basket?" Roger asked turning to Peter.

"No thanks, not now, Pastor Brinkman. I may have something before I start back. So, help yourself to whatever you want. There's plenty more of that when I get home."

"Suit yourself. I will try to leave something for you," Roger said laughingly.

"I know you're a fine preacher and all, Pastor Brinkman, but you don't talk much about your past as a lawman and soldier," Peter said, changing the conversation. "Do you not like to talk about those things?"

"No, Peter, I don't mind talking about them, but it really isn't the best opening line of a sermon to say you shot somebody," Roger replied thoughtfully, recalling one of his previous visits to the Zimmerman home. "I need to gain people's respect as a preacher of the faith, not the law. Although, I carry no shame for what I did before I began my ministry. It's just not in the forefront of what I do know."

"I guess I can understand that," Peter said. "But Matthew, Andrew and I often wonder what life was like for you before you became a traveling preacher."

"I can tell you I never lost my love of the Lord during those times," Roger responded, as he gazed at the distant mountains running parallel to the road. He turned and looked at Peter. "I was troubled that the Lord may have lost His love for me when I found myself in certain situations. But I came to realize I'm really no different than anyone else. Preaching just happens to be what I do now."

"What was it like being a soldier…, if you don't mind my asking?" Peter continued, turning to return Roger's gaze.

"Nothing wrong with being a soldier, Peter," Roger said, "but war is hell. I don't mean to be crude, but soldiering comes with a heavy responsibility. Most who chose that profession are brave and courageous men but they sometimes have to carry a burden much greater than those unwilling to wear the uniform. Soldiers can be called upon to perform heroic acts, while never being considered a hero for doing it."

"I guess it's not as glamorous as some books would have you think," Peter remarked.

"Funny, for as long as I was a soldier the world 'glamor' never crossed my mind," Roger said. "But I can honestly say that making the first part of this trip in the company of soldiers is a very comforting thought for me."

"Was marshaling a lot different? You don't have to answer if you don't want to," Peter said, turning to look straight ahead.

"Marshaling is considerably different," Roger answered. "You're on your own way more than when you're a soldier. "I can't remember ever having more than one other lawman at my side when things got serious, and much of the time I was acting on my own."

"Wow, sounds exciting," Peter said, smiling but noticing Roger wasn't. "I'm sorry, I guess I misspoke."

"Not at all," Roger replied. "I read books that made me think that being a lawman was exciting, but reality is a different story. Now, I tend to use the word fear, rather than exciting, when talking about it."

"There were times when you were afraid?" Peter asked, again turning to look straight ahead and directing the horses off the road. Peter steered onto a wide trail the soldiers used when traveling to and from Fort McRae.

"Yeah, there were, but to be a good lawman you cannot let fear be your guide," Roger said. "A lawman who can turn his fears into appropriate action without drawing his gun each time is my definition of a good lawman."

The ramparts of Fort McRae were now coming into view. Peter thought for a moment and then responded, "Thanks for talking to me, Pastor Brinkman. We don't get to learn about such things out here."

"Let the Bible and your conscience be your guides, Peter," Roger said. "I just hope you follow in your father's footsteps like I eventually did. I think your folks would like to see you do that without taking the long way around as I did."

The two entered the fort grounds, and Peter pulled the wagon up in front of the officers' quarters. Sergeant Chuck Braxton walked out onto the boardwalk in front of the office and greeted the pair.

"Welcome, Pastor, and who do we have here," he said, looking over at Peter.

"He's the son of Paul Zimmerman, one of my top elders. I'm sure you've met him," Roger responded, removing his travel bag, saddlebags, and bedroll. "Peter's the boy's name, although he's nearly a man now."

"Welcome, Peter," the sergeant responded. Chuck Braxton was one of the Buffalo Soldiers assigned to the 9th Cavalry. He had served as an elder at the post for Roger, but was listed among the soldiers who would be transferring to Fort Stockton. "Would you like me to show you around the fort?"

"Oh no, sir, but thank you, sir," Peter said. "I have to be getting back home or my Ma will worry."

"I understand, son," the sergeant replied. "You tell your folks hello, from Fort McRae, okay?"

"Yes, sir. I will do that," Peter said. "Do you have everything, Pastor Brinkman?"

"I've got it all, thank you. I left a little something in your Ma's picnic basket in case you get hungry," Roger replied, extending his hand to the young man. "I'm much obliged to you and your family. I will see you when I return."

"We'll be looking forward to it," Peter said. "Have a great trip."

Roger nodded as the young Zimmerman snapped the reins and turned the horses back toward the gate.

"Are you hungry, Pastor?" Chuck offered.

"No, I helped myself to Mrs. Zimmerman's picnic basket on the ride up here," Roger replied. "Just show me to my quarters, so I can drop this stuff off."

Sergeant Braxton grabbed Roger's canvas travel bag and led the preacher to the guest barracks. It was one room with a bunkbed, washbasin, and water pitcher with a mirror hanging on the wall above. It was spartan, but Roger knew it would likely be the best accommodation he would have for quite a while.

"I've spoken to Carlos Santana Sanchez, and he will take over services here at the fort when we depart for Fort Stockton," Roger said.

"He was here about a day ago getting last-minute instructions," Chuck said. "He's a good man. He thinks the world of you."

"Yes, he and the Zimmermans stood by me when I had to mend fences following my shooting of Gabe Curtain a while back," Roger said throwing his hat on the bunk. "Preachers aren't supposed to do that."

"I hear he had it coming, Pastor. This is a lawless land. You've done your part to try and change and you're still doing it now, only in a different way."

"Life does have its twists and turns all right," Roger said. "By the way, Chuck, we're going to be together for a while. Just call me Roger or 'Hey you.' No need to be formal."

"Okay, pas…, Roger. I'm sure I'll have plenty of time to get used to that," Chuck said, smiling. "In case you haven't been informed, Major Trundell will give us a briefing on our itinerary in his office tomorrow at oh-nine-hundred hours."

"I look forward to it. I traveled with a small detachment once, but never with a troop," Roger said. "How many men will there be?"

"A little over one hundred, not including you and a couple of Indian scouts," Chuck replied. "We'll have plenty of company."

"All Christians, I hope," Roger quipped.

"Mostly, but I can't speak for the Indians," Chuck said. "They're real good men, though. Both are Apache and speak good English – great translators."

The sergeant left Roger with instructions on the mess hall hours and departed.

Chapter 3
Heading for Texas

The next day, Roger joined the troops of the 9th Cavalry for breakfast. The soldiers' day would be spent preparing for the following day's march to Fort Stockton, Texas. Roger would meet with Major Trundell and his officers for a briefing on the troop's itinerary.

Roger left his room early with a plan to meet with Major Trundell and his cadre prior to the briefing. When he entered the officers' quarters, he saw the major talking with his captain and lieutenants.

"Pastor Brinkman, I'm happy you could make it," Trundell called out. "Come in and let me introduce you to my officers."

"Major Trundell, good to see you again," Roger responded. "I guess today you'll be preaching to me for a change."

Trundell enjoyed Roger's levity and began the introductions.

"This is Captain Dan Dunston, my first officer. Dunston served with General Sherman during the war," Roger grasped the hand of the captain. Dunston was shorter than the other officers but had an air of command that was palpable. His face was tanned, with the stubble of a beard. The captain was also well known for his valor in battle and had scars well hidden by his uniform.

First Lieutenant Carl Remington was about as tall as Roger but of slighter build. He was a West Point graduate and a very good administrative officer but did not have much combat experience. Still, he was an excellent horseman.

Second Lieutenant Jeff Liston was fresh out of West Point and was put under Trundell's wing, who was an excellent mentor. Liston was well-liked by virtually everyone and had more appeal as a friend and fellow soldier than he did as an officer. He was athletic and played baseball at the academy. However, he was green as a horse soldier.

"We should have a pretty routine journey," said Trundell, who was middle-aged and heavyset. But he was all soldier and enjoyed his position as the commander of Fort McRae's 9th regiment. He wore a Van Dyke that was well trimmed and flecked with gray. He took to his buffalo soldiers where some officers were a little hesitant to command an all-black troop.

Just then Sergeant Braxton entered the room with Corporal Ronald Sutherland. The major did not bother introducing the men, knowing Braxton was an elder and Sutherland was a regular attendee for Roger's church meetings.

Braxton was the kind of soldier officers would fight for, even among themselves. He was fearless, a virtual horse whisperer, and carried out the major's orders with precision. Trundell not only coveted his sergeant but admired him and did not hesitate to enlist his advice. Braxton was easy to like and never disrespected regardless of what anyone might think of him.

Sutherland was youthful, like Liston, but earned his stripes in the saddle. He was almost a mirror image of Braxton, only smaller, and stuck to the sergeant like a shadow.

"Are the scouts on their way?" Major Trundell asked Braxton.

"Should be right be…" Braxton started, as the two Apache scouts walked in.

"Pastor, meet Nantan and Elan," Major Trundell said. "They have been with us about six months. Both joined our regiment as scouts when they decided peace could never be obtained while continuing to fight. Nantan knows Victorio, a local troublemaker."

"I'm sure it's difficult serving in an army some of your fellow warriors consider the enemy," Roger said, extending his hand to both. "I hope someday we can all live in peace."

"We too," said Nantan. "Good to have a man of peace join journey."

"I pray it helps," Roger replied. "But I think Major Trundell feels

13

we shouldn't run into much trouble."

"I like the sound of that," Trundell said with a laugh. "Now, let's take our seats and begin this discussion. Captain, would you care to get things started?"

"Gentlemen, on the first leg of our journey, beginning at 0900 hours tomorrow, we will enter the Jornada del Muerto lava beds heading southeast and cross the railroad tracks turning northeast. We'll enter the pass through the Soledad Mountains and camp at the Mal Pots Springs," the captain began. "The following day, we will cross the flats until we reach the community of Tularosa where our second bivouac will be."

"That's where we will spend a day or two," Major Trundell broke in. "That is where the Apache Indian Reservation will be established. We will spend some time among the natives there for goodwill purposes. Nantan and Elan will be our spokesmen. And Pastor, I would appreciate your company as well."

"My pleasure, Major," I've gotten to know a little about the Apache since I've been riding the circuit here."

Captain Dunston then described the route that would take the soldiers along the eastern side of the Sacramento Mountains to the Peñasco River. The march would be southeast to the Pecos River and eventually Fort Stockton.

"Well, that about wraps it up," the captain said. "Are there any questions?"

"Sir," Lieutenant Liston spoke up, "are the Apache located on the Sacramento Mountains aware of the proposed reservation, and how do they feel about it?"

The captain deferred to Major Trundell.

"Nothing is to change for the ones who reside there now, and from what I've been told, they don't see the proposed reservation being much different from what they have now. They, of course, will have to remain on the reservation but very few of them wander out of those mountains. Game is plentiful and the reservation is designed to keep intruders out as well."

"May Nantan speak?" the Indian scout requested.

"Of course, Nantan," Trundell said addressing the scout.

"Mescalero are proud people, have great history," Natan began. "But there are forces that divide them. They see it as the Dark Light. White men try to have Apache live as he lives and too soon. It will take time, but white man want changes now."

"Thank you, Nantan," the major said turning to Roger. "I think you can see from what Nantan said, the army's task is a difficult one. We want to assure the Indians we want to help them live without war, but politicians want them to live without Indian customs. It's tough to approach the Apache with an olive branch when there's someone behind you from Washington with a gun at your back."

"I wish I had the solution, but my approach to the Indians has been naïve," Roger said. "I wish I understood their customs better. Perhaps spreading the Gospel among them wouldn't be so difficult if we knew how to assimilate it into their existing culture."

"You seem to have excellent insight into what needs to be done," said Lieutenant Remington, "but what I hear you saying is you, nor anyone else, knows how to get the job done."

"That's pretty much it, Lieutenant," Roger replied. "The Indians are spiritual people, as are men of the cloth, like me, but tying that spirituality together into a single understanding eludes both sides."

"Sounds like you'll have your work cut out for you assisting the major, Roger," Braxton said, "but God bless you for trying."

"Thanks, Chuck," Roger responded. "I could use all of that I can get."

"If there are no more questions, we can adjourn this meeting and get on with our preparations for this trip," Captain Dunstan said. "By the way, Pastor, you will be given an extra horse to carry your belongings since you will be continuing on from Fort Stockton."

"Appreciate it, Captain," Roger said. "And I appreciate the army letting me tag along."

"It'll give you a chance to see how the military half lives," Trundell said. "If you can call it living."

The meeting ended with a hearty laugh.

***

The next morning, Roger rolled out of his bunk as the bugle sounded. It reminded him of when he wore a Confederate uniform. It wasn't a pleasant memory.

Roger had a great deal of respect for the military, himself using it to learn how to fight and eventually kill. The Civil War's supposed purpose to determine whether or not "all men" were created equal was never heard on the battlefield – slave troops excepted. And the Union victory did not put an end to the bitterness, resentment, and prejudice that followed.

While he sat on his bunk, Roger's thoughts turned to stories about the Revolutionary War. A rag-tag, disorganized, and underfunded colonial militia taking on a well-armed, disciplined, and fully-supplied British force – and winning.

And now, the indigenous Indian battles to maintain their ancestral, nomadic way of life. The Indian is disadvantaged, much like the colonists, but they will not win. Ironically, where slaves obtained emancipation, the Indian will be interned. They will shed blood only to end up on a small piece of the land they once freely roamed. Still, Roger could not help but admire the indomitable spirit relentless in its will to fight.

"Are you coming?" Braxton called out, as he burst into Roger's room.

"Whoa, don't tell me I'm holding things up," Roger said, quickly looking up at the sergeant.

"No, you're not that late, unless you want to get something to eat before we go," Braxton said. "I told cookie to keep a plate for you, but he won't hold it all morning."

"Thanks, Chuck. I had better get something in my stomach before we start out," Roger said. "I'll be with you in a minute."

After breakfast, Roger strapped his luggage, saddlebags, and bedroll on the packhorse the army provided and thoroughly checked both horses. Both were good animals, which gave Roger another reason to appreciate the army.

"Roger, why don't you ride up front with us," Major Trundell said, riding up to where Roger was getting ready. "It'll help give us a little more class and it doesn't hurt to have God riding with us as well."

"My guess is He'll be riding with you whether I'm there or not," Roger laughed. "There are times I think I should be in the back of the line."

"Very humble," the major said. "That'll work in your favor."

Roger mounted up and followed the major to the head of the column and soon the formation was out of the fort and on its way.

It was early spring, and the air was chilly. Fort McRae's elevation was more than four thousand feet and there were still traces of snow in areas where the sun seldom reached.

As they descended into the Jornada del Muerto lava fields, Roger could see the Soledad Mountains across a twenty-mile stretch. The early morning sun would not prove brutal crossing the canyon and the mountains beyond reached levels a mile high. Roger figured he might as well soak up as much sun as he could, knowing a night spent at five thousand feet would be cold.

They crossed the railroad tracks and turned north toward an unnamed pass through the mountains. They reached the pass in the late afternoon, and to Roger's pleasant surprise, it sliced below the peaks that rose above them.

As the sun dipped behind the pinnacles above them, the major halted the formation and told the men to set up camp. The chuckwagon had left Fort McRae early and reached the site ahead of the column. By the time tents were set up and campfires burning, the dinner bell rang.

Roger was directed to a tent set up for the officers and the evening meal was brought to them by the cook's assistants.

"Enjoy this meal, Roger," Major Trundell said, "they only get worse from now on."

"You have to admit Cookie is good at rustling up grub on the trail, Major," Captain Dunstan said. "I like to think his meals even get better but, of course, that could just be my imagination."

"No, you're a tough Cookie, Dan," the major quipped. "I think if you'd been with Washington at Valley Forge, you would have considered shoe leather acceptable fare."

"I don't know, sir. I just love it out here," the captain replied.

"So, what do you think, Pastor?" the major asked.

"I ate rattlesnake for the first time while on the trail," Roger said, looking down at his plate with a sheepish grin. "I wasn't going to touch the stuff except I was too hungry not to. To my surprise, it was delicious."

"Rattlesnake, eh?" the major responded. "When did you eat rattlesnake?"

During my training as a United States Marshal," Roger said. "But we also had an outstanding cook, a Wichita Indian named Charlie Blue Feather."

"Son, you were a U.S. Marshal?" Lieutenant Remington said. "When did you decide to become a preacher?"

"When I was probably ten years old," Roger said, with a slight grin.

"And you became a marshal instead?" Lieutenant Liston said, lifting his head in surprise with his eyes wide open.

"It's a long story, Lieutenant," Roger said. "Before this journey is over you'll probably learn some things about me that, well… may shock you."

"I knew you was easy in the saddle," Dunston said. "But then you ride your circuit all the time. Still, you don't ride like you have no other means of transportation."

"All in due time, gentlemen, all in due time," Roger replied, pulling back from the table with a satisfied grin.

"Perhaps a little brandy would shorten that time," the major implied. "Would you care to join me?"

"There was a time I would have given you an emphatic, no!" Roger said laughing. "But that was then. Now my answer is yes."

"I have a few cigars, as well…?" said the major, giving Roger a sly look.

"Don't mind if I do, Major. Don't mind if I do."

Chapter 4
Baptism at Fort Stanton

R oger surprised himself by rolling out of bed at the sound of reveille feeling eager to get on with his day. He had stayed up late talking with Major Trundell and felt no after-effects of that or the brandy and cigars.

He checked to make sure his clerical collar was in his luggage. He had placed it there for safekeeping when the patrol left Fort McRae. However, Major Trundell asked that Roger wear the collar when the company reached the Mescalero Apache community the following day. The Mescalero were scheduled to be moved to the Sacramento Mountains Indian Reservation as proposed by President Ulysses S. Grant.

Roger made his way to the mess tent set up near the chuckwagon. He had a plate of sliced apples baked into sourdough, bacon, sausage, and black coffee. Roger continued to marvel at how good food tasted when prepared in open country. He had become a chef in his own right cooking for himself between stops on his circuit. Still, his fare never seemed to rival that of Charlie Blue Feather's when bivouacking as a deputy marshal with his brother.

"Roger, I trust you are finding the grub to your liking?" said Lieutenant Remington, who stopped for a cup of coffee.

"I've become so spoiled from eating this way that I find eating indoors less tasteful," Roger said. "There's something about throwing ingredients into a Dutch oven and having it simmer over an open fire."

"Perhaps you should have been a soldier," the lieutenant remarked.

"I was, once, but the food then played a distant fiddle to this," Roger said. "That was in the war, where I got my fill of soldiering but not good food."

"What did you do in the war?" Remington asked.

"I was a sharpshooter and just about anything else Lee needed," Roger said. "General Lee, that is."

"You fought for the South?" Remington said with some surprise.

"I'm from Missouri," Roger said, tossing a small stick into the campfire. "Not in favor of slavery, just states' rights."

"Makes sense, I guess," the lieutenant stated hesitantly.

"It's a long story, Lieutenant. Perhaps I'll tell you more about it as time goes on."

"For a preacher, your background seems to say more about you than being a minister," Remington replied.

"The road I traveled to get to where I am today took a lot of turns before I settled on the narrow path," Roger said, as the call to mount up went out and the two men harkened to it and joined the patrol.

"We'll head through this pass and water up at the springs before crossing the salt marsh," Major Trundell called out as Roger and Remington rode up. "Our next stop will be Tularosa. That's where we'll meet with the Mescalero chief and his council."

Crossing the valley between the mountain ranges of Soledad and Sacramento in early April meant miles of white sand mitigated by milder temperatures. The sands and marsh patches also featured a variety of plant life and flowers that helped alleviate some of the ennui of the desert landscape.

"What brought you to New Mexico, Roger?" Major Trundell asked.

"I responded to a calling," Roger replied. "I was hoping for Texas or Oklahoma, but New Mexico was the territory with the greatest need."

"How do you like these mountains, valleys, canyons, and deserts so far?" the major chuckled as he spoke.

"It's not boring, except when crossing an area like this," Roger said. "But I've grown to love this great land. I just wish I had the ability to see more of it."

"You would think there would be enough land for us and the Indians," Remington chimed in. "It sometimes saddens me we have to be at war with some of these folks."

"We do our best to avoid that," Trundell said, as Roger nodded in agreement. "But there are problems and troublemakers on both sides. The army's job is to try and keep the peace, but it isn't always possible."

"It is ironic you should say that, Major," Roger said, eyeing some dark clouds in the distance. "The army, almost by definition, must be prepared for battle."

"We're trained as warriors and asked to be diplomats," said Lieutenant Liston. "We discussed the irony of this at West Point. The real warriors are these Buffalo Soldiers, whose training in diplomacy is what they brought with them."

"History has repeated the tenet of peace through strength," Major Trundell said. "It took a war to secure this country's independence and it seems we are destined to continue that principle."

The major raised his hand to halt the patrol and turned to Sergeant Braxton. "Sergeant, there appears to be a thunderstorm rolling our way. Alert the men to prepare for some wind to kick up the sand. They'll need cover for their faces and those of their horses."

"I guess this place isn't going to be as boring as I thought," Roger quipped.

The wind did slow the patrol's progress, but the storm passed by quickly without incident. They arrived in Tularosa as the sun was setting behind the Soledad Range and the men quickly established camp for the second night.

"We'll be visiting with Mescalero Chief San Juan tomorrow afternoon," Trundell said to Roger, as the two men stood by while the major's tent was being set up. "San Juan is easy enough to deal with, but Chief Caballero will be there also and he's not so easy."

"What's his problem?" Roger said, somewhat nonchalantly.

"Caballero is married to the daughter of Mangus Coloradas, who is a friend of Apache renegade Victorio," Trundell answered. "Caballero does not like the idea of being placed on a reservation, although he has not shown any violent resistance."

"How can I help?" Roger inquired.

"San Juan has been leaning toward the white man's ways and could possibly become Christian with the help of a good man like you," Trundell offered. "I don't expect you to perform any miracles, but your presence could help."

"I'll be happy to be of whatever service I can," Roger replied. "I'll pray for guidance and let the Holy Spirit take charge.

"That would be good," Trundell said. "Apache are spiritual people."

"As are many other tribes," Roger added. "I even had a brief encounter with a Comanche spirit talker a few years back."

"Spirit talkers possess powerful medicine among the Indians," Trundell commented. "I'm sure there is one among the Mescalero as well."

"They can be helpful," Roger said. "The one I met certainly was."

The following day, the company moved north into the Sacramento Mountains. The meeting with Chief San Juan was scheduled to take place at South Fork, where the 9th Cavalry would camp that night. The plan was to reach Fort Stanton the day after to report to Colonel Walter "Buck" Buchwald, commander in charge of establishing the Mescalero Apache Reservation.

The cavalry reached South Fork in the early afternoon, where Chief San Juan and his small entourage were waiting.

"Chief San Juan, thank you for waiting," Trundell said, dismounting along with scout Nantan. "Let us find a cool spot in the shade where we can talk."

Sergeant Braxton took a couple of men and prepared a suitable area where the representatives of the army and Mescalero Apache could sit and talk. Braxton then returned to set up camp for the night.

Trundell introduced his junior officers, along with Roger and Nantan.

"Nantan can assist if we should encounter a language problem during our discussions," the major offered San Juan. "Pastor Brinkman is our spiritual leader in assuring our talks proceed in peace."

San Juan's group included his son Peso and Chief Caballero. There were also three warriors in his company, plus medicine man Gorgonio.

"We bring Gorgonio," San Juan said, waving his hand in the direction of the aging medicine man. "He is spiritual leader for our people."

"Chief, we want you to know that we will do all we can to see you and your people can live your lives as you always have in these beautiful mountains, undisturbed," Trundell began. "Although a mighty warrior, you have been a voice of peace and understanding. And, as a representative of the United States, I can tell you we greatly appreciate that."

"Not all my people feel as you and I do," San Juan said. "There are those who do not feel this land is for you to give. It belongs to the Apache."

"I cannot debate with you the terms of this reservation," Trundell said. "I am sorry we have to be on opposite sides of a war neither of us wants. But white settlers are moving west, and it is the army's responsibility to make this land safe for them."

"You speak of peace, yet come with guns and horses to take what is ours," Chief Caballero cut in. "You say you protect us, but who protect us from you?"

"I agree it's complicated," Trundell responded, turning his gaze away in a search for words. "All I can say is we are here to try and prevent any more killing on both sides. I understand that land is the issue and hope you would understand the land has to be for all people, yours and mine."

"Then why do you not live on reservation away from us?" Caballero said. "You go where you please. We cannot."

"Because wherever you go you make plans to raid and kill settlers," the major explained. "Right now, we are trying to keep the Apache and the setters separated."

"Settlers invade our land. We not invade theirs," Caballero said, waving his arm in contempt.

"San Juan, I appeal to you," Trundell said, turning to the chief. "I cannot argue with Chief Caballero's point of view, but my point is we have to do something to stop this ongoing war."

"Caballero speaks the truth," San Juan said. "I and many of my people only want peace. Those with Caballero do not want to be told where they can live, but you live where you want."

"Chief," Captain Dunston interrupted, leaning forward. "It is the same with you. We tried to bring the Navajo here, but you rejected them. So, the Indian cannot always go where he wants even among his own kind."

"We respect the land of our brothers. You do not respect our land and you do not call us brother," Caballero interjected.

"I'm afraid these talks aren't going as I hoped," Trundell said, turning to Roger. "Do you have any ideas?"

"My job is to appeal to the heart," Roger said. "Perhaps if I could have some time with Gorgonio alone, maybe we could come up with a way to satisfy both sides."

"I've never negotiated with a medicine man before. Perhaps you're onto something," Trundell replied. "Chief San Juan, is it acceptable for our medicine man to speak with yours? I realize this is irregular and I believe we need to let our conversation rest a while."

San Juan turned to Gorgonio and conversed with him in Apache. After a brief conversation, San Juan turned back to Major Trundell.

"Gorgonio has agreed. Best to include Nantan. Gorgonio is limited in your tongue."

"Okay, Pastor, it's your turn," Trundell said, smiling at Roger. "Good luck."

"I'll need more than luck," Roger said, rising from his position and joining Nantan and Gorgonio. The three men walked a short distance until out of earshot of the others.

"Nantan, ask Gorgonio his feelings about what is being discussed," Roger requested.

Nantan and Gorgonio spoke briefly with one another and Nantan then turned to Roger.

"Gorgonio's heart is saddened by the words being spoken," Nantan said. "Peace is what all Apache want but some feel betrayed."

"Like Caballero," Roger uttered audibly. "Ask Gorgonio if he has any visions or spiritual guidance as to what must be done."

After a lengthier discussion, Nantan relayed the medicine man's reply.

"Gorgonio is old and said his visions are not as strong as when he was younger. His visions are not those of peace and the spirits say wars will continue. As for reservation, that will take place but not for long."

"Not for long?" Roger said. "So, the Mescalero will live for a time on the reservation, then what?"

"Apache time short," Gorgonio said, speaking for himself. "Chief San Juan will put people on land, but not long time. Apache betrayed and will fight until no more."

"What's he saying, Nantan?"

"The spirits tell him the war will continue, but San Juan will protect his people on the reservation. Yet reservation will not last, and the Apache will be removed from the land," Nantan replied. "That will be the ultimate betrayal."

"Gorgonio, Nantan, I am going to have to report to Major Trundell what we have discussed here. I'm not sure Trundell will buy into the spiritual visions of Gorgonio, but establishing the reservation will please him," Roger said. "I will discuss the visions with Trundell in private. May I assume Gorgonio has already shared this with San Juan?"

"He has, as well as Caballero and Peso," Nantan answered.

"Gorgonio, bless you for your help," Roger said. "I am amazed your people have remained cordial during this discussion. Allow me to have the last word."

Nantan related Roger's request to Gorgonio, who agreed.

"If I may, Major," Roger said, as the three men returned to the conference.

"Be my guest, Pastor," Trundell responded. "Please, just make it good."

"Chief San Juan, Chief Caballero, Peso and warriors," Roger started. "Gorgonio has enlightened me as to the situation among your peoples and assured me the Apache want peace. However, it is going to be a long road of continued cooperation for all involved, but it will happen. I just hope through your Great Spirit and the God I serve this all ends well.

"Major Trundell, do you have anything more to say?"

"Just this. San Juan, I admire you for your courage in encouraging your people to live on the reservation," Trundell said. "Chief Caballero, I am sorry my assurances do not satisfy you. I would just hope we can end this needless bloodshed once and for all.

"If you wish to stay the night and travel with us in the morning, you are welcome. We will pass through your land on our way to Fort Stanton."

Chief San Juan turned to Caballero and spoke in Apache. They exchanged words and San Juan said his group appreciated the offer, but they would be returning to their village that day.

After a strained but cordial departure, Roger, Trundell, and his officers retired to their camp.

That evening, Roger, Trundell, Dunston, Remington, and Braxton sat around a campfire outside of the major's tent.

"What was all that hocus pocus about visions and such?" Trundell asked Roger.

"It's really not hocus pocus, as you say, George. These people, the Indians in general, are very spiritual. They have a connection that is foreign to us, and their visions seem to carry a lot of truth. I know it's a stretch, but their visions to them are like the Christian Bible to us. We get our guidance through the Word, and they get theirs by connecting to the spiritual world."

"I'm sorry, Roger," Trundell said. "I just can't relate to that."

"But just so you know, Major," Roger said. "According to Gorgonio, this reservation is going to happen, but won't last long. I'm afraid the Apache will be betrayed, again, by our government, and this war with them will continue."

"Seems a waste," Remington said. "I cannot understand why our diplomacy doesn't work better."

"It works better when you've got the firepower," Dunston remarked, staring into the campfire. "I think even the Bible teaches us that, right, Pastor?"

"Not really, Captain," Roger said, also gazing at the flames. "Faith, hope, and love is what it teaches. But man seems destined to set that aside for, as you say, greater firepower."

"Speaking of firepower, we'd better get some rest before starting out," Major Trundell said. "I'm not feeling as optimistic as I'd hoped after today's talk."

With that, the men departed for their tents.

The following morning, the 9th Cavalry got off to an early start working their way north through the Sacramento Mountains toward Fort Stanton. The tallest peaks still held snow, but the lower meadows were already filled with lush vegetation and colorful flowers. The early morning air was cool as Nantan and Elan led the troops around the steep hills and heavily timbered terrain. Following a brief respite for lunch, the company passed through the gates of Fort Stanton. Sergeant Braxton led the soldiers to the stable area while Major Trundell and his officers stopped at the fort's headquarters and dismounted.

"Major Trundell, you made it," said Colonel Buchwald as the men entered the building. "I trust you did not run into any trouble along the way."

The major saluted and then grasped the colonel's hand, "No trouble getting here, but I'm afraid our trouble with the Apache is not over, Buck." The use of Buchwald's nickname was common among his close friends and ranking officers.

"Did your talk not go well with San Juan?" Buchwald asked. "I had hoped for better news."

"Buck, I would like you to meet Pastor Roger Brinkman," Trundell said, turning Buchwald's attention to the preacher. "He assisted our efforts and I think our meeting at least ended on a positive note."

"Welcome, Pastor," Buchwald said, shaking Roger's hand. "I would like to know what you did. Gentlemen, if you will follow me into my office I should like a full report."

The colonel's office had been expanded to accommodate meetings with the Apache since Fort Stanton had been designated as the headquarters for the Mescalero Apache Indian Reservation. Major Trundell and Roger took seats in front of Buchwald's desk, while Trundell's attaché took seats against the back wall. Buchwald called in his adjutant to be present for the report.

"So, tell me from the beginning what transpired during your meeting," Buchwald requested.

"Captain Dunston and I were making pretty good progress with Chief San Juan, but Chief Caballero played devil's advocate," Trundell related. "His issue was over his people being forced onto a reservation when in the past they considered all land theirs, as long as it wasn't occupied by another tribe. Captain Dunston tried to explain that Indians fighting with Indians over land was not much different than Indians fighting us for it. But Caballero wasn't buying it. Unfortunately, San Juan was starting to side with Caballero."

"It is the same scenario we've been getting all along," commented Buchwald. "The Comanche booted some of them out of Kansas and now we are dealing with them in the New Mexico Territory.

"I know there's been opposition to this reservation, but I understand President Grant plans to follow through on establishing it.

"So, Pastor Brinkman, what role did you have in this?"

Roger thought for a moment and then replied to the colonel's request. "San Juan's group included Gorgonio, a long-standing medicine man for the Mescalero. I had some experience with a spirit talker when dealing with the Comanche and thought if I could influence him, he would do the same for San Juan and Caballero."

Roger credited Nantan for his help in interpreting the conversation but indicated that Gorgonio did understand limited English.

"Gorgonio said his vision was for a protracted war with the white man but that it would not go well for the Apache. I asked that he allow me to make some closing comments during the meeting and he agreed," Roger continued. "So I tried my best to let San Juan and Caballero know they had our respect and hoped their Great Spirit would bring peace to the land."

"Apparently Gorgonio's vision does not offer a good outcome for the Apache," Major Trundell said. "I'm afraid we're not going to see peace anytime soon."

"I'm sorry to hear that," Buchwald said. "What is your feeling about how the Mescalero Reservation is going to work out?"

"I believe I can help with that," Captain Dunston spoke out. "If I may have your permission to speak."

Major Trundell nodded his approval and Colonel Buchwald asked Dunston to continue.

"I believe the reservation is going to work for the Mescalero who follow San Juan," Dunston said, "but there will be splinter groups that will fight to the bitter end. I applaud what you're doing here, and hope all goes well. I think where the 9th Cavalry is going will be another story."

"I guess we still have plenty of work to do, George," Buchwald said, addressing the major. "When do you plan to leave for Fort Stockton?"

"I would like to take a little time to discuss this with my men and my officers, as we may meet some resistance on our way there," Trundell responded. "I do not see that trip as taking more than a day or two. We'll resupply and depart shortly thereafter."

"My office is yours, George," the colonel said. "I feel more secure with your men in camp. They're outstanding soldiers."

"That they are, Buck," the major said, rising to his feet. "And thank you."

The next two days were spent in preparation for the journey south.

The morning before they were to leave, Roger was sitting on his bunk reading his Bible when Lieutenant Liston came into the officers' billets.

"Pastor Brinkman," the lieutenant began, removing his hat, "Do you do baptisms?"

"Certainly," Roger replied. "Why do you ask?"

"I've never been baptized, and I think we may run into trouble on our way to Fort Stockton," Liston answered.

"Are you worried, Lieutenant?"

"I don't think any more than the rest of the men," Liston said, "but if anything should happen, I want to know I've been baptized."

"I believe there's a small chapel on the post," Roger said. "I could bless some water and baptize you there."

"I was hoping to be submerged, sir," Liston replied. "I know we'll be coming to a river during our travels."

Roger just looked at the second lieutenant for a minute lost in thought. "I'll tell you what, Jeff," he eventually said. "Let's do it like this. I'll baptize you here at the chapel, and when we reach the river I'll do an immersion baptism with you. Will that work for you?"

"If you think that's best," Liston replied.

"An immersion baptism is for those who have fully repented," Roger said. "The journey to the river will give us time to talk so I can be assured you truly have a repentant heart. The sprinkling is also a holy baptism and will suffice even if we don't reach the river.

"You do realize this is an act of repentance, don't you?" Roger said.

"I do, sir," Liston said. My Ma taught me all about that."

"Good for her. I will make arrangements with the company commander to obtain use of the chapel and we'll perform it tonight in front of witnesses," Roger proposed.

"Thank you, sir. I'll wait to hear from you," remarked the lieutenant.

Roger checked with Major Trundell, who offered to witness along with his subordinate officers. Trundell also accompanied Roger in requesting permission from Colonel Buchwald to use the chapel.

That night, word got out and the chapel filled up with most of the soldiers from the 9th Cavalry and many from Fort Stanton. That night, Roger baptized twenty-three soldiers."

Chapter 5
Nik in Galveston

After Roger Brinkman left Wichita, Kansas, to return to seminary, his brother and U.S. Deputy Marshal Nik Brinkman spent much of his time mentoring former outlaw Willie Warneke. Warneke was once a member of Texas' Sulphur River Gang of outlaws. He had been arrested by Nik and Roger, but after learning of Willie's limited involvement with the gang, the two helped the former gang member in getting paroled and eventually into the U.S. Marshals Service.

When Nik's promotion to chief marshal came through, he was ordered to return to Washington D.C for further training before establishing the Galveston office.

"Nik, I cannot tell you what a pleasure it has been serving with you," Chief Marshal of the Wichita office, Ned Borchers said. "You've done such a remarkable job in such a short time, I'm really not sure what Washington thinks they can teach you."

"Probably, how to push a pencil, like you have to do most of the time," Nik said, grinning to soften the remark. "I'm happy the service is going to let me in Texas. By the time I reach Galveston, Texas will have become a state."

"Well, I just hope our paths cross again," Borchers began.

"That goes for the two of us," Willie Warneke chimed in. Willie was to replace Nik as Borchers' deputy.

"I, too, shall miss you, Marshal Brinkman," Charlie Blue Feather, Nik's Indian guide and chuckwagon master, added. "You taught me enough to become a deputy marshal as well."

"You're the one who taught me, Charlie," Nik said, turning his attention first to Willie and then his longtime companion. "I might not be alive today had it not been for your savvy in the Llano Estacado. And that goes double for my brother."

After the farewells, the four lawmen made their way to the railway station, where Nik boarded the train for the nation's capital.

After arriving in Washington, Nik was introduced to the policies and functions of Congress. He was even introduced to President Ulysses S. Grant, whom Nik had served under during the Civil War.

Shortly before he was to complete his year of training in Washington, Nik received his transfer orders to open the U.S. Marshals Service office in Galveston, Texas.

Galveston had grown into a major port for overseas shipping, but that made it a target for smugglers. The community of Galveston was originally founded by the famous pirate and privateer Jean Lafitte. Because of his assistance to the young nation during the War of 1812, Lafitte was pardoned of his crimes by President James Madison.

However, Lafitte and his band of buccaneers were eventually evicted from Galveston Island by the United States Navy. That action helped Galveston to develop into a prosperous city.

Galveston was later selected as the site for the first United States Bank of Texas. Nik, despite being black, was selected for the chief marshal's job there because of his investigative work in a land-fraud case. His efforts also exposed former Circuit Judge Victor Giles Kensington in northern Texas of being the mastermind of that conspiracy.

Nik recalled Borchers' remarks concerning Galveston.

"At least you won't have to deal with traders trying to smuggle in slaves. Emancipation and the 1808 slave-trade law ended that," Borchers had said. He also said Galveston was a great place for a black marshal to further his career. Although Texas had been Confederate during the war, Galveston made great strides in assimilating former slaves into their culture.

As a young boy growing up in Africa, Nik had been captured and taken to America to be sold as a slave. But he was rescued from that fate by Douglas Brinkman, who purchased Nik at an auction. The Brinkman family lived in Bordertown, Missouri, where Douglas was the pastor of the local church. The Brinkmans "adopted" Nik, and because of his Christian upbringing, Nik found it easy to blend into the white culture.

Nik departed Washington, D.C., and took the train to New Orleans, Louisiana. From there, he had his choice of sailing on a Morgan ship to Galveston or taking the stagecoach. Since Galveston was a seaport, Nik decided to go by ship, despite his memories of the slave ship that brought him to America.

Once the ship was underway, its captain, Sven Olson, emerged from his cabin. The first thing that caught his eye was a passenger leaning over the taffrail with his hat in hand.

"Haven't yet found your sea legs, Marshal?" the captain asked, aware from the ship's manifest as to who it was feeding the fish.

Nik regained his composure and rose up without looking at the officer. "My illness has more to do with my memory than it does your ability to navigate the seas, Captain."

"So, you've traveled by sea before?" Olson responded.

"On a slave ship. I was kidnapped from my native country and brought here against my will," Nik said, glancing at the captain and turning back again to gaze over the open waters.

"I am sorry to hear that. However, it appears you have done very well for yourself, in spite of it," the captain said, moving forward to lean against the taffrail next to Nik. "Becoming the U.S. Marshal of Galveston is quite an accomplishment."

"Thanks, Captain, but that accomplishment is because the Good Lord took me by the hand in the person of a man who became my adopted father," Nik said, turning again to look at the captain. "I'm certain the Lord also had a hand in guiding me to this destination."

"A success story, nonetheless," said the man in uniform. "I am Captain Olson. Have you been to Galveston before?"

"Pleased to meet you, Captain," Nik said, extending his hand in greeting. "No, this is all new to me, except for being a marshal."

"I have found Galveston to be an enchanting destination," the captain replied. "Though, I've never been able to spend more than a few days there before shipping out again."

"What 'enchants' you about the place?" Nik said, turning to gaze out to sea.

"The serenity and the mix of people," Olson answered. "Seaports are notorious for populations made up of people from around the world. I think you'll like it." The captain said, turning to rest his elbow against the rail. "Still, with your initial experience at sea, why did you choose my ship over a stagecoach?"

Nik turned, leaned his back against the taffrail and stroked his mustache between his thumb and middle finger. "To face my fears," Nik said. "As you say, Galveston is a seaport. I thought maybe this trip would help put those memories to rest."

"I assume it did not," mused Olson. "But if I'm any judge of character, and I've seen all kinds, I think you'll do just fine once you get there. You're young and appear to be quite resilient."

"Thanks, Captain. It's my plan to live up to your kind words."

With that, the captain offered a courteous salute and departed to meet some of the other passengers.

It was now late spring when the ship docked in Galveston, Nik's trunk was unloaded and placed on a shuttle wagon. The driver took him to the Globe House where he checked in as a semi-permanent resident. It was late in the day, so the new chief marshal nursed his stomach with a light dinner in the hotel's dining room and retired to his room.

Nik's accommodations were spacious and comfortably furnished. The approaching summer climate prompted the opening of a window to welcome a cooling breeze. Nik's stomach grumbled because of the harbor odors, but the fresh air helped to offset the discomfort.

He retired early, but the constant sounds of the surf made sleep difficult. Several times he was awakened by dreams that left him in a cold sweat. He closed the window hoping to relieve his mind of past memories but to no avail. Morning could not come soon enough.

After a breakfast of coffee and a biscuit, Nik went in search of his new office located in the Galveston's courthouse. There he met Galveston's sheriff, Joe "Duke" Atkins.

"Happy to have you onboard," Atkins said, rising from his desk to greet Nik. "We can use all the help we can get here. A lot of strange things, and people, arrive here by sea."

Atkins had a cherub-like face and was almost as round as he was tall. Nik guessed him to be in his late thirties or early forties. He had an office in the back of the receptionists' space, where two deputies were stationed. After introducing him to the office, the sheriff led Nik into his office.

"You seem kind of young to be the chief marshal here," Atkins stated. "No offense, of course, just observation."

"I've packed quite a bit of life into a short time," said Nik, now in his late twenties. "I fought in the war and was a deputy marshal under Chief Ned Borchers. He's a consummate professional and I learned fast."

"I can tell you that as a federal man you will have your hands full," Atkins continued while sitting down behind his desk and gesturing for Nik to take a seat in front of it. "Do you have deputies who will be joining you?"

"In looking over my orders, I am authorized to hire one deputy to begin with. I also can contract if I need more men," Nik answered. "Unfortunately, I don't know anyone here. Perhaps you could help with that?"

"Hmm, I don't know of anyone off the top of my head, but I may have an idea how you might find someone," the sheriff said, leaning back in his chair and furrowing his brow.

"I'm open to any suggestion you might have," Nik replied.

"Ever hear of Juneteenth?" Atkins asked.

"Can't say as I have," Nik said leaning forward.

"It's a celebration of emancipation here in Galveston, and pretty much throughout the state," Atkins said. "I hope I don't offend you by telling you this, being colored and all."

Immediately Nik thought, "and all what?" However, his response was "I'm a fan of emancipation. So, please proceed."

"Well, that celebration comes up June nineteenth. It takes place on Virginia Point, across the bay from here. June nineteenth was the day emancipation was announced in Galveston," the sheriff said. "They hold a shooting contest there every year and you might be able to recruit a deputy or two from among those sharpshooters."

Nik promised to keep the date in mind and mentioned that his office was also supposed to be in the courthouse.

"I know where it is," Atkins said. "If you follow me, I'll take you to it."

The office was located at the end of the hall in the same wing as the district attorney and circuit judge.

"This here's Judge Jedediah Conklin's office," the sheriff said, pointing to a door with the judge's name on it. "He's not in right now or I would introduce you."

Nik took note as Atkins led him to the end of the hall.

"It's open," the sheriff remarked. "You'll find the keys to the door in your desk. It's a bit smaller than our office, but we ain't had a U.S. Marshall of our own before."

"Thanks, Sheriff, I'll check it out," Nik replied, shaking Atkin's hand. "I will take your advice. I hope it won't be too much bother if I drop in with more questions in the future."

"My door's always open, Marshal Brinkman. Drop in anytime."

The Juneteenth celebration was several weeks away, so Nik spent most of his time getting acquainted with Galveston, introducing himself, and establishing the U.S. Marshals Service Office.

One of Nik's personal priorities was to write to his brother, who was still attending seminary in St. Louis, Missouri, at that time. Uncertain of how long he would remain a resident at the Globe House, he used his office address just in case.

"Dear Roger,

I have reached Galveston and have mixed feelings about being here. For one, this is my first job as a chief marshal, and two, this place is quite different from what I am used to.

Galveston is surrounded by water, and I can literally walk from one coastline to another in a matter of hours. My assignment includes ocean-going traffic coming in from all parts of the world, and I have no experience on how to deal with that. I have met the sheriff, and he seems like a nice guy, but I do not know how much I can depend on his help. His jurisdiction is this town, mine is now spread across the globe.

I am spending my time getting acquainted with Galveston, a town that appears to have an open mind where race is considered. So far, no one has objected to me being the area's marshal, but I think that might be because no one here would want the job. I hope I'm wrong about that since I need to hire a least one deputy and have authority to form a posse as-needed, per my contract.

When I left Kansas City, Willie was coming along nicely, and he and Charlie Blue Feather hit it off really well. I think Willie's experience riding with outlaws serves him well, now that he's riding on this side of the law. Being under Chief Borcher's watch is also good for him.

I hope this letter finds you well and doesn't give the impression I am terribly unhappy, I'm not. I'm just all alone in a new town and miss you a powerful lot. I miss those days we rode together as deputy marshals.

Not a day goes by I don't think of Ma, Pa, and Dolly. The hair still goes up on the back of my neck when I hear the word 'curtain.'

I hope when you're done with school and settled into you new career you'll come and visit. I'm still counting on you baptizing me when you become a minister.

God Bless,

Nik"

Nik sat back from his desk for a minute to think about his days growing up in Bordertown, Missouri, with Roger and their friends. He also mulled over the irony of his preacher-bound brother becoming a deputy marshal and their days hunting for outlaws in Texas.

He leaned forward, folded his letter, and stuffed it into an envelope. After addressing the letter to: In care of the Pastor Glen

Tillotson family, he set the envelope on the back of the desk and prepared to go downstairs for supper.

The next day, Nik arose early, retrieved his letter, and went downstairs. Rather than stop in for breakfast, Nik decided to hail a horse-drawn cab and ride over to the beach stretching along Galveston's seawall. The United States Post Office was also in that direction, where he dropped off the letter. After reaching the beach, he paid the driver and made his way down to the sandy surface. The day was pleasant, and the waves were small and restless.

Nik crouched down to touch the sand and again experienced memories of his past, only this time it did not upset his stomach. It evoked anger, reminding him of the beach where he was taken before being sold to slave traders.

His anger softened when remembering his mother and those who befriended him while chained together. Faces he grew attached to who either met an early death or survived to live life as a slave.

Those memories brought tears, so he hung his head and allowed them to fall into the sand.

"You okay, sir?" a voice asked.

Nik looked up to see the figure of a man silhouetted against the noon-day sun. He stood up straight and was confronted by an elderly black man holding a large bag containing unknown items.

"I'm sorry if I disturbed you," the man added, as Nik quickly wiped away his remaining tears.

"No, not at all," Nik said. "I was just reliving a difficult time in my life."

"That happens out here on this beach," said the man, dressed in a plain shirt buttoned down the front and a light jacket. He also wore trousers that easily exposed his bare feet. His hair was mostly white with a stubble of a beard to match.

"My name's Mosely, Abel Mosely. I come out here to see what folks may leave behind. I just wanted to make sure you were okay. Some people have been known to walk into that ocean and not come out."

"I'm sorry to hear that. This is such a beautiful beach," Nik replied, looking out over the water. "I'm Nik, Nik Brinkman. I'm the new

U.S. Chief Marshal here in Galveston. I assure you, I have no intention of going for a swim."

"New chief marshal, you're a pretty important man," Mosely said. "Where do you hail from?"

"I was originally assigned to the Wichita, Kansas, office covering Oklahoma and north Texas. But, I was promoted and sent here," Nik replied.

"You'll find south Texas ain't much like north Texas, no sir," Mosely said. "We do not have a lot of Indians, but outlaws we have plenty."

"I'm sorry to hear you say that as well," Nik said. "Tell me, do things get pretty wild here?"

"Not as a rule. Things are pretty quiet most of the time," Mosely offered. "But the sea opens things up to some strange goings-on with pirates, smugglers, and the like, secret-like things."

"That's what concerns me," Nik responded. "I'm used to hard-riding, quick-shooting outlaw gangs, not smugglers and pirates. You still have pirates here?"

"Mostly types that used to be. The navy has run most of them off," Mosely continued. "But there are still those who are pirates at heart. The more hardcore ones hide out in Mexico, mostly. But they still come around when opportunity knocks."

"Like what kind of opportunities?" Nik inquired.

"Like rich folks gettin' their wallets lifted, and their throats cut in some cases. Or rich widows raped and plundered. It has happened around here," Mosely answered. "Those old pirates tend to show up in disguise during big events, like the Juneteenth comin' up."

"Juneteenth, I've heard of that," Nik said. "Are folks expecting trouble?"

"It's just one of those opportunities you mentioned. The sheriff has gotten pretty wise to it, though he ain't never caught no one," Mosely said. "The last celebration was pretty tame."

"What about confederates? Are they still around?"

"No, most of them were run off by the army and they've mostly moved north or west," Mosely replied. "Galveston's been pretty good to us black folks."

"Thanks, Mosely," Nik said, looking down at the man's bare feet and thinking to himself. "By the way, Mosely, do you spend a lot of time on this beach?"

"I do. It's how I make my livin', mostly, 'cept for odd jobs I do now and then."

"Would you do something for me?" Nik asked.

"If I'm able, I will," Mosely said.

"Since I'm new here, would you help be my eyes on the waterfront?" Nik said. "You don't have to do anything, necessarily, but I would appreciate a report now and then. Tell me what you've seen going on down here, strange ships at anchor, people coming onto the beach here instead of the harbor. Things like that."

"I could do that, Marshal," Mosely said, his eyes widening as he nodded his head. "I do see some of that now and then."

"Good, I'll try to reward you in some way if what you see helps me and the sheriff keep the peace around here," Nik remarked.

"You don't have to do that, Marshal. "Ol' Mosely does pretty good with what folks leave behind down here," he said, tapping his sack as he spoke.

"Wonderful," Nik said, putting his hand on Mosely's shoulder. "Now I'd better be getting back. I'll stay in touch."

"Yes, sir, marshal," Mosely said, smiling.

Nik waved down another cab and directed the driver to take him to the Galveston livery stable.

Chapter 6
Stanton to the Rio Grande

The day of the 9th Calvary's departure from Fort Stanton started well. There were dark clouds near the horizon that appeared to be dumping moisture, but the rain looked as though it was evaporating before reaching the earth.

Major Trundell took a route that swung wide of the eastern slope of the Sacramento Mountains. He felt it would give his troops time to respond to a renegade attack emerging from the timberline. However, there were areas in the mountains he would have to approach to take advantage of the spring waters that flowed out of the hills.

The sky was clear, but the post-winter temperatures were still mild compared to what the summer would bring. Fortunately, his soldiers were accustomed to traveling in the desert heat of the New Mexico Territory.

"That was a fine thing you did for the soldiers last night," Trundell began. "A lot of those men were baptized in their youth but felt another would not hurt their chances of making it to Heaven. Hopefully, none of them will go any sooner than expected."

"Happy to do it, Major, it's akin to why I'm making this trip," Roger said.

"You knew the men would need baptizing?" Trundell questioned.

"Not at all," Roger said, riding up closer to Trundell's side. "You see, before leaving to finish my seminary training, my brother asked me to return and baptize him once I was ordained. My father was going to do it, but he was killed before he could do it."

"What happened to your father?" Trundell asked, patting his horse on the neck.

"He was shot and killed by a man posing as an army officer. The officer and his men were trying to kidnap my brother, and Pa helped Nik to escape."

"I'm sorry to hear that. Why were those men trying to kidnap ... Nik, I believe you said his name was?"

"Nik was taken into my family as a young lad, who would otherwise become a slave," Roger added. "My father could not bring himself to let that happen and bought him at an auction."

"That was noble, indeed," the major said, turning in his saddle to look at Roger. "So where is your brother now?"

"He's in Galveston, Texas. He's the chief U.S. Marshal there."

"U.S. Marshal? That's a tall order for any man, let alone a black man," Trundell responded.

"Not for Nik," Roger said. "He's an outstanding lawman. He taught me everything I needed to know as a deputy marshal."

"So, you were a marshal before becoming a preacher?" Trundell replied with noticeable amazement in his voice.

"I was," Roger said in a matter-of-fact tone.

"So, whatever happened to the man who killed your father?" Trundell quizzed.

"I shot him," Roger stated in monotone.

"I see," Major Trundell uttered, nodding his head and pushing up his lower lip. He then turned his gaze on the horizon straight ahead.

"Sergeant," Trundell called out, prompting Braxton to spur his horse alongside the major. "Chuck, we're approaching the Eagle Creek crossing. Alert the men of a possible ambush from the mountainside. We'll continue traveling southwest to avoid the hills as much as possible.

"Yes, sir," Braxton replied and rode back down the troop line informing the men of the possible danger.

"You still expect us to be attacked?" Roger asked as the sergeant rode away.

"Anytime, anywhere along our route to Fort Stockton," Trundell responded. "The Apache know this land from birth. And they travel it as a way of life almost as if to strategically study it. Our only advantage is that we often outnumber them. Settlers do not have that advantage."

Nantan and Elan could be seen riding up from Eagle Creek in their direction. When reaching the 9th Cavalry, the Apache scouts reported no sign of a potential ambush at the crossing.

After reaching Eagle Creek, the soldiers watered their horses and replenished their supplies. The company then proceeded to a site called Pajarito Springs and camped for the night without incident. In the morning, they followed a route closer to the Sacramento Mountains staying in proximity to the water resources provided by the mountain springs.

Trundell dispatched Captain Dunston, Elan and three soldiers to ride ahead into the mountains to search for signs of Indians. Some Apache groups were also joining with the Kiowa, neither of which was necessarily friendly toward the army.

That afternoon, the major had the cavalry turn toward the Sacramento Mountains in anticipation of taking advantage of the watershed coming from the hills. Captain Dunston's unit was to meet the company's arrival at a place called the "waterholes."

As the cavalry approached, the captain and his detachment came into view and appeared to be dismounted and enjoying the shade of the mountains. Dunston mounted and rode toward Trundell, positioned at the head of the procession. He reined up and saluted.

"Major, it is clear to approach," Dunston reported. "We have found no sign of hostiles in the area."

"Good work, Captain," Trundell replied, as he surveyed the mountain landscape. "I think the men are beginning to get restless." The major then gave the signal for the troops to follow Dunston's lead on the way to the waterholes.

Roger dropped back and sidled up to Sergeant Braxton's mount. "Are the men becoming restless?" Roger asked.

"They're becoming bored," Chuck stated, offering Roger a slight smile. "I hate to say it, but I think they're itching for action. These long marches allow too much time to think, and their focus starts to decline."

"That doesn't sound good. Are we expecting trouble?" Roger inquired.

"Blood between the Apache and the army is not good and plans to turn these mountains into a reservation have not been well received by some renegade bands," the sergeant said. "Long rides like this, anticipating a pending attack, can make the men antsy."

"I think I'm beginning to feel a little antsy, myself," Roger said, urging his mount to catch up to Trundell.

"We won't stay here tonight," Trundell said to no one in particular. "We'll push south to the Rio Peñasco and camp across the river from the mountains."

"Are you still planning my immersion baptism when we reach the Peñasco?" Lieutenant Liston said from behind Roger as the preacher dismounted.

"If we don't run into any trouble, we'll get it done," Roger said, offering the lieutenant a tight-lipped grin.

"Are we expecting trouble?" Liston asked.

"I'm the wrong person to ask that," Roger replied, leading his horse in the direction of a watering hole. "I can only say I hope not."

"I know some of the men have been talking about a possible ambush, but I understand Captain Dunston and his scouting party have reported no danger so far," Liston said, following behind.

"I would be inclined to take their word for it," Roger said. "They understand these hills, and their inhabitants, pretty well."

Roger stopped at the water's edge and allowed his mount to step into the refreshing liquid and drink its fill.

"I shall pray that holds up after we reach Rio Peñasco," Liston said.

"That's a great idea for a variety of reasons," Roger muttered while leading his horse to where the soldiers were allowing the horses to graze.

After a short break, the 9th Cavalry mounted up and started in a southwestward direction. They traveled toward a ridge that marked the southern end of the Sacramento Range that fed the Rio Peñasco.

The sun was beginning to creep behind the range, but the route Trundell chose kept them east of the growing shadows. Although Captain Dunston and his men found no sign of hostiles during their reconnaissance missions, Trundell still felt more comfortable keeping distance between his troops and the mountains.

As the evening shadows stretched over the procession of soldiers, they came to a pleasant spot on the Rio Peñasco and set up camp. Before long, the cook's campfire was blazing, and dinner would soon be on its way.

"A pleasant spot like this really takes one's mind off his troubles, right, major? Roger said as he gazed at the blooming wildflowers, tall grass, and a mix of pine and deciduous trees. The pastor's cares seem to float away with the sounds of the river's bubbling waters.

"Too pleasant for my liking," Trundell said, as he signaled to his men where he wanted his tent staked. "It's the kind of site that can make a soldier too comfortable. I'm going to have Braxton set up a night watch. I won't feel easy until we're away from these mountains. We'll head due east tomorrow following this river."

"I wish I could soften your worries, major, but you have more experience at these things than I have," Roger said, pulling up a stalk of grass and inserting it between his teeth. "I'll pray for a quiet night."

"Pray that my sentries stay awake, while you're at it," Trundell said, surveying the outlying area around the camp. Other than the foliage that lined the river, the landscape was open, offering a good view of any approaching danger.

"Excuse me, major," Lieutenant Liston inquired, "permission to speak?"

"What's on your mind, lieutenant?" Trundell said, acknowledging the junior officer while continuing his visual survey.

"I wanted to know if Pastor Brinkman, here, could baptize me in the river before we go?" Liston said.

"So, you want to take the full plunge," Trundell replied. "I guess, if Roger is willing, you could do it early tomorrow morning before breakfast – if, and this is a big if, we don't have any trouble between now and our departure."

"We can look for a good spot along the river this evening and 'take the plunge,' as you say, in the morning," Roger said. "It'll be a little brisk, Lieutenant, but I'll be more than happy to oblige."

"Thank you, sir, and thank you, Major," Liston said, saluting Trundell with a broad smile.

"God bless you, son," Trundell said. "May God bless all of us."

Roger accompanied Liston down to the river and found an ideal spot where the water was about waist-deep with a gentle flow.

"This should do just fine," Roger said, turning to the lieutenant," but, like I said, the water will be cold."

"If you can handle it, Pastor, I'm more than happy to," Liston said, kneeling to feel the temperature of the river. "It shouldn't take us long, right?"

"Enough time for the Father, Son, and Holy Ghost to be satisfied," Roger replied. "It shouldn't take much longer than the baptism you had at Fort Stanton."

"I look forward to it, Pastor, and thanks."

Roger nodded and put his arm around the lieutenant's shoulders as they made their way back toward the chuckwagon.

Blessed with restful sleep that night, Roger awoke and was surprised to see Lieutenant Liston nearby waiting for him. The air was cold and steam could be seen rising off the river. There was a ground-level fog hanging close to the water but not enough to delay the baptism. Roger pulled on his boots and retrieved his stole and draped it around his neck.

"I have to admit that an immersion baptism this early, and this cold, is a first for me," Roger said, smiling as he approached Liston. "This will be a baptism to remember."

"I had not thought about the conditions as contributing to how special this is to me," the lieutenant said. "I have asked Corporal Sutherland to be my witness if that's okay?"

"God bless you for standing in, Corporal," Roger replied, turning to Sutherland. "It's a blessing you won't have to get wet on this chilly morning."

"My pleasure, Pastor," said Sutherland. "I think this is a terrific thing you're doing, since you have already performed the ceremony at Fort Stanton."

"The Lord would not have me do otherwise," Roger replied, extending his hand in the direction of the river. "Let us proceed since the major is going to want to leave early this morning."

The three made their way down to the river where the lieutenant took off his tunic exposing a loose-fitting white shirt. He seemed almost impervious to the cold as he awaited instructions. There was also a sentry nearby, who saluted the three men as they passed.

"I will wade out a few feet until I find a suitable spot. You can follow a few steps behind until I receive you," Roger said to Liston. "Corporal, you should be able to see the ceremony through the mist. It's getting lighter now."

"Yes, sir," the corporal responded.

The chill of the water made Roger shiver as he waded in up to his waist. He caught a glimpse of what he thought was a low-flying bird and heard a thud and a splash. He turned just in time to see Liston face down in the water.

"Indians," cried the corporal, as he rushed to the lieutenant's aid calling out to the sentry. "Sound the alarm! We're under attack!"

Roger began wading back toward Lieutenant Liston and reached the wounded man just as the corporal was rolling him over – an arrow was protruding from the middle of the soldier's chest.

The sentry began firing across the river, although the fog still made visual contact difficult. Other soldiers, half-dressed, began racing toward the river.

An arrow creased Roger's back, putting a tear in his shroud as he and Sutherland struggled to get the lieutenant to shore. They made their way toward the shelter of some trees as approaching soldiers began firing their rifles. One pitched forward when an arrow pierced his leg.

An Apache war party had made their way down a tributary of the Rio Peñasco opposite of where the 9th Cavalry was camped. Other members of the band had quietly stationed horses in the trees during the night while the warriors quietly took up positions where they could see the camp. Many had rifles but used bows and arrows for stealth until discovered.

Captain Dunston was already out of his tent when he heard the shooting. He called to Sergeant Braxton to gather a few men to work their way up the river in hopes of flanking the attackers.

Major Trundell came out of his tent in his undershirt and suspenders hanging from his waist and encircling his hips.

"Captain! What the hell is going on?" Trundell called out as Dunston and Braxton passed.

"Ambush! Apaches are across the river. Must have snuck up during the night," the captain shouted over his shoulder, just before he and his small group entered the trees by the river.

"Remington, have some of the soldiers mount their horses for a counterattack by crossing the river," Trundell ordered as the lieutenant emerged from his tent.

The sound of rifle fire began to quiet down and seemed to be coming only from the army's side of the river. Dunston and his men had reached the river and could see the war party was now retreating in the direction of their horses.

"Take your best shot, men," Dunston ordered. "Let's not let them get away with this."

By chance, a running warrior was hit and fell to the ground. However, the rest had leaped onto their horses and were well on their way to safety.

Remington, leading six mounted soldiers, plunged into the river and the horses waded across under the cover of those firing from shore. Once on the other side, they scaled the bank only to see the band of renegades disappearing back into the mountains.

"Lieutenant! There is one warrior down," one of Remington's men called out.

"Englewood," Remington said to one of his horse soldiers. "Ride back and bring Nantan here. Perhaps he can be of service in identifying the fallen man. In the meantime, we'll make sure he's down for good."

After reaching the fallen Indian, Remington checked for a pulse and found none.

"We'll, we got one of them," he said. "We'll wait for Nantan and Elan to see if they recognize him."

The two Apache scouts arrived a short time later and examined the fallen warrior.

"This is one of Victorio's warriors," Nantan said, looking over at Elan, who nodded in agreement. "They must have been following our movements waiting for a chance to attack."

"Let him be," Remington said. "They will come back for him after we're gone. There's not much we can do now."

As Remington and his men entered the river to cross back to the 9th Cavalry's side, they noticed Major Trundell and several other soldiers standing near the trees where Roger and Corporal Sutherland had taken Lieutenant Liston for cover. They could see the major was deeply distressed.

"Ah, Roger, would you do me a favor," the major said, removing his hand from his reddened eyes.

"Of course, George. What can I do for you?" Roger replied.

"Will you just say Lieutenant Liston died in battle," Trundell stated.

"I can certainly do that," Roger replied. "Anything else?"

"I know his parents," Trundell said. "I promised them I'd look after their son. This baptism could be seen as a careless move on my part."

"If you're okay with that I have no reason to dishonor a good soldier's death," Roger said. "It was an ambush. He didn't have a chance."

"Thank you," Trundell said, and turned to walk back to camp. "Lieutenant, did you catch up to any of them?" he asked Remington.

"We got one. Nantan said he was one of Victorio's men," the lieutenant replied.

"Find out for me if we lost anyone else," the major asked. "We'll be delayed depending on how many we have to bury. I'm sure we have wounded as well.

"Roger, will you do us the honor of saying a few words when we know the extent of our losses?"

49

"Of course," Roger said looking back at Corporal Sutherland holding Liston's head in his lap. "It's the least I can do."

Trundell doubled security around the camp and assigned a dozen soldiers to accompany Lieutenant Remington in finding a suitable location for burial. Two other members of the 9th Cavalry had also been killed along with Second Lieutenant Jeff Liston.

Four soldiers had been wounded in the surprise attack and were getting medical attention. Fortunately, none required surgery and their wounds were not serious enough to keep them from riding.

"That hill near the river should do," Remington said to Corporal Sutherland, the non-com in charge of the internment unit. "It's surrounded by trees, and it looks too high to be subject to flooding."

"It looks pristine and peaceful," Roger said, following along with the detachment. "It should also be easy to locate if any of the families want to find it."

"I wish we could send them home," Remington remarked. "We're just not set up to do that. We still have two weeks' journey ahead before reaching Fort Stockton.

"Corporal, have the men prepare three graves on top of that knoll," Remington called out.

"Do you anticipate any more Indian attacks?" Roger asked the lieutenant.

"The only mountains we will encounter on our way down the Pecos River is the Sierra Guadalupe Range. The Mescalero used to occupy the area but were driven out by some of these same men when they rode with the 10th Cavalry," Remington said. "I think things will be quiet now. I would guess Victorio is headed west after yesterday's attack to prevent us from following him."

"Does he know where we are going?" Roger asked.

"It is likely Chief Caballero got word to him when we passed through the proposed Mescalero Reservation. Victorio planned the ambush at Rio Peñasco and then fled."

Once the burial sites were established, some of the men were assigned to dig while others spread out as sentries. The sentries would trade places with the working men to ensure the graves would be ready by the following morning.

"Once the service is completed tomorrow, we'll begin our trek to Fort Stockton," Major Trundell said when Roger approached. "I had looked forward to reaching Stockton, but not so much now."

"You shouldn't blame yourself for what happened, George," Roger offered, deferring to the major's first name. "It was an ambush and the fog helped the Apache catch us off guard."

"That's just it, I let my guard down and it cost me one of my officers. The only one whose family I know personally," the major responded.

"You're a soldier at war," Roger said consolingly. "I know what it is to blame oneself for the loss of someone close, and it hurts. You have too much responsibility ahead of you to dwell on something beyond your control. I'm sure his family knew what he was getting into when he chose a military career.

The major solemnly looked at Roger, lowered his head and nodded gently. "I'm just glad you're here so we can bury them with dignity."

The next day at sun-up, Roger spoke at the graves with all in attendance, excluding the sentries at their posts. He honored each soldier for their service giving each the respect they deserved. He also recognized the heroic efforts of those caught up in the fight, especially the wounded.

He closed with a prayer and soon the 9th Cavalry was on its way, following the Rio Peñasco where it flowed into the Rio Pecos.

Chapter 7
Galveston and Juneteenth

After working out a cooperative plan with the Galveston Livery Stable, Nik Brinkman found a horse to his liking. The stable called the mare Galley and she and Nik became acquainted as the two rode about discovering Nik's new island home. Nik took a special interest in visiting the waterfront because Galveston's history was filled with stories of swashbucklers and smuggling.

After the new chief marshal reached the courthouse, he went in to meet those he would be working with, and locate his office. Nik noticed a buggy in the alley between the courthouse and the jailhouse next door. It reminded him of the one owned by Judge Kensington, who disappeared from Paris, Texas. Kensington had been the subject of a land-fraud case he and Roger investigated together.

Upon entering the courthouse, he scanned the lobby marquis and saw Judge Conklin's name. Conklin was the man he would be answering to. He approached the judge's door and knocked.

"Come in," said a voice from behind the door labeled "The Honorable Jedediah Conklin/Circuit Judge 10th District."

Nik entered to find a tall man in a three-piece suit standing next to a desk where a middle-aged man sat smoking a cigar.

"How may I help you?" asked the man behind the desk, whose hair was white and thin on top. The hair color closely matched his muttonchops and mustache. The man was huskily built but did not appear overweight.

"Sorry to interrupt you, your honor, I assume you're Judge Conklin?"

"I am," said the judge in a voice that would command respect in any courtroom.

"Sorry to intrude, but I'm the new marshal in town and thought I should introduce myself," Nik added.

"I am Judge Conklin. The sheriff was telling me about you," the judge said with a grin. "I hear you're the type of marshal that goes after circuit judges."

"Well, I was …" Nik started, as the judge let out a boisterous laugh, shared by the man standing by the desk.

"Don't mind me, Marshal. I was just having fun. Mr. Warburton and I were just finishing up. Jack, we'll discuss this later, if you'll excuse us."

"Not a problem, Judge," Jack Warburton said, as he put his cigar in the ashtray, retrieved his hat from a nearby chair, and nodded as he passed Nik.

"Sit down," said the judge, "and tell me about yourself."

Nik gave Conklin a brief outline of his past and why he had been assigned to Galveston. He apologized for his reputation as a marshal who goes after judges.

"Not at all, Nik, is it?" Nik nodded to the judge in affirmation. "We have been without federal law here for some time. Sheriff Atkins is a helpful sort, but his jurisdiction is rather limited. I hear you're good at what you do."

"I hope I won't disappoint, your honor," Nik said. "I have not spent any real time covering a seaport."

"How are you getting along here in Galveston?" Conklin said, leaning forward in his chair and putting his cigar between his yellowish teeth. "Is Galveston treating you okay?"

"I have no complaints so far, but I would like to find a deputy to assist me," Nik replied.

"I assume your budget can afford that," the judge said, taking the cigar from between his teeth. "Finding someone might be a little difficult. Are you looking for any type in particular?"

"Just someone I can trust to do a good job," Nik answered.

"Does it matter if they're colored?" Conklin said, leaning back.

"Most of the coloreds are on the mainland. But that shouldn't be a problem for you because some parts of the mainland are also in your jurisdiction."

"I've worked with all… colors, as you say, Dudge," Nik said, hoping his remark would not put him on the wrong foot with Conklin like he was with Kensington.

"Does that term bother you, Marshal?" Conklin asked, reinserting the cigar and taking a big puff.

"No, your honor. I'm just adjusting to my new surroundings," Nik answered. "It's just a matter of learning how others in Galveston feel about me as their new marshal."

"Galveston is ahead of the times, Nik. You don't mind if I call you Nik, do you?"

"It suits me just fine," Nik responded.

"You're going to find there are some who have a little trouble warming up to you, but I wouldn't worry about it," the judge said. "You've got a good way about you and that badge doesn't hurt none, either. If you stick around for Juneteenth, I think you'll find there's good feelings here for all kinds," Conklin said. "We're a major port to the world. When I say colored, I mean we got all colors." The judge barked out, leaning back in his chair to enjoy a good laugh.

Nik smiled and waited for the judge to return to their conversation. "I have heard about Juneteenth and plan to attend. Will you be there?"

"I'm afraid I'll be in Houston that day, Nik. I have attended that celebration before and can honestly say I'll miss not being there this year."

"Well, I won't take up any more of your time, Judge," Nik said, excusing himself and rising to his feet. "I should get over to my office and get some work done as well."

"I think we're going to work well as a team, Nik," Conklin said, also getting to his feet and extending his hand.

Nik stepped forward and shook the judge's hand. He bowed slightly, put his hat on his head, and departed the judge's office.

When June 19 rolled around, Nik saddled Galley and made his

way to the Galveston Bay Ferry. His first thought was to take the train, but accommodating Galley proved problematic and he did not want to be on the mainland without a horse. However, his anxiety about being onboard another boat was beginning to wane. He knew he would have to get used to everything seafaring if he was going to fulfill expectations as Galveston's chief marshal.

Nik found the trip across the bay wasn't nearly as traumatic as being on the open ocean. He disembarked without difficulty and steered Galley in the direction of the Juneteenth celebration.

Nik strolled the open fields of Virginia Point, where the events were being held. He took a special interest in the shooting contest scheduled for that afternoon. The Galveston area was the first in Texas to learn of the Emancipation Proclamation following the end of the Civil War, two years after the declaration had been announced by President Abraham Lincoln.

The community of Galveston had taken it upon themselves to embrace the abolition of slavery and were among the first to establish a school and library for former slaves. Nik couldn't help but silently thank his former boss, Marshal Ned Borchers, for landing the deputy in his new position.

As Nik neared the firing range where the shooting competition was to take place, he noticed a rather large man towering above those gathered at the competitors' station. The marshal was intrigued that a man of that size would also be proficient with a rifle.

"May I help you, Marshal?" came a voice just over Nik's right shoulder.

"I'm not sure," Nik remarked as he turned to face the man smiling at him.

Juneteenth was a celebration largely of the black population, but many whites joined in and even sponsored several of the events.

"I hope I didn't disturb you, but my name is Charles Goldfield," said the man. "I am in charge of the shooting contest, and I couldn't help but notice you were with the U.S. Marshals Service."

"No, you're not bothering me at all… Charles," Nik said, shaking Goldfield's hand. "I'm quite interested in this event."

"Did you want to participate?" Charles asked. "And you can call me 'Charlie,' everyone else does."

"Actually, Charlie, I am interested in watching the event," Could you direct me to a good spot where I can observe it?"

"I can do better than that, Marshal. I will make room for you on the judges' stand."

"That would be terrific, Charlie," Nik responded. "And please, call me Nik. I'm new here in Galveston and still getting used to being the district marshal."

"Welcome to Galveston, Marshal Nik. We look forward to having you here." Charlie said. "By the way, would you like a list of the shooters?"

"That I would, sir. Very much so and thank you," Nik said, broadening his smile.

Nik was escorted to the judges' stand where he was introduced to the five-man panel, two of them black. He was given a chair with an excellent view of the shooting range and even offered a pair of field glasses along with the list of shooters.

Once the competition began, Nik noticed one of the other contestants dwarfed the others, and continued to watch him with keen interest. He wasn't at all sure why he instinctively was drawn to the man and tried to dismiss the feeling since he was mostly interested in the best marksmen no matter who they were.

His mind drifted back to the trial of Lupe and Levi and compared the Leviathan to the one now competing in the contest. Two things stood out to Nik about the towering sharpshooter, he wore a Union jacket and was an excellent shot.

"Who is that tall gentleman in the Union jacket?" Nik said, leaning forward to get the attention of the judges on the panel.

"He's the one listed as A. Tucker," the judge nearest him answered. "He's new here."

As the event progressed, the broad-shouldered marksman took the lead into the final shoot. His closest competitor was a tall, thin black man with graying hair and a closely cropped beard bearing the same shade. The final event was firing a long rifle at two-hundred yards. The targets were enlarged to not only compensate for the added distance but to assist the judges in declaring a winner.

Through his field glasses, Nik could see where the bullets were hitting and wondered if his brother, Roger, wouldn't have trouble beating the two finalists. When the smoke cleared, the taller man was declared the winner by a very thin margin.

Nik rose from his chair, thanked the panel for their fine work, and stuffed the list of shooters into his pocket. He quickly descended the stairs and headed in the direction of the awards ceremony.

As he worked his way through the crowd of onlookers using his badge to help explain his intrusion, he soon made his way to the inner circle. When second place was announced, a young woman emerged from the crowd and hugged the older contestant.

Nik was distracted by the woman's striking appearance. He looked down at the ground to try and shift his concentration, but when he raised his eyes they immediately fixed on the young woman.

He couldn't help but stare at her while the first-place ribbon was being given to the man listed as A. Tucker. When the woman's gaze fell on Nik, the slightly embarrassed marshal smiled and quickly looked at the winner.

As the crowd began to disperse, Nik approached the large shooter and called out to the smaller contestant, who was departing with the young woman holding onto his arm.

"Excuse me, sir!" Nik called out while stepping in close to the winner. "Could I speak to you, please? And to you, Mr. Tucker."

The big man just looked down at Nik, as he waited for the older gentleman and his lady friend to return.

"Gentlemen," Nik began. "I am Chief U.S. Marshal Nik Brinkman. I have been watching you shoot and can only say how impressed I am. So impressed, I would like to offer you both a potential deputy's position with the U.S. Marshals Service here in Galveston."

"Excuse me, what did you say your name was?" the tall man asked.

"Ah, Nik, Nik Brinkman," Nik answered.

"That's only the second time I ever heard that name," the shooting champion said. My name's Tucker, Ambrose Tucker."

"If you're referring to my last name, there are not a lot of Brinkmans around that I know of," Nik replied. "Was it someone you know?"

"I haven't seen him since the war," Tucker said. "We were sharpshooters together, and then went I went Union I was one of the ones who captured him. He was white, though."

"Wait a minute, …" Nik said, staring up at the big man. "His name wouldn't have been Roger, would it? Roger Brinkman."

"That's him. Do you know him?"

Nik laughed, "Yes I know him. He's my brother."

Nik could see the young lady look up at her elderly companion when Nik mentioned "brother."

"But, like I said, Roger was white," Ambrose responded.

"Roger Brinkman's parents bought me and made me one of the family," Nik said, looking back and forth from Ambrose to the elderly man and the woman with him as he spoke. "After the war, we were deputy marshals together before he went off to become a traveling clergyman."

"I left the Confederacy and joined the Union Army," Ambrose said. "I was with the men who took him captive just before the war ended. I never saw him again after that."

"My apologies," Nik said, turning to the elderly man and the woman. "I just got caught up in our discussion about my brother. My primary interest is if either of you would like to serve as a U.S. Deputy Marshal."

"I do not think my father would be up to that," the woman replied. "He is a good shot, but I do not think he would be a good lawman."

"It would not necessarily be full-time," Nik began, noting her protection of the man she referred to as father. "As U.S. marshals, we are required to protect certain national assets as opposed to chasing down outlaws. He would not be required to do that."

"I might be interested in full-time if you have that," Ambrose said.

"I would be delighted with that," Nik said. "I would just have to get authorization to hire you as a deputy marshal. However, I do not think that would take long.

"As for you…" Nik started, pulling the shooters' list from his pocket and scanning it.

"Boatman, Isaiah Boatman, this here is my daughter," the tall, thin man responded. "Under the right circumstances, I might be able to help."

"Are you sure, father?" the woman said. "I would not want anything to happen to you. You're all I have."

For obvious reasons, the woman's remark was very pleasing to Nik. He was beginning to experience certain feelings he had never felt before and was uncertain as to how to deal with them.

"Mam…" Nik began.

"Esther," said the woman. "Esther Boatman."

"Wow, what a pretty name," Nik blurted. "I'm sorry, I did not mean to be so forward. You both have biblical names. I like that." Stumbling over his conversation, Nik was beginning to feel embarrassed.

"Let us think about it," Esther said. "We'll let you know. How can we reach you?"

"If it's any easier, I could come to you," Nik said. "Where do you live?"

"How would you know when we've made up our minds?" Esther asked.

"Oh, …ah, great question," Nik said, feeling like an idiot. "I can be found at the U.S. Marshal's Office in Galveston most any day. Unless I'm gone, that is," The thought of taking out his gun and shooting himself flashed through Nik's mind. He was dying inside wanting the conversation to end but wishing Esther and her father would never leave.

"We'll find you, Marshall Brinkman," Esther said, looking up at her father. "We should be going."

"Of course," Nik sighed.

"Congratulations, Mr. Boatman," Ambrose said, reaching out to shake Isaiah's hand. He then tipped his hat in Esther's direction. "Pleased to meet you, Miss Boatman."

"Congratulations to you, Mr. Tucker," Esther said, extending her hand and smiling. "That was some terrific shooting."

Nik stood by sheepishly grinning, contemplating whether he ought to try to shake hands or just wave. As Esther and her father turned to leave, she turned and gave Nik a big smile. He knew immediately he would never get the vision of that smile out of his mind.

"You seem kind of taken by that pretty lady," Ambrose said, once the couple was out of earshot.

"It was that obvious?" Nik muttered. "I don't suppose I did much to inspire confidence in the Marshals Service."

"I wouldn't worry about it," Ambrose said. "But I would like to be considered for that deputy marshal's job."

"Outstanding," Nik replied. "I'll get on it right away. Just let me know where I can get in touch with you."

"Right now, I'm in between places so I can't give you anything permanent," Ambrose said. "But I can sure find the marshal's office in Galveston."

The two men shook hands and Nik set off in the direction of the temporary corral where Galley was stabled. He thought about what Ambrose had said and turned to look after him, but he was nowhere to be seen. He mounted up and began his journey back to the Galveston Ferry.

As he rode along, he could not get Esther Boatman off his mind. Nik grimaced in embarrassment over his complete lack of composure around her. He had been around women before, but none like her. Had he blown his chances of seeing her again? What if her father accepted his offer, would that help?

Then the thought of Esther turning to smile at him caused Nik to smile to himself. It was a beautiful smile, it certainly appeared friendly. He straightened himself in the saddle and considered the fact he was the territory's top lawman.

"Come on, you're Chief Marshal Nik Brinkman," Nik muttered to himself. "You can rise above this. After all, you've faced dangerous criminals, even bigots, and backed them down. Esther is a woman. You can handle it." Yes, but she's such a fine woman, Nik thought without saying it.

"Agggh, life just isn't fair," Nik called out into thin air. Galley turned her ears back, but kept her pace. "I finally meet someone I could care about and I'm an emotional mess."

Finally, horse and rider reached the Galveston Ferry and were soon putting the final touches on the end of their day.

Chapter 8
Roger Meets Pecos

Still grieving over their losses, the 9th Cavalry made camp on the day before they were scheduled to reach Fort Stockton, Texas. It was mid-May and they encountered no further trouble, but the soldiers wounded in the ambush at Rio Peñasco made slow travel time. All but one would be cleared to return for duty, with the last requiring two days of bed rest before being reinstated.

Roger could tell Major Trundell was troubled by the loss of Lieutenant Jeff Liston and his despondency seem to grow the closer they drew to Fort Stockton. That evening, Roger was able to approach the major as to his melancholy nature.

"George, I can tell something is bothering you and I fear you're still carrying the burden of Jeff Liston's death. Do you want to talk about it?"

"I have come to grips with losing Jeff and sending my regrets to his family, but I'm a little worried about how this will affect my career," Trundell admitted. "I know that sounds a little selfish but being in charge of these Buffalo Soldiers has become a part of me."

"Do you really think this could have a deleterious effect on your distinguished career?" Roger remarked. "These men look up to you and I can't imagine the army interfering with that relationship."

"I guess I just feel guilty about it," Trundell said. "I keep thinking how I would approach the situation if I were the commanding officer of the 9th Regiment."

"So, you feel you would be hard enough on yourself to warrant a demotion?" Roger questioned. "Who is the commander of the 9th?"

"Colonel Edward Hatch," Trundell answered. "He may well be at Fort Stockton when we get there. He served as a general under Grant in the Civil War."

"Is he hard to get along with? I'd be happy to put in a good word or even take the blame for what happened?"

"No, I know Colonel Hatch and he is a fair man. Perhaps too fair," the major said.

"Too fair? What do you mean by that?" Roger continued to inquire.

"I have had a distinguished career and that's what bothers me," Trundell responded. "I cannot help but feel I should have prevented Jeff from going down to that river."

"And the only way for you to be relieved of that guilt is to be punished for being in charge when it happened," Roger said. "I'm sure you've lost men before. As soldiers, death on the battlefield is no anomaly. Do you always feel this way when one of your troops is killed?"

"Nope, this is the first time. And the only reason I can come up with is that I knew the lad before he became a soldier. I have to imagine Hatch will dismiss my being at fault and the family will not bear me a grudge. Yet, here I am agonizing over it."

"A group of Sadducees tried to trap Jesus into explaining the afterlife, something they did not believe in. He answered them by saying his heavenly father was the God of the living, not the dead," Roger replied. "His point was that there is an afterlife and that's where Jeff is now. As for you, you are responsible for those who are still alive here on Earth. Let God take care of those who are not."

Major Trundell listened intently to Roger's words and then his eyes widened, and he leaned back. "You're right. I'm going to have to let that sink in."

"If it's any consolation, I've never had anyone ask to be baptized twice," Roger said. "Jeff's faith was such that he wanted to steep himself in the glory of God. Unfortunately, he died in the process, but I can guarantee you, he was not the first."

"I could use a good man like you, Pastor," Trundell said with a smile. "I don't suppose you'd consider joining the army? You'd make a hell of an officer."

"I've joined Christ's Army," Roger answered, smiling back. "I can't achieve a higher rank than that."

The following day, the 9th Cavalry arrived at Fort Stockton and spent the afternoon settling in. Colonel Hatch was in Kansas meeting with General Guy Henry of the 10th Cavalry Regiment. The purpose of the meeting was to finalize plans for the Mescalero Reservation and to subdue renegade Apache leaders Victorio, Cochise, and Geronimo.

"Well, Roger," Major Trundell began, sitting at the officer's table in the mess hall. "Since I can't talk you into joining the army, I guess you'll be on your way to Galveston soon."

"Now is the hard part," Roger remarked. "I have no horse, and there are no trains out here. Do you have any suggestions, George?"

"I do, Roger," Trundell said. "We have a patrol that will leave here for the Mexico border in a day or two. If you want to tag along, the trip will take you to the Rio Grande. There you can catch a ride on the river south to Fort Duncan at Eagle Pass, the 9th has a detachment there and you can replenish your supplies. Riverboats run from Eagle Pass to the Gulf of Mexico, where you can board a ship bound for Galveston."

"Traveling by water," Roger said, mentally mapping out the major's directions. "I did that once, but I was unconscious the entire trip."

"Were you ill or wounded?" Trundell asked.

"You could say that," Roger said. "I fell into a river and was knocked unconscious. I came to in a strange home and did not know who I was. The lady of the house and her son nursed me back to health and here I am today."

"Sounds like quite a story," Trundell quipped. "I suggest you stay alert for the rest of this trip," Trundell added laughing. "By the way, I'll write a letter you can give to the commanding officer at Fort Duncan. They'll treat you right."

"Much obliged, Major. I do intend to keep my wits about me."

Roger retired to his quarters after dinner and lay on his bunk thinking about reaching Galveston and seeing Nik. It had been a while since he'd spent time in Texas and he wondered if it had changed much since he was there as a deputy marshal. He had never been to southern Texas or visited a seaport like Galveston. He whispered a silent prayer for Nik's success as chief marshal in Galveston and a safe journey for the rest of his trip.

Captain Dunston was selected to lead the patrol headed for the border, along with most of the men in the patrol. Sergeant Braxton and Apache scouts Nantan and Elan were also scheduled to ride along. It would take two weeks to reach the Rio Grande, with a stop at Fort Davis in the Limpia Mountains.

The following day, Roger said goodbye to Major Trundell and was given the letter introducing him to the commander when he reached Fort Duncan. Roger's luggage was in the ordnance wagon, and Trundell laughed promising Roger the army wouldn't blow it up.

There were Comanches in the part of Texas they were scheduled to cross, but most lived in peace with the white man. Dunston said his only concern was a young Comanche warrior known as Quanah Parker. Parker was head of a group of renegades, but a recent report said Parker had moved north into Oklahoma.

"His mother was a white woman, kidnapped by the Comanche when she was a child," Duncan remarked, as Roger rode alongside the captain. "He is also the son of a chief and trained well as a warrior."

"Do you think these Indian wars will ever end?" Roger asked, somewhat absentmindedly.

"They're already ending as more and more tribes move onto reservations," Duncan answered. "There are renegades who resist the reservations, but they are becoming fewer as time goes on."

"How long have you been in the army?" Roger asked.

"Going on twenty years, if you count the Civil War," Dunston said. "After that, I was commissioned as a second lieutenant and sent west. I've been fighting with the Indians ever since."

"I guess that was quite a change for you," Roger said.

"At first it was a huge change. I was used to confronting Johnny Reb head on. Out here I have to look out for sneak attacks and ambushes, like the one that took Lieutenant Liston's life," Duncan continued, as he scanned the horizon. "I understand you were in the war."

"I fought for the South actually, for no other reason than I happened to meet a Confederate Captain before I enlisted. He talked me into joining after my family was killed," Roger said, looking ahead as he spoke. "Not one of it my fondest memories."

"What got you into the ministry?" Dunston asked.

"I was away at seminary when my family was murdered by some men I thought were Union soldiers," Roger stated. "After the war, I joined the U.S. Marshals Service and became familiar with this part of the country. After quitting the service, I went back to seminary and chose the traveling clergy lifestyle for my ministry.

"So, do you resent the Indians as much as you did the Confederates?" Roger concluded.

"It's funny you should ask that," Dunston said. "I didn't resent the Rebs as much as I just wanted to teach them a lesson. Slavery never made much sense to me, and it's been my honor to serve with these Buffalo Soldiers, as the Indians call them.

"As for the Indians, I've come to admire all but the renegades. I can understand their resentment but, as a soldier, I can't let that get in the way of what I've been called upon to do."

"That call to duty carries a lot of weight, all right," Roger responded. "I thought that was the path I was on, but along the way everything got mixed up. However, I do believe I'm on the right path now."

"Losing your family, going to war, chasing outlaws, and now preaching the gospel," Dunston began, "I would say things did get a bit mixed up for you. Though you do seem to have come through it well."

"I cannot overstate what faith in Jesus Christ can do for a man, Captain," Roger said. "Had it not been for that you might have been hunting for a renegade-crazed white man instead of riding alongside a man of the cloth."

"We're going to have to talk more about that, high desert preacher," Dunston said, turning and smiling at Roger. "About faith in Jesus Christ, I mean."

Roger just looked back at the captain and smiled.

Fort Davis was nestled among the rolling Limpia Mountains. It appeared almost in too peaceful of a location to be a fort. But it would play a pivotal role in the final battles against the Apache.

After a brief stay at Fort Davis, the patrol continued west and eventually reached the Rio Grande. The 9th Cavalry was assigned to assist ranchers being raided by outlaws out of Mexico and renegade Indians coming down from the Llano Estacado. There were settlements along the river where Roger could find means to travel on to Eagle Pass and Fort Duncan. Duncan's patrol would turn north and ride to Fort Bliss, before turning back for Fort Stockton.

"We'll be reaching the Rio Grande in the morning," Captain Dunston said, as he poured himself a cup of coffee and set the pot back down on the embers of the campfire. "So, how was it you decided on becoming a preacher?

"My Pa was a preacher in the town where I grew up. It was kind of natural for me to follow in his footsteps and take over his church one day. That's where I'd be right now if Pa hadn't been murdered."

"So, the death of your family led you down a path different from what you had intended in the ministry?" Dunston questioned, between puffs of breath to cool down his steaming cup of coffee.

"That tragedy put me on a course of revenge. It was all I could think about at the time," Roger continued. "Vengeance also took my mind off the horror of what my family went through. I couldn't deal with that until I gunned down my family's killer. As guilty as I felt about doing that as a pastor, it did turn out to be the closure I needed."

"I can't imagine what you must have gone through," Dunston remarked. "I've seen my share of killin', but not of anyone as close as family.

"But you say your brother survived the ordeal and that's where you are headed – to see him?"

"Yes, I made a promise to Nik when I left the marshal service that, once ordained, I would return and officially baptize him," Roger said. "Pa was planning to do it after Nik surrendered his life to Christ, but that plan was brutally interrupted."

"I understand that Nik, your brother, was adopted?" Dunston said after a sip of his coffee.

"Not officially. Nik was brought over from Africa to be a slave when he was just a boy. My Pa saw him at an auction, bought him, and brought him home to live with us," Roger said. "At that time, Confederate laws would not allow for the adoption of slaves. So, we ignored that and took him in as family, anyhow."

"That's quite a story," Dunston remarked. "And he's still a U.S. marshal?"

"He is. Just promoted to chief marshal in charge of the office in Galveston."

"Galveston was once a Confederate hotbed," the captain remarked. "Is he going to be okay down there?"

"My brother is a remarkable man. I've never known anyone to handle prejudice as well as he has," Roger said. "Besides, I've heard that Galveston has gone out of its way to assimilate former slaves into its society."

"Sounds like he was raised well," Dunston said. "I guess you both were."

"What about you, Captain. What's your story?"

"We were poor dirt farmers," Dunston said, looking off in the distance as he spoke. "When I was old enough, I decided to join the army. My Pa didn't take that news very well. I was really the only one in our family that could help on the farm. I had two sisters, but they were too young to help with the farmin'. I tried telling Pa he would have one less mouth to feed and I'd send home some of my wages. He was still bitter when we parted company."

"I'm sorry to hear that, Dan. We're you ever able to make up with him?"

"No, by the time the war was over he'd worked himself to death and died penniless. Ma was able to make it on the money I sent home, and she and my sisters set up a sewing and mending business for Fort Wallace near our farm in Kansas," the captain said, tossing the remaining coffee grounds in his cup onto the fire. "I was stationed there for a while before being assigned to the 9th Cavalry."

"Do you get back to see them?" Roger asked.

"It's been a while," Dunston said. "My sisters are married, and Ma now lives on the post, still sewing and mending."

"Did you have a church there?"

"No. Ma read to us from the Bible now and then. Pa did too before he became bitter and started blaming God for our bad luck," Dunston said. "Pa wasn't a bad man, but he was no fun to be around. I think Ma would have left him if he had not died."

"It's hard to find a happy story out here," Roger said, staring into the glowing embers of the dying campfire. "All I can do is offer a little comfort and pray for all the help I can."

"At least you have that, Roger," Dunstan said. "The army could use men like you, but this definitely isn't God's work.

"Speaking of that, we'd best get some shuteye. Morning comes early this time of year," the captain suggested.

The next day, the patrol came to a small Indian village near the Rio Grande, just north of the Mexican town of San Antonio del Bravo. Dunston told Sergeant Braxton to wait while he and Roger rode into the camp.

"We can inquire as to river travel here," the captain said to Roger. "I'll speak to whoever is in charge of the village. I also have to know if they've been having any trouble."

Roger retrieved his gear from the ordnance wagon and the two men rode into the Indian village. After being greeted by a young brave standing at the edge of the camp, Dunston explained the nature of the visit, introduced Roger. The young Comanche spoke English well and introduced himself as Pecos Catfish.

Pecos had led a small band of Comanche to the site where they now lived after splitting from a larger tribe to the north. When he and his followers chose not to fight against the blue coats, they were told to leave the tribe. They migrated south and eventually made their camp along the Rio Grande.

Not yet twenty, Pecos was nearly six feet tall and muscular with powerful shoulders, one shoulder displaying a three-inch scar. His hair was long and worn without ribbon or braid. He wore buckskin pants lined with fringe down each leg. Pecos also wore a leather vest with nothing underneath. As the band moved down the Pecos River to the Rio Grande, the youthful brave learned to fish. Pecos married a maiden in his group, who traveled with her mother. Both women now lived with Pecos.

"This man Roger Brinkman. He is a man of Great Spirit, like medicine man," Dunston said after introducing himself, using broken English mixed with parts of the Algonquin Language.

"I speak English," Pecos said, as the three men conversed in front of the Indian's tipi. "I am familiar with white man's shaman."

"Wonderful," Dunston sighed in relief, looking over at Roger. "Pastor Brinkman needs transportation down the Rio Grande. Can you help us with that?"

"I may, but does not come free," Pecos said. "We trade with those across river in Mexico and they like white man's money."

"I just happened to have some," Roger said. He was still receiving payments from the sale of his family's farm in Bordertown, Missouri, where he once lived. "How much?" he asked.

"Depends on how far you wish to go," Pecos replied. "I would take you to Eagle Pass. Then I must return. There are those in the Mexican village who would agree to take you but be very careful who you choose."

"So, you could take me to Eagle Pass where Fort Duncan is located," Roger said. "And what would the price be?"

"Forty dollars. It is my trip back that increases price," Pecos said, looking into Roger's eyes.

"I can pay you that. What will we use for a boat?"

"Follow me," Pecos said, stepping past his tipi to one not more than ten feet from his own. He led the two men inside. "This will get us to Eagle Pass safely… if you follow my orders," Pecos instructed, pointing to a large canoe located inside the tipi.

Roger and Dunston began inspecting the craft. It was constructed from light but sturdy wood and covered inside with canvas and outside with birchbark. Also Inside were strips of rawhide stretched tightly so as not to create more weight. The oars were of cedar, light and easy to handle. There were also two thick leather shields leaning up against the inside of the canoe.

"She looks seaworthy enough," Roger said, rubbing his chin and continuing to gaze at the vessel. "Are those shields propped up against the side of the canoe?"

"They are," Pecos answered. "Not everyone is friendly along the Great River. The shields come in handy when Apache attack with arrows."

"So, we'll be fighting Apache on our trip?" Roger inquired, turning to face Pecos. "Do they have guns, as well?"

"Guns usually belong to Mexican Bandidos, mostly river pirates. Shields do not work well if they shoot guns," Pecos said, barely expressing any emotion.

"Attacks from Apache and pirates," Roger exclaimed. "Since these shields only stop arrows, what do we do in case of gunfire."

"We escape from the canoe," Pecos said. "When I say jump it is best to jump."

"So, at that point, it's every man for himself? What then, do I swim to shore and hope for the best?" Roger asked.

"No, stay with canoe. There are places to hold on," Pecos instructed. "Once out of danger, we go to opposite shore to gather ourselves and continue on our way."

"I wasn't expecting a luxury cruise," Roger mused, turning and grinning at Captain Dunston. "But this sounds more like trying to break through enemy lines. I thought we were at peace with Mexico."

"Attacks are not often," Pecos began. "I only caution you because it has happened in the past."

"Well, there's no turning back now unless I join the army," Roger said, managing a slight smile in Pecos's direction. "I've come this far, so I place myself in, what I hope, are your capable hands. How old are you, anyway?"

"Not much younger than you seem, but I trained well as a Comanche and made trip many times," the Comanche guide said, breaking a smile. "Now we eat, and I will answer more of your questions."

Dunston then announced he would be returning to where the 9th Cavalry had set up camp.

"I've enjoyed your company," Dunston said, shaking Roger's hand. "I wish we could have had more time together but duty calls."

"May your path be blessed, Captain," Roger replied. "Who knows, we may run into each other again, some time."

As Dunston mounted and rode off, Roger turned to accompany Pecos to his tipi.

Pecos's wife and mother-in-law prepared the meal while the two men sat by an open campfire discussing details of the upcoming trip. Pecos's community had adopted much of the Mexican style of cooking and Roger was surprised at how spicy the food was. However, it was tasty and there was plenty of it.

"You were introduced as Pecos Catfish. Is Catfish a name the Comanche gave you?"

"After separating from main tribe to the north, we traveled the river and met a man who taught me how to fish white man's way," Pecos began. "I learned to cook fish with smoke. Catfish was popular, and I could sell for money or trade. I was good at catching catfish and soon people began calling that name. I use it now for my second name."

"Did you have a... second name before they called you Catfish?"

Pecos seemed to think for a moment while staring into the campfire. "No," he replied.

Roger knew Comanche did use last names but thought it best not to push the questioning further. The conversation again turned to the river trip until the campfire began to dim.

"You and I sleep in tipi with canoe," Pecos said. "Wife's mother will sleep in my tipi with my wife. I hope you do not snore," Pecos added with a smile

"I don't know. I'm not married and have no one to sleep with," Roger replied, looking up from the campfire. "So, your mother-in-law usually sleeps with the canoe?"

"My mother-in-law is an excellent shot. She does a good job of keeping thieves away from the canoe," Pecos said, grinning. "Plus, I am close by.

"It is getting late. We should get some sleep so we can get an early start in the morning."

Chapter 9
Kensington's Invitation

Paco hurried up the dirt road leading to the modest tenement he and Captain Baudelaire occupied when not visiting the cantina in Campeche or entertaining tourists visiting the Yucatan Peninsula. It was a warm day and the captain was sitting outside the bungalow with his chair leaning back against the adobe wall.

"I have word from Señor Giles," Paco called out as he approached the house. "He wants us to have dinner with him tomorrow night at his hacienda."

Cutlass Baudelaire leaned forward dropping his chair onto all four legs. Maggie, sitting on his shoulder, spread her wings for balance, as Paco approached. "You mean to tell me King Victor was serious about what we talked about at the cantina?"

"Si, I stopped by the cantina to gather messages and the invitation was among them," Paco said, pushing his sombrero back away from his eyes.

"Did we get any other messages that might suggest we pass up his invitation?" Cutlass asked.

"The village musicians said there will be a wedding celebration in town this weekend if we wish to attend," Paco answered. "We could pick up some money our usual way, but I checked it out and I found the wedding is actually scheduled for the day after tomorrow."

"Then I see no reason why we cannot accept the judge's invitation," Cutlass said with a grin. "Can you get word to him that we will be there?"

"It is a pretty good climb up to Señor Giles' hacienda and I have been walking all day."

"Then hitch Maria up to the wagon and ride up that way," the captain said, referring to a burro corralled behind the residence. "She needs the exercise and she'll have to take us up there tomorrow afternoon anyway."

The wagon was small with large wheels and not that hard for Maria to pull. It was the only source of transportation the two men had other than walking. And walking was difficult for the former pirate with his leg bound up so he could attach his wooden leg.

"By the way," Cutlass began, "take the back way to the hacienda. We'll go that way tomorrow. I think it would be best if we kept our visit a secret for the time being. At least until we know what the judge is up to."

The distance to Victor Giles' hacienda was not that far, but Maria was never in a hurry, and neither was Paco. Once the burro was on a familiar road, the driver could let go of the reins and let Maria take the lead. With his sombrero pulled low on his forehead, Paco dozed off with the wagon's gentle rocking and rhythmic squeaking of the wheels. Only the occasional jolt from a sudden bump in the road alerted the driver to his whereabouts.

They eventually reached the front gates of the hacienda. Paco got down from the wagon and pulled on the cord that hung from a bell perched atop one of the tall pillars bordering the iron barriers. Enrico appeared out of the shadows of the mansion's front entrance and approached the visitors.

"Ah, Paco, you have received Señor Giles' invitation for dinner?" Enrico inquired.

"We have and Señor Baudelaire sends his gratitude for the hospitality and gives assurance we will attend."

"Bueno, Paco, Señor Giles will be happy to hear that. Would you like to come in and have some refreshment and water for your burro?"

"Thank you, Enrico, but the distance is not far. Maria and I are expected back right away," Paco replied.

"Of course," Enrico said.

Paco returned to the wagon and climbed onboard. He turned to tip his sombrero to Enrico.

"By the way," Enrico called. "Tell Señor Baudelaire that it is not necessary for him to dress as a pirate for the visit," the judge's companion said with a chuckle while flashing a toothy smile.

Paco nodded half amused and snapped the reins to get Maria headed back home. Sensing where they were headed, the burro made better time on the return trip and soon they were back at the bungalow.

"It is all set, Señor Cutlass," Paco said, approaching the man still sitting in a chair propped against the adobe wall that provided shade later in the day.

Cutlass again dropped his chair on all fours, with the same response from Maggie. "What do you suppose that old gringo is up to?" the former pirate quizzed, reaching over to pet and soothe the parrot.

"It is hard to tell," Paco answered. "His valet seemed happy about us coming to dinner, so I imagine it is more than an effort to get acquainted."

"Get acquainted, ha," Cutlass remarked. "He does not like to hobnob with the likes of us. He wants us for something and I'm not anxious to get drawn into anything that's going to require too much work. Fleecing unsuspecting visitors is all the effort I am willing to spend."

"I doubt he has anything as commonplace in mind as that," Paco said. "My guess is that he wants you and the Tiburon for something much bigger.

"By the way, Enrico said it was not necessary for you to come dressed as a pirate and he laughed when he said it."

"I wouldn't mind seeing that lady back out at sea," Cutlass said, referring to his ship. "But I'm not ready to take up buccaneering again. It may have been profitable, but it was not easy. Running and hiding from the law is much tougher than it was when Laffite was in charge."

"If Señor Giles was interested in something like that, would you do it?" Paco asked.

"It would definitely have to be worth our time and the risk," Cutlass remarked, again leaning his chair back against the wall. "Where would we find such a cutthroat crew as Laffite's these days?"

"We do have our share of cutthroats in Mexico," Paco said. "The difficulty is keeping them from turning on you."

"We don't really know what Giles wants, so I'm not going to worry about what I don't know," Cutlass said. "We'll leave the details up to him or walk away from whatever deal he may have in mind."

"Did you pick up some tequila this morning?"

"When I got the invitation, in my haste to bring you the news I forgot," Paco replied. "But I do believe we still have some left in the house."

Cutlass again rocked forward in his chair. "I will take care of that. Why don't you run into town and complete what you started out to do? I will have a glass waiting for you." Cutlass then got up and entered the bungalow.

Paco watched the man disappear into the house. After releasing Maria from the wagon, he placed her into her corral and headed out for the cantina.

The next day, Cutlass and his valet, Paco, laid out their refined attire. Paco's wardrobe was more of the traditional Mexican style of dress, a complete charro suit complete with boots and a vest. Cutlass had a dark sports jacket that he wore over a pair of plain black toreador pants without medallions adorning the legs. Both had a white shirt to go with their ensemble and both outfits were in good shape, as the two seldom had reason to wear them.

"I am surprised these old clothes still look good on us," Cutlass, said, eyeing his jacket as he turned it on its hanger. "Of course, I do not know if it is necessary that we dress this way for the judge's dinner. Are there other guests invited?"

"Enrico did not say so," Paco answered, laying out his suit on his bed. "I think we only wear these clothes because he has such an elaborate estate."

"I wonder where he got all that money?" Cutlass said, hanging his jacket back in the closet. "I did not think judges got paid that well in the states."

"Perhaps he struck it rich doing something other than judging," Paco said, turning to Cutlass. "They say he is crafty."

"That I can believe," Cutlass remarked with a slight snicker. "I just wonder if he is honest. Why did he move to Mexico in the first place?"

"That is a good question, Señor Cutlass," Paco replied. "Maybe he just wanted a simpler life."

"Simpler life? Living in a house like that? There is nothing simple about that man. He acts like royalty," Cutlass said. "Let's go into the village and see if we can find out more about him."

Cutlass put on his pirate costume and hopped into the back of the wagon to ease the pressure on his wooden leg. He had been thinking of giving up the peg leg charade, although it still inspired tourists who had not met him before. Paco hitched up Maria, took the reins, and started down the road to the cantina.

Cutlass took his usual seat near the window of the cantina as he and Paco waited to see if anyone of interest came in. Before long, Enrico entered to check on messages for the judge. The valet greeted the men with a reminder of the dinner. Cutlass responded by asking Enrico to join them.

"Si," Enrico replied, "but I cannot stay long. I must prepare for tonight."

"Are there others coming besides us?" Cutlass inquired.

"There are two other men of Señor Giles' employ, but they are not really guests," Enrico said. "You two are the honored guests tonight.

"Do you plan to wear something more comfortable?"

"Yes, I will ditch the pirate outfit," Cutlass growled. "I'm just curious what this is all about."

"I cannot tell you since I won't find out until tonight as well," Enrico offered. "I only know that Señor Giles is a shrewd businessman and that you will probably like what he has in mind."

"I hope so because if we don't, we walk, and don't want any hard feelings," Cutlass said, staring into Enrico's eyes.

"I'm sure that is acceptable to Señor Giles," Enrico assured. "He requires loyalty. If he does not get it he parts company and you may walk, as you say."

"Okay, just so we're clear," Cutlass added.

"I will pass this conversation on to Señor Giles," Enrico said. "Now, I must be going."

After Enrico departed, Cutlass turned to Paco.

"I don't know if I like this or not," Cutlass said. "I will listen to what Giles has to say and then decide."

"We can do no more," Paco said.

When evening came, Cutlass and Paco got dressed, hitched Maria to the wagon once more, and set out for Kensington's Hacienda. It was a pleasant evening, but the days were getting longer, and the sun would not be setting for two more hours. Cutlass rode alongside Paco on the driver's seat and was lost in thought.

"I cannot help but think the judge is up to no good. I figure, he thinks we'll throw in with him because of my background as a pirate," Cutlass said.

"Si, I think you are correct, Captain," Paco remarked. "Do you think you would return to those days if his offer is good?"

"It would have to be a knockout idea. We have enough trouble staying out of trouble with our little pickpocket game," Cutlass answered. "If all he wants is the Tiburon, I would be willing to make him an offer."

"It would be exciting to sail her again, Captain," Paco said, looking over at Cutlass. "Maybe Señor Giles wants to put on a show."

"If he's willing to pay for the repairs and our time, I'd be willing to put my blade between my teeth and swing from the poop deck for the audience," Cutlass said with a laugh.

"It would be good to reinforce the mast for that," Paco said, chuckling.

"Hey, I may have put on a few pounds but I'm still strong," Cutlass countered. "Most of my weight is muscle." Cutlass said, slapping his belly and laughing.

When they reached Kensington's Hacienda, one of the judge's staff opened the gate and ushered the wagon through. They rode up a circle drive and encountered King Victor coming down the front steps.

"Greetings, gentlemen," Kensington said. "Let my stable boy take your wagon around back where he will care for your burro. Please come inside and enjoy some refreshments."

After getting down from the wagon, Cutlass and Paco ascended the front steps, following the judge.

"I am delighted that you decided to come. Enrico told me about your meeting him at the cantina. I assure you that if you do not like my offer you are free to refuse at no loss to you. But until then, please come in and relax and have a drink or two before dinner."

Upon entering the hacienda, the two men were greeted by a butler who took their sombreros. The hall was finely decorated with a high ceiling. A balcony rimmed by a white banister nearly encircled the room, halting on either side of the structure's tall front doors.

There was a fireplace straight across from the entrance with a large, immaculately framed portrait of Kensington above it. Off to the right was a smaller portrait of Sebastian Lerdo de Tejada. It hung next to a painting of former president Benito Juarez. Flanking Kensington's image on the opposite side was a picture of Antonio Lopez de Santa Anna, also a little smaller in size than the painting of Kensington.

Standing in front of the fireplace, where a fire was burning to enhance the ambiance, were two smartly-dressed gentlemen. One was American and the other a resident of Mexico.

"Gentlemen, I would like you to meet some good friends of mine, Curtis Packard of Texas, and General Porfirio Diaz, who will likely be Mexico's president one day," Kensington announced with a wave of his arm for dramatic effect. "Curtis, Porfirio, I present to you, Señor Cutlass Baudelaire, and his valet Paco Gutierrez."

"We are honored, Señor Giles, to be among such prestigious guests, are you sure it is Paco and me you expected for dinner?" Cutlass asked, looking at Kensington with a puzzled look.

"Absolutely sure, my good man," Kensington assured. "As I mentioned at the cantina a few weeks ago, I have a plan that I think you might like. And if all goes well you could raise your status considerably by what I have to offer."

"Señor Packard, General Diaz, Paco and I are humbled in your presence," Cutlass began, turning his attention to the two gentlemen he and Paco were introduced to. "I hope you will excuse our, perhaps, crude manners this evening."

"Relax, Mr. Baudelaire, ah … may I call you Cutlass?" Packard began.

"Call me whatever you like, señor, in your presence I shall answer to whatever you like," Cutlass schmoozed.

"As I was saying, I do believe you and I have more in common than you might think. My being a guest here is through my friendship with Judge… Giles," Packard said. "I am a guest here, like you."

"As for me," General Diaz stated, "I am a soldier without rank in this hacienda. What we do here is between us, and as a soldier I intend to see it stays that way."

Cutlass and Paco looked at each other, not quite comfortable with what the general might be implying. But their quizzical looks quickly turned to smiles as they both turned their attention back on Diaz.

"Luis, drinks all around," Kensington called out to his server. "We are all here for a specific reason and that reason makes us all one this evening. Pay no mind to status or standing. We are all equals tonight."

Luis delivered the drinks and the men engaged in small talk. To the amazement of Cutlass and Paco, the two of them seemed to be the subjects of interest of the other three men. After a brief period of getting to know one another, the men retired to the dining room to enjoy an exquisite meal.

At the end of the dinner, the men again engaged in small talk until Kensington began ringing his wine glass by gently tapping his spoon against it.

"Gentlemen, it is time to begin a presentation of what this gathering is all about," he announced. "We shall move to my inner chamber where I will explain everything and why I have invited all of you here."

Enrico then stepped forward bidding the men follow him. They moved away from the grand entrance hall and entered a smaller room, although it contained two couches and four chairs, all over-stuffed and comfortable for sitting. The four men all took their seats and Kensington moved to the front of the room and stood before a large, deep-maroon drape that hung from the ceiling.

"Gentlemen," he announced, "before I pull back this curtain, I would like to warn you that I am going to ask you to take a risk. However, the risk for each of you will be minimal, especially where you could be suspected of being somewhat outside the law."

Cutlass cast a furtive glance at Paco but did not change his facial expression.

"I can see you have your own suspicions," Kensington said, looking at the pair. "Baudelaire, you were a pirate with Jean Lafitte, no?"

"I was, Señor Giles, but that was a long time ago," Cutlass said, hesitantly.

"That is why I say the risk to you is minimal," Kensington reiterated. "You have been making a living re-enacting your role as a pirate and that is pretty close to all that I am going to ask you to do. However, the reward for this performance could be, shall I say, far more substantial?

"Allow me to continue," the judge began. "Mr. Packard and General Diaz have already heard of my plan and are backing it one hundred percent. But your role, as well as Paco's, I presume, will be more active, although not as involved. For that, I assure you that Mr. Packard, General Diaz, and I will pay you handsomely for your performance."

"We have come this far, Señor Giles," Cutlass said, "Please go on with your presentation."

"Wonderful," responded Kensington. "Enrico, please, brandy and cigars all around."

Kensington pulled back the curtain to expose a large map of

Texas, the Gulf of Mexico, and the Yucatan Peninsula.

"Cutlass, Paco, there is an enormous shipment of silver headed for Galveston, Texas. The value of silver is expected to match that of gold, for pressure is being put on the United States Government to buy silver at the same price as gold to increase the worth of the U.S. dollar."

"Is doing that good fiscal policy?" General Diaz asked the judge. "For, one day, I will be governor of Mexico and I would need to know that."

"It's horrible fiscal policy, Porfirio," Kensington said. "And that's why we can depend on the Americans to do it. Throwing away money is what they do best, eh?" the judge added, breaking out in laughter.

Kensington went on to explain that the silver shipment was going to be held at the First U.S. Bank recently constructed in Galveston until the government has it shipped to Washington, D.C., for disbursement.

"Mr. Packard, here," Kensington said, with a wave of his hand toward the former sheriff, "is very familiar with this shipment and how it is to be transported. The itinerary is top secret, but we do know when and where the shipment will be most vulnerable – in Galveston Bay."

Kensington explained that the shipment would be transported by rail to a port on the Texas mainland, and transferred onto a nondescript barge. The barge is to then carry the shipment over to Galveston Island. The reason for doing that, the judge explained, was because security did not trust the rail line that runs from the mainland to the island. It was too vulnerable.

"Therefore, Mr. Baudelaire, Galveston Bay is where you can intercept that precious cargo," Kensington said.

"How could I disguise my ship to keep from being intercepted by the police?" Cutlass asked, looking into his goblet of brandy.

Kensington took a big draw on his cigar and blew the smoke steadily in the direction of Cutlass. "You don't have to," he said. "Your pirate ship will be presented to the police as nothing more than a stage play in celebration of Galveston's famed pirate, Jean Lafitte. We believe they will welcome the attraction, taking attention away from the barge. Ships and small boats crisscross that bay all the time."

"That I can do, but I will need a crew to sail the Tiburon," Cutlass said.

"And you shall have it," Kensington offered. "Hire a few extras capable of sailing the ship and Mr. Packard will assign the men we need to help carry out the plan."

"My men got wind of this pending shipment some time ago," Packard chimed in. "We began recruiting the personnel we needed to pull off this heist. They will be joining you. You have to do little more than transport them to that barge."

"You want me to board that barge?" Cutlass asked.

"Not really," Kensington said, again picking up the conversation. "We want your ship to 'accidentally' sink that barge. Packard's men will do the rest."

"But how can I get away with that?" Cutlass asked, incredulously.

"Don't worry, it will hit you," the judge replied with a broad smile. "Our man will be piloting that barge. You see, you're only there to celebrate Jean Lafitte Day. You know nothing about a boat loaded with silver."

"It still sounds a bit risky," Cutlass said, casting a glance at Paco.

"You will be given what you need to fortify your ship to withstand the collision," Kensington assured. "To allay suspicion, you are to drop anchor and help pick up survivors. After that, just sail away."

"But won't the shipment of silver be lost?" Paco spoke up.

"Galveston Bay is only a few meters deep," Kensington said, curling his lips and slipping his cigar between his teeth. He took a puff and then judiciously removed the cigar to speak. "We have a unique plan for salvaging that shipment of silver."

"But Señor Giles, the U.S. Navy is harbored in Galveston. I doubt the Tiburon could outrun that armada," Cutlass advised, "and what are we to do with the survivors?"

"We have that worked out," Packard again cut in. "The Navy will be asked to stand down during this celebration to open up the bay for the celebration. "I'll let the judge give you the details."

"Thank you, Sheriff," Kensington started. "We will have a trained crew aboard the Tiburon who will lower a rescue boat, but in the confusion will actually retrieve the silver and return it to your vessel. "

"But these survivors we are to rescue," Cutlass said. "What are we to do with them?"

"It is unlikely the Navy would be able to respond in time to retrieve those that end up on your ship, so just bring them with you," Kensington said. "Most will be Packard's men, anyway. And if there are one or two others, we'll deal with them after you get here. Americans have disappeared in Mexico before," Kensington announced with a laugh.

The judge's words did help to pacify Cutlass and Paco, but they were still a little disturbed about survivors onboard the Tiburon.

"It is a well thought-out plan," Cutlass said after a brief pause. "How much time do we have to prepare our ship?"

"Time and money will be at your immediate disposal. The sliver shipment is still months away," Kensington said, setting his cigar in the ashtray and putting his arm around Baudelaire's shoulders. "Take a little time to think it over. But don't take too long, we need to put this plan in motion soon."

With the meeting over, the men returned to the entrance room and the judge ordered the cart to be brought around for Cutlass and Paco. Kensington, Packard, and Diaz escorted the pair outside and down the steps to the driveway.

"Just as a precaution, gentlemen, "Kensington concluded with a smile, "do not share what you have learned with anyone. General Diaz is our security, and he is very efficient."

"We understand completely," Cutlass replied, glancing at Diaz knowingly. "You can rest assured we shall not speak of this to anyone, and you will have our decision soon. We bid you buenos nochas, Señors. It has been a pleasure, I assure you."

After boarding their cart and exiting the gate, Paco turned to the captain and asked, "What do you think your decision will be, Señor?"

"I could have given King Victor my decision tonight," Cutlass answered. "I grow tired of fleecing tourists for a living, and I grow weary of wearing that wooden leg. My knee swells up now and it is very uncomfortable. Our share of that silver would set us for life, Paco. We will tell the judge the Tiburon will be ready to sail when the work is done."

Back at the hacienda, Packard asked, "What do you think, Judge. Do you think they'll do it?"

"I have no doubt," Kensington said, turning his eyes from the departing cart and looking at his companions. "That old fraud will not pass up an opportunity to relive the days he once dreamed of as a cabin boy. This is his chance to actually stand in Lafitte's shoes."

Chapter 10
Ron Lester and Ambrose Tucker

The summer was passing quickly and Nik was getting well acquainted with Galveston. The people were friendly enough, but Nik couldn't help but feel an uneasiness in some folks when he identified himself as the United States Marshal. However, he hadn't encountered any blatant bigotry, but occasional hints of condescension were noticeable.

When Nik entered the courthouse, one of the clerks approached the marshal, informing him that Judge Conklin wanted to see him. Nik thanked the clerk and proceeded down the hallway to the judge's chamber and entered.

"You wish to see me, your honor?" Nik said upon entering the office. He removed his hat and acknowledged the sheriff, who was seated to the right of the judge. There was a second gentleman in the room, who occupied the chair to the left of the sheriff.

"You know Sheriff Atkins, right?" Conklin asked.

"I do. Duke, I believe, is that correct?" Nik said, pulling up a chair to the left of the second gentleman. Atkins nodded in affirmation of Nik's question.

"This is Agent Ron Lester," the judge said, nodding in the direction of the middle man. "He is with the United States Treasury Department, and he has brought to our attention a potential counterfeiting operation being funneled through Galveston."

"Pleased to meet you, Agent Lester," Nik said, turning and shaking the gentleman's hand.

Ron Lester wore a loosely-defined khaki uniform. The top of his shirt was buttoned and adorned with a bolo tie, complete with a silver-and-turquoise clasp. There was a narrow-brimmed western hat hanging on the back of his chair and a pair of black cowboy boots protruding from each pants leg.

"Are you finding your way around, Marshal?" Conklin asked. "It is a little different here in Galveston, nothing like Red River Country."

"I have been making progress and want to say I was pleasantly surprised with the Juneteenth Celebration," Nik said, while repeatedly sliding the brim of his hat through his hands. "I, ah … I, ah met some interesting folks, and found the event unique, unique indeed."

"Good. I am pleased to hear that because Agent Lester, here, is with the recently formed United States Customs Service, a branch of the treasury department," the judge began. "It is my understanding the U.S. Marshals Service sent you here because this is the location of this nation's First National Bank. Is that true?"

"I was considered a good candidate for this office because of a case I worked on concerning land fraud," Nik answered, sitting down in the chair next to Lester. "It involved banking foreclosures."

"That is good, but this situation involves something quite different," Conklin said, leaning forward over his desk. "I'll turn the floor over to Agent Lester, who knows the situation better than I."

"Thank you, Judge," Lester replied, nodding and turning first to Atkins then back to Nik. "As I'm sure you're aware, the currency system we presently have in our country has been on a shaky foundation. Because we do not yet have solid legislation to deal with that issue, the United States has been troubled considerable by counterfeiting across the country. In fact, nearly half the money in circulation at this time could well be counterfeit."

Nik glanced up at Conklin and then turned his attention back to Lester. The agent reached into his pocket and pulled out what appeared to be paper money.

"This, gentleman, is what was referred to as a 'greenback,' printed by the U.S. Government to help finance the war," Lester said, first holding up the currency and then passing it over to the sheriff. "These were intended to be federal bank notes backed by the U.S.

Government, but the policy to redeem them was never legislated. Now congress is considering tying greenbacks to the gold standard and allowing them to be exchanged for real gold. I think you can understand the problem."

"Is this bill counterfeit?" Atkins said, passing it to Judge Conklin. "How can we tell a phony note from the real thing?"

"I wish there was an easy answer to that," the agent continued. "It is very hard to tell, even Galveston's bank has no clear means of determining its legitimacy. The U.S. Bank has been authorized to accept the greenbacks as deposit, but it is not obliged to exchange them for gold – not yet, anyway."

"I've got to admit it looks pretty clean," the judge remarked, examining the bill, "although I have not seen many of these in circulation since the war."

"It is essentially being exchanged on good faith that the federal government will eventually make good on their redemption promise. Congress has issued $450 million of these to stay within the estimated value of our country's gold reserves," Lester said. "Had Lincoln lived, he likely would have taken them out of circulation, whereas congress has been uncertain as to what to do with them."

"But, if congress passes a bill to redeem these in gold and our bank has been given the authority to accept them, counterfeit or otherwise, it could bankrupt the country's gold reserves, right?" Nik said, taking the bill from the judge and studying it.

"Precisely," replied Lester. "But without knowing which bills are good, there is no telling how much illegal money is out there. The bank was going to put a hold on accepting greenbacks, but those customers holding legitimate notes need that money to operate their businesses. They have no way of knowing what's legitimate and what isn't, either."

"So, is there any way to round up this counterfeit currency?" Nik asked, handing the greenback over to Lester.

"There is not," Lester said, taking the bill back from the marshal. "Our goal is to find the counterfeiting operation. Texas and the federal government will have to sort out how to deal with the fake money already out there, which could be in the thousands, if not millions."

"So, where do we start?" Sheriff Atkins inquired.

"We believe Galveston was a target because it's a port city where these bills could be spread around the world," was the agent's answer. "We don't know if they're coming from the mainland or even overseas, for that matter. I have agents working with the banks to keep track of the greenbacks being deposited, but that's all we can do. My assignment is to see if they're being smuggled in."

"You believe these greenbacks could be coming in by ship," Nik replied.

"It's possible, Marshal," Lester started. "Right now were standing on square one. If any of you or your men have any ideas, the treasury department is at your service."

"What do you think, Duke?" Nik said, leaning forward to look at the sheriff.

"I think we should put our heads together so we don't duplicate our efforts," Atkins replied. "I don't know how many men you have, but I have only me and two deputies."

"I'm two deputies behind you," Nik said, leaning back in his chair and looking up at the judge.

"That reminds me," Atkins said, looking over at Nik. "There's a gentleman in your office waiting to see you. I don't know what he wants so I hope you have an answer for him. He's a big man."

"Really?" Nik responded. "I might know who he is. Thanks, Sheriff."

After excusing himself, Nik left Conklin's office and hurried down the hall to see who it was that wanted to see him. After entering, Nik knew almost immediately who the man was sitting in a chair in front of his desk. From the back, the visitor's shoulders were at least six inches wider than the backrest. His hips, though narrow, required the man to sit with his legs spread to maintain stability.

"Ambrose? Ambrose Tucker?" Nik inquired, as he approached the figure in the chair. The man rose from the chair and turned about.

"Oh, sorry, Marshal Brinkman. I guess I sorta' dozed off while I was waiting," Ambrose said.

"Not a problem, Ambrose," Nik responded. "I'm just sorry I kept you waiting. Please tell me you're here because you're interested in a deputy marshal's job."

"I am, sir. I thought on it long and hard, and if the job isn't already taken, I'd be obliged if you'd consider me," Ambrose said.

"You're in luck, 'Deputy Tucker.' You're the first man to step forward," Nik said, smiling widely as he extended his hand to the man.

"I didn't mean to come barging in here uninvited, but when you weren't in I stopped in at the sheriff's office to ask about you. When I told him what I was here for, he was kind enough to unlock the door for me and let me wait," Ambrose said, releasing his grip on Nik's engulfed hand.

"He did right, Ambrose," Nik responded. "I just have to ask you a few questions and then I will swear you in, that is, if you still want the job when I'm finished."

"You'll have to work hard to talk me out of it," Ambrose said, grinning. "Not a lot of job options for folks like me now that slavin's done."

"Have a seat, Ambrose, and let's get this ceremony started."

Nik questioned Tucker as to his experiences in the war. Ambrose again mentioned the time he spent in sharpshooter training with Roger. Nik then emphasized the potential danger of the deputy marshal's job and the low pay.

"I made it through the war on less pay than what you're offering," Ambrose said. "I like it here in Galveston, and this is one way I can continue to stay here."

"That reminds me, once I swear you in I've got an assignment for you. Time is of the essence so you'll have to do a lot of training on the job," Nik advised. "Do you have a horse?"

"No, sir, I'm sorry, but I do not," Ambrose said.

"We'll take care of that through the Marshals Service," Nik said. "The service will pay to get you a horse, but you will likely have to pay the money back over time. A lot of what we do is on horseback."

"That suits me fine, Marshal, just as long as they let me get a good one. I need a pretty good-sized horse."

"Yes, I can see that you would. Do you have any objections to a draft horse?" Nik suggested.

"Long's as it gets me where I'm going, I have no objections," Ambrose said.

Nik then excused himself so he could find a Bible. After retrieving one from the sheriff's office, he returned and swore in Tucker as a U.S. Deputy Marshal. After taking their seats, Nik began telling Ambrose about the counterfeit money issue.

"Our goal is to stop the counterfeiting at its source. If I had one of the bills, I'd show it to you, but I doubt it would help you much though finding out where it came from would."

"I would like to see the money so as to know what we're dealing with, good or bad," Tucker said. "Knowing what one looks like could help lead us to the source."

"You're absolutely right, Ambrose," I hadn't thought of it that way. This is my first assignment, too. By the way, you can call me Nik, if you like. We're in this thing together."

"At times, I may, but I don't feel comfortable calling the boss by his first name. So, please don't hold it against me if I do call you Marshal, most times," Tucker said. "I kind of like the sounds of that."

"Come to think of it, so do I," Nik said with a grin. "I think it was the work of Providence that I met you at the Juneteenth Celebration.

"Speaking of Juneteenth, have you seen any more of the Boatmans since then?" Nik asked.

"I stumbled across them when I stopped at the Covington Plantation to ask about work," Tucker said. "Seems the Boatmans work for the widow Covington. Mr. Boatman's daughter is Mrs. Covington's personal maid, and her father is the handyman, I guess," Tucker added. "Mrs. Covington was nice but had no work for me. I knew then this job was my best choice, though I ain't had no official trainin."

"Neither did I when I joined the service," Nik responded. "I was fresh out of the military, myself.

"The Covington mansion, you say…" Nik mused out loud. "What happened to Mr. Covington?"

"Word is Mrs. Covington shot 'im for cheatin' on her, but I don't know no details," Tucker said, folding his hands in his lap. "Nice lady, though. Didn't seem like the killin' type."

"Infidelity can drive people to do things they ordinarily wouldn't," Nik said, staring absentmindedly at Ambrose as he spoke. "Circumstances can change a person."

Nik and Ambrose then worked out a plan to try and help track down the counterfeiting operation. Ambrose agreed to roam the docks, talking to sea captains and crew members to gather whatever information he could. Nik planned to find Abel Mosely to use his eyes and ears concerning any suspicious activity on the waterfront.

"Now, where are you staying, Ambrose?" Nik asked.

"I've been kind'a camping out," Tucker replied. "I suspect I learned to do that in the army. But I don't know that I could do that here on Galveston Island, though."

"Not a problem. You can stay with me tonight and we'll find you a room in the hotel like I have," Nik said. "We'll find you a horse, too."

"I don't mind walking," Tucker said. "I've done that a lot."

"That's okay for combing the docks, but you'll need a horse if we have to cross over to the mainland," Nik advised. "We'll get you lined up with a horse your size so you'll have one when necessary.

"I want to introduce you to Agent Ron Lester, also. Let's head up to his office. "

The two men left the office in time to see Agent Lester, who was just departing from Judge Conklin's room.

"Agent Lester," Nik called out. "May I see you a moment?"

Lester turned and waited for Nik and Ambrose to approach.

"Could I see that greenback bill again," Nik asked. "My deputy, here, would like to see what it looks like."

"Certainly," the agent replied, reaching into his pocket for the money. "Here, keep it. I plan to distribute these to law enforcement. Although, if you come across a greenback, bring it to my temporary office upstairs for identification. The artwork on these things is too good to discern with the naked eye. Oh, and let me know where and from whom you got it. It could be an important lead."

After getting Ambrose settled in at the hotel, the king-sized deputy set out to cover the docks lining the harbor side of the island. Nik paid a visit to the seaside to see if he could find the beachcomber. Not seeing Mosely when he first arrived, Nik took a minute to sit down in the sand and look out over the ocean. His experience on the sea still made it difficult for him to enjoy the moment, but the roar of the waves and screeching of seagulls was enough to direct his mind back to when he was a boy growing up in Africa.

"Scuse me, sir," came a familiar voice that startled Nik from his thoughts. "Perhaps you would like to buy some of my wares?"

Nik looked up, but Mosely's face was in shadow. However, the man's image was enough to jog his memory.

"Abel, Abel Mosely," Nik said, as he rose to his feet.

"At your service, Marshal," Mosely said, grinning at the officer.

"Abel, glad to see you," Nik said. "I need your assistance, if you're still willing to be my eyes and ears down here."

"Whether you ask me or not, sir, I am on the job all day and most the night," Abel said.

"You can comb the beach at night?" Nik inquired.

"I use my feet at night," Abel replied. "Amazing what one can find that way."

"Like what?" Nik said with a chuckle.

"I'll show you," Abel said, kneeling down to pour out his "treasure sack."

There were items from a gold watch to a pair of shoes that someone apparently left behind after a day at the beach. There was also a rubbery object that tumbled out of the sack with the other items.

"What in the world is that?" Nik said, pointing at the elastic piece.

"Oh, that," Abel said. "I forgot about that. Found that with my feet last night. I found this in it." Abel said, reaching into his pocket and pulling out what looked like rolled up paper.

"Let me see that," Nik said, reaching for the roll.

"I'm sorry, it was all wet when I found it. It's probably no good now," Abel said, releasing the item to Nik.

Nik unrolled it and could see it was in the shape of paper money. The ink was smeared, but it was clear enough to tell it was money at one time.

"You found this stuck in that balloon-type thing?" Nik said, his curiosity aroused.

"Yes. I was excited because I thought it was money, but whatever it was it ain't no good now," Mosely said, with hesitation in his voice, afraid the marshal might think he stole it.

"On the contrary, Abel, this might be what I was going to ask you to look for."

"I don't think it's no good anymore, Marshal," Abel said, somewhat relieved at Nik's comment.

"Abel, do you know what counterfeit money is?" Nik asked.

"I think its bad money, I believe," Mosely answered.

"We think someone is trying to pass this... bad money off as the real thing," Nik answered. "I will have to take this to another authority to make sure, although it may be too obliterated to tell. Either way, I'll try to see to it you get something for your discovery."

"Well, Marshal, you know I would appreciate that," Mosely said. "And I'll let you know if I come across anything else."

"Excellent, Abel," Nik said, smiling at his friend. "And, by the way, I would like to have that balloon, as well. It may be a part of a clue if this stuff is really counterfeit money."

Nik pulled a silver dollar from his pocket and handed it to Mosely.

"This will have to do for now, Abel. If there is more reward money owed you I'll see that you get it."

"Much obliged, Marshal. Glad I could help."

Abel gathered up his other items and put them in his sack.

"That gold watch could be worth something as well," Nik advised.

"I'm thinking I might just keep that, marshal," Mosely said. "I may just learn to tell time."

"How about now?" Nik replied. "Let me see that watch and I'll teach everything you need to know about telling time."

Mosely smiled, retrieved the watch and Nik instructed Abel on how to use it. Afterward, the beachcomber walked away reciting the time to himself as he dialed the hands to each number.

Chapter 11
The Deputized Giant

Ambrose had visited the Galveston Harbor before but didn't pay much attention to it back then. There was nothing that held his interest and he felt no particular love for the sea. He was now tasked with looking for money very few could identify as counterfeit and with trying to determine if it was arriving by ship from somewhere overseas. The only thing he really knew how to do was to learn as much as he could about the territory.

His confidence was bolstered by Marshal Brinkman's exuberance over his decision to become a deputy, but this assignment to investigate the waterfront filled him with self-doubt. He'd spent time searching for the enemy when he was in the war and was good at it. He was determined to show his boss he could do the job and would use his new-found authority to ask questions, but what should he ask – Excuse me, sir, have you seen any ships unloading counterfeit money?

Ambrose nearly laughed at the thought, but it steeled his determination to measure up to the job.

As he walked along the boardwalk, he eyed two sailors walking toward him in the opposite direction. Noticing the big man's interest in them, they stopped to ask why.

"Is there anything wrong, deputy?" said the shorter of the two, while attempting to read Ambrose's badge.

"Oh, no, excuse my staring, gentlemen," Ambrose answered. "I'm new here and not yet familiar with the sights and sounds of this place."

"We'll, you're not the only one," the taller one remarked. "We've noticed several lawmen combing the docks lately. Is there something going on down here that we should know about?"

"You've seen other lawmen?" Ambrose asked.

"Yeah, two sheriff's deputies wanted to take a look at our cargo a while back," said the first seaman. "Aren't you working with them?"

"Well, kinda," Ambrose answered. "But they're with a different department. I'm a deputy with the United States Marshals Service."

"I guess things are getting pretty serious, eh?" said the second. "Would you mind telling us what's going on?"

Ambrose hesitated in his reply. He wasn't sure if it was smart to try and explain to them that he was looking for something he couldn't identify. For all he knew, they could be smugglers and he would be tipping them off as to what he was after.

"Just routine, gentlemen," Ambrose said. "I just signed on with the marshal service and, like I said, I'm just learning the territory."

"We'll let you get on with it, then," said the first, as both gave a nod of their heads and walked away discussing reasons for the increase in law officers.

Although he'd stumbled through his first encounter, Ambrose felt a little bolder about what he was doing. They recognized his authority and that increased his comfort level. But how he had to decide what things he should ask that wouldn't hinder his investigation. Would it be smarter to inquire about counterfeit money, or come up with something less direct? Since few could identify an illegal greenback, he felt it best to save that question for someone he determined had knowledge of the subject.

Tucker continued on his way until he spotted two sheriff's deputies walking down the gangplank of a moored ship. He thought they would be a good start in helping him with his investigation.

"Deputies," Ambrose called out as he drew near. "I assume we're looking for the same things?"

"Depends, Marshal," said the deputy identified as Zeke. Zeke Vincent was middle-aged and had been a deputy before Duke Atkins took over as sheriff. He was a seasoned deputy and had a solid reputation as a lawman. He was also a longtime resident of Galveston and knew nearly everyone and every place in the area. "Are you looking for funny money?"

"That's a good name for it," Ambrose said, wanting to get a little guidance, without giving away his lack of detecting skills. "What methods have you fellas been using in your investigation, so I don't duplicate what you've done?"

"We've been inspecting cargo and looking for anything suspicious," Zeke answered. "You know, routine questions like, 'Where did you sail from? Where are you headed. What's your next cargo gonna be?' things like that.

"How is the marshal service handling this?"

That question caught Ambrose off guard. He held back his inclination to simply confess his ignorance and instead said, "To be honest, Marshal Brinkman thought it best to let you guys take the lead. I was kind of hoping to run into someone from your office to talk to."

"Not a bad plan," Zeke said. "I wish we could be of more help, but we're just scouring the docks looking for leads.

"By the way, my name's Zeke Vincent. This here's Deputy Lenny Alexander. And you are?"

"Tucker, Ambrose Tucker. Pleased to meet you fellas. Let me know if there's anything I can do to help. In the meantime, I'll just follow in your footsteps just in case something was missed."

"Not much chance of that, Ambrose," Zeke said. "This job is like looking for a needle in a haystack. But you're welcome to retrace our steps just in case."

"Much obliged, fellas," Ambrose said. "I'll let you know if I turn up anything helpful."

"See you around, marshal," Zeke said.

"See ya," Lenny said, tipping his hat. Lenny Alexander was a young man with only a little more law enforcement experience than Ambrose. He was smart enough to stay close to Zeke and learn as much as he could, but had a bad habit of telling others of his skills as a lawman. Most could tell he was a tinhorn, but humored him because of his otherwise likeable personality.

Ambrose Tucker ran Zeke's questions through his mind, pleased that now he was armed with something to lead with. Ambrose was not accustomed to using his size to intimidate people, but he noticed that the two sailors he spoke to took as much interest in him as they did in his badge. He admired Marshal Brinkman for his straightforward approach to people in spite of his being black. Ambrose felt if he could gain that same confidence he could become a solid asset to his boss and the service.

Deciding not to board the same vessel the deputies had just inspected, Ambrose moved on until he saw someone in seafaring attire giving instructions to other men working on one of the docks.

"Excuse me, sir. May I have a word?" Ambrose said, approaching the man giving the orders.

The man looked up at Tucker and his look of annoyance soon faded under the shadow of Tucker's image. The sailor wasn't hostile, but Ambrose did discover he had already spoken with Zeke and Lenny, answering all their questions.

"Didn't I already speak to some of your men?" the man asked.

"Oh, you must mean those deputies from the sheriff's department," Ambrose began. "No, I'm from the United States Marshals Service. We do work with the sheriff's department but on a different level."

"So, you're a federal lawman, are you? I guess you guys don't hire the scrawny kids," the dockworker chuckled, recalling Lenny Alexander's frame. "How can I help you? But, if you don't mind, make it quick. I've got to see to it this ship gets unloaded today."

"What does this shipment consist of?" Ambrose asked.

"Like I told the deputies, cotton and wool. We had a few passengers, but they have disembarked and headed into town," the shipping supervisor said. "I told Deputy Zeke about everything we've taken in for the last month. No counterfeit money onboard this vessel."

"You talked with Zeke about counterfeit money?"

"I've known Zeke for years. He grew up in this town," the dock master said. "We know funny money is being distributed, but it's not coming in on these ships."

"Do you have any idea where it's coming from?" Ambrose asked.

"If I did, I would have told Zeke. No, it's a mystery," said the supervisor. "We just hope the bank can sort it out because you feds don't seem to know how to do it."

"The feds?" Ambrose quizzed.

"Congress, they've been bickering over currency since the war," the supervisor answered. "Until they get it sorted out, I accept nothing but gold or silver."

"You've been a great help," Mr. ... Mr. ..."

"Montgomery, Woodward Montgomery at your service, Marshal."

"Much obliged, Mr. Montgomery," Ambrose said.

Ambrose figured he might learn something about shipping while on the docks, but not much where counterfeit money was concerned. He decided to abandon the harbor and turn his attention to the bank.

"Deputy Marshal Tucker," Edgar Pottingham, the First U.S. Bank president began. "I assume you know Customs Agent Ron Lester. He knows as much about this counterfeit money, if not more, than I do."

"I do, Mr. Pottingham, and I've learned that Agent Lester knows a good deal about the money, but not where it's coming from," Ambrose answered.

"I can assure you he knows more than I," Pottingham said, leaning forward over his desk. "I hope you don't suspect me or the bank of doing this."

"Not at all, Mr. Pottingham. I learned in the war, in order to stay alive it is smart to learn as much you can from those who have the information needed," Ambrose started. "I come to you because, I would guess, you ought to know plenty about money in general, even if it is hard to tell the good from the bad in this case."

"You seem like an upstanding sort, and obviously a person who knows what he's doing," Pottingham said. "If this counterfeiting isn't stopped, this bank will have to close its doors. We have customers coming in with greenbacks and for the sake of Texas' economy we can't refuse them. We're becoming a major seaport and if we don't take these bills we're finished. And if we don't help our customers they're finished along with this bank. I hope you can appreciate our dilemma."

"Do you know Madame Tillie Covington?" Ambrose asked.

"Indeed I do," Pottingham exclaimed. "She is one of our top customers. We've done business with her since this bank opened. In fact, that's Madame Covington over there talking to one of our vice presidents," Pottingham added, nodding in the direction of a lady seated at a nearby desk.

"I had the pleasure of meeting Madame Covington. She's a fine lady and it's a relief to me to know her money is safe here," Ambrose replied.

"What we can't do right now is exchange gold for greenbacks," Pottingham said. "We accept all greenbacks for the sake of our customers. But Congress is going to have to get this worked out or we'll have to cut off accepting that money."

"I understand, Mr. Pottingham," Ambrose said. "I appreciate you giving me this time. Good day, sir."

When Ambrose prepared to leave the bank, he noticed the man Madame Covington had been talking too had momentarily vacated his desk to speak to a clerk. The deputy decided to walk over to pay his respects.

"Good day, Madame Covington," Ambrose said, tipping his hat as he gained her attention. "I saw you sitting here and just wanted to pay my respects."

"Oh, my goodness, you're that gentleman who stopped by looking for a job, aren't you?" Tillie Covington replied.

"Yes mam, Ambrose, Ambrose Tucker, mam," the large man responded.

"I see you're wearing a badge, Mr. Tucker," Tillie Covington said. "Were you hired by the sheriff?"

"No, mam, I'm working for the United States Marshals Service," Ambrose said. "I've only been doing it for a short time, though."

"My goodness, I'm going to guess a man of your stature commands plenty respect," she said, as she turned in her chair to stand up.

"Please, don't get up, mam," the deputy implored. "Like I said, I saw you sitting here and just wanted to pay my respects."

"You're kind to do so, and I'm happy to see you are employed."

The bank vice president returned and stood behind his chair while Tillie finished speaking.

"Excuse me sir," Ambrose began. "I just stopped by to say hello to Madame Covington. I'll be on my way now."

"So good to see you, Marshal Tucker," Tillie said, remaining in her chair. "By the way, Esther and her father are waiting outside in the buggy, if you want to say hello to them as well."

"I will do that, mam," Ambrose said. "I'll let you get back to your business now."

Ambrose nodded at the vice president, who sat down when the deputy departed. Upon exiting the bank, Ambrose spotted the buggy where Esther and Isaiah Boatman were waiting. He drew near and stood next to the carriage.

"Miss Boatman, Mr. Boatman, I saw Madame Covington inside and she told me you two were out here waiting and I thought I'd come over and wish you a good day."

"Ambrose," Esther began. "It is good to see you. Are you wearing a badge now?" she responded, eyeing the badge the deputy was sporting.

"Yep, I was hired on with the U.S. Marshals Service recently," Ambrose said, smiling. "I'm just out and about doing my rounds."

"Are you working for that gentleman, Nik Brinkman, I think is his name?" Esther asked.

"One in the same, mam," Ambrose answered. "Are you just escorting Madame Covington or are you doing business too?"

"We're mostly escorting Tillie," Esther said. "When she has banking to do, we usually make a day of it. We visit some of the stores and maybe spend some time on the beach."

"Mixin' business with pleasure," Ambrose mused. "Perhaps you could stop by the courthouse and say hello to Marshal Brinkman. I know he would like that."

"It depends on Tillie, but maybe we can do that if she's not too busy with other things," Esther responded. "What do you say, papa?"

"If time allows," Isaiah interjected. "The marshal seemed like a nice gentleman."

"That he is, Isaiah, and I know he'd love to see you," Ambrose said, widening his smile. "Fact is, I've got to be getting back there to make my report. You two have a wonderful time, you hear?"

"Thank you, Ambrose... or is it Marshal Tucker now?" Esther said, returning the smile.

"Just deputy, but Ambrose to you," the big man said.

After reaching the office, Ambrose sat down to wait for Nik's return. It was not long before the marshal strode through the door.

"Ambrose, how did it go out there?" Nik spoke out.

Ambrose turned in his chair and got to his feet. "I covered some ground, but I'm afraid I didn't find out much," the deputy started. "I talked to one of the dock workers and ran into deputies Vincent and Alexander. They were investigating also, but they hadn't found out much either. I stopped at the bank and talked to Mr. Pottingham. He also didn't have much to say as to help the investigation, but he did tell me this counterfeit thing could be a powerful bad situation for folks if it continues."

"Good work, Deputy Ambrose. I'm sorry you didn't turn up more information but I'm glad you made your presence known in the community."

"By the way, I saw Esther Boatman and her papa, Isaiah. They were waiting outside the bank for Madame Covington," Ambrose continued. "I saw Madame Covington too. She was doing some banking while I was talking to the bank president."

"Really, the Boatmans?" Nik said. "I don't suppose they plan to stop by here? Not sure why they'd do that but it would be nice to see her... them again."

"I invited them too, but they said it depended on what Madame Covington had planned," Ambrose said. "I guess they were accompanying her during her trip to town."

"Well, I doubt the U.S. Marshals Service was on their itinerary.

But I did come across something interesting," Nik began. "A man I have doing some undercover work for me came across some money wrapped in this," Nik said, holding up the balloon. "I took the money to Agent Lester's office for examination. He was pretty sure they were counterfeit bills, but they were damaged by the water. This balloon containing the money apparently washed up on shore."

"A balloon full of money, what do you make of it?" Ambrose asked.

"I don't know, unless someone stuffed the money into the balloon instead of using a sock, like some folks do," Nik replied.

"Maybe they hoped the balloon would keep the money from getting wet if they were going to go swimming with it," Ambrose proposed.

"That's possible. Good deductive reasoning, Ambrose."

"That's just speculation, though," Ambrose said. "I don't think counterfeiters would be trying to swim the stuff ashore."

"And if it was a swimmer just out enjoying the water, it wouldn't make that person a criminal," Nik said thoughtfully, as he took his seat behind the desk. "I like the idea of protecting the money from getting wet, though."

As Nik was speaking, Agent Ron Lester walked into the office.

"We confirmed the money you found was counterfeit, Marshal," Lester said, approaching Nik's desk. "There's seven twenty-dollar bills, four tens, and four fives here."

"That's quite a bit of money for one man to have, but not much for something as widespread as you described, Ron," Nik commented. "Deputy Tucker thought maybe it was a swimmer just trying to protect his money from the water."

"That's a possibility, but that would tell me whoever the swimmer was did not know the bills were counterfeit," Lester said. "You did say this was found washed up on the beach?"

"I did not check out the exact spot where it was found, but I have a man on it," Nik said. "This island is surrounded by water."

The men turned at the sound of footsteps echoing down the hall and approaching the marshal's office.

"Expecting company?" Lester asked.

"I'm not sure," Nik replied. "Could be a couple of Atkins' deputies, Ambrose ran into two of them investigating down at the docks."

"I'm inclined to think this money wasn't lost by a swimmer,," Lester replied. "It makes me suspicious that this cash is being smuggled in by ship and wrapped in these balloons for safekeeping. Maybe the smugglers are storing the money in kegs filled with some sort of liquid."

"Could be," Nik said, interrupted by a knock at the door. Ambrose moved over to answer it. When he opened the door, Esther and her father walked in.

"I hope we're not intruding," Esther said, noting the third man standing with Nik and Ambrose.

"Not at all," Nik spoke up. "Please come in and make yourselves comfortable."

"I'd better get back to my office," Agent Lester said, nodding to the Boatmans as he turned to make his exit."Keep me posted on anything more you might find," he called back as he slid past Ambrose and out the door.

"Will do, Ron," Nik called after him.

Ambrose closed the door behind Lester and started toward their guests, "Esther, Isaiah, I'm so glad you took some time out of your busy day to pay us a visit. Where is Madame Covington?"

"She had some other business to tend to and told papa and me to do whatever we wanted, so we came here to see you two and your office," Esther said, as she and her father gazed around the room.

The office was devoid of any décor. Nothing hung on the walls, and Nik's desk and six wooden chairs accounted for all the furniture in the place.

"I'm delighted that you came to see us, but as you can also see the office doesn't offer much to look at," Nik replied.

"It would not take much to make this place a little homier," Esther said, causing Isaiah to give a sly look in the marshal's direction. "Some drapes on the window, a few pictures for the walls, and one or two more comfortable chairs should do it."

"I'm afraid that's way out of my area of expertise," Nik replied.

"Ambrose, what do you think?"

"I don't recall ever doing anything like that," Ambrose answered. "I've always spent most of my time outside."

"You know what, if Tillie is willing to let me do it I'd be happy to shape this place up for you," Esther suggested. "What do you think, papa? Do you think Tillie would mind?"

"You'd have to run it by Miss Tillie, sweetheart," Isaiah responded. "She's usually open to whatever you suggest."

"What we should do is have you two visit us for dinner one evening at the plantation," Esther said. "We can discuss it then. Of course, I would have to get Tillie's approval to do that as well."

"A home-cooked meal, what do you say to that, Ambrose?" Nik said, turning to his deputy.

"I've had one of Miss Esther's meals before, and I would be willing to do whatever's required to enjoy another one," Ambrose said, patting his stomach with a smile.

"Then it's settled, right, papa? I will talk to Tillie and see if she's all right with the whole idea," Esther said enthusiastically.

"It don't matter to me, none. Miss Tillie is the one who has the final say, though." Isaiah replied.

"By the way, Isaiah," Nik began, speaking to Esther's father. "Have you thought any on being a part of the United State Marshals Service? You wouldn't have to do it full time, just when needed."

"Most of my time is taken up looking after the plantation," Isaiah answered. "However, I suppose under special circumstances Miss Tillie wouldn't mind."

"Excellent," Nik said. "Then we shall wait for word from you as to the invitation and your offer to fix up this place."

"You will hear from us soon," Esther said, with a broad smile. "I guess we had best be going then, right, papa?"

"She may be waiting for us, so it's best we be getting along," Isaiah said.

"Ambrose and I will be expecting to hear from you then," Nik said. "Thank you so much for coming by. I can't tell you how much it means to me that you took time out of your day to do so."

After the Boatmans departed, Nik turned to Ambrose. "Well, how did I do this time?"

"Much better, Marshal," Ambrose said, chuckling a bit. "You seemed much more relaxed around Miss Esther, and that's a good thing."

"Yeah, yeah, I felt a lot better this time," Nik said, with a sheepish grin. "I did feel a lot easier in her presence than I did at the Juneteenth Celebration. In fact, I'm feeling a lot easier about everything now."

"Not too much, I hope. I don't see this counterfeiting thing getting any easier," Ambrose replied.

"You're right about that, Ambrose, I think it best we come up with a plan. Just what did that bank president tell you?

Chapter 12
Lenny's Demise

Ambrose Tucker was standing on the dock talking with Sheriff Atkins and Deputy Zeke Vincent as Nik was tying Galley to the hitching post in front of the boardwalk. It was early morning as the marshal quickened his pace on his approach to the two men.

"Marshal, glad you could make it on short notice, but Deputy Tucker, here, said you would want to be informed on this," Atkins said.

"Thanks for sending for me, Duke," Nik replied as he stepped onto the dock with the three men. "I was told it was urgent."

"Urgent is probably the wrong word in this case, Marshal. The damage has been done, but what might be urgent is getting some answers," Duke advised.

"So, what's up?" Nik said, with a shrug of his shoulders.

"We found Deputy Alexander this morning floating in the harbor," Zeke interjected.

"Floating in the harbor? I don't understand," Nik replied.

"He was dead, Nik," Ambrose said. "When I came down this morning to do my rounds, they were fishing him out of the harbor. I sent for Sheriff Atkins and Zeke when I realized it was Lenny. Way too young a man to end up like this."

Nik could sense that Ambrose was fighting back his emotions. It surprised the marshal a little, knowing that Ambrose had been through the war. He'd seen a lot of young men die.

"Do you have any leads," Nik asked, "any idea how it was that he ended up floating in the harbor?"

"He was on patrol, Marshal," Duke responded. "We split up Zeke and Lenny as a team to cover more ground in our search for this counterfeit ring. If I knew things were going to get this serious I would not have done that. It makes me sick that I made that decision. Lenny was still too green."

"Don't beat yourself up, Duke. As sheriff you've got to do what the job requires," Nik offered. "Lenny was a good deputy and probably didn't want to disappoint you. None of us thought his assignment would come to this."

"He's right, Duke," Zeke cut in. "We've been patrolling these docks for weeks now and coming up empty-handed. Whatever happened must have been an accident of some kind."

"That's what we've got to find out," Duke said. "If it was an accident, then we lost a good man by providence. Not much we can do about that. But if there was foul play here, well, we cannot allow Lenny to have died in vain."

"So, you think Lenny could have been getting close to something? Something big enough that someone wanted him dead?" Nik suggested.

"We won't know until we get the coroner's report as to what actually happened. If he simply drowned, then something else may have been at play," Duke continued. "He was a bit brash, as a young man, but he wasn't stupid. He liked his job too much to do something foolish while conducting an investigation."

"Who all knows about this?" Nik asked

"Some sailors pulled him out," Ambrose said. "We're the only law enforcement that's been involved, so far."

"Good. Gentlemen, if you don't mind I would like to borrow Deputy Tucker for a time," Nik requested, "if you're done questioning him."

"We are, Marshal," Duke said. "We know where your office is if we have any further questions for Ambrose."

"Please let me know as soon as you get that coroner's report," Nik said.

"Well put a copy on your desk," Duke promised.

As the two marshals walked back to the hitching post where Galley was tied, Nik asked, "You seem a bit shaken by this, Ambrose."

"I got to know Lenny pretty good working down here at the docks," Ambrose began. "We kind of worked out a partnership, agreeing to meet every so often to discuss what we'd found, if anything. When he didn't show up yesterday, I figured he'd either gotten delayed or had gone off duty and I didn't pay much attention to it. We had spent so much time down here without incident that I didn't think anything of it.

"Poor Lenny, I had gotten to liking him, even though he was a little brash, like Sheriff Duke said."

"I can see where you might feel a little responsible, somehow, being his senior and all," Nik said. "But the two of you were from two different departments. It's admirable that the two of you were able to work together so well, but he was not your responsibility. Let's just wait to hear what the coroner comes up with, what do you say?"

"Ain't nothin' to say, Marshal. I just feel powerful bad that something like this had to happen so soon into my new job."

"I would like to say it's rare, but I discovered early in life that people near and dear can be taken away and there's nothing you can do about it," Nik consoled, untying Galley's reins from the hitching post. "The best thing you can do is to stay vigilant, the way Lenny would have liked you to. I've found it's the best way to work through these tough times.

"I'm going back to the office," Nik added, as he swung into the saddle. "You can continue your investigation here, or take some time off if you need. Whatever you do, be careful. I can't afford to lose you."

"Thanks, Nik," Ambrose replied. "I'm going to try and find out where Lenny was last seen, if I can."

"Good idea. Just don't try to be a hero. Like I said…"

"I know, Marshal," Ambrose said, looking at Nik as he turned Galley to ride away. "I'll be careful."

When Nik returned to the office, there was a note on his desk from Esther Boatman. It read:

"Dear Marshal Nik Brinkman,"

Hmmm, too formal, Nik thought to himself.

"Madame Covington sends her invitation to you and Deputy Tucker to visit us this Saturday. If you can make it, come in the early afternoon and we will show you around the place.

I have a dinner planned I hope you will like and there will be plenty for you and Ambrose. Madame Covington has also agreed to allow me to decorate, 'spruce up' your office. She also said there were some things she wanted to talk over with you.

Hope to see you Saturday,

Esther Boatman"

Boy, did this come at the right time, Nik thought. Both he and Ambrose had been frustrated in their efforts to find anything that would lead them to the counterfeiters. Although the pressure was also on \ the sheriff's departments in the area, counterfeiting was largely federal. Fortunately for the Marshals Service, Agent Lester and his treasury staff were getting most of the heat. Nik sat back thinking a Saturday spent away from work would do Ambrose and him a world of good. Not to mention they would be in the company of the prettiest woman he knew, and she could cook, too.

As Nik pored over the letter, a county clerk entered and approached Nik.

"I was asked to bring you a copy of the coroner's report, Marshal Brinkman," the clerk said, laying it on his desk. "Sorry if I disturbed you."

"Not at all, Mary," Nik remarked, now familiar with most of the employees in the building. "Let's see what you've got."

Nik picked up the report and looked for the cause of death.

"Blunt head trauma to the back of the skull is believed to be the cause of death," the report read. "No water was found in the lungs, indicating the victim did not die from drowning. All other findings were unremarkable."

Nik lurched forward out of his chair wondering if Sheriff Atkins had gotten back. He hurried down the hall and into Duke's office, where an assistant deputy was the only one in the room.

"Has the sheriff seen the coroner's report?" Nik asked the assistant.

"I can't tell you, Marshal," said the deputy. "All I know is he hasn't been in the office at all this morning."

"Thanks, I'll catch up to him later," Nik called out as he made his exit.

Nik set out for the waterfront to find Ambrose.

He arrived and remained on horseback as he searched the dock for Ambrose. As Galley walked along, Nik made a mental note of the ships resting in port. He was surprised by how many there were. The smaller craft were docked at the west end of the wharf, along with the fishing boats, of which only two were in port. Across the bay, moored at Pelican Island where the water was deeper, there were six ocean-going vessels.

Nik did not see any sign of Ambrose and thought maybe the big man had taken the ferry across to inspect the ships moored off the island. Feeling uncomfortable about Ambrose poking around where Deputy Alexander may have been killed, he turned Galley in the direction of the ferry.

As he neared the area, he was relieved to see a large figure standing near the bow of the transport ship returning from Pelican Island. He had little doubt that it was Ambrose

Having spotted Nik and Galley, Ambrose got off the ferry and made his way over to where they were waiting.

"Was Zeke or the sheriff with you?" Nik said, raising his voice over the clanging of the ferry's bell.

"No, they left to talk to Lenny's family," Ambrose said, as he walked up to Nik. "I decided to talk to as many folks as I could to find out if anybody remembers seeing Lenny yesterday."

"What did you find out?"

"He was out and about, all right," Ambrose continued. "Some folks had talked to him but they knew nothing about his drowning."

"He didn't drown, Ambrose," Nik said. "He was hit over the head and apparently died from the force of the blow."

"I knew he had hit his head, but I thought maybe he slipped and hit it before falling into the water," Ambrose replied. "So, the coroner says it was murder?"

"It appears that way. The coroner's report said no water was found in Lenny's lungs, indicating he did not drown," Nik said. "So, he was apparently done in before being thrown into the bay. Where was Lenny's body taken out of the water?"

"Two fishermen in a small boat found his body floating just beyond where the dock ends. You can see across where a large vessel at Pelican Island is loading," Ambrose began. "I ferried across to talk to the captain of that ship. He and three members of his crew said they had talked to the deputy late yesterday and he seemed just fine."

"So, can we assume he was on this side of the bay when he met with foul play?" Nik asked.

"There was a ship that left Pelican Port just before nightfall. He could possibly have been on that ship when it left. But it's well out to sea by now and it could be months before it returns."

"But it would not make sense if he'd been killed on that vessel that they would dump Lenny into the bay," Nik said, looking out over the water and shaking his head. "It would make more sense for them to take his body out to sea before throwing it overboard."

"You could be right, Marshal," Ambrose said. "All I can make of it, speculating on that coroner's report, he must have found something that troubled someone enough to kill him. Were there any clues other than the blow to Lenny's head?"

"You mean like counterfeit bills?" Nik interjected. "No, nothing like that.

By the way, before I forget, we've been invited out to the Covington Plantation for dinner, Saturday. Do you want to go?"

"If Lenny's funeral ain't that day, I'd love to go," Ambrose said.

"I guess we'll have to wait to find that out," Nik responded. "If you're done for now, let me buy you lunch."

"Oh, I'm done," Ambrose said. "No more ships expected in today."

After the two deputy marshals had their lunch, Nik and Ambrose returned to the office and stopped in to see Sheriff Atkins.

"The funeral will be Sunday after church," Duke said. "We plan to do a little salute to Deputy Alexander, if you two would like to join in you're welcome."

"We'd be honored, Duke, right Ambrose?" Nik inquired, relieved to know the ceremony wouldn't be on Saturday.

"I liked Lenny. He was a good man," Ambrose said. "I'd be much obliged to take part."

"Good, nothing too elaborate, we'll give him a rifle salute," Duke said.

"Not to change the subject," Nik started, "but have you recovered any more information as to Lenny's whereabouts before his death?"

"Not much," Duke replied. "Although, he did mention to his family he thought there was something he was overlooking. Lenny didn't tell them what it was, I guess to keep from worrying them."

"Too bad, it turns out they had plenty of reason to worry," Nik said. "What could he have possibly overlooked, Ambrose, any ideas?"

"I don't have any right now. We did not meet up yesterday like planned, so I don't know what he was up to," Ambrose surmised, looking down and shaking his head. "I should have been more suspicious and gone looking for him."

"Don't beat yourself up, Ambrose. It's too bad he didn't mention to you earlier what it was he thought he'd overlooked," Nik said, grabbing the big man by the elbow.

"I pretty much retraced his steps," Ambrose said. "As best I could tell by what everyone I talked to said as to his whereabouts."

"So, we've got water-soaked false money and a balloon to keep it in," Duke said, rubbing his fingers over his chin.

"The wet cash is something, but the balloon could have been a swimmer's idea of protecting it," Nik added.

"An interesting idea, but I can't say it's a common practice," Duke said.

Agent Ron Lester appeared on the scene, interrupting the conversation. "Duke, so sorry about Lenny, any possible idea who the culprit might be?"

"I wish I did, Ron. For all we know, he might have gotten into a row with someone and came out on the short end," Duke answered. "No telling what might have prompted the blow to the head he sustained."

"I've been to the bank. I secured some treasury funds to keep the bank open a bit longer," Lester said, "but they're reaching their limit of how many more greenbacks they can take in. It's possible they will have to close the bank before this thing is cleared up."

"That would have to be tough on the shipping merchants, would it not?" Nik asked.

"There is money exchanging hands every day in Galveston, especially down at the docks. That's why we've turned our attention there, and now we have Deputy Alexander's demise to make matters worse," Lester responded. "Cotton growers are shipping their crops overseas as we speak. We've been checking the cotton transactions at the docks, but there's a lot of cotton being traded right now."

"The cotton's going out but the money's coming in?" Duke said.

"Some transactions are taking place that we don't even know about," Ron continued. "We're almost certain some growers are being paid in worthless greenbacks. We tried spreading the word, but once those bills are in circulation they're good until they hit the bank."

"Isn't the government planning to honor greenbacks again?" Nik asked.

"Yes, they are," Ron said, "but the treasury doesn't have the gold to cover all the counterfeit cash going around. Now they're bowing to the farmers and planning to start using silver in place of gold."

"Pretty soon our money will be as worthless as Confederacy currency," Ambrose chimed in.

"We had a lot of trouble with that," Duke said. "Texas was a Confederate state for a time. Most won't take that money any more."

"Thank goodness," Ron said. "That's all we need to make this bad situation even worse.

"Look, gents, I'm going to have to get back to the office since I'm handling this bank bailout for now. When's Lenny's funeral?

"Sunday," Duke replied.

"I guess I'll see all of you there." With that, the agent departed.

"We'll get out of your hair as well, Duke," Nik said. "Powerful sorry about your loss."

"I just wish Lenny had let us in on what the little secret was that he overlooked," Duke responded. "Other than a deceased deputy, we haven't made much progress."

After Nik and Ambrose departed the sheriff's office and headed for their own, Nik's thoughts turned to Abel Mosely.

"Ambrose, I've got an errand to run, Why don't you go over to the livery stable and make sure they have that draught horse for you. What did you say its name was?"

"Crusader," Ambrose responded. "Kind of a strange name for a horse, don't you think?"

"Maybe not," Nik replied. "We're on a bit of a crusade right now."

"Whatever you say, Marshal. Shall I meet you back here?

"No, meet me back at the hotel," Nik said, as he began striding down the hall. "Do me a favor and lock up the office."

Nik climbed on Galley and rode toward the beach. It was getting late and he was afraid Mosely might have already gone home, wherever that was. But luck was on his side. As Nik approached the beach, he could see a lonely figure partially lit by the setting sun making its way along the beach, sack in hand.

"Marshal, didn't speck to see you out here this time of night," Abel said, as Nik rode up.

"Abel, I've got a question for you. Did you know Sheriff Deputy Alexander?"

"You mean Lenny?" Abel answered. "Yeah, a bit green for a deputy, but not a bad boy."

"Did you know his body was found floating in the bay this morning?" Nik continued.

"I did hear about that," Able replied. "I was truly sorry to hear about that."

"Have you heard anything about what might have happened to him?" Nik asked.

"Ah, come on down off your horse and I'll tell you what I know," Able said. "Do you want to know what time it is? I have a watch."

Nik swung down off Galley and faced Abel. "No, it doesn't matter now, but I appreciate the offer."

"Anytime," Abel said with a grin.

"So what did you hear? Nik quizzed.

"Not much, Marshal, but I have a friend, whose name I won't mention, who ran into Deputy Alexander last night."

"Last night? About what time?" Nik continued questioning.

"I wasn't there so I don't know, but it was well after dark," Abel said.

"So, what was your friend's encounter with Lenny?"

"Well, my friend, he takes some of what we find on the beach, and other places, and takes it over to the wharf to sell to sailors and visitors who might be interested in our wares," Able began. "While over there, he sees Lenny coming off the ferry and approaches him with some items that a young guy like him might like. Lenny calls out to my friend, whose name I won't mention, and my friend says he's too busy to stop. The deputy said he was following a hunch, but doesn't mention what or where he was going and just disappears into the night.

"I'm sorry, Marshal, that's all I got," Abel added.

"No, that's okay, Abel. At least it's something more than what I had when I got here.

"By the way, what have you got in the sack?"

"I'll show you quick like, since light is fading fast," Abel said, putting his sack on the sand and placing the items he pulled from it onto the cloth.

"Wait, what's that?" Nik said, eyeing something hanging on a chain.

"Oh, that's a sweet necklace I found. Gold, too," Abel said. "It's a locket, but there's nothing in it."

"Perfect, how much do you want for it?" Nik asked.

"I don't know. Like I said, it is gold," Abel said.

"Would you take five dollars for it?"

"For you, Marshal. I sure would." Abel said.

"I'll tell you what. If I find out if it's worth more than that I'll make it up to you," Nik concluded. "Besides, I owe you for the information as well."

"Oh, that wasn't worth much," Able replied. "That's on me."

Nik paid Abel with five silver dollars, thanked him for his time and the merchandise, and rode off.

Chapter 13
Covington Plantation

Nik and Ambrose rode up to the docking area Saturday afternoon, where the Galveston Ferry was loading passengers. Nik bought a pair of tickets and the two marshals led their mounts onboard the vessel. Fall was now in the air but the sky was clear and the temperature warm. After placing their horses into the stabling area, Nik and Ambrose went out onto the deck to enjoy the fresh air.

"I wasn't sure I was going to like it here," Nik said, gazing out over the bay. "But there seems to be an excitement in the atmosphere I kind of like."

"We visited the ocean a few times when I was growing up in Mississippi," Ambrose said, recalling his childhood as he spoke. "Master Latimore liked fishing in the surf and taught me to fish for sheepshead and speckled trout. My momma could cook them to perfection. Course, when my folks were sold off we stopped going fishing."

"I had only one serious experience with the ocean and it's one I wish I could forget," Nik responded, continuing to stare at the water. "Still, I am grateful to the Almighty for how it all turned out. Who knows, one day I might cross back over that ocean and find my original roots."

"Do you miss your folks?" Ambrose asked turning toward Nik.

"I think a lot about my mother, and Ma Brinkman too," Nik said, looking up at Ambrose. "I didn't know my real father, but I wouldn't trade the time I had with Pa Brinkman for the world."

"Funny how those things turn out," Ambrose said, glancing back in the direction of the bay."

The horn for the ferry sounded, signaling the passengers to prepare for docking.

Guess we'd better look after Galley and Crusader," Nik said, turning in the direction of the stable area. The two men retrieved their horses and led them down the docking platform. Other passengers could not help but marvel at the imposing figures of Ambrose and Crusader. When the deputy mounted, he towered over the crowd and all other riders coming off the boat.

After about an hour's ride, the two travelers approached the Covington Plantation. The mansion stood at the end of a half-mile lane that led to the courtyard in front of it. The edifice was nearly all white, except for green shutters, and stood out against the blue sky in the background. There were acres of plowed land that were once covered in cotton, but were recently harvested and already in preparation for the next harvest.

About two hundred yards to the right of the mansion stood a large warehouse, also constructed of wood. Next to it was a carriage house and stable. Hidden from view behind the house was a small cottage where the Boatmans resided. Behind the warehouse were a number of dilapidated dwellings that appeared to be abandoned and in need of repair.

Once the two riders reached the courtyard, Ambrose turned his horse to the left onto a lane leading to the stable.

"This is where we can leave our horses," Ambrose said over his shoulder. "As I remember, there's plenty of hay for our mounts and we can put them in the corral behind the stable."

As the marshals approached the stable, they could see a man inside pitching hay. Nik and Ambrose halted and dismounted.

"Hello," Ambrose called out to the man inside. The man appeared, looking out from behind the lower half of a double door and swung it open.

"Hello to you," Isaiah Boatman called out, striding out to meet the two visitors.

"Good to see you, Isaiah," Ambrose said, extending his hand. After the greeting, Isaiah turned to Nik.

"Marshal Brinkman, so good of you to come," Isaiah said.

"Not at all, Mr. Boatman, it isn't often Ambrose and I get invited to such a fine place for dinner."

"Then you are in for a treat," Isaiah responded. "Bring your horses and follow me. We'll put them in the corral where there's plenty of hay and water for them. I know Esther's been looking forward to your arrival."

After taking care of the animals, the three men started for the main house. As they passed the cotton fields, there was a noticeable foul odor that permeated the air.

"You'll have to excuse the smell," Isaiah said, cracking a smile as he spoke. "But we recently finished planting fish and it takes a while to get used to the odor."

"Planting fish?" Nik interjected.

"For fertilizing purposes," Isaiah explained. "These commercial fishermen catch a lot of menhaden, a fish that ain't much good for eatin' but they make great fertilizer. After the cotton is picked, then we plow up furrows and toss in the fish. Our cotton crops are some of the best in the world."

"I hope the cotton doesn't come out smelling like fish," Nik said, waving his hand in front of his nose.

Isaiah laughed, "No, like I say that smell goes away in less than a week, and, fortunately, you can't smell it in the house."

Ambrose was taking in the scenery as the men walked along. He was familiar with Isaiah's story, having visited the Covington Estate before. As he cast his gaze about, he spotted something that caught his attention.

"Excuse me, gentlemen," Ambrose said, as he veered off the lane and walked along one of the furrows. He looked down for a few moments, then bent over to pick something up on the ground. He returned to his companions.

"Excuse me, Isaiah," Ambrose said, turning his attention to the marshal. Does this look familiar?" the big man announced as he held up a balloon-shaped object.

"Let me see that," Nik replied, reaching out for the item and examining it. "This is similar to what my man on the beach found."

"We came across one of those before," Isaiah chimed in. "We figured maybe they were toy balloons left behind by one of the workers. Don't seem to hurt nothing, though."

"You found one before?" Nik asked. "Was there anything in it?"

"No, nothing," Isaiah responded, "just the balloon."

"If you two will wait here for me, I want to run back and put this where I can take it with me when we leave," Nik said. "I don't want to take it into the house with me because it smells like... well, it smells like outdoors here."

"Just put it with your tack, Marshal. It'll be there when you go," Isaiah said.

Nik returned to the stable, placed the balloon where he would see it when he and Ambrose left. Afterward, he rejoined Isaiah and Ambrose and they approached the mansion and went inside where Madame Covington was waiting to greet them.

The large entryway had a vaulted ceiling with a winding stairway that spread out at the bottom and curled left as it rose to a balcony above. The carpet covering the stairs was red and slightly worn, but clean. A drapery arranged in half loops hung on the wall to the right of the stairs, framing several artworks. To the left of the stairs was the receiving room and the dining room was on the right that led to an adjacent kitchen.

"What a beautiful place you have here," Nik said, his eyes flowing up the staircase to the balcony and the ceiling above. A chandelier hung over the midpoint of the hall leading to the stairs and a hallway on the left that opened into a library, office, and den.

"I would be happy to show you around, but dinner is nearly ready, so why don't we go into the front room and have something to drink first?" said the lady of the house.

The receiving room was elegant and furnished well. It was obvious the furniture did not get much abuse as there were no children or pets in the house. A portrait of Sir Lawrence Covington was prominently displayed over the fireplace.

"Is that the Mr. Covington?" Nik asked absentmindedly.

"That's the bastard, all right," Lady Covington said, casting a glance in the general direction of the fireplace. "I'm sure you know the story by now."

"Oh, ah, how stupid of me," Nik blurted out, disgusted with himself for not thinking before speaking. "I'm very sorry... I..."

"It's all right, Marshal Brinkman. He had it coming to him," Tillie Covington said. "He was forcing himself on the slave girls and I warned him that I would not tolerate it."

"I'm sorry, I really did not come here to meddle in matters of your family's past," Nik said. "I guess when I saw that portrait the question of who it was just popped into my mind."

"One day, he took it too far and I shot him," Mrs. Covington replied, now staring at the portrait. "It was ruled justifiable homicide."

Nik eyed Lady Covington with a countenance that belied his secret admiration for the woman.

"I can offer you a Mint Julep or Old Fashioned," Tillie Covington said, turning to Nik. "What would you like?"

"Just whiskey for me, would be fine," Nik responded.

"Oh let me make you an Old Fashioned," Tillie said, smiling as she moved toward the bar. "That's what I'm having. How about you Ambrose, Isaiah?

"If it's not too much trouble that Mint Julep sounds good," Ambrose responded.

"Nothing for me, right now Miss Tillie," Isaiah said. "I'm going into the kitchen to see how Esther's doing."

"Two Old Fashioneds and one Mint Julep, how delightful," Tillie said. "We just don't get much company anymore, not since the war."

Lady Covington made the Mint Julep, handing it to Ambrose, and began pouring the bourbon for the Oold Fashioneds. She added the bitters and was about to drop a cube of sugar into Nik's drink."

"Ah, no sugar for me, thanks," Nik said.

"No sugar? Then it would not be an Oold Fashioned, maybe a New Fashioned?" Tillie said with a laugh. "My, you must spend a lot of time in the saddle, Marshal Brinkman."

"Please, Madame Covington, just call me Nik, I had to learn to like what was available and I can assure you it wasn't an Old Fashioned."

"I will refer to you as Nik if you will call me Tillie, a deal?" she laughed again and Nik joined in.

"Nik, I have a question perhaps you can answer," Tillie proposed.

"I'll try… Tillie, what is it?

"Are you aware of the counterfeit money being circulated in the area?" she asked.

"Very much so, in fact, we are working with the Galveston Sheriff and the Treasury Department to try to get it stopped," Nik answered.

"Oh that would be ideal," Tillie said, her face more serious now. "I'm afraid I have unfortunately come into possession of quite a sum of greenbacks and the bank is at a loss as to how to honor it. Our cotton sales keep the estate going and my reserve funds cannot cover it. I would hate to lose the plantation."

"I believe the Federal Government is going to try and cover the United States Bank's losses, helping to keep the producers in this area solvent," Nik said.

"But I hear that is limited. How close are you in law enforcement to getting to the bottom of this?" Tillie asked.

"I would like to say close, but that wouldn't be truthful. The sheriff lost a deputy, who we believe was close to uncovering some information we could have used," Nik said. "Unfortunately, his funeral is tomorrow."

"It's partly my fault," Ambrose broke in. Nik gave his deputy a quick look. "Lenny Alexander, that was his name, he and I were kind of partnering in our search down at the docks. I guess I wasn't much of a partner because he got killed."

"I'm sorry to hear that, Ambrose," Tillie consoled. "Do you have any idea what he might have discovered?"

"No clue, mam. If I'd gone looking for him like I should have he might still be alive," Ambrose said, "and then we'd know."

"Ambrose, you may have been working with Lenny but you weren't officially his partner," Nik cut in. "You guys had been hunting for clues for weeks and had come up with nothing. Why would you think he was onto something now?"

"Because he did not show up at our usual meeting place," Ambrose said, looking down at the oriental rug covering the receiving room's floor. "I should have looked for him but I thought he'd just gone home – stupid of me."

"Please don't blame yourself, Ambrose," Tillie said. "Carrying a burden like that won't make you a better investigator."

"She's right, Ambrose, and I need you at your best in order to crack this case," Nik said with a stern tone in his voice.

"I understand, sir. I know this isn't helping nobody, especially me and you," Ambrose said. "I'll pay my respects tomorrow and be done with it."

"Good man, I need you now more than ever," Nik started…

"Dinner's ready, if anybody's hungry," Esther called out, standing in the entryway of the receiving room.

Nik was suddenly lost for words and simply gazed at Esther. Ambrose motioned for Tillie to lead him into the dining room. The big man glanced back at Nik,

"Are you comin'?" Ambrose remarked in Nik's direction.

"Oh, yeah, I guess I was lost in thought," Nik said, looking up at his deputy.

"Yes, sir," Ambrose said as he turned to follow Tillie.

Esther flashed a smile and then led the three into the dining room. Isaiah and Esther set the dishes on the table and Isaiah motioned for his daughter to take a seat while he served.

"You'll have to forgive Isaiah," Tillie said to Nik. "It's usually everyone for himself around here since the slaves were freed. Isaiah, here, insisted on serving tonight since we have company."

"My family was the same," Nik said, recalling his life with the Brinkman Family. "I was considered part of the family and learned to pull my weight just like everyone else. I can't say I was never served because Mrs. Brinkman was always looking after everybody."

"I would say she did a very good job," Esther said, as she passed a platter of what looked like biscuits to Nik.

Nik took one and put it on his plate.

"Take two, maybe three," Esther instructed. "They're quite small and I think you'll find they're quite good."

Nik took two and stopped to take a bite out of one. "Say, these are good. What kind of biscuits are these?"

"They're called hush puppies," Esther said with a broad smile.

"Hush puppies," Nik repeated. "I can't say I've ever heard of them."

"They're popular in the south, Nik," Esther continued. "The hunters used to make them when sitting around the campfire. When the coon hounds started to howl, the hunters would throw these to them to keep them quiet."

"So, we're eating dog food," Nik said, with a bewildered look on his face.

"No, that's just how they got they're name. The hunters made them for themselves, but found their hunting dogs liked them as well," Esther said. "They go great with fish and that's what we're having tonight. I would not feed you dog food."

"I seem to make a habit of sticking my foot in my mouth tonight," Nik said with a sheepish grin. "I hope you'll forgive me."

"I have a hunch you spend a lot of time alone, Nik," Tillie broke in. "You're very courteous and polite but small talk does not seem to be your strong suit."

"I'm afraid I cannot argue with that," Nik replied. "Since my... , I left home, I spent a lot of time by myself, being out on the trail and all. I did have an Indian friend who traveled with me on occasion , but he didn't talk much."

"I'm sure that, as a marshal, you have to be... out on the trail, as you say," Tillie said, helping herself to more hush puppies.

"That's right Madame ..., er, Tillie, but that brings me to a question," Nik said. "You mentioned you came into quite a sum of greenbacks. Do you mind telling me how?"

"There's a merchant friend of ours we deal with who buys our cotton. He also volunteers to deliver our fish fertilizer when he comes out, saves us from having to do it," Tillie explained. "Both products are handled through a co-op on the mainland and that's apparently where the counterfeit money comes from. The sheriff has spoken with our merchant friend and the folks who run the co-op, and both were apparently unaware they were dealing in worthless paper, because they are in trouble with the bank like we are."

"It sounds like this counterfeit ring is dealing on a commercial scale," Nik said, sitting back in his chair. "Have other cotton growers experienced the same?"

"Some have, but not all," Tillie said. "We don't all go through the same merchants or the co-op."

"And you're certain your friend and the co-op are clean?" Nik said.

"As far as we know," Isaiah interjected. "I try to keep track of the plantation's transactions and this sort of snuck up on us. We've been dealing with these folks for years."

After dinner, Nik offered to help with the dishes.

"You don't have to do that," Esther said.

"No, I want to," Nik quickly responded. "I, ah… after all the gaffs I've made tonight it's the least I can do. Besides, Ambrose and I have to be getting back soon and I thought, well … since you've kind of been left out of the most of the conversation, I didn't want to be rude and all."

Esther looked at Nik for a moment and smiled. "Okay, you can help with the dishes. Poppa, why don't you look after Miss Tillie and Ambrose? We won't be long."

While the other three departed for the front room, Nik helped Esther clear the table and take the dishes into the kitchen. Esther kept eyeing Nik and he kept trying to appear nonchalant.

"Now, Nik Brinkman, you appear to me to have something more on your mind than doing the dishes."

"Well, no… I was just… you're right. I just wanted to spend some time with you," Nik confessed. "I hope that doesn't offend you… and calling me Nik is adequate. No need for Brinkman or Marshal."

"You haven't done this sort of think often, have you… Nik?"

"I guess it kind of shows," Nik said. "I haven't done this sort of thing at all."

"Relax. I don't bite. And I don't entertain very often, either," Esther said.

"I know this invitation was kind of spur-of-the-moment," Nik began. "But I had to get you aside and ask if I... well, maybe could do this more often."

"You liked my cooking that much?" Esther said with a grin.

"Oh, the food was great. No doubt about that, but... no, that's not what I'm talking about."

"I'm just teasing, Nik. I like you and I like your company... but..."

"But what? Nik said, picking up the conversation. "That's a good start, isn't it?"

"You don't quite understand, I'm afraid. You see, I really don't think it's a good idea that we get too involved," Esther said, forcing a tight-lipped grin after she spoke.

"Ahh, I understand. There's someone else, isn't there?" Nik responded. "I should have known..."

"No, there isn't someone else," Esther said, looking up and away with a stressed expression. "It's just... well, it's Poppa, you understand, I'm sure."

"Your father?" Nik said. "I'm not talking about anything he might not approve of. I mean, I just would like to spend time with you, and if Poppa has to be there too I'm all right with that."

"No, I... I'm afraid I'm giving you the wrong impression," Esther said, holding her hands in front of her and wringing them slightly. "It... it's complicated and I probably shouldn't have suggested this dinner thing."

"I've come on too strong and offended you," Nik lamented. "My whole evening's been going that way. I'm sorry, I probably read too much into this, like a jerk."

"You're not a jerk and I wanted you to come, as well as Ambrose. I... I, listen, I can't explain it now but if you'll give me some time I will," Esther said. "I'll come by your office sometime, sometime when you're not busy, all right? I did promise to do some decorating to your office."

Ahh, sure, that would be terrific," Nik replied with a slightly hurt but somewhat relieved look. "Anytime you want to come by is fine with me."

"Maybe when this counterfeit thing is cleared up, would that be okay?" Esther said, waving her hand as if to try and dismiss the conversation as soon as she could.

"Like I said, Esther, anytime," Nik paused looking at Esther as she cast her eyes on the floor. "Look, this has been a real treat for Ambrose and me, but we should be getting back."

"Of course, Nik, thank you both for coming and I promise I'll… I'll get in touch with you soon."

"Sure, Esther," Nik said. "I will look forward to it."

Esther stayed in the kitchen as Nik went in search of the other three to retrieve Ambrose and say goodnight. Isaiah accompanied the two to the stall and helped them ready their horses for the ride home.

Isaiah spotted the balloon Nik had set aside. "Did you want to take this with you, Marshal?" he asked.

"Oh, definitely," Nik answered. "Thanks, Isaiah, if you hadn't spotted it I'm embarrassed to say I would have forgotten it."

"You've got bigger things on your mind than toy balloons, Marshal," Isaiah said, with a slight glance at Ambrose.

"Is it that obvious?" Nik said, with a slight blush in his cheeks. "Look, Isaiah, I can't hide that I have feelings for your daughter. If you do not approve, I'll back off. I think that may be what Esther wants, anyway."

"Oh, don't be too sure of that, Marshal," Isaiah replied with a sly smile. "Esther's pretty good about hiding her feelings. You have my blessing to see my daughter but I'm not surprised she may seem standoffish. She has her reasons.

"Give her time, Marshal. I think she'll come around."

"Your blessing is encouraging, Isaiah," Nik said. "If there's one thing I have it's time."

The three men concluded the evening with a laugh, and Nik and Ambrose mounted up and headed out into the night.

Nik and Ambrose made good time in getting back to the ferry

and spent very little time in talking with each other. Once on the ferry, they saw a couple vessels heading into port some distance from the boat.

"Someone's working late," Nik commented.

"It's a busy place, all right," Ambrose said, as the two stood leaning on the rail of the ferry. The big man's thoughts were on Lenny's funeral scheduled for the next day.

Chapter 14
Lenny's Clue

United States Marshal Nik Brinkman and his deputy, Ambrose Tucker, sat silently listening to the eulogy being delivered at Lenny Alexander's memorial service. Nik could see that Ambrose was agitated, realizing that his deputy was still wrestling with the notion he had abandoned Sheriff Deputy Alexander prior to Lenny's body being found floating in the bay. Once the eulogy had completed, an offer was extended to anyone wanting to say a few words on Lenny's behalf. Ambrose began to tremble.

"Relax, Ambrose," Nik whispered to his companion. "No one thinks you had anything to do with this."

Ambrose looked at Nik and the marshal could see he was filled with emotion and holding back tears.

"I've got to do this," Ambrose said in a trembling voice that rose above a whisper.

Several folks sitting nearby glanced over in the direction of the two marshals.

"Yes, sir, I'd have something I'd like to say," Ambrose blurted out, as his enormous frame rose above those seated around him.

"Then, please come forward, my good man," the preacher offered.

Ambrose ran a sleeve across his face as he squeezed past Nik and into the aisle. Many heads turned in the deputy's direction as he walked toward the podium on the altar. Very few among the mourners were familiar with the new deputy and what he might have to say. Ambrose approached the lectern, placed his large hands on its edges and leaned forward with his head bowed.

"My…, ah…, my name is Ambrose Tucker. I'm a U.S. Deputy Marshal here in Galveston," Ambrose began. "I got to know Deputy Alexander because I'd been working with him on a case we were both investigating. We were both frustrated because we were not getting anywhere and a lot of folks were counting on us. Even some that didn't know it.

"You see," Ambrose continued, raising his head to look out over the audience. "We were looking for bad folks printing bad money and that money was threatening the good money the fine folks of Galveston had saved up. Although Lenny was with the sheriff's office and I with the Marshals Service, we formed a team to watch each other's backs and share information hoping we could make some headway together. The night Lenny… umm passed away," Ambrose lowered his head and his shoulders shook from the sobs he tried to choke back. "I was to meet him that night and I didn't do it. I… I went home instead."

Ambrose turned his back to the audience in an attempt to gain his composure. The preacher came forward to assist and Nik sprang from his seat and joined the two men at the podium.

"Folks, I'm Chief Marshal Nik Brinkman and Ambrose here is my deputy. I fear this fine man thinks himself responsible for what happened to Lenny and I hope you can find it in your hearts to let him know the circumstance he speaks of is the kind of thing many of us share. I know, I found myself in that same situation many years ago. I, like my deputy here, carry that guilt even though there was nothing I could do about my situation, or Ambrose can do about his.

"What I will say is that Deputy Lenny Alexander was a good man and a solid lawman. If he were not, my deputy here would not feel the way he does about Lenny's loss. I do not know what all of you do for a living, but lawmen, such as ourselves," Nik said, turning to look at Ambrose, who was now standing with the preacher and listening intently to what Nik had to say. "We form a special bond no matter what our titles say or if we work in separate offices. Ambrose had that special bond with Lenny, although they did not know each other all that long. That makes no difference, we lost a fellow soldier in Lenny Alexander and we cannot help but carry the burden of it even if it was something that happened beyond our control."

As Nik spoke, Sheriff Atkins approached the podium and stood next to Nik.

"Folks, most of you know me," Atkins began. "And what Marshal Brinkman says is true. I was Lenny's boss, and though I was not there that night, I too have to carry some of the burden the marshal speaks of. Like a parent, I wish I could always be with my men when they get into dangerous situations, but it just isn't possible. If we all stayed in the same place we would never be able to solve a case. But even… even in death… Lenny spoke to us and gave us a glimpse of what we're up against."

Sheriff Deputy Zeke Vincent and one assistant deputy came forward and stood behind Nik and Atkins, along with Ambrose and the preacher.

Following the sheriff's words, many in the audience came forward to express their sympathy toward Ambrose, as well as Lenny's parents. That day, Lenny Alexander got the honor he deserved and Ambrose the support he needed to carry on.

After the ceremony, everyone gathered at the Galveston Cemetery for Lenny's burial. A twenty-one gun salute accompanied the interment and then all but Lenny's immediate family began to drift away.

The next day, Nik took the balloon recovered from the Covington Plantation and presented it to Agent Ron Lester.

"They certainly look similar," Ron said. "You say you found this in a cotton field?"

"I know no children put it there," Nik interjected. "There aren't any kids within miles of the place and it's miles from the beach as well."

"There may not be any connection here, but I will try and track down where these balloons came from," Ron suggested. "Perhaps whoever makes them can tell us who is buying them."

"Solid idea, Ron. Ambrose and I will step up our vigilance. We've now got a murder on our hands to solve as well."

Weeks passed without any leads being turned up by either the sheriff's department, U.S. Marshals Service or U.S. Treasury Department. However, Agent Lester did report tracking down where the balloons were manufactured and presented his findings to his law-enforcement allies.

"If it's any help to this investigation," Agent Lester began, "We believe these balloons were made in Mexico. Apparently the Indians down there, centuries ago, discovered a tree that produces this rubbery substance called latex. When treated, this latex can be molded into balloons, which are good for waterproofing, as you have already discovered, Marshal Brinkman."

"That's great," Nik started. "That might explain how it washed up on Galveston's beach, but not how it ended up in a cotton field."

"No, but it does help to explain why those counterfeit bills were placed in one of these balloons," Sheriff Atkins cut in. "Could these balloons be made bigger so as to hide thousands of counterfeit dollars under water?"

"I know this stuff has been used in hot-air balloons, so I'm sure they could be made to size," Ron said. "But a balloon that size would be quite noticeable unless kept underwater. It would then have to be retrieved and brought onto land. That could prove to be quite an undertaking."

"The distribution, which seems to be in smaller amounts, ended up in a balloon the size of the one that washed up on shore. Or like the one Ambrose and I found on Covington's Plantation," Nik mused out loud.

"And there was no money at all in the one you found in that field?" Ron asked, directing his question to Nik.

"None, right Ambrose?" Nik said, turning to his deputy.

"No, sir, just that small balloon." Ambrose answered. "Nothing in it, but I was thinking…" Ambrose paused.

"What were you thinking?" Nik asked.

"I don't want to interrupt with sayin' something stupid," Ambrose answered, embarrassed that he even spoke up.

"Nonsense, Ambrose, we need every idea we can get right now."

"We know money was inside the first balloon found on the beach, right?

Everyone in the room nodded in affirmation.

"And we found a second balloon, although there was no money in it," Ambrose continued. "My thought is maybe the balloon was being used to hide the money inside barrels of water or something."

"So, you're saying we may have been on top of the money all along but missed it because it was submerged in something," Ron interjected. "Like a pickle barrel or keg of rum?"

"Just sayin'," Ambrose said, again feeling embarrassed at his remarks.

"No, deputy, you may be onto something there," Ron said. "We did examine the contents of some barrels onboard several ships and on the docks. But we didn't open those containing liquid, assuming money would not be kept in there," Ron's expression began to change as he spoke, "unless wrapped in something watertight."

"That's good thinking, Ambrose," Nik added. "You never cease to amaze me."

"Well, gentlemen, keep digging," the sheriff said. "Let's head back and check out those liquid barrels, turn 'em over and empty them out if necessary. Judge Conklin and the bank are breathing down my neck over this. We've got to cut off this phony money supply because it is spreading."

"I'll have Ambrose continue combing the docks," Nik offered. "In the meantime, I'm going to follow up with that coroner and Lenny's family."

"What do you hope to find?" Duke asked.

"Any lead possible," Nik answered. "We've got to retrace every step we've taken so far in hopes of turning up something we may have missed."

As the group split up to pursue their collaborative investigations, Nik asked Ambrose to help the sheriff and his deputy in checking out any cargo being shipped in watertight containers. Meanwhile, Nik decided he would continue with his hunch to visit the coroner and talk to pathologist Dr. Elias Klotman, who examined Lenny Alexander's body.

"I do not know what more I can tell you, Marshal," Klotman said, leaning back in his chair from behind his cluttered desk. "It's all in the report... most of it anyway."

"Most of it?" Nik repeated.

"I got to thinking about it later. It seemed too unimportant at the time and perhaps would interfere with the entire investigation," Klotman answered.

"We're looking for anything right now," Nik said. "We've been running up blind alleys and coming back empty handed. Any additional information you could give us would help."

"Well," the coroner began, "when the Alexanders came by to pick up Lenny's belongings, I noticed what looked like the tail of a fish sticking out of the pocket of the deceased's trousers. I was going to say something but the family was so distraught I thought better of it. Later, I did wonder what it was but those thoughts were interrupted by the arrival of another body to examine, unrelated to Lenny's case."

"A fish, you say," Nik responded.

"I cannot say for sure, but it did resemble the tail of something," Klotman said. "Perhaps even seaweed or something like that."

"I will follow up with the Alexanders, just in case," Nik said. "

Nik did not relish the idea of having to invade the grieving family's privacy but knew it had to be done. Feeling emboldened by Ambrose's suggestion, Nik felt determined to track down every clue they had, even one as insignificant as finding a fish in a deceased deputy's pocket.

As Marshal Brinkman approached the Alexander's house, he could see the partial outline of someone's face peering at him from behind a window curtain. The image disappeared as soon as Nik looked in its direction. The immediate withdrawal of the face gave the lawman an uneasy feeling but he pressed on with what he had to do.

There was a ring on the post of the front gate and Nik tied Galley to it. He opened the gate and tried to maintain an unthreatening posture as he approached the door. It opened before he knocked.

"Marshal, we did not expect to see you again so soon," Sylvester Alexander, Lenny's father, said from behind the partially opened door.

"I am sorry to interrupt, Mr. Alexander, but I'd just like to ask you some questions concerning Lenny's case."

"Lenny's case? What about it?" Sylvester said, still refusing to open the door any wider.

"We need to find Lenny's kil … the man who took Lenny's life," Nik said, trying to guard his words. "I promise not to take up too much of your time. Believe me, I know how you feel."

Sylvester stared at Nik briefly before stepping back and completely opening the door. Nik entered and saw Bea Alexander sitting on the front room sofa with a black veil hanging down from the hat she was wearing. However, her clothes were not dark in color.

"Please, have a seat, Marshal," Sylvester said, as he walked past to sit by his wife. Nik took a seat opposite the aggrieved couple.

"Coroner Klotman said you picked up Lenny's clothes, is that right?"

"Yes," Sylvester said, and Nik could see Bea's head bob in the affirmative.

"Did you find anything strange about Lenny's clothes? Something in the pockets perhaps?" Nik started.

"No, nothing," Sylvester said with an almost perturbed tone.

"Anything, anything at all," Nik persisted. "We want to find who did this to Lenny and we can use any clue you might have discovered."

Nik could hear a soft whimper come from behind Bea Alexander's veil. Sylvester looked in her direction and then back at Nik.

"Like I said, there was nothing."'

"I'm sorry to have to bring this up, but the coroner said he saw something like the tail of a fish sticking out of one of the pockets of Lenny's trousers," Nik responded. "Did you find anything like that?"

Mrs. Alexander let out another sigh, louder than the first.

"A fish, no there was no fish in Lenny's pockets," Sylvester said.

"That would be kind of strange, don't you think, Marshal?

"Perhaps strange is what I'm looking for, Mr. Alexander," Nik replied. "We have very little to go on right now."

"There really is nothing more I… we have to say, Marshal," Sylvester said, glancing over at his wife. "As you can see, we're still grieving over this."

"I understand that, but…"Nik started.

"I'm sorry, Marshal," Sylvester cut in. "It would be best if you would go."

"Go on Pa! Tell em!" rang out a voice from behind the curtain hanging in the doorway that led to the kitchen. "Tell him about the fish in Lenny's pocket. We need to know who did this to Lenny." A young girl stepped out from behind the curtain that Nik recognized as the face he had seen in the window when he rode up.

"Mary Beth, you keep quiet, you hear," Sylvester said, rising up from the couch and turning to the girl.

"No, Pa, you need to tell 'em," the girl continued.

"Pay no mind to my daughter, Marshal," Sylvester said, turning to Nick. "She's distraught and likely to say anything."

"Wait a minute, Mr.…." at that moment, Bea began to openly sob, pressing her hands against her veil.

"Now you've gone and done it, Mary Beth," Sylvester said in a tone approaching a shout. "You've upset your poor mother."

"I don't care. The marshal needs to know," Mary Beth said, mimicking her father's tone.

"Whoa, let's take a minute to compose ourselves," Nik said, trying his best to intervene between the two. "Mrs. Alexander, I'm powerful sorry about all this but if you're hiding something you may be violating the law. You don't want that added to the pain you already feel over Lenny's unfortunate death, do you?"

Sylvester's attempt to sit back down on the couch appeared more like a collapse. He cupped his hands over his face and said nothing.

"Let's take a moment to collect ourselves and start again," Nik said in as calm of a tone as he could. "What about the fish? And I don't care who tells me but I need to know."

"Pa…" Mary Beth began.

"All right, now that you have laid it out in the open, I… I'll tell the marshal what we found," Sylvester directed his words to his daughter. Mrs. Alexander let out a slight wail and continued to cry.

There was a pause and Mary Beth moved out from the kitchen and into the front room, in a determined effort to get her father to tell the truth.

Sylvester took in a deep breath and began. "We did find a fish and we threw it away," he said.

"Pa, tell him everything," Mary Beth demanded.

"Mary Beth, I swear…" Sylvester said, turning to her.

"Mr. Alexander, please, you have to tell me or I will have to subpoena you for the information in court," Nik said, trying not to threaten. "If you tell me now none of that will have to happen."

Sylvester looked down at the floor with a long pause and then spoke. "There was money in the fish." Bea again let out a tearful wail.

"Money? You found money in the fish?" Nik asked in a confused voice.

"Yes," Sylvester said, sitting back, turning his head, and pushing his hands forward on his legs.

"So, where is the money now?" Nik asked.

"I don't know," Sylvester said.

"It's buried in the backyard, Marshal," Mary Beth blurted out.

"Mary Beth, I swear…" Sylvester said, again turning in his daughter's direction.

"Buried in the backyard?" Nik quizzed. "Can you show me where?"

"I cannot take anymore," said Bea, rising from the couch and disappearing into another room.

"Now see what you've done…" Sylvester said to Mary Beth.

"Mr. Alexander, show me where you buried that money and I may be able to end this agony for you," Nik said. "I need to see that money."

Almost in slow motion, Sylvester led Nik outside, casting a sad, hurt glance at his daughter as he passed. Once outside, Sylvester grabbed a shovel, approached a freshly overturned plot of ground and began digging. Before long, he turned up a wad of bills stuffed in an all-too-familiar latex balloon. He handed it to Nik.

"Thank you, Mr. Alexander," Nik said, taking the item. "Why were you so reluctant to tell me this?"

"Well, because obviously Lenny stole it," Sylvester said.

"Lenny stole it? How do you now that?"

"Because Lenny never made that kind of money," Sylvester continued. "Sure, he was a good deputy but deputies don't get paid that much. There's more than a hunnert dollars there."

"If Lenny stole it, why in the world would he try to hide it in a fish and put it into his pocket?" the wheels in Nik's head were turning as he spoke. "Wait a minute, no, Mr. Alexander, Lenny didn't steal this money. No, he found it in the fish and put both in his pocket as evidence. Don't you see? Lenny found how the counterfeit money was coming into the area and in the process... I fear, that's why he was killed."

"So, my son didn't steal that money?"

"I seriously doubt it's real money, Mr. Alexander, I believe it's counterfeit," Nik replied. "As a deputy sheriff, he had been searching to find out where this money was coming from, and he did."

"I need to tell my wife," Sylvester said, with a smile. "When we found that money we thought Lenny was a thief and we did not want his memory marred by that. That's why we hid it back here in the yard."

"You're son not only was not a thief, he was a hero," Nik said, with a wide smile. "Lenny may have single-handedly cracked a case that had at least three law-enforcement agencies baffled. No, Mr. Alexander, you're son was one fine, honest, deputy. You, your wife, and Mary Beth should be proud."

"Thank you, Marshal. I can't wait to tell Bea the good news," Sylvester said, shaking Nik's hand.

"I should be thanking you, and Lenny, and I will let you go because I need to get this information back to my colleagues," Nik said. "And, by the way, don't breathe a word of this. For now, this is just between us."

"We've kept it quiet this long, we can do it as long as you need, marshal." Sylvester said, turning and running toward the house.

Nik secured the money in his pocket, and started to walk around the side of the house to retrieve Galley. He glanced over as Sylvester ascended the porch stairs to go into the house and was confronted by Mary Beth. Sylvester stared at his daughter momentarily before wrapping his arms around her and hugging her.

Nik smiled to himself as he continued on his way and mounted Galley, who was trying to get at what little grass remained on the Alexander's front lawn. Nik pulled up her head, turned her around, and galloped off in the direction of Galveston Courthouse.

Chapter 15
Counterfeit Fish

Nik arrived at Galveston Harbor, where he tethered Galley and went in search of Ambrose and others that might be inspecting ships with cargos of liquid-filled containers in their holds or unloaded on the dock. He spotted Sheriff Atkins talking rather heatedly to a ship's captain whose vessel had recently docked.

"Duke," Nik called out excitedly as he drew near. "I'm sorry to interrupt, but I have some important information for you."

Atkins and the captain turned to Nik, and the marshal could see the two men were not in the best of moods.

"Again, gentlemen, I apologize for my rude intrusion on your conversation, but I may be able to help."

"I hope so," said the ship's captain. "I'm not about to stand by and have my cargo dumped out looking for what I do not have."

"I can use the help," Duke said, "What have you found out?"

Nik took the sheriff by the arm and pulled him away, asking the captain to give them some privacy. The captain did not answer and turned to walk in the direction of his ship.

"Duke, I think we're looking for the wrong cargo. We need to be checking the fishing boats," Nik said.

"The fishing boats? I don't understand, Nik."

"Look at what I have here in my pocket," Nik exclaimed, pulling the cash-filled balloon from its location.

"Oh, you found some more," Duke said, surprised at what Nik was holding in his hand. "Where did you find it?"

"In a fish," Nik said with a broad grin. "The counterfeit gang is stuffing the money into fish using a latex balloon to protect the bills from deteriorating."

"Whoa, slow down, Nik. How and where did you find this out?"

"I visited the Alexanders and discovered that the clothes Lenny was wearing the night he was killed had a fish in the pocket of his pants," Nik began. "That fish contained what I am holding in my hand."

Nik went on to elaborate on the discovery to further convince the sheriff the money was being hidden in fish.

"So, how does the money get distributed from inside the fish?" Duke inquired.

"That I am not sure of," Nik answered. "But I believe it is coming ashore in the stomachs of fish."

"That means our search of liquid-filled barrels is in vain and we need to be investigating the fishing vessels," Atkins conjectured.

"Apparently so, do you know where the rest of the men are right now? Nik asked.

"My men, Ambrose and the customs agents are boarding ships insisting they be allowed to inspect any liquid-filled containers," Duke said. "All we need to look for are some very upset sea captains and we'll know where our deputies have been."

The sheriff's suggestion proved prophetic as he and Nik saved a number of their inspectors from a potential fist fight. All except Ambrose, who had no trouble convincing the captain any altercation would not be in the skipper's best interest.

Each law officer they found was instructed to meet back at the sheriff's office. After clearing the harbor, they all met at the courthouse to discuss why they needed a new strategy. Ron Lester had been informed and was also included in the gathering. Nik led the meeting, explaining what he had found and why it was believed the phony money was being smuggled inside fish.

"We can be reasonably sure the money is reaching U.S. soil hidden inside of fish," Nik instructed. "What we don't know is how it gets from the fish into the hands of those distributing it."

"So, should we be checking fishing boats instead of shipping vessels?" one of Lester's agents asked.

"That seems to be the most logical place to start," Nik answered. "Hopefully, if we can find the boats these fish are coming in on, we'll also discover the counterfeiters' means of distributing the bills."

"If I may, Marshal," Agent Lester spoke up, "most of these ships will contain tons of menhaden fish, the most prolific fish of the Mexico Gulf. As we have learned, these fish are generally small, even small enough to fit into a man's pocket. That means we may have to inspect a lot of fish before finding those containing balloons full of money. I say this so you won't be discouraged if you do not find the smuggling operation right away."

The group agreed to delay their inspections until late afternoon when the fishing vessels return with their day's catch. Because of Lenny's death, the men were instructed to not board a fishing vessel alone or unarmed.

Later that day, when the fishing boats began to arrive, the law officers informed each captain of the necessity to inspect their catch. They felt if they encountered some resistance, it would indicate an attempt to hide something. However, each captain agreed to an inspection as long as it did not hinder the unloading process. The lawmen were instructed to inspect menhaden-laden vessels only, to help save time. However, many of the boats carried a variety of marine species, slowing the inspection operation.

The crews worked late into the night with little success, and limited hostility.

"I wonder if we were not misled, somehow, by that fish in Lenny's pocket," Sheriff Atkins remarked to Nik.

"Misled how," Nik answered, a little troubled by Duke's comment.

"Maybe Lenny was set up into thinking he was onto something by finding money in a planted fish, perhaps to throw him off," Duke added.

"I guess that's possible, but why kill him and throw him into the bay if that's what they wanted us to think," Nik responded. "Besides, if each fish contained several hundred dollars it wouldn't take much to pour thousands of counterfeit dollars into the system. I'm still convinced that Lenny was onto something."

"I have to admit that I want to think that same thing. At this rate, we won't have the manpower to examine all these fish."

"Perhaps not, but someone does, otherwise this fish smuggling scheme cannot work… wait a minute," Nik said, thinking out loud and turning to Atkins, "where do these fish go? What are menhaden fish good for?"

"They're not necessarily good eatin', most are used for fertilizer," Duke answered. "The Indians taught us that and most are sold to the fishery co-op. They're sold by the ton, so somebody would have to know specifically what he's looking for."

"That's an excellent point, Duke, but someone on this end has to be doing that," Nik replied. "Is it possible some of these boats are picking up the cash-filled fish from somewhere and transporting them separately? It's hard to imagine they would be stuffing fish at random."

"So, you're saying there could be a ship with a specific cargo of fish and dropping them off at a distribution facility?" Duke responded, picking up on Nik's train of thought. "I guess that would make more sense than randomly stuffing a few select menhaden at sea and hoping they fall into the right hands."

"To me, it only makes sense since we know thousands of fish are unloaded here," Nik mused. "If the distribution base is here then I'm guessing someone from that facility is picking up those fish. I suggest we regroup back at your office and lay out a new strategy."

Much to the relief of those lawmen examining hundreds of fish, they were all called back and told to meet again in Sheriff Atkins's office.

"Gentlemen," Duke began, "It has come to our attention that the fish containing the counterfeit money are likely not among the thousands harvested, but are stored separately from the rest. We believe the counterfeiting ring would have the same trouble examining all those fish that we do."

"If that's the case," Customs Agent Lester chimed in, "we're looking for a specific shipment of fish and not some that are scattered amongst the many?"

"Duke and I came to that conclusion after witnessing our failed effort to find any fish containing cash among all those boats in the harbor," Nik said. "At least one ship must be picking up the counterfeit fish, bringing that shipment here and handing it off to someone who knows what's in them."

"But don't they all go to the fertilizer co-op?" Deputy Vincent asked.

"We now think that is not the case," Duke answered. "Other than the eating establishments, there must be another facility that's taking some of these fish. Menhaden are edible but they're not very good."

"Not unless prepared properly," said one of Lester's agents, speaking with a foreign accent. "These menhaden, as you call them, they are related to herring, are they not?"

"Menhaden is a species of herring native to gulf waters," Lester advised.

"In my country, pickled herring is a delicacy," the agent said. "Do you have such a canning facility here?"

"There is Johansson Canning Company on Pelican Island." Zeke offered.

"That's true," Sheriff Atkins responded, "but I've known the Johanssons for years. They run a first-class operation. There's no way they are involved in this thing."

"Perhaps not the Johanssons, Duke," Nik said, "but someone who works for them. How many employees work there?"

"I'm not sure," Duke answered. "But they do run a pretty big operation. They ship many of their products overseas."

"It would not hurt to pay them a visit, since they do take in a limited number of menhaden," Agent Lester said.

"I would be happy to follow up on that lead," Zeke said. "I've known Felix and his wife for quite some time. I think I can approach him without giving him a reason to think he's suspected of anything."

"Do exercise caution," Duke advised."I do not what to upset the Johanssons or tarnish their reputation in any way. They're pretty proud of their business. Maybe keep your badge in your pocket to help make them feel they're helping us as opposed to being investigated."

"Got ya, chief," Zeke said. "I'll do it first thing in the morning."

"In the meantime," Nik concluded, "continue working on whatever you have been but be extra careful. The word is out now that we're examining virtually every ship in the harbor. And don't board any vessel without a companion, no matter how suspicious the boat may appear."

After the meeting broke up, Nik and Ambrose returned to their office.

"Ambrose, unless you have something pressing to do, why don't you come with me. There's someone I'd like you to meet," Nik said.

"I figure, since we're going to wait until Zeke reports back about that canning company," Ambrose replied, "I'm in your hands and would be glad to meet this person."

The two rode over to the ocean side of Galveston and out onto the beach. After riding a short ways, Nik spotted Abel Mosely moving along the shoreline. He was inspecting the surf as it washed over his bare feet and flowed back out to meet the next wave coming in. When he spotted Nik and Ambrose, he quickened his pace and called out a greeting, Nik dismounted and Ambrose followed suit.

"Abel, I want you to meet my deputy, Ambrose Tucker," Nik said, smiling and clutching Abel's hand.

After releasing Nik's hand, Abel stepped forward to grab the one Ambrose was extending.

"Pleased to meet you, deputy," Abel said smiling. He called back to Nik. "My, Marshal, you sure do pick 'em big."

"Happy to meet you, Abel," Ambrose replied, looking up at Nik with an amused expression. "Is this the gentleman that found the first balloon filled with money?"

"He is," Nik responded, and turned to Mosely, "Abel, do you have anything for me?".

"I do, Marshal," Abel said, reaching into his sack and pulling out a fish. "Some of these washed up on the beach. Most folks ignore them and move away to other locations on the beach. They do not smell good when lying in the sun for a time."

"But you decided to pick one up anyway," Nik said, grinning.

"I did, but when I examined it I put just the one in my bag and ignored the others. I think the city is going to pick them up and dispose of 'em, eventually." Abel said.

Nik reached into the fish's mouth and extracted a balloon with cash in it.

"You say more of these fish washed up on shore, where?" Nik asked.

"They're up where the ocean flows into the bay. Not too many on this beach, more of 'em toward the north near the channel," Abel said.

"Ambrose, ride back to the office and find Agent Lester. Inform him of this," Nik instructed. "He may want to wait until morning, but I think he and his men are going to want to see this."

"Yes, sir," Ambrose said, "Nice to meet ya, Abel," Ambrose said to Mosely, as he turned and mounted Crusader.

"What do you make of it, Marshal?" Abel asked.

"I don't yet know what to think, Abel," Nik answered, looking up from the fish in his hand. "That balloon washing up on shore was one thing, but if those other fish you mentioned are filled with money, why all of a sudden? Let's walk up there and see what we can find."

"I think you best ride, marshal. It's quite a ways up there."

"Let's both ride, Abel. Galley can carry us both."

As the riders neared the north end of the beach, Nik could see dozens of objects scattered all across the shore. No one was in the area, so Nik kicked Galley into a gallop.

"You okay back there, Abel?" Nik called out.

"I'm hanging on just fine, Marshal. Besides, it's not far now," Abel responded.

As they drew nigh, the odor of dead fish was heavy in the air. The men dismounted and began inspecting fish as they walked along. They found a few with balloons containing greenbacks, but not many. When it grew too dark to see clearly, Nik turned back to Abel.

"I'll take the ones I found containing money. I'm guessing Agent Lester and his crew will arrive in the morning," Nik said. "Can I give you a ride somewhere?"

"Not necessary, I'm close to my beach hut now. I can walk the rest of the way," Abel said.

"In that case, I'd better be getting back," Nik said. "Thanks again for your help, Abel. I'll appropriate some money to pay you for your services."

"Much obliged, Marshal," Abel said. "But ain't no hurry. I do pretty good selling what I find."

"Just don't sell any fish," Nik said with a laugh. "We've got to stop this, somehow."

The two men parted and Nik rode back to the livery stable, dropped off Galley and headed for the hotel. Ambrose was already there.

"Did you get hold of Lester?" Nik asked.

"He wasn't in his office and showed up late," Ambrose said. "I explained to him what was found. He said he and his men would investigate in the morning. Since everyone's waiting until tomorrow, I figured I'd come back here and wait too."

"Excellent work Ambrose," Nik said, taking off his hat. "Let's go downstairs and get something to eat."

The next morning, Zeke put his badge in his pocket and headed for the ferry that would take him across to Pelican Island. He scanned the waterfront for signs of anything suspicious, but it seemed to be business as usual. He boarded the ferry for the short ride to the island, disembarked, and rode off in the direction of the Johansson Canning Company.

The business had expanded since Deputy Vincent's last visit, and when he entered he could see a line of men and women processing fish on a large butcher-block counter. Some of them looked up when Zeke entered but few paid any real attention. Zeke looked over at the familiar stairway leading up to a small office perched on a landing situated above the work area and briskly walked over to climb it.

"Felix Johansson," Zeke called out as he entered the office and approached a heavyset man seated at a desk studying some papers. The man looked up when Zeke spoke and squinted in the deputy's direction.

"Zeke, Zeke Vincent," Felix responded. "I have not seen you for ages. What brings you to the cannery?"

"Just passing through and thought I'd drop in," Zeke began. We've been investigating Deputy Alexander's death. I imagine you heard of it."

"I did," Felix replied. "What a tragedy. Do you know what happened? He was a good boy, as I understand."

"He was, Felix. It was a blow to the office, this town and the Alexander family," Zeke said. "We don't yet know what or who was behind it, but we'll keep searching until something turns up."

"I understand. That must be hard," Felix said.

"It is, but that's not why I came by. I just wanted to stop in and see how things were going with you and Elsa, and the canning company."

"Business has been great," Felix said, "except for a setback or two."

"Setback?" Zeke inquired. "Have there been some problems?"

"Nothing serious, I hope," Felix replied. "But we had a shipment of fish we had to throw out. It's something that almost never happens."

"A shipment thrown out? How does that happen?" Zeke said, trying to sound curious but not suspicious."

"Oh, this fishing company we get our choicest fish from did not give us the quality fish they usually do," Felix started. "They delivered fish, but not the choice ones they usually do. I inspected them but I could not bring myself to use them. My products are too good.

"I had to sell that batch to the co-op at a loss."

"I don't understand," Zeke said, trying not to sound too interested. "Fish are fish, aren't they?"

"Oh, why am I boring you with this?" Felix said. "We can talk old times. How are you and your family doing? How about Sheriff Duke? We haven't seen him in quite a while either."

"Oh, you know, we get caught up in our work too, and before you know it a year or two has passed," Zeke replied, anxious to keep the conversation going. "Say, Felix, would you mind showing me around the cannery? If you have time, of course, I see you've grown and I've never seen your operation up close."

"If you want, sure," Felix said, rising up from behind his desk. "Let me take you on a tour."

Felix led Zeke to the front of the warehouse where his butchers were preparing the meat. Then they moved to where several women were adding spices and herbs into jars filled with pickling solution and pieces of menhaden herring. After observing the station where the jars were sealed, the two headed back to the office. When they reached the bottom of the stairs, Zeke hesitated.

"What goes on behind that thick curtain hanging just below your office?" Zeke asked.

"Oh, that's the dressing station. We bring the fish in there where they are put on ice until morning. Then they are gutted, scaled, and washed clean. Not much to see there, especially today," the cannery owner said.

"But no fish today," Zeke said, expressing a frown.

"Like I said, we received an inferior shipment, so I sent the workmen home. I could not bring myself to process anything that doesn't meet my standards," Felix lamented.

"So, were your employees upset about being sent home?"

"They would have been," Felix added, with a slightly hurt look. "They are good men so I promised to pay them anyway. I cannot process inferior fish. We have our reputation to think of."

Felix started up the stairs. "We have a contract with Sea Serpent Fisheries. They promise us the best of each catch, for which we pay top dollar," Felix said, turning back to Zeke as he ascended the stairs behind him. "Last night, they sent me fertilizer fish."

"So, this Sea Serpent Company tried to pawn off run-of-the-mill fish on you?" Zeke asked.

"It is the first time it has happened," Felix said, as the two men entered the office. "I inspect the fish for quality when I arrive in the morning, before my crew comes in. I had to reject last night's catch and sell them to the co-op, at a loss."

"How often do they ship?" Zeke asked, sitting down in the chair he occupied when he first arrived.

"Usually once a week, sometimes ten days, but I cannot wait any longer than that," Felix answered, taking his place behind the desk. "I ship much of my product overseas. I contract with those ships as well. I have to pay for the space when a ship sails empty."

"Would you like us to look into it?" Zeke said, choosing his words carefully, knowing all the lawmen in Galveston were already doing that.

"Oh, no, I do not want to bother you folks. You are busy with other things, like that poor boy's demise," Felix responded. "This is a business matter. If necessary, I will find another fishing company to contract with."

"Well, don't be too hasty," Zeke said with a smile, hoping his words didn't sound too apologetic for a company he knew nothing about. "I'm sure things will get straightened out."

"They will or I will straighten them out," Felix said with a boisterous laugh.

Zeke smiled and thanked Felix for giving him the tour. He bid his friend farewell and descended the stairs. At the bottom, he paused momentarily to gaze at the "dressing area," then left. He mounted up and rode off at a gallop.

After reaching the courthouse, Zeke hurried inside and headed for the sheriff's office. He was met by a room nearly empty except for the jail guard.

"Where is everybody?" Zeke asked, as he stopped in the middle of the room to look around.

"They've all gone down to the beach," the guard said, looking up at the deputy.

"The beach, what is this, some kind of holiday?" Zeke uttered rhetorically. "What is everybody doing at the beach?"

"Picking up fish is what I've been told," the guard said, leaning back in his chair. "I'd be there too if I wasn't in charge of the cells."

"Picking up fish? I don't get it."

"You will if you go down there, and prepare yourself to help pick up dead, smelly fish," the guard said with a chuckle.

Zeke's mind was spinning as he left the office and rode off in the direction of Galveston Beach. At first, the strand appeared empty but as he rode along he could see activity at the east end near the channel. As soon as he arrived where the men were gathering fish, he swung out of the saddle and approached where Nik, Duke and Agent Lester were working.

Duke raised his head to see his deputy approaching. "Hey, Zeke, good to see you, we can use the help," he called out.

"What's going on, Duke? What's with all the fish?

"They started washing up on shore last night. Nobody thought too much about it until someone found a fish with money in it," Duke said.

"Money, you mean counterfeit bills?" Zeke asked somewhat absentmindedly, as he thought back on his visit to the Johansson Canning Company.

"Yeah," Duke replied. "Not sure what they're all doing here but it seems the marshal was right about how this money was being brought in. But we're all puzzled as to why they're washing up on the beach. Surely, this cannot be how they expect to distribute the bills."

"How much money have you found?" Zeke asked.

"Around two thousand dollars," Duke answered, "and all of it inside balloons and stuffed down the throats of the largest fish. The smaller fish were mostly empty. What did you find out at the cannery?"

"Little more than to believe the cannery has nothing to do with the counterfeiting, although Felix did complain about his last shipment of fish," Zeke said, rubbing the back of his neck. "In fact, he rejected the whole batch, said he could not damage his company's reputation canning fish fit for fertilizer."

"It's too bad he didn't get these beauties," said the customs agent who had suggested the cannery idea earlier. "These fish would not have hurt his business in the least. It's too bad they've been out here on the beach, otherwise they'd be excellent for canning."

Nik, who was listening while examining fish and placing them in a gunny sack, dropped the bag when he overheard the conversation.

"Zeke, you say the cannery owner rejected the last shipment he got?" Nik inquired.

"Yeah, Felix wasn't happy either. He said he had a contract for only the finest fish, but that's not what he got. He said his driver later told him the captain apologized, but it was the best he could do. Felix had to send some of his employees home because of it."

"Wait, let's think this through," Nik said, pondering the situation as he spoke. "We're finding cash-filled fish here on the beach. And Ron, your agent said these fish would be suitable for canning, but Felix got rejects. Do you think maybe this fishing outfit the Johanssons deal with got wind of what we were up to and dumped these fish before reaching the harbor?"

"That would make sense," Lester replied. "Zeke, how upset were Felix's employees he sent home?"

"Felix said they were too valuable to lose, so he paid them anyway," Zeke responded. "What are you suggesting?"

"You said this Felix, the company owner, is likely innocent?" Lester asked. "Does he supervise the cleaning of the fish?"

"He inspects them, but he's too busy to supervise everything. Elsa looks after everything on the canning side of the curtain," Zeke said, remembering how the butchering station was set up.

"Other side of the curtain, what curtain?" Lester asked.

"The fish are put on ice behind a heavy curtain that separates the cleaning area from the canning area," Zeke answered. "When the fish are cleaned, they're moved into the canning area for processing."

"So, these cleaning guys are behind a curtain," Lester said, with a concerned look on his face. "Other than Felix's inspection, they work out of sight cleaning the fish."

"Are you thinking what I'm thinking?" Nik interjected.

"It sounds like a perfect set-up to extract the money behind the curtain and then send the fish off to the cannery," Lester said. "I was wondering how upset Felix's employees might be being denied about two thousand dollars in counterfeit cash. At this point, we don't know if Felix knows about this or not."

"Now hold on a minute," Atkins cut in. "The Johanssons do too well to dirty their reputation with something like this. However, I can't say all of his employees are clean, or this fishing company either.

"Zeke, what did you say the name of it was?

"I didn't," Zeke said, "but as I recall, Felix referred to it as Sea Serpent Fisheries."

"Sounds fitting," Nik interjected. "Duke, I think we need to pay this Sea Serpent Fisheries a visit. Zeke, what can you find out about those men behind the curtain cleaning fish?"

"I'm on it," Zeke replied.

Chapter 16
Letter from Home

After the fish were cleared from the beach and turned over to Agent Ron Lester and his customs agents, Nik and Sheriff Atkins laid out a plan of how to tie the Sea Serpent Fisheries Company to the counterfeiting ring. They found that the fishery company was located on the coast of Louisiana just across the tributary separating Louisiana and Texas. Nik offered to get word to the U.S. Marshals Office in that state to investigate the company concerning Johansson Cannery's contract with them. Meanwhile, Zeke, Ambrose and some of Duke's assistant deputies would be on hand to inspect all Sea Serpent fishing vessels unloading menhaden for the Johanssons.

"I'll pay Felix another visit and ask to see the cleaning process," Zeke announced. "I can't help but think that's where the counterfeit money is being extracted."

"Good idea, Zeke, but don't let Felix know why," Duke said. "I hate to say it but at this juncture the Johanssons could end up as suspects in this case."

"If they are, I would not want to make the arrest, Duke," Zeke replied. "I've known them all my life."

"I hope they are innocent as well," Atkins said. "But we can't take that chance. If Felix gets suspicious it could hamper our investigation."

"I'll keep it under my hat, boss. But I think the real fishy business is going on behind that curtain," Deputy Vincent responded.

Ambrose and an assistant deputy named Russell Talbert offered to visit the docks that night to inspect any Sea Serpent fishing boats that docked at Pelican Island.

"Just be careful, Ambrose," Nik said. "Lenny taught us these folks mean business."

"Russell and I will handle it just fine, Nik. I've gotten pretty familiar with those folks down there."

That evening, Ambrose and Deputy Talbert took the ferry over to Pelican Island just as a fishing boat was pulling in. It was not of the Sea Serpent fleet, but Ambrose and Russell made a casual inspection of it anyway. While they were checking a couple menhaden, another vessel pulled alongside marked "Sea Serpent III."

Ambrose shot a quick glance at Russell and the two made their way over the other ship just as a wagon from Johanssons was pulling onto the dock. The two lawmen waited patiently watching as several fishermen disembarked carrying buckets of fish and dumping them into the back of the cannery wagon. When it appeared the wagon driver was set to leave, Ambrose and Russell emerged from the shadows.

"Excuse me, driver, we'd like to take a look at your cargo," Russell called out.

The heavily bearded driver turned to look at the approaching pair. The driver was huskily built, wore a black hat and was wearing an apron.

"Is somethin' wrong, deputy?" the man growled.

"That's what we're here to find out," Ambrose said, as he approached the back of the wagon. "There's nothing wrong as far as we know, but we just need to take a look at a few of your fish."

"Help yourselves," the driver grumbled, "but I ain't got all night."

Ambrose and Russell extracted several large fish from deep in the stack piled in the wagon. As they rammed their fingers down the throats of the selected menhaden, the driver eyed them with a scowl on his face. However, he did not look surprised or inquire as to what they were looking for. After several minutes and a dozen fish checked by each, Ambrose spoke up, "Looks good. I guess you can go now."

"'Bout time," the driver grumbled. "I've got to get these critters on ice." With that he snapped the reins and his team lurched forward. Before long, the wagon disappeared into the night.

"I guess I'm not surprised we didn't find anything," Ambrose said. "I have a feeling they're on to us by now."

"Why do you say that, Ambrose?" Russell asked.

Ambrose pushed his hat back on his head as he spoke. "I think those fish that washed up on shore were dumped on purpose. This batch came in clean. We'll see what Zeke finds out, but I've got a hunch the funny money shipments have been put on hold."

"You think so?" Russell quizzed. "If that's so, how are we going to catch these folks red-handed?"

"We ain't if they know we've got their operation figured out," Ambrose replied. "I'm afraid we discovered this thing too late to catch them in the act. I'm guessing Lenny did, but he paid for it with his life."

"It's a shame Lenny didn't live long enough to alert us to what was going on," Russell lamented, shaking his head.

"It's a shame in more ways than one," Ambrose countered, lowering his head, "but at least we may have stopped the money from coming in by boat if they're afraid we'll be inspecting these shipments.

"Unfortunately, I'm going to guess they'll find another way to do it," the deputy marshal added, rubbing his chin.

"So, I guess that means we'll be back where we started," Russell said, looking up at the big man.

"Nik and Duke ain't gonna like this, but our hand's been played," Ambrose said, as the two men sat down on a bench to watch for any other fishing boats that might pull in.

As the hour of midnight drew near, the two men heard someone walking toward them. As they peered into the night a familiar figure emerged; Marshal Nik Brinkman.

"Gentlemen, did you turn up anything new?" Nik asked.

"Afraid not, sir," Ambrose said. "However, it still might be worth it to check out that fish cleaning operation at the cannery."

"So, you've already checked the load coming off the last ship?"

"We did," Deputy Tucker replied. "We made a random search in case there was an attempt to bury those filled with money and came up empty handed."

"I'm not surprised," Nik responded. "Whoever is responsible for this knows we're onto this caper and will likely lie low for a while. "So, will we continue to inspect fish in hopes they'll make a slipup?" Russell interjected.

"I don't think we can do that," Nik said. "As long as we're checking fish they won't make that mistake again. My guess is they'll use another tactic or quit counterfeiting altogether."

"Then we do nothing?" Ambrose commented.

"We can't continue this. I've got a deputy in Louisiana looking into the Sea Serpent Company now," Nik stated. "That may lead to something. As for now, we'd better start back. The ferry is making a run to Galveston and won't be back here for several hours."

Disappointed, the three men made their way back to the ferry and returned to Galveston.

The next day, Nik and Ambrose stopped in Sheriff Atkins office to get and update on the cannery from Deputy Vincent. Zeke reported that he was allowed to view the fish-cleaning process taking place behind the heavy curtain. He also obtained employee profiles on those working in that area. The deputy said he also ran a check on each one, but there were no outstanding warrants or prior records on any of them.

"However, I can tell you it would be easy pickin' for those guys in the cleaning area to extract that money," Vincent told the others. "I came clean with Felix and he seemed surprised and almost fascinated at the fish-smuggling idea. He was totally cooperative and didn't hesitate to turn over those employee profiles."

"Can we look through those files?" Nik asked. "The Marshals Service might have something on one of them."

"No problem, Marshal, just bring them back and put them on my desk when you're done," Zeke replied.

"Since you've already gone over them, it shouldn't take us to long to do the same," Nik said. "That cleaning area does sound ideal for extracting money. It disheartens me that we didn't handle this thing better."

"So, Nik, any plans as how we proceed from this point on?" Sheriff Atkins inquired.

"I'm still waiting for a report from our deputy in Louisiana. I'm hoping that turns up something. Until then, we'll just have wait until more counterfeit money shows up."

"What about making spot checks on those Sea Serpent vessels? Atkins suggested.

"I would not do that, Duke," Nik answered. "If they're onto us, which is an almost certainty now, they'll either find another way to bring that money into Texas or stop altogether. That would help the bank and this state, but it would throw cold water on finding Lenny's killer.

"Perhaps we could station an undercover deputy in Johansson's cleaning area," Deputy Talbert said.

"Unless all those guys doing the cleaning are in on the counterfeiting they would not be doing the extraction when cleaning," Ambrose replied. "My guess is it is done at night before the cleaning crew shows up. If that surly guy driving the pickup wagon was in on it, he likely would have warned the others."

"Ambrose is right," Nik chimed in. "There's too much suspicion about us right now. I imagine even Felix Johansson has to talk to his crew about it by now."

"So, we just wait?" Duke offered.

"I'll get hold of Ron Lester and let him know we're at an impasse," Nik proposed. "Maybe he's got some ideas.

"In the meantime, Ambrose, why don't you help Zeke with those files and I'll go see Ron."

Nik was troubled, not only that the counterfeit trail had gone cold, but they were also no closer to finding Lenny's killer. He wondered if they'd gotten too eager and played their hand too early. The load of fish on the beach was a clear sign Sea Serpent was now aware of the investigation. Nik whispered a little prayer that the officer in

Louisiana would turn up something.

After returning to his office, Nik found Ambrose going over the Johansson Cannery employee files.

"Find anything suspicious?" Nik asked, coming through the door.

"A cowboy, two former fishing boat deckhands, a cook, and a guy who dabbled in real estate," Ambrose answered. "No past run-ins with the law that I can see."

"I wonder why the fishing boat deckhands decided to start cleaning fish for a living," Nik said, as Ambrose vacated Nik's seat and moved around to the front of the desk.

"Maybe the hours are better at the cannery than on a fishing vessel," Ambrose said. "I don't think the pay would be any better though."

Nik took his normal position behind his desk and his deputy sat in front of the desk. Nik leaned back folding his hands over his midsection and looked over at Ambrose.

"How would you feel about going to a baseball game in Houston?" Nik asked.

"I ain't much familiar with baseball," Ambrose answered. "I wouldn't mind seeing Houston, though."

"We've been keeping some pretty hectic hours and haven't much to show for it," Nik mused in a somber tone. "We know how they were getting the money into Galveston but we have no real suspects. And to make matters worse, we have one dead sheriff's deputy and no clue who did it.

"That's why I think we need a break," Nik said leaning forward, putting his hands on his desk and shoving aside the employee files. At that moment, the county clerk entered the office.

"Marshal Brinkman, I have some mail for you sent from the Marshals Service in Louisiana," Mary said, approaching the desk. "It just came in today."

Nik's face lit up as he reached out to receive the envelope. "Thanks, Mary."

Nik sat back down and immediately pulled out a penknife from his desk and cut open the packet. He pulled out the contents and began poring over them.

"Anything we can use, Marshal?" Ambrose asked.

After a short pause as Nik continued reading, he tossed the letter down and pushed his chair back. "No, it appears Sea Serpent is clean. They've got about six fishing boats that set sail, one each day. By the time the first one returns the last one is preparing to take out again. They do have a contract with Johansson's and apparently have to search the entire gulf region to find menhaden palatable enough to convert into pickled herring.

"The captains are excellent seafaring men and none have committed any serious crimes, other than an occasional drunken brawl."

"Maybe seeing a baseball game would be good for us to do," Ambrose said as Zeke walked into the office.

"If you guys are done with those files, I plan to make another trip to Johansson's cannery and I'd like to return them," Zeke said.

"Sure, Zeke, Ambrose, are you satisfied you've seen enough of these?" Nik said, glancing over the files as he gathered them. He stopped suddenly when his eyes caught something familiar.

"I didn't see anything..." Ambrose started.

"Wait a minute, let me take a closer looked at this file," Nik said, mostly to himself, as he slid a file from the pile of folders and began reading it.

"Something wrong?" Zeke asked.

"I just noticed this Harper, Nolan Harper, used to work for Confederate Enterprises," Nik said, as he scanned the document.

"Is that important?" Zeke again inquired.

"Yes! Real Estate," Nik nearly shouted. "Why didn't that ring a bell with me when you said it, Ambrose? I know this company. They were trying to swindle homesteaders in Mount Pleasant."

Nik slowly lowered the file and looked up at Ambrose and Zeke. "The head of Confederate Enterprises killed my family."

"Oh my God," Zeke said in a near whisper. "Do you think this Harper fella had anything to do with that?"

"That I don't know. I did see the men who did it, but I was scared back then and things were pretty much a blur," Nik recalled. "Maybe if I saw this Nolan Harper I might recognize him."

"Terrific, why don't you ride along with me tomorrow and hopefully he'll still be working when we get there," Zeke said.

"Good idea," Nik responded. "Ambrose, I guess we'll have to postpone that trip to Houston."

"No problem, boss," Ambrose said, "I just hope you can bring those folks to justice for what they done."

"If he's crooked like you say, Nik, he might be in on the counterfeit ring," Zeke said. "But you might want to use caution. I would guess if you recognized him you'd want to kill 'im."

"You're right, Zeke. I don't want to jeopardize this case," Nik said.

Nik and Ambrose accompanied Zeke back to the sheriff's office and explained to Duke Atkinson what they found among the hired help files at Johansson's cannery. After giving some thought to Nik's dilemma as suggested by Zeke, the sheriff offered his solution.

"I agree it would not be wise to jeopardize this case, but I would suggest this," Duke began. "I don't think anyone at Johansson's knows many of Ron's boys. If we could get a customs agent to go undercover and keep an eye on this Harper character, he might lead is to the source of this counterfeiting ring."

"I think we could set the agent up in the front office as an accountant or consultant," Zeke suggested. "That way he wouldn't have to really do anything more than keep an eye on Nolan."

"Let's run this idea by Ron and see if he's got an agent qualified to do this," Duke said.

After hearing the proposal from the two law officers, Agent Lester nodded in agreement and introduced the men to the agent of his choice.

"Gentlemen, this is Agent Foster Letterman," Ron said, after calling Letterman into his office. "Foster actually worked as a Union undercover agent and then transferred to the Treasury Department. He then requested a transfer to customs."

"I once met one of those treasury agents who helped us break up a land-fraud deal involving a bunch of homesteaders," Nik interjected. "I have to admit his expertise was invaluable in the case."

"Sebastian Mason," Letterman said.

"Yeah, that was the guy," Nik said. "Did you know him?"

"We worked together on a number of cases. He was also a Union undercover agent and a good one," Letterman continued. "I would have accompanied him on the Judge Kensington case, except I was busy with another fraud case in Nebraska."

"Then I think we have the right man," Nik said, turning to Lester with a grin and extending his hand to Letterman. "Welcome aboard, Letterman. Nik Brinkman's my name."

"Sebastian spoke highly of you and your brother, Marshal Brinkman," Letterman said, eyeing Nik's badge. "Just call me Lester, or whatever name you give me for this job."

The men settled on the name Bill Williams, making it easy to remember.

Zeke offered to speak to Felix Johansson and have Foster "Bill Williams" installed in the front office. The men decided to give the undercover agent as much information as possible over a two-week period before presenting him to the cannery to allay suspicions. They also decided to back away from making cursory checks on Sea Serpent's cargo of fish in hopes of getting the counterfeiters to let down their guard.

After returning to their office, Nik and Ambrose went to work on some of the minor assignments the U.S. Marshals Service were commissioned to perform. The office clerk placed subpoenas, warrants, and court bills to be paid onto Nik's desk, courtesy of Judge Conklin. When not heavily involved in a case, Nik and Ambrose would divide the service requests rendered and carry out the duties of the office.

When Nik reached his hotel near day's end, the clerk presented Nik with a letter. It was from his brother, Roger. He hurried to his room, tore open the envelope, and began reading the letter.

"Dear Brother Nik,

I hope this finds you well. I think by now you have reached your new assignment, but I sent this letter on to Ned Borchers in Wichita asking him to forward it to you, since I do not know for sure where you are.

I have graduated from seminary and have become a circuit preacher in the New Mexico Territory. The people here are good, God-fearing folks and have helped me a great deal in setting up my circuit. I have nearly eight congregations. I stop between churches to help out where I can. Some Apache Indians have joined two of the congregations.

I must tell you that I was involved in an incident unbecoming to a preacher's duties. While servicing my congregation in Palomas, my good friend Paul Zimmerman asked me to help some homestead folks getting a raw land deal, similar to what we dealt with in Mount Pleasant, in a place called Alamosa.

When I arrived, I met with a nice Mexican man named Carlos Sanchez Santana. We were discussing the homestead problem when a man interrupted us. It was someone you know, Colonel Gabriel Curtain.

I shot him, Nik. It was a fair fight and he lost. I did not feel as happy as I thought I would and I later grieved my actions. I returned to my church in Palomas. I asked that congregation for forgiveness and they gave it to me. I hope you are not disappointed.

To complete what I feel I need to do, I am planning to travel to Galveston in the near future to find you, once I know you are there. I plan to baptize you like Pa said he was going to.

If this letter finds you, you need to tell me where I can find you. Write to me in care of Paul Zimmerman, Palomas, New Mexico Territory. I will get the letter there. Once I know where to find you I will send a letter as to my departure date and will come your way.

Your Loving Brother,

Roger"

Tears were rolling down Nik's face when Ambrose entered the room.

"You all right, Marshal?" Ambrose asked.

Nik quickly wiped his faces with his sleeve and nearly fell into the chair behind him.

"Yes… yes, I'm fine, Ambrose," Nik said looking up hoping his tears were gone. "I just read a letter from my brother."

"Is he… your brother… is he all right?" Ambrose said, hoping the answer was yes.

"He's fine, too," Nik answered, once again swiping his sleeve across his face. "He's a preacher, you know, and he still carries a gun."

"Was he shot or something?" Ambrose said, drawing closer and wanting to offer more comfort to Nik.

"No, he shot someone," Nik said with tears welling up in his eyes again. "It should'a been me who done the shootin'."

"I guess I don't understand," Ambrose began.

"You see, Roger killed the man who killed our family back in Missouri," Nik said, the tears now rolling down his cheeks again. "You see, Roger is a preacher and should not have been the one to have to shoot that man. It should have been me."

"I'm sorry, sir, I'm powerful sorry," Ambrose said, seating himself in a chair near Nik.

"No, it was more Roger's cross to bear," Nik said, now staring straight ahead at nothing in particular. "I should have been the one to do it in order to save my brother from doing what a preacher ought not have to do. But it needed doing."

Ambrose quietly rose from his chair and silently slipped out of the room leaving Nik to his thoughts.

Chapter 17
Silver Shipment Orders

In the absence of any further information concerning the counterfeiting case, U.S. Marshal Nik Brinkman and Deputy Marshal Ambrose Tucker spent their days doing routine work for District Judge Jedediah Conklin. Nik busied himself with work, but could not get his brother's letter out of his mind. All of it was good, except for Roger's killing of Colonel Curtain. Among his mixed feelings over the news was that of shame.

Nik had been on the Brinkman farm when his adopted family had been murdered by the colonel and his men. The colonel's plan was to kidnap Nik and put him back into slavery, but his "adopted" father, Douglas Brinkman, sacrificed his life to allow Nik enough time to flee safely into a nearby wood. Ensconced in a tree, Nik witnessed the carnage that included the burning of the farmhouse that took the lives of his Brinkman mother and sister.

The feeling that he would be the one to track down Colonel Curtain and his men and bring them to justice – his way – burned deep within the new chief marshal of Galveston. Although he felt great pride in his brother's killing of the outlaw, Nik felt a little cheated that he was not the one to do it. With the thought that Johansson Cannery employee Nolan Harper might have been one of the men riding with Curtain that fateful day, Nik's desire to confront that man grew.

Several days following his reading of Roger's letter requesting Nik send him his address, he sat down at his desk to do so. He tried hard to suppress his disappointment over the colonel's demise and sincerely welcome his brother's offer to fulfill a promise and baptize him.

"Dear Roger,

So you put that scoundrel Curtain in the grave where he belonged. Good for you …." After a short pause to reread what he'd written, Nik crumpled up the sheet of stationery and threw it into the waste basket. Perhaps he wasn't ready yet to write the letter but he continued.

"Dear Brother Roger,

My address is U.S. Marshal Nik Brinkman, Hotel Galveston, Galveston, Texas. Folks here know who I am, so all future correspondence to that address should reach me.

I would so love to see you again and look forward to your baptism. I met your former sharpshooter military friend Ambrose Tucker. He is a fine man. I made him a deputy marshal and he is working out well.

We have been working on a case involving counterfeit money. I cannot tell you much about it because it has not yet been resolved. You must tell me all about your shootout with Colonel Curtain.

I hope all is well. Let me know when you plan to be here so I can prepare for it.

Your Brother, Nik"

After reading over the letter several times, Nik decided to send it hoping his disappointment would not show through. He quietly vowed to change his feelings about the killing before Roger's arrival so their meeting would one of joy as intended.

When he returned to the courthouse, he was given notice that Conklin wanted to see him in the judge's office. After entering the judge's chambers, he noticed another man sitting to the side of the magistrate's desk.

"Marshal Brinkman, let me introduce you to Senator Ashley Maxwell," Conklin said, as the senator turned and looked at Nik with near shock on his face and quickly turned away. "The senator fought in the war also, but now represents the great state of Texas."

"Senator," Nik said, nodding at the back of Maxwell's head. The senator said nothing. Judge Conklin, looking briefly at the senator, quickly turned his attention back on Nik.

"I have an assignment that is going to require your full attention," Conklin began. "However, I must caution you that what I am about to say be kept in the strictest confidence."

"Of course, your honor," Nik said. "One thing I've discovered is that I'm at my best when I keep my mouth shut," Nik replied, thinking back on his awkward conversation when he met Esther Boatman for the first time. Nik also noticed the senator's shoulders shake following his remark indicating a slight chuckle, although Maxwell sat stoically and said nothing.

"Indeed, Marshal, in this business the less said the better," Conklin responded. "So, I will try to make this as brief and to the point as I can.

"As you know, we have what is the First U.S. Bank of Texas. The bank was originally the Island City Bank Savings before the change. It has an excellent vault, and for that reason was selected for charter as a U.S. Bank." Conklin turned to nod in Maxwell's direction, who nodded back. "The senator and I have been discussing the Sherman Silver Purchase Act being put forth in Congress," the judge continued. "If that becomes law, sliver will become as valuable as gold. I will not go into detail about that but will tell you that a substantial shipment of silver is headed for our bank here in Galveston. We need to see to it that it gets here safely." Conklin paused as if waiting for a response.

"What would you have me do?" Nik interjected.

"Reconnaissance tells us there has been a leak about this shipment that is supposed to arrive here by rail from Houston in a few days. Because of that leak, our plans have changed."

The plan Conklin laid out was to take the silver from the train in Houston under the cover of darkness and transfer it to a barge. The transfer was prompted because the train trestle that ran from the Texas mainland to Galveston was too vulnerable to attack. Instead, the shipment was to be transported across Galveston Bay on a barge designed to look like a typical ferryboat.

"We believe that change will avoid any effort made to sabotage the train as it crosses the trestle," Conklin continued. "Your job will be to stay close to that shipment and see to it nothing unfortunate happens to that silver. By the way, there will be armed guards at your disposal to assist you."

"Do we know these armed guards can be trusted?" Nik said, instinctively. "And there is the danger that too many guards might draw attention?"

"Some of the guards we've enlisted served with Senator Maxwell during the war. We have no reason to believe they would not do their duty in the face of any danger," the judge said, leaning back in his chair and folding his hands across his midsection. "As far as how many guards you think you'll need, it is up to you, Nik."

After a brief pause, the senator broke his silence and said in a rather boisterous voice, "Do you think you can handle it … Marshal?"

Nik looked up a little surprised by the remark.

"I will do my best, sir," Nik offered.

"Your best, humph. Your best may not be good enough," the senator again said in a louder than necessary tone.

"Now, Ashley," Conklin said, straightening up and leaning across his desk in the senator's direction. "Marshal Brinkman has an excellent record with the service and comes highly recommended."

"I'll rest easier when that silver is in the bank," the senator remarked, lowering his tone.

"Nik, when that shipment arrives in Houston you will have to go there and meet the men who will assist you," the judge instructed. "Sheriff Ed Ellsworth will be your liaison and he has plenty of experience in commanding men."

"Fine man, Ellsworth," the senator said. "He served under me in the war, hell of a soldier and a damn good lawman."

"I'm sure, sir," Nik said. "I look forward to meeting him." A feeling of dread came over Nik, giving him the feeling he would eat those words.

Conklin turned in Nik's direction. "I would like you to work up a plan of action and consult me with it as soon as you can. After that, when the silver shipment arrives in Houston you'll have to be ready to go."

"I understand, your honor. I'll get on it right away," Nik answered.

"Then you may go. Oh, and remember," the judge added, "this is top secret."

Nik felt tempted to salute and click his heels together but quickly thought better of it. He placed his hat on his head. "You can count on me, sir… senator," Nik said, turning in the direction of Maxwell and touching the tip of his hat.

After leaving the judge's chambers, Nik returned to his office and found Ambrose there sorting through some of the paperwork left there by the clerk.

"Ambrose, glad you're here. It looks like we'll have to shift our attention to another assignment. We're being asked to help guard a shipment of silver that is to be deposited in the First U.S. Bank of Galveston," Nik said. "When it arrives in Houston, you and I will take the train up there. While there, we will meet a security detachment already assigned to the silver. We will then board the train to accompany that shipment."

Nik explained about the shipment being removed from the train and placed on a barge moored at Virginia Point disguised to look like a ferryboat.

"The crossing will have to be done during the day to avoid suspicion. I can only take two guards with me so I'll need you to stay on the train," Nik said. "I'll stay with the silver as it crosses the bay.

"Be prepared for trouble because word has gotten out that the silver would be onboard the train, inviting a possible attack when crossing the trestle."

"When is this to happen?" Ambrose asked.

"My understanding is soon," Nik answered. "It is supposed to be on its way to Houston from wherever it was mined. We're to be informed as to its ETA so we can be there when it arrives."

"Should we maybe go up to Houston so we can survey the situation?"

"That's not a bad idea," Nik said. "Maybe we'll take in one of those baseball games we talked about. It'll give us an excuse for being there.

"By the way, when the train carrying the silver reaches Galveston, I'll need you to meet us when the boat docks to help deliver it to the bank," Nik added.

"Until then, I guess we'll have to keep busy with these warrants and subpoenas," Ambrose said, glancing at the desktop. "Some folks really don't like getting these things, especially those that have to come back to the courthouse with me for processing."

"Any problems?" Nik inquired.

"None, I just tell them come along peaceably or I'll have to carry 'em in." Ambrose said, smiling.

"I can see where that would be very convincing, big guy," Nik said with a laugh.

At that moment, the office door opened and a head peeked in.

"Is it okay if I come in," a familiar voice said.

Recognizing the voice to be that of Esther's, Nik jumped up from his desk and started for the door. "By all means," he called out, meeting Esther as she entered. "What a pleasant surprise. What brings you here?"

"I hope I'm not disturbing you but I've come to keep my promise as to making your office a little homier," Esther said.

"You do that just by being here," Nik said, while absentmindedly smoothing down the corners of his moustache.

"You're too kind, Marshal," Esther said with a slight blush.

"Uh-ah," Nik said. "It's Nik to you, my lady," He took Esther's hand and led her into the room. "I have enough trouble getting my deputy to call me by my name so I do not want to have to keep reminding you."

"Good to see you, Miss Boatman," Ambrose said, now standing to greet their guest.

"Since we're exchanging first names, Ambrose, please do the same for me, both of you," Esther said with a broad smile. "Can I go about brightening up this place without you two or do I have to work around you"

Nik wanted to say something about Esther's presence brightening the office but thought better of it. "We do have work to do and would be happy to leave you to your magic."

"I would hardly call it magic," Esther replied.

"It would have to be if Ambrose and I tried it," Nik said, laughing. "Ambrose, are you ready to oblige the lady?"

"I am, mar... Nik," Ambrose responded, frowning at using his boss's first name. "I have to head over to Pelican Island to serve a warrant so I'd best be going."

"I'll tag along, Ambrose," Nik said, as the two marshals moved toward the door. He then turned back to Esther. "I want you to know how much we appreciate this."

"A promise is a promise," Esther said.

"Yes, that it is," Nik said with a slight smile as he and Ambrose tipped their hats and went out the door.

As they two lawmen stepped outside to untie their horses, Nik suddenly stopped.

"Ambrose, I just remembered there is something else I have to take care of," Nik said as Ambrose mounted Crusader. "You go on. It's probably best I don't visit Pelican Island just now. It's too close to the cannery and I might be tempted to drop in for visit. I think I'm going to look up Abel Mosely and talk to him."

"I hear ya," Ambrose said with a knowing smile, turning Crusader in the direction of the harbor.

Nik went back into the courthouse and straight to his office. He stopped at the door, thought for a minute, took a deep breath and walked in.

"Marshal! I mean... Nik, back so soon?" Esther said, turning from the window frame she was measuring. "Did you forget something?"

"Yes," Nik began. "Look, Esther, I know you said you needed some time but I can't get my mind off of you. I would like to court you, gentlemanly-like, but until that is settled I'm going to be distracted."

Esther paused for a moment looking a bit forlorn at Nik. Nik's heart sank as he tried to brace for her rejection.

"Yes, I needed some time and I told myself to break this off before it goes too far," Esther started. "But I couldn't get you off my mind either. Why do you think I'm really here? I have to get this... this feeling I have settled as well." With that Esther walked over to Nik, threw her arms around him and kissed him hard on the mouth. Then she quickly pulled away leaving Nik in a complete state of ecstasy and confusion.

"Nik," Esther began again. "There is something you need to know before this goes any further. I..." Esther looked down at the floor."I... I don't know any other way to say this. I was once raped!"

Nik appeared stunned by her remark but, in truth, he was still thinking about the kiss. "What?"

"I was the victim of a rape. So there, now you have it and you know why this cannot work out."

"Wait a minute, you were the victim of a rape?" Nik asked. "Who, I mean, why... why did you take so long to tell me?"

"What woman likes to go around telling men she cares for that she's been raped?" Esther said, almost shouting.

"No, no, Esther, I understand that," Nik said pleadingly. "I don't care. I mean, I do care, but I don't care as far as my feelings for you are concerned. Esther, I've never felt before in my life the way I feel about you. I'm powerful sorry about, what I guess, is what has been holding you back from giving me any sign of hope.

"Right now, I want to celebrate. I've never been kissed like that before."

Nik paused, gazing at Esther, who now had tears in her eyes. "Look, I don't really need to know the details about all this. I just want you to know how I feel about you and the rest... darn it, the rest be damned!

"I'm sorry, I probably should not have said that."

"Do you mean it?" Esther said, as she began to openly cry.

"Hell yes... I mean, shucks yeah. I guess I'm not being very gentlemanly," Nik was stammering as he tried to process it all.

"Oh, God, Nik," Esther said, as she rushed to the partially stunned marshal and kissed him again. They embraced with both crying and tears running down their cheeks.

As they talked, Nik learned that Esther had been raped by Lawrence Covington while she was still serving as a slave. Esther had battled with the guilt and avoided Covington whenever she could. One day, the plantation owner snuck up on Esther and grabbed her from behind, thinking they were alone. As Esther struggled, Millie Covington walked into the room with a rifle and shot her husband dead. From that time on, she became like a mother to Esther.

"What about your father, did he know?" Nik asked.

"He figured it out and was going to kill Sir Covington himself, but I talked him out of it," Esther said. "I begged him not to because I knew he'd be hanged if he were to do that. Feeling my pain the way he did nearly broke him. He's not the man he used to be."

"Is he willing to let another man into your life now?" Nik said, again stumbling over his words for fear of the answer.

"Whatever would make me happy is what makes him happy," Esther said, to Nik's relief. "I'm afraid that's the only joy he knows now."

"I will also have to be honest with Miss Tillie," Esther said. "She will have to know these feelings we have for each other."

"Of course," Nik said. "Do you think she will object?"

"Object? No, she saw this coming and even encouraged me," Esther said. "She knew I would never be completely healed until I was able to let a man back into my life."

"And you're sure your father's all right with this?" Nik repeated.

"He's never done anything but support me in everything I do," Esther said. "The Lord blessed me with him."

"I think I'm the one in this process being blessed," Nik said, with a joyous laugh as he spoke.

After their exchange, Nik let Esther get back to her work while he went in search of Abel Mosely. He stopped at the sheriff's office to let them know he had a "decorator" working in his office and not to be concerned. He also told Mary, the clerk, in case anyone else asked.

After reaching Galveston Beach, Nik walked along the boardwalk until he noticed a lonely, familiar figure sitting on the beach looking out over the ocean. After making his way onto soft sand, he approached the figure and sat down beside him.

"Admiring the waves?" Nik asked.

"Something alluring about the sea, Marshal," Mosely said. "It's like fire. One can gaze at it for hours and yet, in moments, it can consume you. But you cannot help but admire its power."

"Among other things, you dabble in philosophy, too?" Nik said, with a half smile.

"I was a sailor at one time," Abel started. "Something always churned inside me when I went to sea. It was a mixed feeling of fear, anticipation, and adventure. It seems funny though, it always turned out to be a lot of work and very little adventure. That was when I began to admire being on the beach more than the water, and I found those first feelings returned as I searched the sand. But now and then I have to just sit and watch those waves and sort through my memories."

"My experience with the sea was one of sheer fear, Abel," Nik said, looking out over the restless expanse where the ocean meets the sky. "The first time I was on as ship, it brought me to this country as a slave. But the Good Lord had a different plan, thanks to my family."

"Do you still see your family?" Abel asked.

"They're gone now, Abel. I lost them years ago, and the day I lost them still haunts me," Nik said, turning to look at Abel, "Wwhich is why I'm here."

Abel looked back and Nik thinking about what his friend had said. "What can I do for you, Marshal?" he said.

"Do you know a man by the name of Nolan Harper?" Nik asked.

"He works at the cannery on Pelican Island," Abel said, again turning to look out over the sea. "Word is, he was once mixed up in a swindle of some sort. I hear he is working out just fine at the cannery, though."

"Is that all?" Nik pressed.

"Folks I know say he just showed up here one day on one of the fishing boats. Funny thing was, he got off the boat and before you know it he was working at Johansson's Cannery cleaning fish," Able said.

"Really?" Nik responded. "Do you know what boat?"

"No, 'cept it was one that brought fish for the cannery. I know he still talks with the folks on those boats now and then," Abel continued. "I don't know what about though."

Nik looked at his companion. "I think maybe I do, Abel. I think maybe I do." Nik again looked out over the water.

"Are you going to tell me?" Abel asked.

"It's not important, my friend. But what is important is a favor I have to ask," Nik said. "I need you and your connections to help keep an eye on this Harper fellow. You don't have to approach him or anything, just watch his activity when he visits the fishing boats. We have a man at the cannery watching him, but to avoid suspicion he cannot follow the man around. Can you do that for me?"

"Doesn't sound too hard," Abel said, with a slight smile. "Anything you need, I'm happy to help."

"Great," Nik said, reaching into his pocket and pulling out five silver dollars. "Here, these are for you," Nik added, extending the money to Mosely.

"You don't have to do that, Marshal. Ol' Mosely does just fine."

"Please, take it," Nik said. "Consider it additional payment for that necklace you sold me and for the work you do, even if you don't consider it work."

Abel smiled and took the money. Nik got to his feet, thanked his beach companion and departed.

Chapter 18
Intrigue and Romance

Deputy Sheriff Zeke Vincent met with Felix Johansson to discuss the hiring of Bill Williams, who was actually undercover agent Foster Letterman from the customs office. Felix was disappointed that his business might be connected in some way to a counterfeit ring but he was more than happy to cooperate.

His wife Elsa questioned the need for another employee, but Felix assured her the hiring would not strain the company's budget. What he had not told her was that "Williams" was being paid by the U.S. Customs Department and not by Johansson Cannery.

"Do we really need an accountant consultant?" Elsa asked Felix before the hiring. "And why has Deputy Vincent been coming around?"

Felix got up from behind his desk and walked past his wife with his finger over his lips. He then shut the office door behind her.

"Elsa, my love," Felix said in a low whisper. "Williams is an agent trying to catch criminals printing counterfeit money."

"So, why...?" Elsa started but ceased when Felix put his finger to his lips once again. She lowered her voice. "So, why is he here?"

"They think the money may be being smuggled in the fish we get. They believe Deputy Lenny Alexander found out about that and that's why Lenny was murdered," Felix whispered.

"Are we crooks, Felix?" Elsa's voice rose as she spoke, prompting Felix to raise his finger to his lips again.

"No, Deputy Vincent said it could be someone they believe already works here," Felix said in a low voice. "The new man is here to see if he can catch him."

Elsa Johansson was visibly shaken by the news and Felix led her to a chair so she could sit down. Once Felix assured her that they and the company were not under suspicion, she recovered and went back to her station but had trouble concentrating on her work.

Customs Agent Ron Lester sent word to Nik and Sheriff Duke Atkins that the hiring of Letterman as an accountant consultant had been approved by Washington, D.C. They used his being an account as the best way to keep other cannery employees from engaging him in unnecessary conversations. However, the employees were told he may ask them questions from time to time.

Initially, Letterman spent his time roaming aboard Sea Serpent ships talking to captains and crews, while observing the operation. What he discovered was that none of Sea Serpent's six captains remembered delivering an inferior selection of menhaden to Johansson's cannery.

On the day Harper was to pick up a load of fish, Williams went along with him.

"Do you remember the day Sea Serpent gave you an inferior load of fish that had to be thrown out?" Williams asked Harper.

"Ahh, not really," Harper answered.

"You don't remember? It was the day Mr. Johansson had to send all the prep employees home," Williams said. "Surely you remember that. It wasn't that long ago."

"Oh, yeah, I guess I do remember," Harper answered, staring down at the horses. "Felix was good enough to pay us anyway."

"Do you think you could tell me the captain that apologized to you about that?" Williams inquired.

"Ahh, no, I don't think so," Harper mumbled. "I don't see the captains that often."

"So then, wouldn't you remember the one that apologized? Since getting a poor grade of fish is rare?"

"Are these accounting questions?" Harper said, turning to look at Williams.

"They are," Williams countered. "Losing an entire batch of fish is a big deal."

"Yeah, well, I thought Felix would accept them anyway," Harper said. "So I guess I didn't pay much attention."

Williams decided not to push Harper any harder and simply observed the loading routine. He noticed how efficient it was, even in the early hours of the evening. He spotted someone onboard the fishing boat holding up a lantern. The man called out.

"Tell Felix Captain Blair says hello," the man shouted. "He'll be happy with this catch. We ran across a quality school of menhaden."

Harper just shrugged his shoulders, snapped the reins, and headed the team back to the cannery.

Williams had trouble getting the picture of the man holding the lantern out of his mind. His face was quite clear in the light of to the lantern.

"Was that the captain who apologized to you when he unloaded the poor grade of fish?" Williams asked.

"Huh, what... no, I dunno. Like I said, I don't pay much attention," Harper answered, "Maybe."

"Well, at least Felix should be happy with this load," Williams said. "If you'd like, I'll pass along the captain's message to Felix in the morning."

"Yeah, fine," Harper said, while keeping his eyes on the road.

After they reached the cannery, there were two men waiting to help Harper unload and put the fish on ice.

"I've got some bookkeeping to catch up on. I'll catch you later," Williams said to the men, and then disappeared behind the heavy curtain.

After the menhaden were unloaded and the three employees departed, Williams went down to inspect the fish. None had been cut open, but all were a favorable size for stuffing money into. Although a little bothered by his experience with Harper, the agent was disappointed he did not find out more. Williams locked up the cannery and left.

Letterman had been told that Harper's profile showed his previous experience had been as a crewmember on a fishing vessel. It was listed along with his brief employment with Confederate Enterprises in Mount Pleasant several years ago. He decided to interview Harper again in the morning.

"Did you learn to clean fish when you were working on a fishing boat?" Letterman, now using the undercover name Williams, asked Harper the next day.

"I worked mainly with other fish," Harper answered. "We rarely cleaned menhaden,"

"Why did you leave the fishing boats for this?" Williams asked, trying not to appear too nosey.

"I didn't like being on the ocean, and fishing is hard work," Harper said, while expertly gutting a fish. "When I heard about this job I left it behind."

Letterman was coming to the conclusion that Johansson's cannery was not involved in smuggling counterfeit money into the county. He decided that either the fish smuggling was put on hold, or that it never existed. Still, he wondered, why was Deputy Alexander killed with a fish containing money in his pocket, and what were all those fish, some loaded with money, doing on the Galveston shore?

The following day, Nik received an urgent message from U.S. First Bank President Edgar Pottingham. He hurried over to the bank and found Agent Lester was already there, talking with Pottingham.

"Marshal, so glad you could make it," Pottingham said in greeting. "I was just telling Agent Lester here of the bank's predicament."

"I'm sorry if I've held you up," Nik responded.

"Not at all," Pottingham said. "Ron and I were just exchanging small talk. So, let me tell you my situation.

"Gentlemen," Pottingham started, "we have received a large deposit of greenbacks made by Mr. Christopher J. Wellington. Because of the size of the deposit, I asked Mr. Wellington how he came into so much money."

Pottingham went on to explain Wellington was working at a silver mine and did very well selling his ore to the local assay office, mostly in Confederate currency. He was apparently approached by a broker who offered him twice as much for his silver as the assay office offered, if he would accept payment in greenbacks. The broker convinced him the federal government would make good on the greenbacks, having set aside almost five-hundred million in gold to back its currency. Wellington knew this to be true and accepted the greenbacks.

"What we don't know is whether his small fortune of greenbacks is genuine," Pottingham continued. "This counterfeit issue has us in a quandary."

"Allow my office to examine some of Wellington's notes," Lester said. "It's true that counterfeit greenbacks are coming ashore, but they're almost impossible to detect, unless they come in by fish," the customs chief said, turning to Nik.

"I don't understand," Pottingham replied.

"Mr. Pottingham, we have reason to believe the counterfeit money is being smuggled into Galveston inside the bellies of fish," Nik explained. "We have found fish containing greenbacks that most certainly would not be genuine currency."

"Are you serious?" Pottingham said, pushing himself back from his desk slightly and widening his eyes.

"I'm afraid so, Edgar," Lester cut in. "The best we can do right now is to estimate how many of the greenbacks in circulation are genuine. Because of that, I suggest you accept the greenbacks as legal tender until we know for sure. I'm sure the U.S. Treasury will keep the bank solvent."

"How close are you to busting this fish-smuggling ring?" Pottingham asked.

"Thanks to Ron's agents and the outstanding effort of Deputy Alexander, we feel we're pretty close now," Nik advised. "We have someone in our sights we believe is a part of this."

"That's a shame about young Alexander," Pottingham said. "His loss must have come as quite a blow to his family."

"And the sheriff's department," Nik offered.

"Has your agent turned up any more information at the cannery?" Nik asked, turning to Lester.

"The cannery?" Pottingham said, glancing at both men.

"Please do not jump to any conclusions just yet," Lester said, leaning forward in his chair. "As for your question, Marshal, Letterman is leaving no stone unturned, I can assure you."

"Perhaps it's time to turn up the heat on Harper," Nik responded, giving Lester a stern look.

"He will, but it's best we do not overplay our hand any more than we have, Nik," the customs agent said. "If Harper becomes too suspicious of us he may bolt."

"Just the same, we need to keep an eye on him," Nik said.

"Speaking of the treasury," Pottingham said, speaking to Lester. "What's the latest news about Congress raising the value of silver?"

"They're being pressured by a group of farmers lobbying as the Greenback-Labor Party," Lester answered. "They are a powerful organization, so I would not be surprised to see legislation raising the price of silver to that of gold."

"That could really jeopardize this shipment of silver," Nik muttered, turning his eyes away from both men.

"What was that, Marshal?" Lester asked, leaning forward and looking at Nik.

"Oh, nothing really," Nik said. "I was just thinking how difficult it would be to ship silver if it was as valuable as gold, just a U.S. Marshal's comment. A lot of folks have died trying to protect gold, let alone silver."

"Good point," Pottingham said, casting a wary eye Nik's way.

"Look, I need to get back to work," Nik said. "So, unless there's anything more we need to discuss, I should get going."

"I wish you gentlemen luck," Pottingham said. "This counterfeit situation is making me nervous."

"Speaking of that," Lester said, rising from his chair, "I'd like to take a look at some of those greenbacks Wellington brought in."

"Certainly," Pottingham said, also getting up from behind his desk.

The men bid each other farewell and parted company.

Agent Foster Letterman, working under the assumed name "Bill Williams," was in Felix Johansson's office contemplating his next move. A thought struck him, prompting him to run downstairs and pass behind the curtain where the prepping crew was working.

"Harper," Williams called out, "could I see you a moment?"

The two men went back on the other side of the curtain to talk.

"Harper, I know I have been kind of picking on you, but I see you as an integral part of this business," Williams said. "I want to make it up to you by taking you to lunch, what do you say?"

"Ahh, that's kind of you, but you don't have to do that," Harper responded. "I'm fine concerning your questions."

"No, it would make me feel a lot better," Williams said. "Besides, Felix said it would be a nice gesture."

Harper gave in, and the two men rode over to a nearby diner where visitors to the island would stop to eat. The two men engaged in small talk as they ate. When they were done, Williams got up to pay for the meal.

"How stupid of me," Harper said, searching his pockets. "I've left my money at the office. Would you mind paying and I'll reimburse you when we get back to the cannery."

"I suppose so," Harper said, reaching into his jacket pocket and pulling out a roll of greenbacks. "How much?"

"Oh, leave five dollars that should more than cover everything," Williams replied, "Thanks."

Williams made good on his promise and returned the money. However, he now had something to go on. When the time drew near for the fish-cleaning crew to leave, Williams again went behind the curtain to catch Harper before he left.

"Say, Nolan, thanks for having lunch with me," Williams said. "Something has occurred to me I would like to discuss. Could you stay behind for a few minutes before going home?"

"I ... I really should be going," Harper said, "I have something ..."

"Let me level with you, Nolan," Williams began. "I saw that roll of greenbacks you pulled from your coat pocket this afternoon at the eatery. I am a U.S. Customs Agent and you had best tell me where those bills came from."

Harper's eyes widened as Williams spoke. Williams could see he was becoming visibly shaken.

"Look, Nolan, I have reason to believe you are not guilty of anything, but if you don't come clean I can make things difficult for you."

"It was money a highwayman gave me," Harper blurted out. "I had to take it."

"Whoa, wait a minute, a highwayman gave it to you? That doesn't make sense," Williams said. "Highwaymen usually rob people, not give them cash."

Harper went on to explain that the night he ended up with the inferior load of fish, he had originally received a quality shipment. But on his way back to the cannery, he was held up and forced to switch wagon loads with an unidentified assailant.

"I was unarmed, since that sort of thing has never happened to me before," Harper said. "It was strange, I know, but the man gave me the money telling me I'd better not tell anyone about this. If I did, he'd kill me. After the exchange, he rode off with my wagon of choice menhaden, leaving me with the cull batch."

"This person held you up, stole your wagon of fish, and gave you money to keep quiet," Williams said, a look of bewilderment on his face.

"I did as he said and came back here with the bad load," Harper said. "I had no choice but to unload it, knowing the fish would go bad if I left them in the wagon, but I figured Felix would reject them."

"What did Felix say to you about this?" Williams asked.

"He didn't know. I left the man's wagon and horse at the cannery," Harper said, "but when I came in, Felix's wagon and horse had been returned and the others gone, so Felix never knew what happened, other than the bad fish."

"So, the man paid you in greenbacks. Can you describe him?"

"Not really," Harper said. "He was a well-spoken man, a lot like you, but it was dark and I was unable to see him all that good."

"Nolan, listen, don't breathe a word of this," Williams said. "As best I can tell, you have nothing to worry about. I believe you were set up and are innocent in this thing.

"But one more question: have you or any of your crew ever found money in the fish you clean?" Williams asked.

"Money in the fish? No, never," Harper said. "I guess I don't follow..."

"It's not important," Williams said. "Remember, this is just between you and me."

Nik and Ambrose returned to their routine work. There were no further breaks in the counterfeiting case and no word as to the arrival of the silver shipment. Nik told Ambrose he would take the warrants, subpoenas and other court documents involving the mainland so the deputy could remain on Galveston Island. Nik was planning his time wisely so he could stop by the Covington Plantation and visit Esther.

"My brother is going to be coming here to visit," Nik told Esther, while the two were out riding in a buggy trying to find a spot to enjoy a picnic.

"You've not said much about him," Esther responded. "How long has it been since you've seen him?"

"It's been several years now. We used to be deputy marshals together until he decided to go back to seminary and become a preacher," Nik said, surveying the road for a turnoff to Clear Lake, a body of water that fed into Galveston Bay. "Pa was going to have me baptized just before he was killed, along with my Ma and sister, Dolly. I made Roger promise that when he became a preacher he would return and baptize me. I got a letter saying he was going to do it."

"That's wonderful, Nik," Esther said. "I've never been baptized either. Do you think he would baptize me too?"

"I don't see why not," Nik replied, smiling at his pretty passenger. "We've never talked much about religion and such. Are you a Christian?"

"My mother and father raised me that way," Esther said. "But there was no church for colored folks around here so we never went. Miss Tillie used to go, but after shooting her husband she grew tired of the stares and whispering that went on at church."

"Makes no sense for folks to do that," Nik said. "Maybe I can talk Roger into staying and starting a church around here for white and colored folks. It's not American to be separate all the time."

"We're somewhat fortunate here," Esther commented. "After June-teenth, many of the barriers came down that separate us. You seem to get along well in Galveston."

"I do. I have to say one thing for the South. They tend to either like you or they let you know they don't," Nik said. "Other places, they pretend they're okay with us when they really aren't. That's hypocritical."

"You seem to know a lot about black and white relationships," Esther suggested.

Nik halted the buggy and turned to his companion. "Esther, I was raised in an all-white family, a Christian all-white family. That doesn't mean there weren't stares and whispers when I was growing up as well, but my family taught me to face it head on as being nothing more than ignorance."

"I guess that's all we can do," Esther replied.

"By the way, Esther, I don't think I've thanked you proper-like for the decorating job you did in our office," Nik began as he started to chuckle. "It looks all white now."

Esther laughed, "Don't forget, Mr. Know-it-all Brinkman, I was raised in an all-white mansion so what did you expect?" The two broke into laughter as Nik snapped the reins and turned the horses down the lane to Clear Lake.

The following day, a letter arrived in Nik's mailbox from Roger. It was short and to the point that his brother had made all the arrangements and would be headed for Galveston. The letter took several weeks to arrive, so Nik figured Roger was well on his way to Galveston.

With his spirits up, when Nik arrived at the courthouse, he was surprised to see Duke, Zeke, Ron, and Ambrose sitting in his office. They did not look happy.

"What's up?" Nik said, surveying each face separately.

"Agent Letterman's dead," Agent Lester said.

"Whaaat …?" Nik said, almost breaking into a smile thinking this was some kind of joke.

"No, seriously," Sheriff Atkins cut in. "Our undercover agent was found floating in the bay, dead."

"No, no way. How? How could that happen?"

"Looks very similar to Lenny's death," Zeke offered. "I was beginning to think this counterfeiting operation had ground to a halt."

"Any clues? Do you suspect Harper had a hand in this?" Nik asked in an exasperated voice.

"We don't know, Nik," said Duke. "Zeke rushed out to the cannery this morning and everyone showed up for work, including Harper, all except for Letterman, of course."

"And you questioned them?" Nik said rhetorically.

"Everyone, including Harper, Felix, Elsa, all of 'em," Zeke said.

"And nothing? How did Harper look? Did he flinch when you questioned him?" Nik rambled off, with an incredulous look.

"He actually came across more innocent than the rest," Zeke said.

"That's a clue," Nik said, almost shouting. "He may have prepared himself to show an innocent demeanor."

"You have a point, Nik. Now all we need is a motive," Ron cut in. "Letterman was to do no more than keep an eye on the place. If he went beyond that we don't know."

"So, what? A blow to the back of the head, like Lenny?" Nik continued. "Was there anything in his pockets, fish, phony money…?"

"It's just a clear case of homicide, like Lenny's death," Duke said. "Unfortunately, Letterman left no clues in his pockets or anywhere else."

"Zeke, did you look for bloodstains at the cannery or maybe on the dock?" Nik asked.

"I sent Deputy Talbert to scour the place," Duke said. "Ron sent an agent with him as well,"

"It's got to be that Harper character," Nik said, as his eyes scanned the floor as if some clue might pop up there. As the marshal pondered the situation, his mind drifted back to the conversation he'd had with Abel Mosely. "Gentlemen, if you'll excuse me, there is something I need to do."

"You're not going to go out and try and shoot Harper, are you?" Duke said quickly. "We really don't know if he had a hand in this."

"No, just something I need to take care of," Nik responded, as he pulled open the office door and then turned to his deputy. "Ambrose, you tag along with Duke and Zeke. I'll catch up to you later."

Nik rode Galley onto the beach and then galloped along the wet sand just short of the water. He got to the end of it where the fish had washed up on shore several weeks ago. He stood up in his stirrups to scan the area, but no Mosely. Then a feeling of dread ran through his body.

What if Mosely had gotten too close and ended up in the bay as well? A feeling of guilt rode over his conscience when a voice called out, "Looking for me, Marshal?"

Nik wheeled around in his saddle to see Mosely standing behind him. A wave of relief swept over him.

"Abel, am I glad to see you."

"Why? Did you think something happened to me like that poor fellow last night?" Abel said.

"Then you know? Nik asked.

"Word travels fast on this beach, Marshal," Mosely said. "My eyes told me a Sea Serpent fishing boat was in the harbor last night. Appears two men, could have been anyone, it was too dark to tell, boarded that vessel. Eyes said only one got off. The ship sailed away this morning," Mosely related.

"Two men got on and only one got off?" Nik repeated.

"It was dark, all right, but my eyes can count," Abel said.

"When you say 'eyes' Abel, are you referring to your eyes?" Nik asked, trying to decipher Abel's testimony.

"Not my own, Marshal," Abel said. "No – other eyes. Too many know I talk to you on the beach. It wouldn't do for me to be sneaking around."

"Thank goodness," Nik said, almost to himself. "But can you trust what these 'eyes,' as you call them, saw?"

"They're better eyes than what ol' Mosely's got, Marshal. I shared that five dollars with 'em."

"You are a smart and crafty man," Abel. "My hat is off to you."

"I told you I'd been to sea, marshal. You can learn a good deal out there."

"Maybe I ought to try it sometime," Nik muttered, "as a sailor, not a slave."

"Oh, one more thing, Marshal," Mosely said. "It may not be important but it was strange. My eyes said he saw someone drive a wagonload of fish onto the ferry last night. Not sure why, eyes said he'd never seen that before."

"Thanks, Abel," Nik said with a shrug of his shoulders, "could be something to it. I'll check it out."

Nik then bid Mosely farewell and rode off in the direction of the courthouse.

Chapter 19
Roger and the Rio Grande

Before the sun was up, Roger Brinkman and Pecos Catfish took the canoe belonging to the Indian guide from its tipi and transported it to the banks of the Rio Grande. Roger and Pecos did a mental check of their gear and the Comanche guide repeated his instructions.

"Best you put your weapon and gun belt into the bottom of the canoe, along with your saddlebags and luggage" Pecos said. "If we have to take to the water you do not want those things to get wet. But keep your gun within arm's reach."

Roger did as Pecos instructed, and soon the two river travelers were on their way downstream. As the rising sun began to dance off the waters, Roger kept his eyes ahead to avoid the blinding flashes that glanced off the surface. The river was calm that day and the weather warming up, and were it not for the need of his paddle, Roger might have drifted off to sleep.

Near mid-morning, the two approached a stretch of river with leafy foliage along the western bank.

"Prepare yourself," Pecos said. "This is a dangerous part of the river."

"How so?" Roger said, turning his head to view Pecos sitting in the rear of the canoe.

"Ambush," Pecos replied. "The Apache hide in the bushes sometimes to ambush unsuspecting river travelers."

"Well that sounds like fu…" just then an arrow hit the side of the canoe, stopping Roger in mid-sentence.

"Grab the shield down by your foot," Pecos called out. "Stay low. Let the river carry us."

Just as Roger pulled up his shield an arrow glanced off of it.

"Young Apache," Pecos said. "Their weapons are inferior, fortunately."

Pecos had no sooner gotten the words out of his mouth than a flaming arrow sank into the side of the canoe.

"Jump out to the left," Pecos called out, "and hang onto the side of the canoe."

Roger tossed his hat into the bottom of the canoe, dropped his shield, and rolled into the water. Pecos did the same with both hanging onto the handholds on the left side of the vacated canoe.

"When I say, push up on the canoe," Pecos said.

"What for?" Roger asked instinctively.

"Put out the arrow's flames, of course," Pecos barked out. "Ready, push!"

The canoe rocked and a hiss could be heard.

"Hold onto the canoe while I check on the flames," Pecos said. The guide then dove under the canoe and looked up from underwater to see if the flame was out. An arrow struck the water in front of Pecos and quickly lost momentum. The guide then resurfaced next to Roger.

"We are nearly past the danger," Pecos said. "The arrow no longer burns and others are falling short of the canoe. Try swimming for the bank while holding on to the canoe."

Their swimming efforts worked, as they reached a shallow part of the river and were able to walk the canoe onto the east bank. They pulled the canoe onto the shore and inspected it for damage.

"Remove your jacket and trousers, rinse them out and we'll stop to eat while they dry out," Pecos said.

Roger obliged, although he felt a little silly eating in his underwear. After a short meal of cornbread and dried catfish, Roger donned his still-damp clothes and the two men set out again upon the water. As the sun rose higher in the sky, Roger's clothes began to dry and the trip turned pleasant again.

The first few days of the trip went without incident, until they came to a wide spot in the river. Pecos instructed Roger to paddle to shore where they would again spend the night.

Pecos's wife had packed plenty of food for the trip but Roger was growing tired of cornbread and dry fish.

"What are the odds we could shoot some wild game for dinner?" Roger asked Pecos.

"It could draw attention, but this area along the river is pretty peaceful if you're willing to take the chance," Pecos advised. "Game is plentiful if you are a good shot, are you?"

"I've been known to hit a bull's eye or two," Roger said, "even when it was running."

"Plenty of jackrabbit, but they run fast," Pecos said, smiling as he handed Roger his rifle.

"Your catfish is great," Roger said, "but when I'm hungry for something different, it's hard to outrun me."

Pecos laughed. "I'll set up camp and start a campfire. You bring home the dinner," he said.

True to his word, Roger's hunting skills came back into play and he soon had two hare for the spit. Pecos had the rabbits cleaned in short order and soon they were feasting on roasted jackrabbit – and cornbread.

"We'll be coming into a wide part of the river. There are Mexican river pirates in this area that are known to go after small boats like ours," Pecos said. "They use firearms instead of bows and arrows. It can be risky."

"To think I could have taken the train," Roger said, "but the stopovers and rail connections by stagecoach simply did not appeal. Besides, I wanted to see this country. I have never been on the Rio Grande before."

"These pirates are a bit amateur," Pecos said, "but they are dangerous all the same."

"Is that where you got that scar on your shoulder?" Roger inquired.

Pecos looked over at the three-inch mark and turned back to Roger, "No, no it is not."

"I don't mean to pry, Pecos, but you told me after we first met that you broke away from your original tribe an migrated to where you live now," Roger reminded his companion. "Why did you do that?"

"It is a long story, white shaman. I'm not sure you want to hear it," Pecos responded.

"You carry yourself with great dignity for such a young man," Roger said. "On the contrary, you said you were familiar with 'white man's shaman,' how familiar?"

Pecos paused, picked up a stick and poked the campfire. "Because you are shaman, I trust you do not go further with it. Since you asked, I am Pecos Parker, brother of Comanche Chief Quanah Parker. Our mother was white woman, last name Parker, captured during a Comanche raid."

"I've heard of your brother, a great warrior as I understand," Roger said, "so, why the secrecy?"

"Quanah is wanted by the army," Pecos answered. "I, too, was wanted and got this scar during a battle. The word was that I died. It was then I decided to break away from my brother and join the band I now live with."

"Our mother raised my brother, sister, and I half Indian and half white. She was eventually retaken by white soldiers to live among her kind. But she longed to return to us and eventually died of a broken heart."

"I'm sorry, Pecos, that's quite a story," Roger said.

"My story is for your ears only. My life is better that way," Pecos said.

The next day, Roger and Pecos reached the wide part of the river. The current was much slower and so was the speed of travel. However, all went well until they reached the halfway point of the calm waters. They were startled by a loud bang, followed by a whistling sound, and a splash near their canoe.

"Small cannon fire," Pecos said. "I told you they were amateur. They try to intimidate us with cannon but will use rifles to get us to halt."

Roger had turned in the direction of the explosion and saw a small, white billowing sail growing on the horizon.

"It looks like they're going to try and overtake us by sail," Roger said.

"Keep paddling. We are okay as long as we stay out of rifle range," Pecos said.

In spite of their efforts, the sail grew larger and soon rifle fire could be heard.

"What do they think they're going to get from a two-man canoe?" Roger asked.

"Nothing, it is sport for them," Pecos said. "Otherwise, they have to work their father's farm and they would prefer to be on the water."

"Sounds like a parenting problem," Roger said, ducking as a bullet hit the surface of the water nearby. He looked back and could see the boat was still gaining. Roger placed a shield in the front of the canoe propping it up against the crossbeam and between the sides of the canoe.

"What are you doing?" Pecos asked.

"Just hand me that rifle. I have an idea," Roger responded.

With the rifle in hand, Roger turned around and leaned against the shield.

"Get down," he said to his paddling companion. Pecos complied as the bullets were beginning to come closer.

Roger took careful aim and fired. His shot hit just below where the makeshift spinnaker was attached atop the mast. He took aim, fired and hit just above the spinnaker, knocking away a part of the upper mast. The vessel was now well in range and Roger's next shot dropped the spinnaker into the boat covering the three men operating it. The pirate ship quickly faded into the distance.

"That's some fine shooting, preacher man," Pecos said, grinning.

"And it wasn't even running away," Roger said, with a laugh.

With the danger now behind them, Roger and Pecos reached Eagle Pass without further incident. They pulled the canoe onto shore and Roger retrieved his belongings, turned to Pecos and grasped his forearm. "Thank you, my friend. May you and your family find peace."

"Before you go, I have something for you," Pecos said, reaching into the pouch he was wearing over his shoulder and then extending his hand. "I do believe this is yours."

Roger looked down and saw a white stone in Pecos's hand. The preacher's expression changed from one of mystery to one of confused delight.

"Yes it is, but how did you get it?" Roger inquired, breaking into a smile.

"It fell when you removed your gun belt while we were loading the canoe at my village. I thought it might be valuable to you so I kept it safe during our journey," Pecos explained. "Is it important?"

"It is my touchstone, so to speak," Roger said, tears welling in his eyes. "It keeps me in touch with my family, like your secret keeps you in touch with yours."

"Then I am happy to return it, Shaman Brinkman," Pecos said. "I hope your brother appreciates what you're doing for him."

"And I hope yours appreciates what you're doing, Pecos. May God go with you."

"And with you," Pecos said smiling, as he returned to his canoe. "You can replenish your supplies at Fort Duncan. It is easy to find, just ask anyone in Eagle Pass," Pecos called out.

"And you?" Roger replied.

"I have all I need. Farewell, my friend," Pecos said as pushed the canoe into the water and paddled upstream while staying close to the bank.

Roger watched Pecos "Catfish" Parker as he swiftly negotiated the stream and was soon out of sight. Roger threw his saddlebags over his shoulder and picked up his bag as he started for Eagle Pass. He walked down the main street until he saw a sign that read "River Trips," in the window of a small store. He went in.

"What are the chances I can catch a ride to Brownsville?" Roger asked at the counter of the store.

A slightly-built gentleman wearing a visor that failed to cover his bald spot on the back of his head was rearranging items on a shelf behind the counter. He turned when Roger spoke.

"Can I help you, sir?" the man said, peering over a pair of spectacles that rested on the bridge of his nose.

"Yes, I'm trying to get to Galveston and was told if I reached Brownsville I could make my way up the coast," Roger said.

The man stared at Roger for a moment, but Roger could see he was thinking more than he was looking. "There are flatboats from here that can get you to Brownsville. There are hostile Indians but the flatboats always seem to make it through," said the man, who apparently was the storekeeper. "As for Galveston, I would suggest you make port in Roma instead of Brownsville and catch the stage from there to Corpus Christi. You can continue on by stage all the way to Houston, if you wish, but if I were going that way I would find a yachtsman in Corpus Christi to sail me up the coast to Galveston. Just my suggestion, you understand, that's how I would do it, I reckon."

Roger kind of nodded his head as he tried to process the man's suggestion.

After a moment, Roger said, "Then, can I catch a river ride to Roma?"

"It's seventeen dollars, but it's a good way to travel, considering the hostile Indians and all."

"When could I expect to catch this ride to Roma?"

"The River Rat is expected this evening and will depart in the morning. Captain Schlutterman would be your host. Andy's a fine river pilot," the man continued. "I know the name of his craft doesn't sound t'all pleasing, but it's a fine craft nevertheless."

"I look forward to meeting this... this Captain Schlutterman and catching a ride," Roger said, taking seventeen dollars from his saddlebag. "By the way, I take it those buildings I see just outside of town would be Fort Duncan?"

"Certainly is," the storekeeper said. "Will you be staying there? You don't dress like a soldier."

"It's an arrangement I made with the cavalry. I've been traveling with them," Roger answered. "I'm a circuit clergyman, actually. Though I'm sure my attire would not give you that impression."

"A clergyman," said the proprietor. "Welcome to Eagle Pass."

Roger slipped his trip ticket on the River Rat into his saddlebag and set out for Fort Duncan.

"Colonel, there is a Mr. Roger Brinkman here to see you, sir," the corporal at Fort Duncan said with a salute.

"Sounds like the man Major Trundell was talking about," Lieutenant Colonel Schafer said.

"Yes, sir, a preacher man, I think, sir"

"Send him in, corporal," Schafer said. "Send him in."

"Pastor Brinkman," the lieutenant colonel greeted, rising from his chair and waving his hand at the one sitting in front of his desk, "please, have a seat."

"Thank you, colonel," Brinkman said, positioning himself in the chair. "I'm sorry to bother you, but I was told I could replenish my supplies here. I am to catch a riverboat tomorrow morning."

"That you can, pastor, we also have accommodations for you to stay the night," Shafter said, sitting back down. "Where are you headed?"

"I'm making my way to Galveston. I am to meet my brother there. We have not seen each other for quite some time."

"A reunion, that should be nice," Schafer said. "How did you make it to Eagle Pass?"

"By canoe, sir," Roger said. "It was quite a ride."

"Were you transported by Pecos Catfish?" Schafer asked.

"Yes, a very capable and accommodating man," Roger replied.

"I wish more Comanche were like Pecos. Although, I do believe he is from a warring tribe in Indian Country," Schafer said. "We've had no trouble with Pecos or members of his village up near San Antonio del Bravo."

"I doubt you ever will," Roger said, with a sigh, somewhat fatigued by the long river trip. "Pecos told me he sees no future in fighting the white man."

Schafer smiled at Roger and called out, "corporal!"

"Yes, sir, colonel," the corporal said, as he strode up next to Roger and saluted.

"Please show Mr. Brinkman to his quarters," Schafer said. "Oh, and direct him to where mess will be served, too."

"Yes, sir," the corporal saluted again.

"Thanks, colonel," Roger said as he rolled out of his chair and fell in behind the corporal.

The corporal led Roger to a non-com's billets, where Roger dropped off his gear. The corporal then directed Roger to the mess hall, where Roger looked forward to a meal of something besides catfish and cornbread, even if it was army chow. After eating what did not taste like what it was called, he decided to just drop into his bed for the night.

"I hearsay you're headed for Galveston," came a voice from the shadows on the other side of the room.

Startled, Roger rose up from the bunk on his elbows. "I'm sorry, I didn't know anyone else was in here."

"No problem, this is the non-com's accommodations," said the man, who wore sergeant's stripes on his arm. "We don't often have many visitors who stay here.

"What's in Galveston?" the sergeant asked.

"My brother. I'm a preacher and plan to baptize him while I'm there."

"That's good. I heard there was a soldier killed on the Rio Peñasco during a baptism a while back," the sergeant said, lying supine and looking up at the ceiling as he spoke.

"I was there," Roger responded, "I was asked to baptize the man before that unfortunate incident befell him."

"That's a kind thing you were going to do," said the sergeant. "I'm just sorry it turned out the way it did."

"Perhaps we should have been more careful," Roger said, fighting back the memory of the incident. "It was a hard thing for all the men."

"We get used to it after a while," the soldier offered. "It was good they had a man of God with them."

"I'm not so sure," Roger said, assuming the same position as the sergeant. "I'm afraid my presence may have caused more trouble than if I hadn't been there."

"No, I don't think so. We soldiers need more men like you in our ranks," the sergeant said, almost in a whisper. "The Indians could have showed a little more respect, though."

"They didn't know," Roger said. "Our ways are not necessarily their ways."

"Pecos knew enough to return that white stone to you, didn't he" the sergeant remarked.

Roger immediately raised himself onto his elbows and said, "How did you know..."

Roger stopped in mid-sentence, staring at an empty bunk where he had clearly seen the stripes on the sergeant's sleeve. His mind raced back to visions he'd seen before, in his past.

He lay back down in silence and soon drifted off to sleep.

When he awoke the next morning, he took time to shave before making his way to the mess hall to have breakfast before leaving. After filling his plate, he spotted the corporal and sat on the bench opposite across from him.

"Good morning, pastor," the corporal said. "Did you sleep well?"

"I think I may actually have passed out. Slept all night," Roger said, cutting a slice in his pancakes. "By the way, do you know if someone else slept in my quarters?"

"No one, sir," the corporal answered, while concentrating on his own meal.

"That was the non-com's billets, right?" Roger said, between bites.

"It was at one time sir, but that room has now been set aside for guests," the corporal replied."

"Must have been a dream I had," Roger muttered before taking a drink of coffee.

"Sir?" the corporal responded.

"Nothing, nothing at all, corporal, I just want to thank you and Fort Duncan for all your hospitality."

"Yes, sir, it was good to have you here." The soldier then excused himself and left the mess hall.

Roger finished eating, picked up his plate, utensils, and coffee cup and returned them to the mess counter. He returned to his billets, glanced at the empty bunk across the room, and gathered his gear. He stopped to thank the colonel and set out for the river.

"Welcome aboard, Pastor…, a, ah, Brinkman, I believe it is?" said the man standing at the end of the gangplank that extended from the dock to the flatboat resting on the waters of the Rio Grande that passed by Eagle Pass. "I'm Captain Andrew Schlutterman," he continued, shaking Roger's hand as he came aboard. "We don't get many folks of your kind in these parts."

"Pleased to meet you, Captain Schlutterman," Roger responded. "By my kind, you mean…"

"Ah, men of the cloth, preacher-types, no we usually get trappers, buffalo hunters, prospectors, and an occasional Indian fighter, but very few preacher men. Just call me Andy, if you've a mind to. The captain thing is just 'cause I own the River Rat, this boat that is."

Andy Schlutterman was a man of slight build. He was clean shaven and wore a broad-brimmed hat to protect him from the sun. However, his face was ruddy in color, mainly from the glare reflecting off the water. He wore a red shirt draped with an open vest and both hung loosely on his frame. He wore high-top black boots and suspended cotton trousers.

The boat was crude but well built. Its main features were a single-sail mast in the middle and a tent-shaped, log structure that sat to the rear of the craft for sleeping and supplies. The helm was placed in front of the structure surrounded by logs extending from the sleeping quarters, like an open closet. In the bow was a large metal bowl with a grill on top. Next to the bowl was a thick wooden table with a butcher knife stuck into it and a flat spatula dangling from it.

Schlutterman's crew included a heavyset man dressed similarly to the captain, known as "Fingers," and a large, muscled black man they called "Cutter." Roger learned later that Cutter was the cook and Fingers got his nickname after losing a digit during a dispute over Cutter's cooking.

Fingers showed Roger the accommodations and where to store

his gear, while Andy finalized arrangements with the shopkeeper. Once the captain was back onboard, the River Rat made sail down the river.

Chapter 20
The Tiburon

Judge Victor Giles Kensington, otherwise known as King Victor, sat in his elegant coach with his back to the driver. In front of him were General Porfirio Diaz and former Texas sheriff Curtis Parker. The judge's valet, Enrico Peralta, sat up front with the driver.

"We have nearly everything set for what promises to be the most spectacular silver robbery in history," Kensington said, as the three gentlemen puffed on expensive cigars. "I have every reason to believe that Baudelaire, or Cutlass as he likes to be called, will soon have his ship ready. The authorities in Galveston have already been notified and have approved our 'Celebration of Jean Lafitte.'"

"My men tell me the silver shipment is on the move again," Packard said, leaning against the back seat. "I just hope this 'pirate ship' idea works as planned."

I received word from Baudelaire nearly a month ago that she was ready. That is why I set up this meeting. You will be able to see the ship and the work that has been done on it," the judge said. "We were able to hire some very capable maritime workers to get the job finished."

"This money should be all I need to secure my election as president of Mexico," Porfirio said. "Once I take over, money will no longer be an issue," the general concluded, exhaling a cloud of blue smoke.

After going several more miles, the carriage turned toward the ocean. After passing over a road lined with palms, sycamore, coral vine, and maguey plants, the buggy rolled into a cove complete with an exclusive white beach. Sitting on large scaffolding with its bow completely out of the water was the fully-rigged pirate ship Tiburon, including a Jolly Roger waving in the gentle sea breeze atop the foremast.

Two men were on the scaffolding applying the final touches to a figurehead adorned with a bust of the pirate Jean Lafitte plated in bronze. A sheet of metal wrapped around the bow just below the figurehead added the strength necessary to withstand a collision.

"Welcome, gentlemen," Cutlass called out as he walked across the beach toward the men in the carriage. "Would you like to come onboard?"

"No," Kensington said, "we're just here to make sure the Tiburon is seaworthy and ready to go."

"She is more than seaworthy," Cutlass said laughingly. "She is worthy of sinking a barge to the bottom of the sea. And thanks to Mr. Parker, his men are also seaworthy and ready to sail.

"Have all the arrangements been made?"

"You should run into no trouble at all," Kensington said, grinning and shaking the "pirate's" hand. "The word is being spread throughout Galveston and the surrounding area about this week-long celebration of Jean Lafitte. Billing the event as a week-long event allows for any delays that might hold up the shipment of silver."

"We shall look forward to your return and your cargo of treasure," Diaz said, extending his hand to Cutlass. "This appears to be the perfect place to hide the ship and unload the booty, so to speak," Diaz added, laughing.

"Are you sure you wouldn't like to come aboard and see the Tiburon, now that it is seaworthy again?" Baudelaire said, waving his arm in the direction of the ship. "She will be the star of the celebration."

Kensington relented and the new arrivals boarded the ship. Cutlass explained how they would handle the chests of silver once they were onboard. Baudelaire also gave them a tour below deck, where several mattresses were stored.

"Why the mattresses?" Packard asked.

"If we are delayed, the men have a place to sleep," Cutlass said. "And when the balloon lowers the chests of silver we shall use them on deck in case a chest should accidentally fall."

Judge Kensington flashed a quick glance at Packard and Diaz. Turning back to Baudelaire he said, "That's good thinking, Cutlass. One cannot be too careful with such a valuable cargo."

"Unfortunately, we have no way to practice how this is to be done," Cutlass said. "Mr. Packard's men said they know how to handle the transfer so I am leaving it up to them."

"Yes, my boys know what they're doing," Packard interjected with a broad smile and glancing at Kensington. "They have talents that even surprise me."

"We have made arrangements for you to dock in Galveston Harbor until the time is right for you to sail," the judge instructed. "In the meantime, Cutlass, dress up in your finest Jean Lafitte regalia and parade through the streets of Galveston to get folks in the mood. We've got volunteers from the city who will be doing the same. They're proud of their connection to the pirate.

"You knew him, did you not, Cutlass?"

"Yes, our town, Campeche, was the name of Lafitte's village on Galveston. However, I was just a lad and served as a cabin boy for the renowned pirate, but it was after the United States Navy ran him off the Island," Baudelaire answered. "However, I remember his dress well and have fashioned a costume after him."

"W have told Galveston officials that you once sailed with Lafitte, so you will be welcomed as somewhat of a celebrity," Kensington said. "Enjoy yourself, but once you set sail and have your… ah… cargo onboard, just keep sailing west through the bay and get back here as soon as you can."

"You said you do want me to pick up survivors from the wrecked barge, right?" Cutlass asked.

"By all means," the judge added. "We're not doing this to hurt anyone. We're doing this for the silver. As for the survivors, we have accommodations for them."

"Besides, two of them will be my men," Packard said. "They will be on the barge preparing the cargo for the balloon to pick up once you've sent their boat to the bottom."

"What if there are other boats on the bay resembling the barge?" Paco, Cutlass's companion, asked. "We would not like to sink the wrong ship."

"If there's any question, my men will be onboard the barge to signal you," Packard advised. "Besides, you will have received an accurate description of the barge prior to sailing."

"It sounds like you folks have thought of everything," Cutlass said, smiling.

"That we have... Jean Lafitte," Kensington said, laughing out loud.

The men concluded the tour and the judge, former sheriff, and general climbed back into 'King Victor's' elaborate carriage. Once they were back on the road, Dias spoke up.

"He does not appear to suspect anything."

"All he expects is a cut of the booty we'll be getting," Kensington said, turning his attention from admiring the landscape to his two companions. "Besides, what he doesn't know won't hurt us," the judge said, again breaking out into laughter and being joined by his companions.

Chapter 21
End of the River Trip

As the River Rat drifted farther south on the Rio Grande, the day's temperatures increased, prompting Roger to remove his coat and hang it over his arm. One warm day, he leaned against the log-framed sleeping quarters near the helm where Andy was standing behind the wheel.

"I don't know what you experienced coming down the northern part of the river," Andy, whose sleeves were rolled up, remarked, "but the days will be getting' a tad warmer the closer we get to the gulf, more humid too."

"I spent most of my time around the Red River and in Oklahoma," Roger answered, while looking past Andy at Cutter positioned at the side of the craft checking his fishing lines. "Do you get many storms down here?"

"An occasional squall passes through. Plenty of thunder and lightnin' but, for the most part, not much rain," Andy answered. "Our cozy quarters provide shelter enough and I wear my slicker when it rains so I can stay on the helm."

Just then Cutter pulled a big catfish out of the water, hooked to one of his fishing lines.

"Breakfast," Cutter called out, turning toward Roger and Andy while holding up the fish.

"That sounds good," Roger said to Andy, "I was wondering if we were going to get something new to eat this morning."

"I take it you're getting a little tired of dry, salted meat," Andy replied. "It helps when he gets lucky like this. That way we can save the red meat for the evenin' meal.

"By the by, do you shoot?"

"I picked up a ribbon or two when I was younger," Roger said, thinking back on his early days in Bordertown, Missouri," "Why?"

"I'm guessing you never ever shot a man before, bein' a preacher and all," the skipper said with an expression of doubt.

"I fought in the war and was a U.S. Deputy Marshal for a time," Roger said, dodging the question. "I didn't turn to preaching until after that."

"I only ask 'cause there are times when local Injun tribes object to us passing through on the river," Andy said, while keeping his eyes trained downstream. "Sometimes passengers help out when that happens. But don't think ya' have to. No, Fingers, Cutter, and me, we do just fine."

"If that happens and you have and an extra rifle, I'm willing to do my part," Roger said, swinging his jacket over his shoulder.

"You're sure a different sort of preacher, aren't you Mr.… Pastor Brinkman?"

"Not when it comes to preaching, but when it comes to survival I pray that the Good Lord will give me the ability to shoot straight," Roger answered with a slight laugh.

"Sounds like you're the right kind of man for doing what you do in this part of the country," Andy said, offering a little grin in answer to Roger's remark.

"I hope so," Roger said. "If you'll excuse me, I think I'm going to check on how Cutter's coming along."

Cutter had stoked the coals under the grill and was whittling away on the catfish he'd caught. When he had pared each cut of meat to his liking, he rolled it in a pan of cornmeal mixed with spices. After covering the meat with a good coating, he placed the cut of fish onto the barbecue.

"Man, that smells good," Roger said, as he approached the front of the boat.

"All my cookin' smells good," Cutter said, turning toward Roger with a broad smile. "It's just that sometimes there are those who don't think it tastes as good as it smells." Cutter chuckled, turning his eyes on Fingers, who was poling the raft away from two tree branches hanging low over the river.

"I have never been so impolite as to complain about vittles anyone prepared for me," Roger answered. "My mother would have boxed my ears if I had complained about her cooking. But I can honestly tell you, I never had cause to complain."

"My momma taught me to cook and we ate just about anything the Good Lord provided," Cutter said, turning back to his grill and turning the meat. "I don't know why I paid so close attention to how she did it, but I'm glad I did."

Once the fish were done, everyone ate their fill and offered zero complaints. Fingers' approval was a grunt and Roger's only gripe was there not being more of it. To satisfy his hunger, Roger concluded the meal by munching on an apple.

As the day wore on, clouds started to gather, the darkest ones off in the distance. The captain suggested the crew prepare for possible rain and each, in turn, donned their wet-weather gear.

"If we get some rain, you might want to climb into the cabin," Andy called to Roger, who was standing near the west side of the craft scanning Mexico's landscape.

Cutter placed a large piece of metal over the cubbyhole containing fuel for the grill, and poured several buckets of water onto the grill to cool it down. Afterward, he covered the entire thing with canvas and tied the corners down with twine.

Almost out of nowhere, a strong wind started blowing up the river from the south ahead of the dark clouds. Roger pulled down on his hat to keep it from blowing off and slipped back into his jacket.

As the wind picked up it brought with it a mix of rain and spray from the river. Roger made his way into the storage cabin just as a flash of lightning lit up the darkening sky. It was followed almost instantaneously by a clap of thunder and a sudden torrential downpour.

Safe inside, Roger whispered a little prayer for the crew. Fortunately, the cabin was watertight, but each time lightning flashed,

Roger was certain he could hear the river sizzle. But just as suddenly as it began, the rain stopped and the rumble of thunder grew distant. That encouraged the River Rat's lone passenger to step back onto the deck.

"Well, that was exciting," Roger said, reaching the front of the cabin where Andy was still at the helm.

"It could get even more excitin' if that rain continues north," the skipper said, with rainwater dripping from the brim of his hat. "If it causes flashfloods, we might get some of that wash rollin' down the river."

"Is that bad?" Roger quipped.

"Not so much the water, but it can carry a lot of junk, like fallen trees, limbs, rudderless boats – even saw a body float by one time."

"That sounds encouraging," Roger muttered, half to himself.

"Fingers will move aft to pole away anything like that that might come our way."

As the afternoon wore on, a minor rise in the river was noticed but nothing floating by that posed any danger. Roger busied himself by assisting the crew where needed.

Toward evening, Cutter got his fire going again and pulled out a large griddle to place atop the grill. He pulled out some fry bacon from storage and began mixing pancake batter. Following an unusual but excellent dinner, Roger told Cutter that if he was in the eatery business instead of preaching he would hire him as his chef.

The rest of trip continued without incident, until the River Rat was within five miles of Laredo, Texas. Roger was again standing off to the side of the helm talking to the captain when an arrow hit the top log on the left side of the helm's enclosure.

"Injuns," Fingers shouted, as he ran for the doorway of the shelter.

Roger looked up, and less than one hundred yards in front of the boat he could see what appeared to be two Indian warriors, partially concealed in the brush on the east bank. He also noticed Cutter duck down behind his barbecue and pull out a pistol from his utility cupboard.

"Cutter, I'll handle this," Roger shouted. "Fingers, hand me a rifle."

Using the cabin as a shield, Roger took the rifle from Fingers just as two more arrows landed, one in the side of the cabin and the other on the deck. Roger then moved behind the cabin and positioned himself so he could see that attackers. He took aim at a rock near where the Indians were partially hidden and fired. Dust flew from a rock about ten feet from where the warriors were positioned.

"You're going to have to do a little better than that," Cutter called out.

It was hard to tell, but the two attackers appeared to laugh when the shot hit the rock.

After whispering a short prayer, Roger's next shot took the feather from atop one of the Indians' head, sending it into the air. Both warriors disappeared into the bushes.

"Your aim was too darn high, preacher," Andy shouted, standing at the wheel with an arrow protruding from the cabin wall behind him, the shaft extending just over his right shoulder.

"Nope," Roger called back, as he moved around to the right side of the cabin near the helm. "I was right on target."

"But your first shot hit that rock. It wasn't even close," Andy exclaimed.

"Just sighting in the rifle," Roger said. "It was off about an inch. As the river drew us closer, I was pretty certain where the proper aim should be."

"So, you're sayin' you meant to hit that warrior's feather instead of his forehead?" Andy queried, as Cutter, keeping a low profile, hustled back toward the helm and Fingers peeked out from the cabin. "Why?"

"Did you get a good look at those two?" Roger replied. "They were not young braves. In fact, I would say they were a couple old warriors trying to prove they still had some fight left in them."

"I guess that kind of shootin' is impressive," Andy said. "But this arrow over my shoulder tells me those two were playing for keeps."

"I'm sure they were," Roger said. "But the pattern of their arrows told me their skills were sorely lacking."

"He's right," Cutter chimed in. "Three of their arrows didn't even hit the Rat."

"Still, I got a scar on my leg that could have been prevented by a skilled shooter like you, preacher man," the captain said, reaching down to rub his thigh. "And it was right near this spot too, right, Cutter? It could even have been those two."

Cutter nodded his head in the affirmative.

"How long ago?" Roger asked.

"Oh, I dunno, maybe fifteen, twenty years ago," the skipper said.

"Those two warriors would have been about fifteen to twenty years younger then," Roger said, grinning. "My guess is they could see and shoot a lot better back then."

Cutter and Fingers had a good laugh at that remark, but the captain was not amused.

Sailing on, the River Rat eventually docked in Laredo, where the crew made a closer inspection of the craft to determine if any further damage had been done during the attack. The arrows appeared to be a mix of Comanche, Kiowa, and Cheyenne.

"My guess is, those two we met up river borrowed those arrows," Roger said. "I doubt they have the ability to fashion their own anymore."

"Perhaps you're right, preacher man," Andy said. "But I make it a point to never underestimate an Injun. I don't care how old."

Roger laughed and put his arm around Andy's shoulder. "Come on, if there's a tavern in town I'll buy everybody a beer."

"I'll be danged, if you ain't like no other preacher man I've ever knowed before," Andy said, joining in the jocularity.

After Roger and the River Rat's crew returned to the flatboat, they again set sail downriver. The farther south they went the warmer the days grew, until they reached the port of Roma. Roger said his farewells to Captain Schlutterman and his crew, blessed the River Rat, and carried his belongs into the small outpost known as Roma.

He stopped into one of the businesses that lined the main street of the town and inquired about the stage.

"The stage is due in two days and departs on the third," said the heavyset proprietor, wearing a small derby hat with red suspenders holding up his loose-fitting trousers. "We have accommodations here, nothing fancy, just a place to stay until the stage arrives. Two dollars a night, plus one dollar for food each day, you can get your plate and eat in your room, if you like. Out back is a place to eat if the weather's pleasant, has been for a while now."

"How much for passage on the stage line?" Roger asked.

"Depends on where you want to go. It's twenty dollars to Alleyton, which is on the way to Houston," the clerk said. "Stage stops in King Rancheo, San Patricio..."

"I want to reach Corpus Christi. I was told I could find a boat that would take me on to Galveston from there," Roger interrupted.

"In that case, I recommend passage to King Rancheo," the proprietor said. "Corpus Christi is just a short distance from there. You can get a horse from the livery stable in King Rancheo and ride over to Corpus Christi."

"How much to King Rancheo?" Roger asked.

"Seven-fifty, there's a junction where you'll have to transfer onto the stage out of Brownsville," the clerk said. "Shouldn't be any trouble, but I see you wear a gun. That's good."

"Why is that good?" Roger inquired.

"It doesn't happen often, but Indians have attacked the stage-coaches from time to time," the owner of the business said. "Most passengers aren't carrying much of value so robbers haven't been a problem."

Roger took twenty dollars out of his saddlebags and handed it to the clerk. "This should cover my expenses. If not, I'll make up the difference before I board the stage."

"Thank you...Mr....

"Brinkman, Roger Brinkman, and you are?"

"Peloton, Price Peloton," the proprietor replied.

Roger spent the two days, before the stage arrived, collecting his thoughts and preparing for the final leg of his journey. The food at the small inn where he stayed was satisfying, although not much for variety. It was pancakes and eggs in the morning, soup at lunch, and a potato and entre in the evening, usually venison, buffalo or fowl.

As Roger prepared to leave, he stopped at Peloton's desk to enquire about his bill. The innkeeper said he had change coming, but Roger told the innkeeper to keep it as credit. Roger said he might be passing by this way again in the not-too-distant future.

Roger took his saddlebags and luggage out to the stage and handed it to a man on top of the rig, who secured to the roof. As Roger stepped to the side of the stagecoach to enter, he noticed the security rider's weapon lying across the man's knee.

"Is that a modified Stoeger you have there?" Roger shouted up to the fellow.

"Yes, sir, the best," he said.

"And ol' Dutch, here, can knock an acorn out of a squirrel's paws at twenty paces with that thing," the driver called out with a laugh.

"Thirty paces," Dutch growled.

"That's great," Roger shouted back, then lowered his voice to say, "if we're attacked by squirrels armed with acorns."

"What's that?" the driver called back.

"Oh, I was just wondering if there were any weapons available inside the coach," Roger answered.

"Yep, there's a Colt single-shot rifle with ammunition in the coach carry compartment," the drive said. "Do you know how to use one?"

"I do, thank you," Roger said, as he pulled himself inside the coach, wondering why people kept asking him that question. He guessed it was because of his clerical clothes.

The trip to the junction was a little rough, but otherwise peaceful. After stopping at the junction, Roger transferred over to a second stagecoach waiting there. The one he was on then lit out for Brownsville as he started out for King Ranchero. He took his seat across from two women dressed as if on their way to church.

"Ladies," Roger said, slightly tipping his hat as he sat down. The women both nodded but said nothing. The three passengers rode along in silence, as Roger gazed out one of the openings on his side of the stage. When he turned back, he saw the older of the two women staring at him. As she continued looking at him, she spoke.

"Are you a preacher?" she asked.

"Momma," the younger woman said, softly pushing her mother's arm.

"I am," Roger answered. "What gave me away?"

"Just the way you carry yourself. We met a preacher in California and you kind of reminded me of him."

"I hope he was someone you liked," Roger said, glancing over at the younger woman, who was smiling. The younger woman was pretty, like he remembered Gloria, his former girlfriend, but the young passenger appeared more refined. Gloria had been raised on a farm in Missouri, with little time, or money, for the finer things in life. Roger could not help but wonder how uncomfortable it was for these ladies to be riding in a dust-laden stagecoach, on a warm day, wearing dresses buttoned all the way to their necks.

"He was a fine man, but he was a Catholic," the woman answered. "Catholics don't marry, as I'm sure you know."

"I was trained a Lutheran, so I do know," Roger said. "Was that important to you?"

"My Pricilla could have married a fine man like that priest, but it was out of the question," the woman continued.

"Momma," the young girl, referred to as Pricilla, said while looking at her mother.

"We were living in California, until my husband, Pricilla's father, decided he was going to run off and discover gold. I told him if he did that we would return to Philadelphia and wait for him there," the lady continued. "By the by, I'm Margaret Wiggins. This fine young lady is my daughter, Pricilla."

"Pleased to meet you both, I'm sure," Roger responded. "Roger Brinkman is my name. If I might ask, what are you doing here in southern Texas?"

"The ship we sailed on was damaged in a storm just off the coast of Mexico. We had to dock for repairs that would have taken weeks. Pricilla and I decided to catch this stage out of Brownsville and see if we couldn't make our way to Galveston and board a different ship to take us home."

"I'm headed for Galveston as well," Roger replied. "However, I've been advised to book passage on a shuttle ship out of Corpus Christi rather than travel by stage. It's safer that way."

"And probably a whole lot more accommodating than this rolling cloud of dust," Margaret said, waving her hand past the open window of the stage. "I don't suppose you'd consider letting us tag along."

"It's not for me to say, mam," Roger answered. "I have to find a captain willing to sail up to Galveston and I'd be delighted if you…"

Just then a shotgun blast interrupted Roger's offer and the thud of an arrow hit the back of the stagecoach.

"You ladies get on the floor, quickly," Roger ordered.

Frightened by the sudden outburst of gunfire and shouts coming from outside the coach, the women complied. Roger reached over them to pull down the Colt rifle and a box of shells from an inside compartment. When he sat back, an arrow whistled through the window and hit the opposite interior wall of the passenger cabin, just missing him.

Another shotgun blast sounded as Roger placed a shell in the chamber. He stuck the barrel of the gun out the window and fired. A warrior went sailing over his horse as the animal crumpled to the ground. He reloaded and put another warrior on foot. Following another shotgun retort, the attack was over.

The stagecoach continued rolling at high speed for another mile before the driver slowed his team to a halt. The man known as Dutch jumped down while the drive set the brake and leaped from his perch at the front of the coach.

"Are you folks okay?" the driver shouted, as Dutch opened the opposite side of the carriage and looked in.

"I think you ladies can get back in your seat now," Dutch said, as Roger reached down to help up the two women. "Thanks for your help, parson," Dutch added.

"Glad I could help," Roger said, as the driver inspected the inside of the cabin.

"Sorry about that, folks," the driver said. "I think we'll be okay now. Just the same, I'm going to make a little better time than before just to be safe. The ride may be a little rougher, but I want to make sure you folks reach King Ranchero in one piece."

"If I end up in pieces I'm going to want my fare back," Margaret grumbled, dusting herself off. The driver and Dutch ignored the remark and climbed back onto their seat and set the team into a trot.

"If you were about to tell us it would be fine with you if we sailed to Galveston instead of traveling this way, we accept," Margaret said.

"Did you really shoot those Indians?" Pricilla asked.

"No, mam," Roger said. "I just saw to it they'd have to chase us on foot if they wanted to keep up the attack."

"You shot the horses?" the daughter exclaimed.

"I assure you, they were clean shots. No animal suffered," Roger responded.

"Never you mind, girl," Margaret said, smiling at Roger. "We're alive and that's what matters."

Although the ride into King Ranchero was every bit as uncomfortable as the driver warned, everyone on the stagecoach was grateful to reach their destination alive and in one piece.

Chapter 22
The End in Sight

"I s Ron in?" Nik Brinkman inquired, pushing open the door to the Customs Office.

"Sorry, Marshal," said an agent scanning currency bills with a magnifying glass. "He had to go to Houston to meet with some federal agents there."

"Has there been a break in the counterfeiting case or the two murders associated with it?" Nik asked, knowing what the answer would be.

"Not that I've heard of, Marshal. I'm sure Agent Lester will inform you if anything positive comes our way," the agent replied. "Shall I tell him you were here?"

"It's not necessary. I'm just trying to keep an open mind with this thing. Trail's been dead and I also have to go to Houston, but on a different matter," Nik answered.

Nik left the Customs Office and headed back to his own. Upon arriving, he found Ambrose going through some paperwork.

"I just got orders from Judge Conklin that the shipment will be arriving in Houston any day now," Nik said. "I've picked up our train tickets and we are expected to be in Houston this afternoon. No need to pack much. I don't imagine we'll be there long."

"What about weapons?" Ambrose asked. "What should we take with us?"

"A pistol and rifle, as far as I know," Nik said. "Most of the arrangements are being made in Houston. If we need to pack more artillery I assume they will supply us with it. We'll go over our roles again on the train."

The two men boarded the train for Houston about 11 a.m., informing the conductor as to the nature of their business. The conductor placed them in a car where there were only two other passengers, whom the conductor suggested they move to a different car.

"I don't know when the shipment will arrive in Houston or exactly when they will move it on to Galveston," Nik began, speaking across the aisle as the two sat in opposite seats across from one another. Ambrose's size was enough to fill an entire seat.

"I'm told there's a hotel where we can wait until that shipment arrives. We'll then be briefed on our assignments, although I'm pretty sure what they are," Nik said. "You'll remain on the train and I'll be stationed on the barge with the shipment. This has been kept hush-hush, so I don't expect any attempted robberies."

"What would anyone want with all that silver?" Ambrose asked. "To my recollection, it isn't worth nearly as much as gold."

"It's the currency thing, Ambrose. There is word that Congress is going to raise the price of silver up to that of gold. The Farmers Union is demanding they do it so it can be added to the money supply. It ties in somewhat with this counterfeiting case we've been dealing with."

"So, Congress can do that?"

"It appears so. It seems they're always doing something they shouldn't. Printing too much money is what has gotten us into the mess we're in now," Nik concluded.

After reaching Houston, the two marshals inquired as to transportation in and around the city. They were told Houston's new municipal trolley system was the best way to travel.

"Best way to get to the sheriff's office is to take the trolley," the clerk at the railroad ticket office said, stamping the marshals' tickets. "Just tell the driver where you want to go and he'll announce when you've reached your destination."

After a short wait on the depot deck, a trolley pulled up and both lawmen got on board. Nik informed the driver they wanted to be dropped off at the sheriff's office.

"That would be on Baker Street," the driver responded. "It's near my third-stop station. Just walk east on Baker Street and you'll see the sheriff's office."

Nik and Ambrose sat silently observing the busy city as they rode along. After reaching their destination, they disembarked and started down Baker Street until they reached the building marked "Houston Sheriff Office." They entered and were greeted by a clerk sitting behind a desk near the front door.

"Can I help you folks?" the clerk said, looking up.

"We're with the U.S. Marshals Service out of Galveston," Nik said, approaching the man. "We're here on assignment and were told to report to the sheriff's office."

"Have a seat if you will," the clerk said. "I will let the sheriff know you are here." The clerk walked to the back of the outer office where three men sat behind their desks either conversing with one another or studying wanted posters. He turned and entered the office marked "Sheriff" and disappeared behind a closed door.

"Sheriff Ellsworth, there are two marshals here from Galveston," the clerk said to a man of average build and sporting a handlebar mustache. He wore a leather vest that his badge was attached to. His hair was thinning on the top, while the hair on the crown of his head hung down almost to his shoulders. "But I must tell you, they are not white and one's as big as a house."

The sheriff looked at the clerk for a moment before speaking, "I've heard of them," he said, shaking his head. "Send them in."

After returning to the front office, the clerk told the two marshals to proceed to the door marked "Sheriff." They walked past the stares of the three men identified as deputies by the stars on their shirts. Nik and Ambrose entered the sheriff's office.

"What can I do for you folks?" the sheriff said, without looking up.

"We've been asked to help protect the silver shipment that is supposed to arrive here any day now," Nik said, leaving his hat on, while Ambrose removed his. "We were told to report to this office for further instructions."

The sheriff looked up and leaned back in his chair. "I believe you are a little early," he said. "Our latest information tells us the shipment will be here tomorrow. I have called a meeting of all law officers involved to meet here in the morning. I take it you did not get that information."

"No, we did not," Nik said. "However, we can wait until morning if you would be so kind as to direct us to the nearest hotel. What time do you plan to hold this meeting?"

"I figure most will show up after breakfast. First train isn't due until around noon. I 'spect the shipment will be on board that one," the sheriff said, leaning forward. "The Carriage Inn at the edge of town will take you, I believe. Did you arrive on horseback or take the train?"

"We took the train," Nik answered.

"Then the trolley is your best bet to get to the inn. It stops near the west end of Baker Street."

"We're familiar with the trolley," Nik said, using the same condescending tone as the sheriff. "We know where it stops. Unless you have anything else to say, we'll be on our way."

"Nothing," the sheriff deadpanned.

"Ambrose, put your hat on your head. It's a little chilly in here," Nik said, smiling at his deputy. He then turned and started for the door as Ambrose followed.

They again strode past the three deputies. Just as the two marshals reached the exit, one of the sheriff deputies called out.

"What kind of law do they have in Galveston, anyway?" The other two chuckled.

"From what I can tell, one considerably better than what you have here," Nik answered. "Good day, gentlemen." With that, Nik swung the door open as he and Ambrose departed.

"Not the friendliest, I'd say," Ambrose remarked, as the two walked along.

"Typical southern types," Nik responded. "Texas fought with the Rebs, like you did at first. We can be happy we marshal in Galveston."

After reaching the station where the trolley stopped, Nik glanced over the schedule posted on the back of the bench set up for waiting passengers.

"It looks like we've got a while before the trolley we need shows up," Nik said. "Want to take a look around?"

"Sure," Ambrose remarked, "It may not be the friendliest town but it is fascinating."

With light luggage in their hands, they strolled the main streets of Houston. It was a western town like most in Texas but was growing rapidly. They reached a section of the city where most of the residents they saw were black. While there, they decided to visit a small eatery from where the aroma of a barbecue was emanating.

"What do you say we grab something to eat?" Nik suggested. "My guess is the folks here are friendlier."

"Oh, sounds terrific, boss, I'm powerful hungry."

The two took a seat in the back of the small cookhouse and sat down. A young lad approached and explained to the two men what was available on the limited menu.

"We have ribs, rice, and greens," the young man said. "We also have cold tea if you have a mind for that. We don't serve beer."

"Three plates for us," Nik said, smiling at Ambrose. "I'd like to try that cold tea, how about you, Ambrose?" Ambrose nodded in the affirmative.

"Three plates, sir?" the young waiter asked.

"Two for my friend," Nik said, smiling at the young man. "If you're generous with your meals, we won't need a fourth," Nik added with a laugh.

While the two men were eating, the chef came out to greet them.

"How do you like the barbecue?" the proprietor asked. "I have not seen you before, are you new in town?"

"We are new and if you keep serving meals like this we may grow old here," Nik said, rising to his feet to shake the man's hand.

"Name's Rudy, Rudy Leathers," the man continued. "I see you are lawmen. Is there trouble brewing?"

"We hope not," Nik said, while Ambrose continued eating. "We're here mainly for a visit, perhaps a day or two."

"Where you staying?" Rudy asked.

"The Carriage Inn was recommended to us," Nik answered. "We were told they take our 'kind.'"

"Nonsense," Rudy said. "They'll put you in the basement on a dirt floor. Stay here in Freedmen's Town at the Cotton Gin, it's just down the street from here and the accommodations are fine – just fine."

"My name's Nik Brinkman. This is my deputy, Ambrose Tucker," Nik said. "Thanks for the advice. I think we'll take you up on that … Cotton Gin, I believe you said. Is that a hotel?"

"Mostly a large house, but they got plenty of rooms and hospitality galore," Rudy said, nodding and smiling. "Now, you'd best be getting back to your meal before those ribs get cold and the tea warms up."

After they finished dining, Nik and Ambrose checked out the Cotton Gin and made up their minds to stay. They left their small carry bags in their room and continued touring Houston. After leaving the section in which they were staying, Ambrose spoke up.

"Isn't that Agent Lester up yonder?" Ambrose said, looking ahead and across the street.

"I think it is," Nik said. "I remember one of his agents told me he was in Houston for a meeting or something. I thought maybe it was the same one we are supposed to attend tomorrow."

"Maybe he's here for something else," Ambrose said. "He just went into that building over there." The two men crossed the street and tried the door to the building the man appearing to be Ron Lester went into, but it was locked.

"That's funny," Nik said. "There's still plenty of daylight left. I wonder why the place is locked. We just saw whoever it was go in."

"I can't tell what's inside," Ambrose said, squinting to peer through the building's only window. "I don't see anyone. It looks like there's another door in the back of the front office. That may be where Agent Lester went."

"Let's go around back and see if there's another entrance," Nik suggested.

The alley that ran alongside the building went quite a ways before coming to the back, piquing Nik's curiosity. Once they reached the rear of the structure, they saw two huge double doors, big enough to drive a buckboard wagon through. Unfortunately for the two marshals, the doors were sealed with a padlock and chain. Nik pounded on the doors, but no answer.

"Ron, are you in there?" Nik called out. The two lawmen stood silent for a moment but heard no sound coming from inside. "I don't know. Maybe there's an upstairs and he can't hear us."

"How bad do you need to catch up to him?" Ambrose asked.

"It's not real important, I just wanted to ask if Washington had taken any action concerning Foster Letterman's death, but it can wait.

"Let's head back to… what did Rudy call it… Freedmen's Town? It seems a lot friendlier than the rest of Houston."

"I'm with you," Ambrose said, as the two went back to the street side of the building and turned back toward Freedmen's Town.

✶✶✶

Roger had rented a carriage large enough to transport himself and the two women he'd met on the stagecoach to Corpus Christi.

"Why are you going to Galveston, Pastor? Are you going to start a church there?" Margaret asked.

"No, mam. I'm keeping a promise I made to my brother, who is the chief U.S. Marshal in Galveston," Roger said, looking over at the woman in the seat next to him.

"And what promise was that?" Pricilla asked from her seat in the back of the buggy.

"He made me promise when I finished school and became an ordained minister I'd come back and baptize him," Roger explained, turning his eyes back on the road.

"Were you baptized when you got to school?" Margaret asked.

"No, mam. I was baptized by my father when I was a boy. My Pa was the pastor in the town where I grew up."

"Why didn't your father baptize your brother as well?" Pricilla inquired.

"My brother didn't come along until later and my parents were murdered before Pa got around to it," Roger said, turning to Margaret and glancing back at Pricilla.

"Oh, my, that's terrible," Pricilla said, raising her hands to her face.

"It was a while ago," Roger said, looking ahead again. "The man who did it was brought to justice though."

"That must have given you some comfort," Margaret said.

"Not as much as I thought," Roger replied, as his shootout with Colonel Curtain flashed through his mind. "It didn't bring the peace I thought it would. I'm still searching for that."

"You poor man," Pricilla said. "That has to be a terrible burden for a man of your principles."

"I do find myself calling on the Lord quite often for help," Roger said, letting out a sigh.

"Hush, now, Pricilla. Let the man tend to his driving," Margaret said, turning from glancing at Pricilla to look straight ahead.

After reaching Corpus Christi, Roger pulled the carriage up to a tavern that overlooked the bay. After halting the horses, he excused himself to go inside and inquire about booking passage on a sailing vessel.

"You're going in there to ask?" Margaret said.

"That's where the sailors hang out, mam," Roger said, tipping his hat and smiling, while continuing on his way.

"And call me Margaret, for Heaven's sake," the woman called out. "Mam's too formal. Never did like being called that."

After entering the tavern, Roger inquired about transportation to Galveston at the bar. The bartender pointed to a man sitting at a table by himself with a mug of beer in front of him. As Roger approached, he could see the gentleman was dressed as one would imagine a sea captain to be. He wore a captain's hat, a dark-blue wool jacket and trousers to match, with black boots protruding at the bottom.

"Sir," Roger said, when he reached his table. The man looked up slowly and with interest in Roger's dress. "I'm looking for passage to Galveston for three passengers."

"Galveston, why Galveston?" the man said in a gravelly voice. "Corpus Christi is a nicer town for a preacher, if that's what you are. Not so many folks here and more peaceful, except for a bar fight now and then, when visiting sailors have had too much to drink."

"Sage advice, sir, but I have good reason to want to go to Galveston, as do my companions," Roger said.

"Three passengers, you say," the man replied, waving his hand for Roger to sit across from him and then drawing it back to his chin. "I charge twenty dollars a head. Bring your own food. It will take two to three days."

"I believe we can swing that. What is your ship like?"

"Sweetest sloop on these waters," the captain began. "It'll accommodate all three of you comfortably. Are your companions family?"

"Actually, no," Roger answered. "They're two women I met while traveling here. They're from California and want to reach Galveston and book passage to Philadelphia."

"So, they'll need separate quarters from you, I take it?" the captain said.

"That would be appropriate," Roger responded. "Can you accommodate that?"

"Sure, the Texas Belle, that's what I call her, is more than fit for that situation," the man continued. "The name's Samuel Rice, but you can call me Sam. The crew refers to me as skipper."

"It's a pleasure, Sam," Roger said, reaching across the table to shake the captain's hand. "When can we sail?"

"I'll need some time to put together my crew, but we should be able to sail by tomorrow afternoon," Sam said. "If the wind is with us we'll reach Galveston Bay about this same time two days from now."

A murmur rippled through the room causing Roger and Sam to look up. Margaret and Pricilla had entered and were looking about for Roger, and trying to ignore the sailors who were busy admiring them.

"Excuse me, Sam," Roger said standing up and starting toward the Wiggins ladies. "The women I've been traveling with just came in. I will fetch them over to meet you."

Sam stood up and waited for Roger to return with mother and daughter in tow.

"Captain Rice, I would like you to meet Mrs. Margaret Wiggins and her daughter, Pricilla."

"It is with great pleasure that I greet you, ladies. And please, call me Sam. Captain Rice is reserved for my crew," the skipper said with a slight bow. "Please allow me to get you both a chair."

After all were seated, Roger explained to Margaret and Pricilla what the captain had offered in accommodations.

"It sounds like a pleasure cruise after what we have been through," Margaret began. "We sailed on a fine ship out of San Francisco to Panama, where we had to cross by rail. It was dreadful hot and miserable, and the ship we boarded on the west coast of Panama was more of a wreck than a sailing vessel."

"Now, momma," Pricilla protested. "It wasn't that bad."

"It barely got us to Texas before it had to be dry docked for repairs," Margaret retorted, glancing over at Pricilla.

"I can assure you the Texas Belle is as you described," Sam cut in. "Like you say, a pleasure cruise. As I explained to Pastor Brinkman, passage is twenty dollars per passenger, food is up to you, and I can show you the best place to shop for it. It's only a two to three day trip but avoid food that quickly spoils.

"Would you ladies like something to drink?"

"I think we need to find a place to stay first, so it's best we be going," Roger said. "Where should we meet you tomorrow?"

"If you stay at the Fisherman's House on the bay, the best accommodations in Corpus Christi, you can walk from there to the harbor where the Texas Belle is located," Sam said. "Their rates are reasonable and the owners are friendly. Good food, too."

"We'll take you up on that," Roger replied.

As Roger and the two ladies were walking out, Margaret asked, "Do you not drink liquor, Pastor?"

"I do, but I'm too tired and need to get some rest," Roger replied. "I guess I forgot my manners and spoke for you in the tavern. I'll be happy to escort you back in. I'm sure Captain Rice would not mind the company."

"Nothing of the sort," Margaret responded. "We're as tired as you are. I was just curious as to your habits."

They boarded the carriage and soon found the Fisherman's House. It was a Victorian home converted into separate rooms for travelers. It was clean, comfortable and offered a pleasant view of the bay. It was owned by a widow name Isabelle Taper. Her husband did much of the reconstruction on the house and the two ran the place together until his passing about a year ago.

After signing in, Margaret and Pricilla were given a room with a double bed. Roger's room was smaller and contained a single-wide bed. Once inside, the preacher took off his jacket and set out to walk along the shore before the dinner bell rang.

He watched the seagulls search for food on the beach, then fly away as he approached. The rumble of the rolling breakers had a soothing effect, but being near the ocean was new to Roger. The atmosphere offered a rich mixture of smells different from anything he'd experienced. He tried to imagine what being on the sea would be like.

"There's nothing like the ocean to help you forget your troubles," said a voice from behind. Roger turned to see Pricilla. It surprised him to see her in an open-collar shirt and riding pants tucked into high-top brown leather boots. The bonnet she wore was gone and her hair gently flowed in the late-afternoon breeze.

"Pricilla, I'm sorry, I didn't know you had a mind for this sort of thing or I would have invited you."

"I wasn't going to bother you," Pricilla said. "I got the impression you like spending time alone, but I couldn't resist. It's such a pleasant evening."

"My solitary nature comes with the territory," Roger said. "I think too much, otherwise I enjoy company as much as the next man. Especially with someone as pleasant as this evening."

"Why, pastor, you make me blush with such talk," Pricilla said, smiling at the compliment. "I have to confess, I am somewhat of a loner too. I wasn't very sociable living in California. It was too rowdy and untamed for my liking."

"Then I highly recommend you don't try the New Mexico Territory," Roger said, laughing. "Though, I have to admit, I have a lot of good, down-home parishioners there."

"It must get quite lonely there," Pricilla said."Why did you choose New Mexico to start your ministry?"

"I spent some time in Oklahoma and Texas before I went back to St. Louis to finish up my Bible training," Roger replied. "I had a longing for the west after I was ordained, and the church wanted someone to spread the gospel there, so I accepted the mission."

"What did you do when you were out here before?" Pricilla asked.

"I was a U.S. Deputy Marshal, chasing bad guys and Indians," Roger said, turning his gaze out over the bay.

"From a lawman to a preacher man," Pricilla responded, "that's quite a transition, I'd say."

Roger stopped walking and looked back at her. "It's a rather long story how it all came about," he started. "I was pegged to be a preacher while I was still a boy, but things got messed up. Before I knew it, I had fought in the war, was drawn to marshaling, and finally got back to what I was meant to do in the first place."

"That's quite a journey, and yet you're still young," Pricilla said, looking into Roger's eyes.

"I reckon on the outside," Roger replied. "I'm a lot older on the inside."

Their conversation was interrupted by the ringing of the Fisherman House's dinner bell.

"Guess we'd best get back," Roger said, extending his arm to needlessly show the way back. The two then walked together up to the Fisherman's House.

The next morning, Roger and the Wiggins stopped at the mercantile store to buy provisions.

"If you're settin' out to sea, I recommend plenty of fruit, bread, and some crackers. You don't want things to upset your stomachs," said the proprietor.

"We're used to it," Margaret said. "Give us some of that beef jerky, as well."

It was the first time Roger had given thought to being on the ocean. He had heard about seasickness but it hadn't crossed his mind until now.

"How rough are these seas?" he asked.

"Depends on how far you're going," the clerk said.

"To Galveston," Roger responded, searching the man's expression.

"No problem there," the owner said. "Who you sailing with?"

"A Captain Samuel Rice," Margaret offered.

"Oh, you could not have done better. Rice is a sailing man. Former officer in the U.S. Navy, that man. Salt of the earth, and the sea for that matter," the clerk replied. "He fell in love with Corpus Christi and his ship, the Texas Belle, and settled here. That is one fine craft."

"So it should be a pretty calm trip?" Roger asked, seeking assurance.

"As far as Captain Rice and the Belle are concerned," was the response. "I can't speak for the ocean, though. You never know what's brewing out there."

"Do you have anything for seasickness?" Margaret asked. "Just in case."

"I have this here stomach elixir. I hear its real good," the proprietor offered, putting the bottle on the counter. "If you are all worried, I might suggest three bottles. And a little hard candy helps, too."

"The candy sounds good, but one bottle will do," Margaret replied. "It's a pretty short trip."

After gathering their groceries and luggage, the three made their way to the harbor. The Texas Belle was long and sleek and not hard to pick out from the other boats. Captain Rice was standing at the head of the gangplank and walked down to assist with the luggage.

"Welcome aboard. Are you folks ready? I've been told the weather should be full in our favor for this voyage," Rice said.

"I hope so," Roger mumbled.

Chapter 23
Sebastian and Silver Shipment

Nik and Ambrose were up early and had a Texas-style breakfast at Rudy Leathers', complete with leftover barbeque rib trimmings mixed in the scrambled eggs. Rudy added complementary hot cakes and coffee on the side. Ambrose, again, had them bring two plates.

Rudy came out to greet the two lawmen and chat a bit.

"You cook the evening meal and then you're back for breakfast?" Nik asked. "Doesn't that make for a long day, Rudy?"

"It's what I do, gentlemen," Rudy answered. "This place is me and has been ever since I opened it."

"Are you married?" Ambrose inquired.

"I am and the missus, she does all the shopping," Rudy answered. "She's the big reason folks like eating here at our place."

"So, do the two of you get any time to yourselves?" Nik chimed in.

"We will when we retire, sell this place, and do what other folks do – travel," Rudy answered.

"I wish you the best, but I hope you don't retire while I'm still able to visit Houston," Nik said, smiling.

"It will be a while yet, Marshal, it will be a while yet," Rudy answered.

After the meal and another cup of coffee, the two retraced their steps to the spot where they were dropped off by the trolley. As they approached the building where they'd seen Ron Lester, they noticed a wagon sitting in the street out front. They crossed the street hoping they would run into him.

When they were a short distance away, Lester came out of the building carrying two large sacks and threw them into the wagon. He then mounted the driver's seat and shook the reins to set his team of horses moving.

Seeing the wagon pull away, Nik called out to let Lester know they were behind him. Lester turned around as if in answer to Nik's voice but quickly turned back and urged his team into a gallop.

"What was that?" Nik said, astonished at what he had witnessed.

"I don't know," Ambrose said. "I kinda thought he saw us, but had no mind to stop."

"He did seem to be in kind of a hurry," Nik said. "Let's see if anyone's in the place now. We can ask them about what business Lester has with them there and where he was headed so fast."

Upon reaching the front of the building, with Lester's wagon well in the distance, Nik tried the door and found it was locked. He knocked, and after a brief wait, knocked again, but no answer.

"I don't know what to make of this," Nik said. "Let's check in back again."

After reaching the back of the building, they again found the back door chained and padlocked.

"Could I help you, Marshal?" Nik picked up on a slightly familiar voice coming from the shadows. A figure stepped forward into the sunlight and Nik's eyes widened.

"Sebastian? Sebastian Mason?" Nik said out loud.

"In person, my dear marshal," said the impeccably dressed man, also wearing a smile. "I guess I should not be surprised. I remember perceiving you as a man with a sharp mind. And who is this mammoth deputy with you?"

"Let me shake your hand, you sharpie," Nik said with a broad grin, while extending his hand. "This is my right-hand man, Ambrose Tucker," Nik added, turning to his deputy.

"Pleased, I'm sure," Ambrose said, removing his hat with one hand and extending the other to grasp that of Mason's.

"No, the pleasure is all mine," Sebastian replied. "In fact, I would say serendipitous. It is my good fortune to find you two here."

"It is more of a shock for us to see you here," Nik said. "Aren't you still stationed in Washington, D.C?"

"That I am, my dear marshal. However, I am on assignment, undercover for the Secret Service, if you will," Sebastian advised. "I can only assume you are in search of Agent Ron Lester?"

"We are. Do you know him?" Nik asked.

"Indeed I do," Sebastian answered. "We were employed together in the hallowed halls of our nation's capital. But it is keenly important that he not know I'm here."

"I'm a little confused, Sebastian, but my deputy and I have an important meeting to attend," Nik explained. "Can we meet up with you sometime later?"

"It would be to my great benefit to do so, Nik," Sebastian said. "Do I recall your name correctly?"

"Speaking of sharp minds, of course you recall my name correctly," Nik said. "Are you familiar with Freedmen's Town on the street out front?"

"Indeed I am," Sebastian said. "I have spent quite a bit of time there since my arrival here in Houston. Should we meet somewhere there?"

"We're staying at the Cotton Gin Hostel," Nik said. "We can meet you there."

"Consider it done, my friend and cohort," Sebastian said, extending his hand again. "I shall await your return."

After Nik and Ambrose were out of earshot, Ambrose asked, "Who was that?"

"Sebastian Mason is a treasury agent," Nik said, as they approached the trolley waiting area. "He helped us expose Judge Victor Kensington's land-fraud deals. He and my brother worked together to bring in two members of a gang in north Texas we were pursuing. One guy was about your size."

"So, is this Judge Kensington still at large?" Ambrose asked.

"He disappeared right after Roger and I broke the case open. The U.S. Army found a burned wagon we knew he was apparently trying to escape in, but there were no signs of a struggle or a body. We think the judge may be hiding out in Mexico."

"And you can't go after him in Mexico?" Ambrose continued.

"Not without permission from the Mexican Government," Nik replied, as the two lawmen reached the trolley waiting area. "We've alerted Mexico that he's wanted, but so far we've not heard anything back."

"Do you think that is why that treasury agent is here?"

"Good question, but I think we'd have been notified if Kensington had been found," Nik said. "It's possible his presence may have something to do with the counterfeiting case we've been working on."

The trolley arrived and soon Nik and Ambrose were headed to the sheriff's office. After disembarking from the trolley, the two men walked down Baker Street and entered the Harris County Sheriff's Office.

"They've been waiting for you," the clerk said. "You're quite late."

Nik and Ambrose went straight into Ellsworth's office. The sheriff was seated behind his desk, with Judge Conklin seated off to his right. About ten other men were either seated or standing around the room.

"Well, glad to see you could make it… finally," Ellsworth said. "We were about to break up the meeting."

"My apologies to you all," Nik said, maintaining his hat upon his head. "We got a break in another case and spent a little too much time following up on it."

"Another case?" Ellsworth interjected. "What case are you following up on in Houston, Marshal?

"Nothing that concerns you, Sheriff," Nik answered. "Ambrose and I ran into someone here who had information concerning a case we're dealing with in Galveston."

"And that's something more important than this silver shipment?" Ellsworth asked sarcastically.

"Let me break in here," Judge Conklin said. "I think we can cut this short.

"Nik, as you know we're diverting the shipment from the train to a boat, which I expect you to be on. Deputies Wyatt and Nelson will accompany you," the judge continued, waving a hand toward the two men.

Wyatt wore a ten-gallon hat over muttonchops that culminated into a bushy mustache under a crooked nose. His pants were tucked into his scuffed brown boots, and he said nothing in response to the introduction.

Nelson wore a seaman's hat and a worn pea coat. He appeared middle-aged with wool pants that did not quite reach his dull black shoes. Red and white striped socks covered his ankles.

"As you can tell, Al Nelson has experience sailing. Casey Wyatt is an expert marksman and served in the war with Senator Maxwell," Conklin continued. "We do not anticipate Wyatt's services will be needed, but just in case.

"These other men will be stationed at the train depot. Ted Vickers and Bart McIntyre will travel on the train with you and will remain on it with your deputy, Nik."

"Perfect, it doesn't sound like anything's changed from what we discussed earlier, Judge," Nik said. "When do you expect the shipment to arrive here in Houston?"

"We're expecting it by seven tomorrow evening," Ellsworth said. "That train has a good reputation of running on time, too."

"Which means we should have the cover of darkness when we unload the cargo to transport it to the bay," Conklin said. "The barge has already been positioned to receive the cargo. The captain of it is a longtime trusted citizen of Galveston and used to work on a Mississippi steamer. So he knows his way around boats."

"I think my deputy and I understand our duty, sir," Nik said. "You can count on us."

The remark brought a derisive smirk to Ellsworth's face, but he quickly looked away and got to his feet. "I think we can all go back to work. Marshal, did you two find the accommodations at the Houston Hotel to your liking?"

"As luck would have it, we found a place we liked better, Sheriff. If you need us, we're staying at the Cotton Gin in Freedmen's Town," Nik answered, smiling.

"Freedmen's Town, figures," Ellsworth mumbled.

"Excuse me," Nik said, "Did you say something, Sheriff?"

"Just that I hope you enjoy your stay at the Cotton Gin," the sheriff shot back.

"Well thank you, Sheriff," Nik responded, turning to the judge and touching the tip of his hat."Good to see you, Judge. Where are you staying?"

"Oh, I'm heading back to Galveston. I have business to tend to," the judge said. "We have that Jean Lafitte celebration starting tomorrow, pirate ship and all, should be fun."

The meeting broke up and the two marshals made their way back to Freedmen's Town.

After everyone cleared out of Ellsworth's office, the sheriff closed the door and walked back to his desk, but hesitated before sitting down. "You can come out now. The office is empty," Ellsworth spoke out quietly.

Emerging from a door located behind Ellsworth was Ron Lester. "I think that pesky marshal might be on to me," Lester said in a low voice.

"What fool thing have you done now?" Ellsworth asked.

"What I've been doing all along. I thought you sent that marshal and his deputy to the Houston Hotel. What's this about the Cotton Gin in Freedmen's Town?" Lester said in a heated voice under his breath.

"How did I know those two would stumble into Freedmen's Town? I directed him to the Houston Hotel. You should have been more careful," the sheriff said with similar conviction. while keeping his voice down. "You knew they were going to be in town."

"They may have seen me, but they do not know what's in the print shop or in the back room here," Lester said. "I can make some excuse as for me being in Houston but this could hamper our operations."

Sheriff Ellsworth thought for a minute and then said in a soft reassuring voice, "Don't forget, that marshal will be on the barge when it's hit. Those dark boys aren't good swimmers, you know."

Both men chuckled at the remark.

After getting off the trolley, Nik and Ambrose headed for the Cotton Gin to see if Mason had stopped by. To their good fortune, the treasury agent was there reading a newspaper in the lobby.

"Sebastian, I'm glad you're here," Nik said, approaching the agent.

Mason lowered the newspaper and said, "Is there somewhere we can go so we can speak in private?"

"Our room, it's small but cozy," Nik said. "It's not likely anyone will disturb us there."

"Excellent," Sebastian said, rising from his chair and tossing the newspaper on the lobby coffee table. He followed the two men down a short hall and into one of the rooms at the end of it.

"Make yourself at home," Nik offered, removing his hat. "Can I get you anything?"

"Just lend me your ear, Marshal," the agent replied, taking a seat in a corner of the room. "I have much to tell you and to discuss."

Nik pulled up a chair and Ambrose sat on the bed.

"You have been working with Customs Agent Ron Lester, is that correct?" Mason began, as Nik and Ambrose nodded in the affirmative. "Let me give you a little background on Agent Lester.

Sebastian went on to explain that, during the war, Lester had worked in the Treasury Department. Mason and Lester were acquainted but did not work in the same areas. Lester had artistic talent and worked in minting.

"When the legislation came down to mint greenbacks to finance the war, Lester was called on to help design the plates," Sebastian continued. "The authorization was for four-hundred and fifty million dollars in fives, tens and twenties – all redeemable once the national reserves returned to specie."

"I'm sorry, Mr. Mason but I don't think I know what that last thing you said means," Ambrose interjected.

"In this case, it means gold. These greenbacks were not backed by gold, only the faith and credit of the federal government," Sebastian answered. "We investigating agents knew that could lead to trouble... and it did."

"Leading to the counterfeiting we have going on here?" Nik chimed in.

"Precisely," the treasury agent said.

Mason continued, telling the lawmen that after the authorized amount was reached, congress was divided over stopping the process. There was a group representing agriculture who wanted the government to continue printing the bills. In fact, they created their own political party called the Greenback Party to keep the money flowing.

"Congress wanted to return to the reserve note but the currency battle continued. It was about that time the new Customs Department was started and Lester transferred to it," Mason said. "It was also when they created the Secret Service, to which I am now affiliated."

"Was that unusual?" Nik asked.

"Not at all, but when the counterfeit greenbacks began showing up here in Texas, the Secret Service was notified to investigate," Mason said. "That was when we learned that Lester had been transferred to Galveston."

"So why have you not been to Galveston?" Nik asked.

"We have been," Sebastian replied. "My fellow agent, who I believe you knew as Foster Letterman, was acting undercover as a customs agent. When he turned up dead floating in your bay I was dispatched here to find out why."

"So, what role does Lester have in this?" Ambrose inquired.

"Very astute question, deputy," the agent went on. "Putting two and two together, we now believe Lester used his knowledge of greenbacks' design to set up this counterfeit operation you have going on here."

Nik and Ambrose looked at each other in almost disbelief.

"So our seeing him here in Houston was no coincidence?" Nik said. "This kind of blows our fish story apart."

"Fish story?" Sebastian asked.

"It's a long story," Nik said. "Please go on with yours."

"To make my long story short, I believe Lester is printing counterfeit greenbacks in that very building where we met this morning," Sebastian answered.

"So, why don't we just bust in there and find out?" Ambrose exclaimed.

"Not prudent, my dear deputy," Sebastian said. "We do not have proof that Lester is behind this just yet, and we have a murdered agent to account for as well. We also believe he has accomplices to help distribute those greenbacks. If we move too fast our entire investigation could be compromised."

"This really turns things upside down," Nik said. "And Ambrose and I have a silver shipment to deal with tomorrow."

"I've heard about that," Sebastian said. "That could turn out to be a very valuable cargo."

"How so?" Ambrose said.

"These same greenback advocates want congress to price silver equal to gold and mint coins with silver," Sebastian answered.

"So, where do we go from here?" Nik quizzed.

"We need to come up with a plan to trap Lester into a confession and that won't be easy," Sebastian said. "That's why I haven't allowed myself to be discovered."

After a discussion that lasted well into the evening, the three men reached a tentative plan on how to proceed. They would put the plan into action after the silver shipment was safe in the First Bank of Galveston. Sebastian bid the marshals goodnight, and left the Cotton Gin Hostel.

The following day, Nik and Ambrose revisited the Houston Sheriff's Office to see if there was anything new concerning the silver shipment. They were told it was on time and should arrive at the depot by seven that evening. Those assigned to guard the shipment were advised to board the train separately so as to not raise suspicion.

Nik and Ambrose spent the rest of the day riding the trolley and learning as much about Houston as they could. They disembarked near Freedmen's Town and had lunch at Leathers' diner. They avoided the building where Lester had been seen the previous day.

By late afternoon, they were back on the trolley headed for the Houston Train Depot. They kept an eye out to avoid any lawmen they might recognize as being part of the silver-shipment task force, so as not to arouse anyone's suspicions.

It was dark when the train carrying the silver arrived, giving the posse the cover needed for the final leg of the cargo's journey.

After leaving the depot, the train ran at a reduced speed so the stop to unload the two chests would be less noticeable. After steaming to a slow stop near Clear Creek, Nik and Ambrose parted company as the marshal climbed aboard the wagon used to transport the shipment to the vessel docked at Clear Lake.

"See you in Galveston," Nik said in departing.

Casey Wyatt was in the wagon, sitting on one of the chests of silver as Nik climbed onto the seat next to the driver. Nik recognized the driver as one of the men in Ellsworth's office during the briefing the day before. The man said nothing, only snapped the reins as the team started the wagon rolling.

"Wasn't there another man assigned to this shipment?" Nik said, turning in Wyatt's direction.

"He's at the boat, along with the pilot," Wyatt said.

"Just be ready if anyone tries to stop this wagon," the driver said.

"I had assumed this detour from the train was to avoid that?" Nik said.

"Ya' never know, never know," the driver grumbled.

After a quiet and uneventful trip, the wagon turned off the road toward a small light in the distance. As they drew near, Nik could see the light was coming from a campfire with two men standing beside it. One was Al Nelson, the sailor introduced at the meeting. Nik would soon learn the other was the barge skipper, Captain Clifford Kruger.

What caught Nik's eye, even in the dim light of the campfire, where two large, rolled-up objects on the ground behind the two men.

After introductions, Nik asked, "What are those?" Nik tipped his head in the direction of the two rolled-up objects

"Something ingenious, Marshal," Nelson said. "Those are the balloons we are to attach to each chest of silver."

"This is new to me," Nik said. "Why two balloons?"

"Precaution, Marshal Brinkman," Kruger instructed. "We are a seafaring vessel and subject to sinking. Should that happen, these balloons will mark the spot where the chests of silver are located."

"But don't they have to be filled with air in order to keep them afloat?" Nik said incredulously.

"We use the heat from the steam engine that is onboard to inflate them, which we will do just before we reach the train trestle," Nelson said. "That is where we think the most danger lies concerning this seaward transport."

The barge was a sixty-foot sailing vessel that had a half-enclosed area near the rear of the boat containing a small steam engine that powered a paddlewheel. It was used mainly to get the barge into open waters where it would convert to sails.

After loading the two chests onto the craft, Nelson secured the two rolled-up balloons to the chests using two ropes coiled up in the bottom of the boat.

"How high do you expect those balloons to go?" Nik asked, judging the length of the two ropes.

"It's just a precaution since we do not know how deep the waters will be if we do lose our cargo," Nelson said, as he moved into the sheltered area of the boat containing the steam engine. "We will belay the ropes to the sides of the ship to keep them from releasing too soon."

"How will that not be conspicuous?" Nik inquired.

"They will be, but there is a celebration going on at this time and we will likely look like part of it," Nelson answered as he started the engine and the paddlewheel began to churn.

"By the way, would those things keep this boat afloat?" Nik said, trying to add humor to his enthusiasm for the idea.

"Depends on the damage, Marshal," Kruger answered.

Soon, the ship was in open water heading for Galveston Bay.

Nik fought to keep his mind off the ocean voyage he made as a slave. He was pleasantly surprised that he didn't feel the seasickness he suffered during his trip from New Orleans to Galveston. He was anxious to get this shipment into the bank and concentrate on the plan he, Ambrose, and Sebastian had devised to solve the counterfeiting case. He was hoping it would also bring closure to the deaths of Deputy Lenny Alexander and Agent Foster Letterman.

Nestled in a corner of the bow with his rifle across his lap, the rhythmic splash of the paddlewheel soon had him dozing off.

Chapter 24
Pirates and Balloons

The air was brisk, a sharp contrast from that inside a dusty stagecoach. Roger Brinkman sat almost motionless, moved only by the perpetual rocking of the Texas Belle. The travelling clergyman found he felt just fine, as long as he didn't move himself.

"You'll get your sea legs in time," Pricilla said, hanging onto a strand of the rigging as she smiled down at Roger. "The more you sail the more natural it becomes."

Roger took a deep breath and let it out slowly. "I'll let you know when I have those legs you mentioned," Roger said without looking up at the woman. His eyes were fixed on the mast that bobbed with the ship, but otherwise didn't move.

"Mother and I were miserable when we first set sail for California. On our last trip, we were comfortable enough to bypass the train trip through Panama and continue by ship. We weren't properly warned about Cape Horn, though," Pricilla said, recalling their trip around the southern tip of South America. "After that experience, the thought of a train ride through Panama didn't seem so bad."

"Pretty rough, was it?" Roger asked rhetorically.

"It was dreadful and cold," Pricilla continued. "We were not at all sure our ship was going to make it. We had reason to believe the captain had doubts as well, although he didn't say it.

"After that trip, one like this is like a gentle ride in a canoe."

"I wish I was in a canoe right now," Roger muttered.

"Oh, you'll be all righ..." Pricilla began.

"Anybody interested in eating before bedding down for the night?" Captain Rice called out as he approached the pair. "I don't know what you brought with you, but we have some fresh scallops and oysters in the galley, if you'd like."

With that, Roger leaned over the side of the sloop and relieved the nausea he had been holding back.

That evening, while most were below preparing for bed, Roger remained at his post resting against the side of the ship. He was feeling better, but did not have much of an appetite. He looked back at the pilot who had just begun his four-hour shift behind the wheel. Roger was grateful that the pilot didn't talk much.

When he turned to watch the horizon gently rise and fall, he was greeted by a large orange moon just beginning to rise. There was something about the moon that always fascinated him, even as a boy growing up in Bordertown, Missouri.

"It is beautiful, isn't it?" said a familiar voice from behind. "It looks somehow larger coming up over the ocean than it does rising above land."

Roger turned slightly, aware that Pricilla had come on deck to observe the astral show.

"Maybe it's the reflection off the water," Roger mused out loud. "I've never seen it like this before."

"How are you feeling," Pricilla asked, "any better?"

"I think maybe I've gained one of those sea legs you mentioned," Roger answered. "I'm working on establishing the other one now."

"What are your plans for the future," Pricilla said. "Do you plan to continue as an itinerant clergyman?"

"For the foreseeable future, yes," Roger said. "If the time comes when I no longer feel the need to spread the gospel in this amazing country, perhaps I will start a church somewhere and settle down."

"Do you think you'll ever marry?" Pricilla prodded.

"There was certainly a time when that was the plan," Roger said, dropping his right arm over the side of the sloop to feel the cool spray coming off the water. "But being on the go so much, I haven't given it much thought. It's not often I meet anyone willing to put up with these untamed parts of America.

"How about you, is there someone in Philadelphia waiting for you?"

"Perhaps, but I'm not anxious about it," Pricilla said, turning her head to gaze at the moon and feel its glow on her face.

"Not your type?" Roger asked.

"He's a lawyer and someone my mother introduced me to," Pricilla said, letting go of the rigging and seating herself on the raised deck covering the galley. "At first, mother thought he would be a good catch, being a lawyer and all, but the more we got to know him the less desirable he became."

"Was there a problem?" Roger inquired.

"His first love was himself. Oh, we got along well enough, but I never felt I meant that much to him," Pricilla said, shaking her head. "Mother could see it too. That's when she insisted I come to California with her and father."

"Your mother mentioned your father went out to California to search for gold, is that right?" Roger asked.

"No, not originally," Pricilla answered. "He was invited to San Francisco to join a law firm, but it proved too risky. Father also had to give up a lucrative law practice in Philadelphia to go. So, mother and I suspected he was drawn by the gold rush, and not practicing law.

"It did not take long before the lawlessness of the west turned his thoughts to prospecting. After the war, he went at it full time. He was away so much that mother and I decided to return to Philadelphia."

"Will you see him again?" Roger said.

"I'm sure we will. When he tires of his desire to strike it rich in gold," Pricilla lamented. "He loves us, but he has to get that gold fever out of his system.

"That passion has infected many a man," Roger replied.

"Yes, and sleep is beginning to infect me, Pastor. I think I shall turn in," Pricilla said.

"By the way," Pricilla, you can call me Roger. You won't violate my calling by doing so."

Pricilla laughed. "Goodnight, Roger."

Roger woke up the next morning with a hearty appetite and two legs that felt as if they had grown accustomed to the sea. He went on deck and was greeted by a stiff, cool breeze. He spotted Sam, who was at the wheel.

"Good morning, Pastor Brinkman," Sam greeted. "You slept well, I hope."

"Surprisingly well," Roger responded. "I even have an appetite, but not for those things you mentioned last night."

Sam laughed. "No, the galley mate has made up some tasty cornbread. I recommend that."

"That sounds good," Roger commented. "The wind seems more brisk today, or is it just my imagination?"

"Brisk enough to sail us into Galveston Bay," Sam said. "It picked up last night and we have made excellent time. If it continues, we could reach the bay by noon."

The ocean was also reacting to the change in weather, throwing spray above the taffrail. However, Roger felt surprisingly comfortable, with a touch of anxiety realizing he would soon be reunited with his brother.

✱✱✱

The barge carrying the silver had departed the inland waters and was now well into Galveston Bay. The transport vessel was making good time and Nik could see the train trestle up ahead.

Nelson emerged from the pilot house and made his way into the engine shelter. He began loading wood and soon had a blaze going.

"Do we need that now?" Nik called out to him. "We're making good time under sail."

"Yep, captain and I agreed that we might need it to pass under the trestle," Nelson shouted back.

"I'm sure we would fit under the trestle. I've seen taller masts than this pass through," Nik said.

"Winds can change in that underpass and this barge is small," Nelson shot back. "We have to lower the sail to prevent that and switch to paddle power."

"Well, I guess you guys know what you're doing," Nik said, partly under his breath. "I certainly don't."

As soon as the barge passed under the trestle, the captain began scanning the bay through binoculars. After his surveillance, he turned and nodded at Nelson, who began blowing up the balloons attached to the chests of silver.

"Hey, marshal, Wyatt, lash the ropes to those cleats on each gunwale," Nelson shouted, as he began filling one of the balloons with heat from the fire. He looked up to see Nik and Casey standing still with confused looks on their faces.

"The rope," Nelson called out, "tie it around those double-pronged hooks on the rail of the ship."

With a clearer understanding of Nelson's request, Nik and Wyatt each grabbed separate ropes and began winding them around the cleats.

"Pull the rope tight," Nelson said. "We don't want these balloons getting away, not yet anyway."

"Do we really need those balloons," Nik called back. "Won't that make us conspicuous?"

"Look yonder," Nelson said, tipping his head toward the west end of the bay. "Not any more conspicuous than that."

Nik peered into the distance and saw a small dot in the sky that seemed to be moving toward them.

"What is that?" Nik again shouted.

"It's an aerial balloon," Nelson said, as he tied a length of rope the two balloon ropes. "It's probably part of this celebration to Jean Lafitte. You see them over in Europe a lot."

"Why are you tying those two ropes together?" Nik quizzed Nelson.

"If anything should happen, we want these balloons to stay together. We don't want one going one direction and the other in another direction," Nelson said.

Nelson began inflating the two balloons with hot air, as the distant aerial balloon was slowly coming into view. Nik could now make out the bright red color of the airborne object decorated with flags and other ornaments.

"I've never seen one of those before. Have you, Casey?" Nik asked.

"Can't say as I have, Marshal, looks kind of pretty up there, though," Wyatt answered. "But look over toward the harbor. I'll bet that's the pirate ship that's supposed to be sailing around the bay that afternoon."

"There was more to this celebration than I imagined," Nik said, turning to see the "pirate ship" sailing in the opposite direction of the balloon's trajectory. "I just hope everybody knows where they are going."

✶✶✶

"We're entering Galveston Bay," Captain Rice shouted to his passengers, now on the deck. "If you look off to our right you can see a United States Navy ship."

"Why is the navy here?" Margaret asked.

"I'm not sure about that, Mrs. Wiggins," Rice answered. "But they do have a presence here in Galveston. They were responsible for running the pirates off the island."

"There were pirates on the island?" Margaret interjected.

"That was some time ago, mam. They've been long gone for some time now," Rice said.

As they sailed forward into the bay, Roger spotted another large ship headed in their direction.

"Is that navy, too?" Roger called out to the captain.

"No, I'd say that's some sort of show boat of some kind," Rice said, picking up a nearby set of field glasses. "Ha, it appears to have a Jolly Roger on its mainsail. I'm guessing they're celebrating the famous pirate Jean Lafitte who used to reside on the island. He's still quite a popular figure among the Galveston folks."

"I wonder what Nik thinks of all this," Roger said rhetorically.

"How's that?" Rice called out.

"Oh, nothing really," Roger said. "It's just that my brother is the marshal of this territory and his office is located in Galveston."

"You don't say," Rice said, laughing. "One brother a lawman and the other a man of the cloth, I guess you both represent the law in one form or another, right?"

"I'll bet you'll be glad to see him, won't you, Roger?" Pricilla said, as she moved beside the pastor.

"It has been a while," Roger said. "I'm almost as nervous as I am excited."

"Why is that?"

"A lot has happened since he and I have seen each other," Roger commented. "But I know there's still a lot of love and respect between us."

"Nothing bad happened, I hope?" Pricilla inquired. "Not really, it's just that things out here in the West can happen in a relatively short period of time," Roger said. "There's nothing bad that's gone on between my brother and me, though."

✳✳✳

On board the pirate ship, Captain Cutlass Baudelaire was slyly smiling as he spotted the barge with the two balloons flying in back.

"Do you see the barge, 'Jean Lafitte?'" Paco laughingly called out to the pirate captain. Paco was wearing a red scarf on his head and a red and white T-shirt. His trousers were cut off just below the knees and his buckled shoes were heeled with lifts.

"Aye, first mate," Baudelaire answered, laughing back. The 'pirate' was wearing a large plumed hat, red vest, and a long double-breasted coat with Maggie, his parrot, on his shoulder. Maggie stretched out her wings and added a squawk to the conversation. "I think we have the Tiburon square on target." Baudelaire added, smiling at his pet bird.

"Is everything ready?"

"I see the balloon approaching," Paco called out, as he peered at the airborne object through a telescopic lens. "The crew is at their posts ready to receive the booty!"

✱✱✱

"Captain, do you see the pirate ship headed this way?" Nik called out to the pilot at the wheel. "It looks as if she's coming right at us."

"They have seen our balloons and know to avoid us," the captain shouted back. "We are making good time now."

"I guess I'll have to take your word for it," Nik said, with a tone below what the captain could hear. "All this is a little too crazy for my liking."

"This was all worked out before you arrived at the meeting in Houston," Nelson shouted. "Sorry that you missed it, but your job was to guard the shipment, which you are doing."

Nik nodded his head at Nelson's remark but could not take his eyes off the approaching pirate ship.

Meanwhile, Roger was watching the proceedings and noticed that the boat with the two hot-air balloons on the back appeared to be on a collision course with the pirate ship.

"Captain Rice, does it not look like that boat with the balloons is getting kind of close to that pirate ship?" Roger said, turning back to look at the man at the wheel of the Texas Belle.

"I hope those two vessels have spotted each other," Rice answered. "That smaller craft looks as if it's determined to cross right in front of that larger ship. It's possible that boat with the balloons is a party boat, complete with liquor on board.

"I'll set a course to follow behind the barge just in case."

✱✱✱

"Captain, I'm not experienced enough to tell you how to pilot a boat, but I swear that pirate ship is headed right for us," Nik said, moving into the pilothouse.

The captain seemed almost oblivious to Nik's comment and kept silent as he steered his craft straight ahead. The ship off to the left was now only about two hundred meters away and closing fast. Nik ran to the port gunwale and began waving his arms at the closing pirate ship but got no answer from anyone on board.

Suddenly, the captain of the barge turned and ran out of the pilothouse.

"Abandon ship!" he called out, stripping off his coat. "Every man for himself."

Nik turned to see Nelson frantically unfastening the balloon ropes as the spheres quickly rose above the barge. He heard wood start to splinter as the pirate ship crashed into the starboard bow of the barge. Nik dropped his rifle and frantically ran toward the back of vessel, as the captain and Nelson dove into the water.

A quick glance in Wyatt's direction told Nik the deputized cowboy was virtually frozen with fear.

"Jump!" Nik screamed at the man, just as the barge tipped over and threw them both into the water.

✳✳✳

"Give her full sail, boys" Captain Rice called out to his crew. "We'll try to rescue the folks on that barge."

Margaret and Pricilla were watching in horror as the pirate ship sliced right through the barge, throwing its four passengers into the bay. The pirate ship began to slow as the large red balloon above them sailed over in the direction of the crippled craft.

The two balloons attached were now well into the air. The chests of silver were dangling below, as the large balloon approached. Roger watched as a man in the basket threw out a tethered grappling hook that went over the tether line. He and a second man began drawing the smaller balloons toward them.

"What are they doing?" Pricilla asked Roger.

"I really don't know," Roger replied. "Maybe it's part of the cele-bration show, but I would say something has gone terribly wrong."

***

"Drop those sails and lower the anchor for drag," Baudelaire commanded. "Two of you lower the lifeboat like we practiced and pick up the survivors. The rest of you prepare to take those chests of silver on board when the balloon sails over us."

However, the balloon with the smaller balloons in tow appeared to be sailing in a direction opposite to the pirate ship.

"It's not coming this way," Paco said. "It's headed in a different direction."

"It must be blown off course," Baudelaire answered. "We must chase it."

"But we're dragging anchor so we can save the survivors, Captain," Paco called out. "I will keep an eye on the balloon with the tele-scope and maybe we can see where it's headed."

"This is not good," Baudelaire said in a low voice.

"Awk, not good," Maggie cawed.

As the Texas Belle closed in on the sinking barge, Roger had grabbed the captain's field glasses and was scanning the water for those in the water. He suddenly stopped and shouted.

"That's my brother," he called out, peeling off his jacket and lean-ing up against the cabin to remove his boots. "He's struggling out there."

Rice turned his ship in Nik's direction and was closing in fast on the struggling swimmer. Roger dove into the water. He came up swimming and was soon close enough to assist Nik.

"Roger! What are you (gulp) doing here?" Nik gasped between breaths.

"Trying to rescue you," Roger answered, putting his arm around

Nik's chest and under his arms. "What's the matter with you? I taught you to swim better than this."

Nik coughed and spit out some water. "I can't seem to get my (cough) feet to work."

"Your feet?' Roger said, said, kicking his foot against Nik's to determine what the problem might be. "Nik, you've still got your boots on. Why don't you kick them off?"

"Are you (glub) kidding?" Nik replied. "Those things cost me fifteen (gargle) dollars. I'm not leaving them behind."

"For the love of…" Roger said, struggling to keep Nik afloat. "I'll buy you a new pair. Keep paddling while I remove them."

Roger dove down and pulled Nik's boots off as the lifeboat from the pirate ship approached. Roger tossed Nik's boots into the boat as the rescuers pull them onboard.

✶✶✶

"Captain, you're going right by Pastor Brinkman," Pricilla called out.

"I can't risk hitting them, and Roger seems to know what he's doing," Rice answered. "We'll try to rescue the others."

Using a lifeline, Rice's crew was able to pull the barge captain onto the Texas Belle. The captain then made a large circle to turn back toward the area where Roger and Nik were.

Meanwhile, the lifeboat off the Tiburon had pulled Nik, Roger, and Nelson out of the water and made its way back to the pirate ship.

"Bring them all onboard, and hurry!" Baudelaire shouted. "Raise those sails and haul up that anchor. We need to get out of here."

As the three men freshly fished from the water sat gathering their wits, Roger stood up to see where the Texas Belle was. He noticed that the pirate captain was bearing west and leaving behind the sloop he was on.

"Captain," he called out to Baudelaire, "Let that ship behind us catch up. My belongings are onboard that vessel."

Neither Baudelaire nor Paco looked in Roger's direction. They seemed determined to chase the balloon that was rapidly floating out of sight.

"Captain, where are you going in such a hurry?" Nik chimed in. "Take us back to the harbor and drop us off."

Nelson stepped back, as Nik and Roger approached Baudelaire.

"Captain, didn't you hear us?" Roger said in a voice he knew Baudelaire could hear.

"I am sorry, but you are onboard my ship and I have a mission to complete," Baudelaire said. "I am afraid you will just have to come along for the ride."

"I don't know where you intend to go in such a hurry, but I doubt you'll get far," Nik said, "I've got a hunch that Navy frigate dead ahead is going to want to talk to you."

Baudelaire took his eyes off the vanishing balloon and stared at the navy vessel pulling into the west end of Galveston Island. It was obviously sailing in the direction of the Tiburon.

"He's right, Captain," Paco said, now training his telescope on the frigate. "It is a U.S. Navy ship and it is coming our way."

Baudelaire's face dropped, as he watched the approaching warship.

"Wait a minute," Nik said, "Just what is going on here? Did you deliberately ram the boat we were on? And why are you dead set on chasing that balloon?"

Baudelaire took his eyes off the navy ship and turned to look at Nik. A melancholy expression came over his face.

"Just what role did you play in this pirate celebration?" Nik continued.

"Nik, do you think this ship deliberately ran you over?" Roger asked. "What was on that boat of yours, anyway?"

"Silver, Roger, nearly a million dollars worth of silver," Nik answered. "And now it's sailing away hanging from a balloon. A million dollars I was supposed to guard."

"Captain Black Beard, or whoever you are, were you aware that barge you ran over had that shipment of silver on it?" Roger asked, helping Nik piece together what had just happened.

"Paco, we've been had," Baudelaire said, turning to his companion. Paco's face drooped as he looked down and just shook his head.

"What do you mean you've been had?" Nik asked. "Look, I'm a U.S. Marshal and I think you'd better come clean as to what's going on here."

"Maybe we ought to throw these two back overboard," Nelson said from behind them. "No need for anyone to confess to anything."

"You too, Nelson?" Nik said, turning to face the seaman.

"They're just excess baggage, Captain," Nelson said. "As far as anyone else knows, this was all a big accident."

"I wouldn't be too sure about that," Roger began. "You're not going anywhere once that Navy frigate gets here. And that sloop following us, everybody onboard knows I'm on this vessel with my brother, a U.S. Marshal."

"I don't want to hang for this," Baudelaire lamented. "I didn't really mean any harm. We stopped to rescue the survivors, at least the three of you."

"You don't have to hang," Nik said. "If you've been had, then that means someone else put you up to this. My brother and I have been through this before and an honest man always stands a better chance than someone like Nelson here."

"You're not dragging me into this," Nelson said, making a quick turn and running to the side of the pirate ship and leaping back into the water.

"Do you want me to go after him, Nik?" Roger asked.

"No, I know who he is and I doubt he'll get far," Nik said. "But as for you, Captain, what's it going to be, a hanging or a confession?"

"I'll tell you what I know," Baudelaire said, as the Navy frigate pulled up alongside and informed the Tiburon it was about to be boarded. "This was not my idea or any of my crew.

"By the way, did you say this man is a U.S. Marshal and your brother? Baudelaire asked Roger. "Are you both marshals?"

"Nope," Nik said, "my brother, here, is a minister."

"But you are brothers?" Baudelaire again inquired.

"It's a long story... Captain," Roger answered.

"Don't bother," Baudelaire said, "I'm French, I understand completely."

The Brinkman brothers both laughed, bringing a weak smile to Baudelaire's face as well.

After the U.S. Navy took the Tiburon into custody, Nik explained to them the situation. Baudelaire and his crew were arrested and placed in a dinghy that transported them to the Navy vessel.

"Do you gentleman want to come on board with us or stay here?" the Navy lieutenant asked. "I'm leaving a crew to sail this ship back into the Galveston port."

Nik and Roger looked at each other. "No, I think we'll sail back into port on this 'pirate ship' if you don't mind, officer," Nik said. "It will help us to feel like we're a part of the celebration."

"Welcome to Galveston, Texas, Pastor Roger Brinkman," Nik said, gabbing Roger's hand. "I'll bet you weren't expecting a greeting like this?"

"So good to see you, Nikkumbaba Brinkman," Roger said, laughing and pulling Nik into a hug. "You folks do put on quite a show here."

"Boy, I haven't heard that name in a while," Nik said. "We definitely have some catching up to do.

Chapter 25
Counterfeit Plan

The Tiburon pulled into Galveston Harbor with Nik and Roger leaning over the starboard bow gunwale. Roger spotted Pricilla, her mother and Captain Rice waiting on the dock and he waved to them.

"Someone you know?" Nik asked.

"The two women are Pricilla and Margaret Wiggins. I met them on the stagecoach that took us to Corpus Christi," Roger said, looking down at the trio on the boardwalk. "The gentleman in the captain's cap is Sam Rice, an ex-naval officer who owns the ship that brought us here. You can see it a couple bays over. It's a beautiful boat."

"You'll have to tell me more about your trip," Nik said. "I would guess it was a rather intriguing journey."

"I could probably write a book about what I experienced during that time," Roger quipped.

"I'd rather you told me about it than have to read it," Nik said. "I think we both have some interesting tales to tell."

"Gentlemen, the gangplank has been lowered if you would care to disembark," the ship's chief officer called out.

Roger and Nik thanked the crew for their help and made their way to the dock where Pricilla, Margaret, and Rice were waiting.

"Folks, I'd like you to meet Galveston's chief marshal, my brother, Nik Brinkman," Roger said.

The three did not look shocked but were obviously taken aback by Roger's introduction.

"Let me help you out, here," Roger said, breaking into a smile."Nik is my adopted brother. We grew up together and he was my mentor when I served as a deputy marshal."

"This is a distinct pleasure," Sam Rice said, stepping forward to shake Nik's hand.

"You did take me by surprise. Thank you for explaining," Margaret Wiggins said. "Now that I know, I'm not surprised at all. Marshal Brinkman, I offer you my hand."

Nik took Margaret's hand and gave a slight bow.

"How foolish I feel," Pricilla chimed in behind her mother. "I'll bet you get a lot of this when you introduce each other.

"But I have to admit, knowing Roger and meeting you, Marshal, I am not surprised at all," Pricilla said, smiling widely and offering Nik her hand. "In fact, I am delighted."

"Now that we've gotten that out of the way, may I offer you some refreshment at my resident establishment, the Globe House?" Nik said. "Roger, I did not reserve you a room because I did not know when – or how – you would arrive. However, I'm sure the hotel will accommodate your stay."

"Are you thinking of finding a more permanent place to live than a hotel?" Roger asked, as the five retreated from the landing dock.

"I am, but that's another story for another time," Nik said.

After reaching the hotel, the five entered the lounge and took a seat. Drinks were ordered and the conversation immediately turned to what had just happened on Galveston Bay.

Nik explained what he was doing on the barge and why it was decided to go by water rather than rail. He told them he was totally taken by surprise and may have drowned if it had not been for Roger's help.

"You can't swim wearing your boots," Roger quipped." Would you really have chosen to drown rather than take them off?" That brought a laugh from the others, including Nik.

As the laughter quickly quieted, Nik spoke up in a sober tone, "Do you know how hard it is to find a good pair of boots these days?" That brought a laugh as well.

"Did they, whoever they were, really get away with all that silver?" Pricilla asked.

"Apparently," Nik answered. "It turns out one of the guys on the barge was in on it. However, I think he was taken into custody when he swam to shore."

"Captain, you're a former naval officer," Roger said, turning to Rice. "What will the Navy do with those pirates they arrested?"

"They will hold them until the proper authorities decide what to do with them," Rice replied.

"By the way, there were two other men who did not end up on the pirate ship," Nik said. "Did you see either of them?"

"We fished out a man who claimed he was the pilot of the wrecked vessel, but we did not see anyone else," Rice said.

"That means he may still be in the bay, somewhere," Nik commented. "It seems bodies floating out there are becoming a common occurrence around here," Nik said, taking a sip of his beer and wiping the foam from his mustache.

"There have been others?" Margaret asked.

"We recently had a sheriff's deputy and a customs agent found floating face-down in the water," Nik said. "However, they did not die from drowning. They were both murdered."

"That sounds dreadful, Marshal. Is this the sort of thing you have to deal with very often?" Pricilla asked.

"Please, call me Nik. It wasn't until we were informed of a counterfeiting ring flooding the local area with greenbacks that the deaths occurred. Counterfeiting was a serious enough problem without adding murder to it."

"Not to mention the theft of those two chests full of silver," Roger added.

"Anyone for another round," Nik asked, changing the subject.

"Not for me, thanks," Rice said. "I have to get back to my boat and prepare it for the trip back to Corpus Christi."

"By the way, what happened to that pilot you rescued?" Nik asked.

"I'm not sure," Rice said. "After we docked, he said he had business to attend to and disappeared."

"Pricilla and I had better find accommodations. Do you think we could get a room here?" Margaret said.

"I don't see why not," Nik said. "This is not the busy season, yet."

"It sounds like it is for you," Pricilla offered. "Are you going to find time to be baptized?"

"That's right, Nik," Roger said. "And that little episode we had in the water earlier today doesn't count."

All had another good laugh with that remark. Afterward, everyone departed to take care of other matters. Nik then booked Roger into a room at the Globe House, while Roger accompanied the Wiggins to retrieve their belongings off the Texas Belle.

When Roger and Margaret and Pricilla Wiggins returned to the hotel, Nik was waiting for them in the lobby with Ambrose Tucker.

"Ambrose Tucker," Roger called out upon spotting the giant former sharpshooter. Roger took long strides in getting over to grab Tucker by the hand. "Tell me you haven't gotten bigger since I saw you last."

"I don't think so, Roger. I understand you are a preacher man now."

"I am, and I would like to introduce you to Margaret and Pricilla Wiggins," Roger said. "I made their acquaintance during my trip from the New Mexico Territory."

After introductions, everyone with luggage was shown to their rooms and promised to meet later in the dining room.

"So, this is where you live, Nik… Ambrose?" Roger said. "They're nice enough rooms, are they enough for you?"

"Ambrose and I live downstairs in larger accommodations that the hotel maintains for temporal purposes," Nik said. "Ambrose and I have not had time to try and find something long term."

"I gather, you are pretty busy now."

"Especially since we lost that silver shipment. I don't even know where to begin on that one," Nik said. "We're also in the middle of a counterfeiting case that includes two murders. The possible loss of one of our guards in that boating accident may be a third, unrelated to the counterfeiting problem."

"Wow, you are busy," Roger said, putting his belongings in the room's amoire cabinet. "How do you plan to squeeze in your baptism?"

"What I'm more concerned with now is how I can squeeze you into helping me with the two cases I have on my hands," Nik said.

"Whoa, I have some parishioners back in New Mexico waiting for me," Roger said, with a slight smile. "I'm not sure what I can do for you."

"You are a good lawman, at least you were," Nik began. "I know you brought down Colonel Curtain after becoming a minister, so I know you still have it in you."

"About that, Nik," Roger countered. "I probably shouldn't have done that but I just could not let him get away. I tried to get him to turn himself in but he drew on me."

"I'm not asking you to shoot anyone, but I've got to lay a trap for the one we believe is behind the counterfeiting racket," Nik said. "The culprit knows the three of us, but he doesn't know you."

"The three of you?" Roger questioned.

"There's a third who just recently joined the party, and you know him pretty well," Nik said, with the hint of a smile.

"I do? Who would that be?" Roger asked.

"Our good friend from the treasury department, Sebastian Mason," Nik answered, breaking into a broader smile.

"Mason! He's back again. What brings him to Texas this time?"

"The counterfeiting case, and the murder of the customs agent. The agent actually worked with Mason," Nik said. "The three of us have worked out a pretty good plan to solve the counterfeiting case. However, I could definitely use your help."

"Woah, I didn't think I would do much more here than see my brother again and baptize him," Roger said, mulling the situation over in his mind.

"As I said, you don't have to shoot anybody. Besides, I think it's my turn now," Nik assured.

"Were you hurt by the news that I had killed Curtain?

"I was, Roger, but I'm not completely sure why," Nik answered. "You see, at first, I think I was a little bit jealous. But when I pictured you in your clergyman collar having to shoot the man, I felt sorry for you and frustrated. But all along, we both knew you would do it if you had to. My guess is, even God knew that and will likely set aside a mansion in Heaven for you and burn that vile, detestable Curtain in hell."

"Ha, I don't know about that – the mansion in Heaven, that is," Roger said, with a smile of relief. "But I'm sure Curtain's burning in hell right now."

"If you two are done," Ambrose broke in, "I think two ladies may be waiting for us in the lobby."

The three men hurried down to the lobby where the women were, indeed, waiting. After apologies, the five of them entered the dining room and were soon eating. During the meal, the women announced they would be leaving the following day to sail back to Philadelphia. Roger could see Pricilla was uncomfortable by her mother's announcement and was hoping to get a chance to talk with her, alone.

Just before the dinner party broke up, Roger asked Pricilla if she would like to go for a walk along the wharf. She brightened a bit at the invitation and accepted.

"I'm sorry the two of you have to leave so soon," Roger said as the two strolled along just as the moon was rising above the horizon. "We were just getting to know each other."

"Perhaps it's best, Roger," Pricilla said with a sigh. "I think I was beginning to enjoy your company a little too much."

"What an amazing capacity you have for enjoyment," Roger replied. "Since we've known each other, we've ridden in a dusty stagecoach, complete with an Indian attack. You consoled me while I was seasick on the Texas Belle, and witnessed the boat my brother was on get cut in half by a pirate ship."

"It has been an adventure," Pricilla said, smiling as she revisited the scenes Roger described. "Perhaps that's what intrigues me so. I did like the frontier atmosphere of California, but I never met anyone there like you."

"I could say that was to your benefit, but I really don't feel that way," Roger said, turning to Pricilla and gently gabbing her shoulders. "I have to confess that I really don't want to say goodbye, but I do know my brother has a lot more in store for me than baptism."

"Are you going to go back to being a lawman?" Pricilla asked.

"Not in the strictest sense of it, and only temporarily, but apparently Nik does need my help," Roger said, noting the reflection of the moon in Pricilla's eyes. "Judging from our previous experiences, I doubt I'll have time for anything more than that."

"I know that, Roger," Pricilla said, as she turned and began walking again. "What about after that? I mean the baptism and all. Will you go back to being a traveling clergyman afterwards?"

"It is my calling, Pricilla," Roger answered. "I'm more than willing to assist my brother but not in leaving the ministry."

"Don't you ever get lonely?" she asked. "I mean, traveling all the time?"

"Funny you should say that. I think I'm feeling it right now. I do have to return to New Mexico, I have a flock there that needs tending to. But I have to confess, it is a lonely calling."

"Will you never marry?" Pricilla prodded.

"Oh, I can't say that," Roger replied. "I had plans to marry at one time, but Providence changed all that."

"What happened?"

"A man murdered my family and I swore revenge. I became a soldier to learn how to kill and later became a U.S. Marshal to carry out that plan," Roger explained. "The strange thing about it, I didn't finish the job until I after I became a preacher."

This time, Pricilla stopped and turned to Roger. "You killed the man who murdered your family? It feels strange to me, but I actually admire you for that."

"That's the conflict, Pricilla," Roger said looking down at her. "Saving people is what I should be doing, not shooting them."

"But you didn't shoot those Indians who attacked the stagecoach. You shot their horses instead."

"I don't hate Indians. I just wanted them to stop chasing us," Roger continued. "Hate doesn't fit into my profile now. But I do have to live with what I've done."

Pricilla put her hands on Roger's shoulders and pulled his head down to kiss him. After pulling away she said, "I hope you will take that kiss as it was meant. I was hoping I'd get a chance to do that before we parted and give you something to remember me by. And, I would like to write to you, even if you don't write back."

"I will remember that kiss, and I would like it very much if you wrote to me. It would give me something to hold onto during those lonely nights in New Mexico," Roger said. "Here's something else to remember…" Roger pulled Pricilla up and kissed her in a far more passionate way.

"You're definitely not like any preacher I ever knew," Pricilla said, after Roger released his arms from around her. "I think we'd best be getting back to the hotel now. Mother might start to worry."

Roger laughed. "I can't make any promises," he said, "but don't be surprised if I answer your letters."

The following day, Roger, Nik and Ambrose escorted Pricilla and her mother to the dock where their ship was waiting.

"Thank you for last night," Pricilla said to Roger before walking up the boarding ramp. "Take good care of that flock of yours."

"And you take care of your mother," Roger said, as the two women ascended the ramp. "When the moon rises over New Mexico, I'll think of you – both."

"Must have been a pretty special evening the two of you had, eh brother?" Nik said when the women were onboard and out of earshot.

"I got a lot off my chest last night," Roger answered. "I feel a lot better today, and I can't say I completely know why."

"Maybe it wasn't what you got off your chest but something you felt inside of it," Nik said, flashing a smile at Roger.

"Okay, Dr. Love, I know what you're thinking. Pricilla and I are friends and have an understanding. She'll be in Pennsylvania and I in the New Mexico Territory. I would say that qualifies as a long-range relationship."

"You have a relationship with God and he's all the way up in Heaven," Nik said laughingly. "You don't seem to have a problem there."

"Nice try, Brother Cupid, how about we discuss the help you need, and fulfilling the promise I made to you."

Nik and Ambrose escorted Roger to the Galveston Courthouse where Nik introduced his brother to the officers in the sheriff's office. The trio then gathered in Nik's office to discuss strategy.

"As I mentioned, Sebastian Mason is in Houston where he thinks the printing press for rolling out counterfeit greenbacks is located. Ambrose and I have been to the site and tend to agree with Mason," Nik began. "We were led to believe the money was being smuggled in on fishing boats inside fish."

"Inside fish? Sounds a little messy to me," Roger quipped.

"Not when the money is put into a latex balloon-like pouch and inserted into the fish," Nik countered.

"Wow, this sounds sophisticated," Roger said. "How did you find this out?"

"It gets even more sophisticated," Nik said. "It now appears the fish smuggling scheme was all a ruse. And two men died because of it."

"I am sorry to hear that. I hope no one you were close to," Roger replied sympathetically.

"Closer than I would have liked," Ambrose inserted. "Deputy Alexander and I were working together the night he was killed."

"It wasn't Ambrose's fault, although he's had a hard time believing that," Nik chimed in. "Alexander, Lenny as we called him, was found floating in the bay with a wound to the head. The coroner believes the blow to the head is what killed him. The kicker, though, is Lenny was found to have a fish in his pocket containing a balloon with money in it."

Nik explained that Lenny's "clue" led them into an investigation that eventually took the life of a customs agent as well. The marshal also related that the customs agent turned out to be an undercover treasury agent and a friend of Sebastian Mason's. Nik added that Mason had remained incognito because he was known by Customs Agent Ron Lester.

"It seems Lester was one of the original designers of the greenback used to fund the Union cause in the war. They were discontinued after the war with the government on the hook for four-hundred and fifty million dollars."

"So Lester, and whoever he's working with, has been printing these bills and using them for money? Roger asked. "Is he in need of that much money that could eventually end up to be worthless?"

"We don't know Lester's complete scheme here," Nik said. "He could have used some of that money for his own purposes but that would have aroused suspicion if discovered. Sebastian thinks he has other motives, like forcing the government to cover the counterfeit greenbacks or turn them into the reserve currency."

"Sounds complicated," Roger said. "So, what would you have me do?"

"I'm sending you and Ambrose to Houston to meet with Agent Mason," Nik instructed. "I will stay here and give Lester the impression I really wasn't sure he was the man we saw pulling away from that warehouse in a buckboard. I want to hear what his excuse is.

"I'm deputizing you so you won't violate your professional standing. I promise not to ask you to do anything that would lead to that," Nik added.

"I'll pray on it, brother. As long as I'm upholding the law, I can't see where I would break any sacred vows," Roger replied.

"Ambrose," Nik said. "Be sure to let Sebastian know we have a man of God on our side."

"I'm sure he'll be happy to know that," Ambrose said.

The following day, Roger and Ambrose boarded a train bound for Houston. Upon arrival, they took the trolley and arrived in Freedmen's Town. After a short walk, they entered the lobby of the Cotton Gin, where Mason was again perusing some of the local literature.

"Well, if my eyes don't deceive me, it is Deputy Marshal Roger Brinkman," Sebastian said, glancing up from his reading as Ambrose and Roger approached.

"Good to see you, Sebastian," Roger said, as Mason rose from his chair. "Ironically, this is my first day as a newly deputized deputy marshal."

"Come again?" Sebastian responded.

"I left the service and became a Lutheran Minister, like my father was before me," Roger said, smiling and shaking the Secret Service agent's hand. "I came to visit Nik and, before I knew it, I was a deputy marshal again."

"You are a man of incredible flexibility, considering the disparity in your chosen professions," Sebastian said, laughing. "I trust Nik has filled you in with some of the details of what we are planning."

"Yes, somewhat," Roger said.

The three men moved out onto the patio where they could speak in private.

Chapter 26
Preacher Man, Lawman, Spy

Roger Brinkman, Ambrose Tucker, and Sebastian Mason sat on the patio of the Cotton Gin hostel discussing the most expedient way to bring justice to the Houston-Galveston area. An estimated million-dollar shipment of silver had been carried off by a lighter-than-air balloon, an episode that possibly resulted in a least one death. And, two men had already died trying to solve a counterfeiting operation wrapped up in a fish tale.

"In your estimation, the counterfeit money was not smuggled into Galveston on fishing boats delivering fish stuffed with cash," Roger replied in response to Mason's assertion to the contrary. "I believe your suspicion is that a government customs agent is printing the stuff here in Houston?"

"I'm almost certain of it, Deputy Brinkman," Mason answered. "Ambrose, Nik and I have worked out a temporary plan. When Nik mentioned your pending arrival, we thought if you would agree to go undercover, you could help us bring this caper to a close."

"I am willing to do whatever the Good Lord and my conscience will allow me to do," Roger stated, "in order to help my brother in whatever way I can. I came here to baptize him and instead he deputized me."

"Fortunately, we're not organizing a posse to go after the bad guys with guns blazing," Mason said, offering a faint smile as he spoke. "We also have murders to solve and we do not know for certain who is responsible for that. We think that you can be a big ally because most of the various players in this performance don't know who you are, especially those nefarious ones."

"However, it's possible you may have been seen with me or Nik," Ambrose said.

"I, too, am incognito only because my number-one suspect knows me," Mason continued.

Mason went on to explain how he, Nik, and Ambrose decided to create a false identity for Roger. It required the cooperation of the U.S. Government to create a profile listing Roger as a rehabilitated former outlaw. The profile would include the Treasury Department recruiting Roger to help bring other criminals to justice.

"Since you may have already been identified as being in the company of Marshal Brinkman and Deputy Ambrose, your role here should deflect that suspicion," Mason said. "Your authorization papers are already on their way from Washington and should be here by tomorrow. Nik and Judge Conklin will introduce you to Agent Lester. Your job will be to gain Lester's confidence and convince him you can be bought because of your previous disreputable background."

"Since my Roger Brinkman name would be an obvious giveaway, who will I now be?"

"They've given you the name Rodney Eugene Brown. I know that may sound like a mouthful but it bears your actual initials R.E.B. That's code for the department to keep track of you," Mason said.

"Rodney sounds a little bit like Roger," the undercover deputy remarked, "Isn't that a little risky?"

"It's helpful to have an assumed name close to your own. It helps to prevent failure to respond to your new appellation," Mason instructed. "Your life could depend on it."

"I'm not sure I like the sounds of that. So, just who is this Rodney Eugene Brown?"

Roger was told that Brown is on file as a Confederate Army deserter who pilfered fifty thousand dollars in Confederate currency. He was caught and escaped hanging when the war ended but he remained in prison. He was brought before a Union court and remained incarcerated until determined rehabilitated. Brown was then recruited as a treasury agent to assist in currency fraud cases.

"This should give you all the cover you need. Since you are a former Confederate soldier you are familiar with their protocol," Mason said. "Lester will introduce you to the counterfeit bills. I suspect those bills are for his cover story, because he has created near-perfect replicas of the original greenbacks."

"And, as for the murders?" Roger asked.

"Nik will fill you in on that," Mason replied. "I, too, want to know, but I cannot expose myself at this time. Oh, and an official shirt and badge will also arrive tomorrow, so you can dress accordingly."

Mason gave Roger an allowance to purchase other clothing more in line with his position as a customs agent.

"We'll stay here tonight, if that suits you okay… 'Rodney Brown,'" Ambrose said, grinning. "We can shop for clothes and then head back on the train tomorrow.

"I also know a great place to eat not far from here" Ambrose added.

Sebastian then parted company with the two deputies with plans to return the following day with the supplies Roger would need. Ambrose checked in with the hostel desk clerk, obtaining a room for two – Ambrose Tucker and Rodney Eugene Brown.

In the morning, Mason delivered everything as promised. Roger donned his new uniform and he and Ambrose departed for the Houston Train Depot. After reaching Galveston, Ambrose and "Rodney Brown" were met at the depot by Nik. Roger explained the details of his cover story.

"All right, 'Rodney,' I've got a horse for you," Nik said.

Nik had picked up a horse for Roger at the livery stable, along with Galley and Crusader. They rode together toward the court-house.

"We have to be careful," Nik said. "Baudelaire and his crew are being held in Sheriff Atkins's jail and could recognize you, Rog … er, Rodney Brown. I'll invite the sheriff up to my office to meet you. It's probably best you steer clear of the sheriff's office, however, Judge Conklin has been told who you are, just in case."

"Just in case what?" Roger asked.

"Just in case something should happen to Ambrose and me, or Sebastian, you would need someone of authority to identify you," Nik said. "At first we weren't going to let the judge know, until we considered that possibility."

"I appreciate you looking after me, Nik," the preacher-man-now-spy said. "Do you think this Agent Lester killed those two men found floating in the bay?"

"Right now, it's our best guess because he's the only known suspect we have," Nik answered. "There are very likely others helping Lester and we're hoping you can find out who."

"And Sebastian tells me I'm not to wear a gun unless I'm involved in an arrest. What if I want to arrest Lester?" Roger said.

"Don't, is all I can tell you. Leave that to us, right Ambrose?" Nik said.

"Yeah, Agent Brown, your job is to gain information," Ambrose answered. "I don't think the Good Lord would be happy with us if we let anything happen to you."

"Ambrose, I don't know if you're a praying man, but I know Nik is," Roger said. "Follow his lead and help say a few words on my behalf. It can't hurt and it just may get us through this alive."

"Oh, I can pray," Ambrose said. "Momma made me do it every night, and I prayed even more when she was taken away."

"Did you ever make contact with your parents, Ambrose?" Roger inquired.

"I have not. I came west hoping they might have migrated out here after the war. But no one I know has seen nor heard of their whereabouts," Ambrose said. "I pray one day I will, though."

Roger could see Nik was thinking about what Ambrose had said and guessed his brother was wondering about his natural mother as well. However, something inside Roger told him not to ask.

After stopping at the U.S. Marshals office, Roger and Ambrose waited while Nik retrieved Sheriff Duke Atkins and Deputy Zeke Vincent. After a cordial greeting, the sheriff and deputy left and Nik escorted Roger to Judge Conklin's office.

"Your honor, I'd like you to meet Customs Agent Rodney Brown,"

Nik said. The judge looked at Nik out of the corner of his eye and Nik nodded his head in the affirmative.

"Just call me Rodney, your honor," Roger said.

"It's a pleasure… Rodney," the judge said. Then in a hushed voice he asked, "I hope this is not asking too much of you, since you are a man of the cloth."

"Not at all, Judge. My cloth has been soiled more than a few times. I'm sure Nik has told you about me."

"He has and we're grateful for what you're doing. Just be careful."

"The best help is on my side, your honor," Roger said softly.

After that introduction, Nik took Roger upstairs and introduced him to Lester.

"A new agent?" Lester said in surprise. "I was unaware the department was sending me a new man."

"I'm sorry to hear that," Agent Brown responded, "although, I do have all my paperwork with me. It should fill you in on most details and I'd be happy to supply you with whatever it might not show."

"I guess they wanted to get you a replacement for Agent Letterman as soon as they could," Nik cut in. "Hopefully all the necessary paperwork is there."

"Yes, it all looks good and we can certainly use the help," Lester said, leafing through the portfolio. "Nik, I appreciate you bringing Agent Brown up here. How did you know he was coming?"

"Oh, I didn't know," Nik quickly answered. "Ambrose and I were at the depot when Agent Brown arrived and we recognized his badge. After introducing ourselves he told us you would be expecting him, so we offered to bring him with us."

"Thanks, Marshal, appreciate that," Lester said, continuing to glance through the government documents. "If you would excuse us, Nik, I'd like to get to know Agent Brown a little better."

"Of course," Nik said, turning to Roger. "Rodney Brown, welcome aboard," Nik said, extending his hand to shake Roger's.

"Yes, most folks just call me Rodney, pleasure to meet you, marshal."

Nik left and Roger followed Lester into his small office.

"You'll have to excuse the accommodations. We haven't been in

Galveston all that long and this was the only space available at the time," Lester said. "How long have you been with the service?"

"I'm relatively new," Roger answered. "I was assigned because of my past experience with money. I guess they thought I could be of help with the counterfeiting problem here."

"Past experience with money, do you mind elaborating on that?" Lester probed.

"If you look deep enough you'll find I have a rather sordid past," Roger began, explaining his role as a deserter from the Confederate Army.

"We had stolen a good sum of Confederate currency and planned to turn it into greenbacks."

"How did you plan to do that?" Lester continued his questioning.

"My partner was the brains. We stayed in the South and bought items at inflated prices using that stolen money. We later sold those things below value as long as we received greenbacks in exchange. When we could no longer buy anything with Confederate money, my partner made off with the greenbacks and left me holding the bag, so to speak."

"What happened to you after that?"

"I was arrested and close to hanging, but the war ended and I was turned over to the Yanks, who threw me in prison for a time. So, I spent as much time as I could educating myself. After a spell, they let me out on good behavior and hired me to help sort out all the money exchanges being made following the war."

"Was there any special reason why they sent you here?"

"I would have to say it's the counterfeiting thing," Roger answered. "And probably my criminal experience and thinking like an outlaw. They felt I might be able to help out in some way."

"And are you happy being a customs agent?"

"It puts food on the table. It'll have to do until something better comes along," Roger continued, trying to give Lester the idea he was open to other means of supporting himself. "I kind of got into the habit of spending big."

"Do you know anything about fishing?" Lester quizzed.

"I used to do it as a boy, why?"

"No reason, I just thought we'd wrap this up with that. Welcome aboard, Agent Brown. Do you prefer Rodney or Rod?"

"Odd, but I'm best known as Rodney, Agent Lester. Just tell me what you'd like me to do and I'll do it."

"To start, why don't you stick close to me," Lester said. "Perhaps you'll pick things up faster that way."

Roger spent the rest of day reviewing office procedures and met Lester's two other agents, Cole Grady and Reggie Fredrickson. Lester also had Roger go over a number of greenbacks, instructing him on how to tell a counterfeit bill from legal tender.

"I would have to say that whoever is doing the counterfeiting thing is doing a good job. Even with your instructions, I'm having a hard time telling the difference," Roger said.

"Your profile says you spent time trying to help resolve the issue of Confederate money mixed into the economy after the war, did you not, Agent Brown?" Lester asked.

"I did, Agent Lester, but I was more concerned with taking the Confederate currency out of circulation than trying to determine its value," Roger answered.

"I understand. But still, you must have gotten pretty good at recognizing inconsistencies between bills," Lester said. "And, by the way, you may call me Ron. We're all on a first name basis in this office."

"Thanks, Ron, I did, but most attempts at counterfeiting back then were more obvious than these bills. These greenbacks are… I have to confess, incredible forgeries," Roger responded.

"Who was your commander in the war?" Lester said, out of the blue.

"General Jackson, at first," Roger answered, relieved to hear a question he was familiar with. "I got into a little trouble with him and I ended up with General Lee."

"That's top brass, as far as the Confederacy was concerned, right?" Lester continued.

Roger marveled at how well his experience in the war aided his cover. "Lee is where I got into real trouble that left me with no choice but to desert," Roger began, carefully formulating his answer. "My troubles began when General Jackson accused me of dereliction of duty. He sent me to Lee for correction and I managed to get along well enough with the Southern Commander. I became Lee's attaché. He was the one receiving the bulk shipments of pay for the rebel troops. That's when my friend, John, talked me into helping him steal the Confederate cash and making off with it.

"It later occurred to us that not only would Lee be upset, but we had the entire Northern Virginia Army mad at us. It was only by Providence I escaped hanging."

Roger felt good after that speech. His description tying the truth with his cover story had to convince Lester that he really was Rodney Eugene Brown – "former crook."

"We'll spend some time at the wharf after this," Lester said. "Did Marshal Brinkman fill you in on counterfeit money being discovered in fish?"

"Ah," Roger figured he'd best play dumb with that question. "No... counterfeit money in fish?"

"It's our best lead right now, but we've hit a bit of a dead end," Lester said. "I'll fill you in on the details later.

"I think I'll also take you to Houston with me and introduce you to some folks who are assisting us in that area."

"Whatever you say, Ron," Roger said, smiling up at the lead agent. "You're the boss."

"Where are you staying, by the way? Lester asked.

"Oh, ah, Marshal Brinkman was kind enough to book me into the Globe House... nice place." Roger answered.

"That was quick. I guess you'll be near the marshal," Lester said, with a wry smile. "Be sure to let me know whatever is going on with him and his deputy, won't you?" Lester concluded.

"Sure, whatever helps," Roger responded, hoping he hadn't triggered any suspicion with the lead agent.

The day ended with Roger riding back to the Globe House. He decided not to stop at Nik's office for fear of appearing too close to the marshal. He felt his first day went well enough and hoped he'd gained some of Lester's confidence, even if it did end on a weak note.

Roger left a message with the clerk, requesting Nik visit him in his room and to make certain he wasn't seen doing it. Although the relationship between a customs agent and a U.S. Marshal would not appear too suspicious, still, Roger was supposed to be new in town. Roger took some comfort in Lester's remark to report back on what the marshals were up to. That would be easy enough to do, with whatever information Nik wanted Lester to know.

While relaxing in his room, Roger heard a soft knock at the door and rose to answer it. Nik was standing in the hall. He glanced in both directions before quickly entering the room.

"So, did you learn anything today?" Nik asked.

"I think I managed to lead Lester into thinking of me as a potential ally, if he shows any signs of needing one," Roger said. "However, I'm still a long way from gaining his full confidence. I think, what will help is he asked that I give him some inside information as to your operation."

"That could play into our hands very well," Nik said, taking a seat by a small table in the room. "Coordinating this with Sebastian in Houston is going to be tricky. However, Sebastian said he'd do his best to find out what is in that locked warehouse and leave us to concentrate on Lester."

"Lester said he wanted me to visit the harbor with him tomorrow. I suspect I'm going to get an earful of that fish story," Roger said, taking a seat opposite Nik. "Can you give me something to pass onto him that will help draw me more into his trust?"

"Tell him we have received some information on one of the fishing boats that we intend to investigate," Nik said, tapping his finger against the top of table, as if thinking out loud to the rhythm of the tapping. "That should give him the impression we're still buying that fish story. "What we need to know, if he's printing that money, as we suspect, we need to know how he profits from it. There may well be others involved but we do not know who."

"Lester intends to take me to Houston and introduce me to some friends of his there," Roger offered. "He wasn't specific about who these 'friends' are, but I have a sneaking suspicion it's part of his plan to scrutinize me."

"Give him plenty of rope, but don't hang yourself with it," Nik advised. "We believe this guy's already killed two men, I definitely don't want to add you to the list."

"You've got to stop encouraging me like that," Roger replied, chuckling. "However, I do have the advantage that you should know my whereabouts, for the most part."

"We'll use these little rendezvous to keep apprised of what's going on," Nik said. "If anything changes, there are three other men you can trust with your information, including the judge."

"I'd best get back to my room."

Roger pushed himself up from his chair and walked to the door. "I'll step out and make sure no one is around. Then you can head back to your place."

With Nik gone, Roger lay down on his bed to speculate on the variables performing in a role he never expected to play.

After breakfast the next morning, Roger retrieved his horse from the livery stable and rode to the courthouse. When he entered the customs office he found Reggie studying a stack of twenty-dollar bills.

"Find something interesting?" Roger asked as he approached the agent."

"Nothing here," Fredrickson answered. "These are genuine as far as I can tell."

"What do you do with them once you've inspected them?" Roger inquired, without thinking.

"Apparently, you've never done this before," Reggie responded, looking up at Roger. "I thought you were a money man."

"Mostly Confederate," Roger quickly answered. "But my interest is more in where these greenbacks go once they've been inspected."

"Back to the bank," Reggie replied. "These come to us from the bank to ensure they are good. If they're not legal, we hold them as evidence."

"That makes sense," Roger said, trying to appear nonchalant. "Is Agent Lester here?"

"No, he's down at the wharf. He said to have you go down there and meet him when you showed up," Reggie said.

"The wharf's a pretty big place," Roger said. "Did he offer anything more specific than that?"

"I would say just ride until you see a sorrel horse tied to a hitching post bearing a saddle with 'U.S.' stamped on it. Ron will likely be somewhere near there."

"Thanks, Reggie, I'll let you get back to work."

Roger took Fredrickson's limited advice and rode nearly the length of the harbor until he came to the ferry boat landing. He did not see a horse of any kind, so he dismounted, tied up his horse and walked to the end of the pier. He could see a ferry approaching the dock and watched as it maneuvered into position and the gangplank was lowered. It was then he saw Lester leading the sorrel he was supposed to identify coming off the ship.

"I'm glad you are here," Lester said, as he approached the clergy-turned-lawman. "I had to go across the bay and was afraid I would miss you. Thanks for waiting."

"Not at all," Roger said. "I used my time to familiarize myself with the harbor. This is quite a place. What's on the other side over there?"

"Oh, that's where most of the fishing vessels dock," Lester answered. "I did an inspection but didn't find anything suspicious, like I had hoped."

"According to Marshal Brinkman, he said he received information about a fishing vessel thought to be attached to this case. Is that what you were checking on?" Roger questioned.

Agent Lester looked at Roger with an odd expression. "I, ah… yes, I was checking on one of the fishing boats in question," Lester answered. "Unfortunately, I didn't find anything worth noting.

"By the way, Rodney, I stopped at the Globe House to pick you up this morning and they told me no one by your name was staying there. Did you move?"

That question left Roger stunned for a moment. Thinking back he remembered Nik had checked him in, likely under his real name. "Really, I'll have to check that out because I haven't moved. Oh, you know what, Marshal Brinkman checked me into that hotel as a friendly gesture. He may have checked me in under his name. I'll have to square that with him."

"I guess that makes sense," Lester replied, looking a little bewildered. "At any rate, let's mount up and I'll give you a tour of the island."

The two spent most of the day sightseeing and talking about things unrelated to the counterfeiting case. Roger relaxed and allowed Lester to do most of the talking, listening for any clue he might let slip. They stopped for a sandwich near the beach on the opposite side of Galveston Harbor. It was a warm day and there were quite a few locals on the strand taking advantage of the weather and enjoying the cool breeze coming off the ocean.

"I've made arrangements to take you with me to Houston tomorrow," Lester announced. "We'll take the train and be gone most of the day, unless you have other plans."

"Until I learn more of what I need to know," Roger said, giving Ron a slight smile, "I'm in your hands."

"Good," Lester said, finishing the last of his lunch. "Houston it is."

That evening, Roger told Nik about not being registered at the Globe House under the name Rodney Eugene Brown.

"Overlooking a detail like that isn't good," Nik said, rolling his eyes. "Look, I'll fix it so it is under Brown. If Lester says anything more about it, tell him you told the clerk that I recommended the Globe House and he listed the room under my name by mistake."

"As 'Roger' Brinkman?" Roger questioned.

"Say Roger's my real name, Nik's a nickname," Nik said, a little frustrated by the unfortunate error. "If Lester gets any nosier than that, I'll have to shoot him."

Chapter 27
The Roundup

Customs Agent Ron Lester and Roger Brinkman, posing as Customs Agent Rodney Eugene Brown, boarded the northbound Galveston, Houston and Henderson Railroad. Roger could tell Lester was bothered by something but the agent did not appear nervous or act suspicious. After some extensive praying, Roger had come to terms with his new role and was feeling more comfortable about being "Agent Brown."

"You seem a little preoccupied," Roger said, as the two men took their seats on the train. "Anything I can help you with?"

"Oh, sorry, Rodney," Lester said, giving an almost sheepish smile in Roger's direction. "I'm... ah, I'm just running some things through my head as to what I would like to get accomplished on this trip."

"You know, Ron," Roger began. "I ran into Agent Fredrickson, who was searching through a stack of greenbacks yesterday. He said all the bills were legal currency, but confessed he was frustrated by how hard it was to determine a counterfeit from the real thing. That's got to be a real dilemma for you guys."

Lester turned his head toward Roger with an almost perturbed look.

"I'm assuming that's why you're here," Lester said. "By the way, I did receive confirmation notice from Washington that you would be coming. I'm puzzled why that took so long. Transfer employees typically take weeks or months to arrive following confirmation of their impending arrival."

"Washington's pretty bogged down now trying to reconcile the South and they're either behind in their work or simply overlooked it," Roger said. "Meanwhile, I guess somebody's getting rich off these counterfeit greenbacks."

"The West is a lawless place, Rodney. People are able to get away with a lot of criminal behavior out here," Lester answered, turning his gaze forward.

"Whoever's forging those greenbacks has got to be making a fortune," Roger added. "How do you suppose they are profiting from it?"

"Don't you know? Lester asked. "You were tasked with sorting the good from the bad. There's only so much specie gold to back up the legal tender. If you can reproduce what the government prints, people will accept your phony bills. What the crooks have left over they'll probably try to exchange for gold.

"You were in that business, to an extent."

"Almost wish I was again," Roger quipped, trying to act flippant.

"What?" Lester questioned, turning to pull his shoulders back to express surprise at Roger's remark.

"Oh, I'm sorry," Roger said. "I didn't really mean that. I was just thinking about the cash my friend and I were rolling in before we got caught. It was a lot more money than I make now."

"Isn't your salary enough to support you?" Lester asked.

"Oh, it's all right, I guess," Roger saw an opening but hoped he wasn't laying it on too thick. "It's just that a guy with my background ends up with lot of debt."

"Really, anything I should know about?" Lester queried.

"Nothing I'd want to bother you with, Ron. It just means I have to be extra careful how I spend my money, that's all."

"Yeah, it can be rough out here on a government salary," Lester said, turning and leaning back in his seat. "It's smart to be careful."

Roger knew enough not to say more. He had planted the seed about his desire for more money, and Lester was aware of "Brown's" past. Getting too bold could tip his hand. He was content to let the agent return to his thoughts.

After reaching Houston, the two boarded a trolley and got off at Baker Street. Following Lester's lead, the two men soon reached the Houston Sheriff's Office.

"Is Ed in?" Lester inquired of the clerk at the front of the outer office.

"He is, Agent Lester, I think he's expecting you. You'll find him in his office," the clerk replied.

Houston's two deputies were in the outer office and glanced up at the two men as they walked by. They nodded a casual hello, obviously acquainted with who Lester was. They did not seem overly concerned as to who Roger might be.

"Ed, I've got someone I'd like you to meet," Lester said, as he and Roger entered Sheriff Ellsworth's office. "He's a new customs agent sent from Washington to help us with the counterfeiting case. Rodney Brown is his name."

"Really," Ellsworth exclaimed, offering Lester a quizzical look as he pushed back his chair and got to his feet. The sheriff walked around the desk to shake Roger's hand. "I was unaware that Washington was sending someone new."

"Took me by surprise, too," Lester said. "He has a bit of a past, considering the war and all, but his credentials say he knows his way around money."

"Pleasure, Sheriff," Roger said, shaking Ellsworth's hand. "I guess this counterfeit cash is working its way up from the gulf."

Ellsworth glanced over at Lester.

"The sheriff has been our lookout for counterfeit greenbacks in Houston," Lester responded. "The smuggling is Galveston's jurisdiction. That's where the U.S. Marshals Service comes in."

Ellsworth moved behind his desk and sat down. "Please, gentlemen, have a seat," he said. "So, Ron, what should we discuss in order to help Agent… Brown, I believe is the name?"

"That's correct," both Roger and Lester responded in unison.

"We have been tracking the greenbacks in this town but we're having a difficult time separating the good from the bad," Ellsworth continued, again glancing over at Lester. "So, Brown, you're an expert on currency identification?"

Lester nodded in the affirmative, but Roger cut in, "I hesitate to consider myself an expert. I must confess, if Ron hasn't told you, I was a convicted Confederate war criminal and only escaped with my life when the North won the war. I have to thank the Good…" Roger hesitated a moment, "…good fortune for coming out of my situation as I did."

Lester encouraged Roger to complete the story of his ordeal before becoming a customs agent, which the undercover deputy did.

"That's quite a story, Agent Brown," Ellsworth commented. "So your job was separating good money from bad?"

"I have to confess that my nefarious ways led me to the position I now hold," Roger concluded.

"So, what's the plan, Ron?" Ellsworth asked.

"Ed, why don't you have one of your deputies show Rodney some of Houston's sights," Lester said. "That way you and I can discuss details."

"Good idea," Ellsworth said. "I'll get Mac to do it."

Ellsworth got up from his chair and walked over to the door separating his office from the outer one. He opened it and called out, "Mac, come in here for a moment, will you?"

Deputy Bart McIntyre entered the office and stood behind Roger and Lester.

"Agent Brown, this is Deputy Bart McIntyre," Ellsworth said to Roger and then turned to his deputy. "Mac, I would like you to take Agent Brown here up to the diner for a cup of coffee, if you would. Fill him in on what goes on around here. Agent Lester and I have some things to discuss."

"Sure, boss, whatever you need," McIntyre said.

Roger stood up and extended his hand, "Please call me Rodney I'm happy to make your acquaintance."

"Likewise," McIntyre responded. "How do you like your coffee?"

"Cheap," Roger blurted out, regretting sounding too obvious.

"In that case, I'll buy," McIntyre said, grinning.

After Roger and McIntyre departed, Lester and Ellsworth got

down to business.

"I hope this new recruit isn't going to throw a horseshoe into things," Ellsworth quipped.

"The jury's still out, Ed, but I do know he's got a dark side. He's even hinted he wished he was doing the counterfeiting. If he's good, he might be helpful in making our product foolproof."

"How do you propose to do that?"

"I don't know, not yet, anyway," Lester responded. "The guy could be a plant like Letterman was. I'd like to set him up here in your office monitoring bank deposits. It's going to take some time for him to recognize the flaws in our cash

"His presence might also put the bank president's mind at ease. I think he's suspicious that my assessment of these greenbacks isn't all that good. He's even pointed out a few discrepancies that I've had to make excuses for."

"What if Brown turns out to be too good?" Ellsworth queried.

"If Brown is corrupt, we may be able to use him," Lester started. "If he's really good, he may be able to correct those plates and whip those Chinamen into shape.

"If he's too good, we may have to turn him into fish bait, as well."

"Maybe we should just stop it now," Ellsworth stated.

"Not yet, if we can correct the errors we can take our next print and disappear into Mexico," Lester countered. "The U.S. has agreed to reimburse Mexico for the greenbacks found there. Then we can abandon this operation,"

"I don't want to go to Mexico," Ellsworth said. "I like the deal I have here."

"There's no need for you to go. I'll handle the Mexico end," Lester said. "I have friends there who just made off with a huge shipment of silver. Our greenbacks will go hand-in-hand with that shipment."

"It still makes me nervous," Ellsworth said. "I'll keep doing the distribution as long as the money's available. My end of the operation is still above suspicion."

Together, the two men settled on a means to determine Roger's value, or the danger he might pose.

Deputy McIntyre and Roger sat at a table in a small Houston diner and ordered coffee.

"What brings you to Houston, Rodney?" McIntyre said, swirling his spoon in his coffee.

"I guess you could say I'm a parolee trying to straighten my life out," Roger said, looking across the table to study the deputy's expression.

"Parolee, being a parolee brought you here?" McIntyre questioned in surprise.

"It's a long story, Bart," Roger said. "I was a Confederate war criminal and the Union got me off the hook in exchange for helping in this counterfeiting case."

"So, you were passing bad bills in the service?" McIntyre continued. "You can call me Mac, by the way. Everyone else does."

"Actually, Mac, a fellow war criminal I knew was the mastermind, I just did the grunt work," Roger said, trying to sound nonchalant but sincere.

"What happened to him?"

"He got away scot free," Roger answered. "I was the one who got caught and now I'm the one paying for it."

"What grunt work did you do that made you valuable to the Yanks?" McIntyre asked.

"I was helping to exchange Confederate money for greenbacks. We had to be careful because there was counterfeit money on both sides," Roger said, feeling more comfortable with his cover story. "They sent me here to help Agent Lester crack the case."

McIntyre let out a chuckle, sat back in his chair and eyed Roger. "Help Lester, huh, is he making any progress?"

"It seems the phony money may be coming on shore inside fish," Roger started, causing McIntyre to nearly spit out his coffee.

"Sorry, Rodney, the coffee was hotter than I thought. Please go on."

"Well, I guess the counterfeit currency is showing up in Houston, as well," Roger stated, watching McIntyre closely. "I'm guessing Sheriff Ellsworth and you deputies are helping track it down."

McIntyre cleared his throat, "Yes, but it's been difficult. Here,"

McIntyre said, tossing a greenback onto Roger's side of the table. "Can you tell if this is genuine?"

Roger hesitated a moment, then picked up the bill and took a hard look at it as if he really knew what he was looking at. "Not without a magnifying glass," he responded.

"Yeah, it's tough to tell," McIntyre said with a slight smirk. "Now you know what you're up against."

At that moment, Ellsworth and Lester entered the diner, spotted McIntyre and Roger, and came over to their table.

"Agent Brown, I'm going to assign you to help Sheriff Ellsworth," Lester said, with a half smile. "You'll have to work here in Houston though."

Roger thought a moment about visiting Nik in Galveston, but bit his tongue. "If that's what you need, Ron, I'll need a place to stay."

"We can put you up at the Houston Hotel," Ellsworth chimed in. "My department will help out with the additional expense.

"We'll arrange some space for you at the sheriff's office, since you will need security. My men will transport greenbacks from the bank to the office and you can inspect them there."

"I, ahh, I guess that will work out just fine. Whatever you men need," Roger said.

"Not at all," Lester offered. "You'll be doing us a huge favor and saving us plenty of time."

"Can I go back to Galveston with you to get my things?" Roger said, realizing he would have to get word to Nik.

"Not a problem. We'll head back this afternoon and you can report to Sheriff Ellsworth in the morning. The Henderson's got a nine o'clock commuter you can catch if you're ready."

"I'll see to it. And thanks again," Roger said.

On the train ride back to Galveston, Roger noted that Lester seemed to be more at ease and less distracted.

"I take it your discussion went well with Sheriff Ellsworth," Roger said to get the customs agent's attention.

"Oh, yeah," Lester responded, turning toward Roger. "I was happy we were able to get you set up with the Houston Sheriff's Department." With that, Lester turned back to face the front of the car and fell silent. Roger did the same.

After returning to the hotel, Roger got a note from Nik saying he would be in his room when he returned. Roger went up to his own room and then retreated to the area below the lobby where Nik's apartment was located. After knocking, he was invited in.

"Well, James Dunwoody Bulloch, did you crack the counterfeiting case?" Nik said, smiling and holding out a glass of brandy. "Won't you join me?"

"I will," Roger said, as both laughed, considering Roger's past history imbibing alcohol. "Who knew I wouldn't learn to handle the stuff until I became a preacher?" That brought a second laugh, as Nik poured his brother the spirit. "By the way, who did you call me?"

"James Dunwoody Bulloch," Nik repeated. "He was the Confederate spy who got the British to help finance the South during the war."

"Oh yeah? Whatever happened to him?" Roger asked advisedly.

"You know, I don't know," Nik said. "He's probably still prowling around London, I suppose."

"Or floating in the Thames," Roger cracked.

"Seriously though, did you find out anything?" Nik asked.

"I am going to be the chief counterfeit bills inspector for the city of Houston. By the way, what do you know about Houston Sheriff Ed Ellsworth?"

"He's a bigot, what more do you need to know?" Nik answered.

"Other than that, is he a straight shooter, a good lawman?" Roger quizzed.

"He's got a great job, a fine office, plenty of deputies and apparently lives well," Nik said. "He was always rude to Ambrose and me, but I never thought of him as a crook."

"He and Lester are pretty cozy, and they put together this job for me. I'm not sure how I'm going to be able to fake reading counterfeit bills," Roger added. "Also, I'll be living in Houston and working out of the sheriff's office.

"By the way, I think Lester is aware his fish story is beginning to smell," Roger said.

"Sebastian said he has something to help you identify those bills," Nik started. "He's also been watching that warehouse in Houston that Lester seems to frequent. If Ellsworth is in on this, I think you may be able to take the lid off this mystery."

"By the way, his deputy, Bart McIntyre, nearly spit his coffee on men when I mentioned the stuffed fish angle."

"Just do what you can, brother," Nik said. "Where will you be staying in Houston? We'll set up a meeting in the next day or so, maybe at the Cotton Gin, and decide on our next move."

After a brief toast and farewell, Roger departed to his room.

The next day, the new deputy-turned-customs agent took the train to Houston and the city's sheriff's office. Ellsworth was out but the office clerk showed Roger his designated office. It was adjacent to the sheriff's office and filled with dozens of boxes containing reports and old wanted posters.

After shoving several boxes aside, Roger noticed a door near the rear of his "office" leading into a small room behind Ellsworth's office. Roger tried to open it, but the door did not budge.

Toward the front of the office, a few feet from the entrance, was a desk and chair that had been recently brought in. Roger assumed it was his and attempted to remove as much clutter from around it as he could. There was nothing on the desk, and after inspecting the drawers, he found them empty as well.

The space was spartan, but Roger thought some of the stored records might prove valuable. However, he knew he couldn't take the chance of getting caught rifling through them.

After his initial assessment, Roger simply sat with his hands folded on his desk. It did not take long before Ellsworth burst into the room.

"I see you've made yourself at home," the sheriff said, almost laughing at the cramped quarters. "I'm sorry about the mess, but this serves as our storage room. Arrange things as you see fit. If you need anything, just ask Jake at the front desk. He's been told to get you whatever you need – even coffee."

"Thanks, Sheriff," Roger said. "I think I will start with that coffee."

"I'll let Jake know, Rodney, and please call me Ed. The sheriff thing is too formal."

"Thanks again… Ed," Roger replied. "Ah, when can I expect to receive some of that bank money?"

"The bank holds those greenbacks until there's enough to make the delivery worthwhile," Ellsworth said. "In the meantime, acquaint yourself with Houston. I think you'll like it. Stop in at the bank and introduce yourself. Jake will give you directions.

"I think Ron made arrangements for you at the Houston Hotel, so check that out sometime today. Until then, I'll be in and out so catch me when you can should you need me."

"I'll take you up on all that, Ed. I'm sure I can find my way around just fine. Thanks again."

Ellsworth retreated, leaving Roger to continue settling in. The office clerk, Jacob Doberman, entered with a cup of coffee. Doberman was a slightly-built, middle-aged man sporting a trimmed mustache and a bald pate left uncovered by a shaded visor. He had on a pair of sleeve garters and looked every bit like a clerk should.

"Thank you, Jake is it?" Roger said, as the office attendant set Roger's coffee on his desk.

"Yes, sir, Jacob Doberman, but folks call me Jake," Doberman said. "Can I get you anything else?"

"Not just yet," Roger replied. "I'll probably need some things after my real work begins."

"Just ask," Doberman said. "I'll be out front until I leave for the day around five o'clock."

Roger had noticed a small window directly in the back of the office and made his way close enough to look outside. In the open space behind the office sat a buckboard wagon he assumed was used to transport evidence – even a dead body or two.

He heard Ellsworth's voice in the outer office and hurried back to his desk. The sheriff spoke a few words to the clerk and said he would return later. With Ed gone and little to do, Roger decided to head over to his hotel and check out his room.

"I'm Rodney Brown," Roger said to the clerk at the Houston Hotel counter. "I believe you have a room for me."

"Mr. Brown, a U.S. customs agent, right?" the clerk said, turning to the rack of keys behind him. "Room 215 – just up the stairs and to your right. By the by, there's a telegram for you as well."

Roger took both the key and telegram from the clerk and started for the stairs. Before he started up, he saw an older gentleman come out of a door located behind the stairwell. As Roger glanced at the telegram, he heard the older man speaking Spanish to the clerk. The clerk responded in Spanish and the old man returned and vanished out the door he came through.

"Pardon my curiosity," Roger said to the clerk. "Where does the door that gentleman went through lead to?"

"That's hotel steerage," the clerk said, with a slight smile. "It used to be the hotel's livery stable and we now use it when Mexicans or former slaves need a place to stay, even had an Indian stay down there once. Don't worry, they are not allowed on the main floors."

"I see," Roger said, turning toward the stairs to the second floor. "I'll try not to worry, thanks."

After reaching the landing and turning right, Roger again glanced at the telegram.

"COTTON GIN BOARDING HOUSE – STOP – 7 PM – STOP – NB – STOP"

Roger grinned and made his way to room 215, stepped inside, and locked the door behind him.

After putting away what few things he had, Roger took a short walking tour of Houston. He visited the Bank of Houston and introduced himself to its president, John Halliburton.

The bank president told Roger there were three mercantile stores in Houston that operated as branch banks. They all sent most of their day's deposits to the Bank of Houston for safekeeping. The Houston Bank separated out greenbacks and sent them to the sheriff's office for inspection.

"Any gold, silver or other bullion is shipped by rail onto the First National Bank in Galveston," Halliburton said. "We do try to keep an eye on the counterfeit currency that has been circulating. We didn't discover the problem until about the time your boss, Agent Ron Lester, showed up. He's been a good deal of help to us."

Roger thanked Halliburton, departed, and crossed the street to the livery stable and retrieved a horse. He asked the stable manager for the shortest route to Freedmen's Town.

After reaching the village, he entered the Cotton Gin, where Nik was waiting for him. Nik nodded his head, giving Roger directions, and the two disappeared into the hallway. At the end of the hallway, Nik knocked three times on the door farthest from the lobby and walked in, Roger followed.

"Ahh, the Brinkman brothers," Sebastian Mason said, rising from his chair to greet the former deputy marshal. "Roger, I can't thank you enough for the assistance you give us, both spiritual and statutory."

"Sebastian," Roger said, removing his hat. "Your presence gives me greater pleasure knowing Nik is in the company of such capable assistance."

"I will reserve comment until we wrap up this counterfeiting corruption. I do hope your presence will help bring justice to this misdeed," Sebastian said. "By the way, I have something for you."

Agent Mason reached into his pocket and produced a small en-cased eyepiece. "This will help you. It was specially developed to detect these counterfeit bills. When you peer through this ocular piece, you will be able to detect forged from genuine. A government issue greenback will appear blue under the eyeglass, a counterfeit bill will remain green."

"Terrific," Roger responded. "I was worried they would discover me as a fraud, since I would have had no idea how to make that distinction otherwise."

"Take good care of that monocle. Lester is unaware of it, for good reason. We want him to think he's getting away with his criminal chicanery." Mason added.

"What should I do if the bills I inspect are all counterfeit?"

"Report it," Nik broke in. "Chances are that is all you will find. We only want to see what Lester does with the money after that."

"I would not do that," Mason interrupted. "Discovering that his counterfeiting operation was compromised could be dangerous. If Lester has already killed two men to cover up his crime, why not make it three?"

"Good point," Nik said. "I spoke much too soon."

"Roger, my guess is you've been trying to convince Lester that you're willing to join in his nefarious operation. I believe he will test you by mixing a few good bills with the spurious cash to see if you can tell the difference," Mason continued. "After stating that all the bills you've inspected are genuine greenbacks, give Lester two bills, one good and one bad, requesting his opinion. He will know one is genuine and will either fire you or take you into his confidence.

"If he fires you, you're done. If he agrees with you, you're in."

"Meanwhile, we'll keep watch on that warehouse," Nik said, "That way we'll be close if you need us."

"We're closing in, gentlemen," Mason added. "Remain vigilant but also be very careful."

Chapter 28
Blood Justice

Roger Brinkman, masquerading as U.S. Customs Agent Rodney Eugene Brown, carried a magnifying glass for show and an eyepiece for authenticity into the Houston Sheriff's Office. He was greeted by Doberman, the clerk.

"Agent Brown, I was asked to tell you that a shipment of money will be delivered here for your inspection. I'm, told Deputy McIntyre is on his way with it."

"Excellent," Roger responded, now confident in his ability to identify counterfeit greenbacks. "I'll be in my office when they get here."

Roger entered the office and sat down at his desk. He reached into his pocket to make sure he had the monocle Sebastian Mason had given him. He also pulled out McIntyre's five-dollar bill the deputy had handed him at the diner.

Roger scanned the bill with the ocular device and wasn't surprised that it did not appear blue. He wondered if McIntyre knew it was counterfeit, and that was why he didn't ask for it back.

Roger's thought pattern was suddenly interrupted by the sound of a wagon pulling up in back. He peered outside to see McIntyre lift two moneybags out of the wagon and disappear through the backdoor of the room next door. A moment later, he entered Roger's office and laid the sacks on his desk.

"Have fun, Agent Brown," McIntyre said with a sly smile. "We'll be anxious to hear what you find."

"By the way, here's that five-dollar bill you gave me yesterday," Said Roger.

"Hang on to it," McIntyre said. "Let me know if you can figure out if it's good or not. If it is, I'll reclaim it."

After the deputy left, Roger laid the magnifying glass on the table along with several bills. While going through them, he discovered a blue ten-dollar bill. He used the magnifying glass to examine it. After comparing it to a counterfeit ten, he could detect minor differences but nothing conclusive. He took each over by the window to examine them side by side with the naked eye and was amazed at how similar they were. Returning to the rest of the money, Roger also found a blue five-dollar bill and a twenty.

It was exactly as Mason had predicted, the genuine greenbacks had been planted. He placed the good bills into his desk drawer along with matching counterfeit ones, keeping them separate. He then refilled the money sacks with the rest.

"How is it coming, Agent Brown?" Sheriff Ellsworth said, bursting into the room without knocking.

"Oh, Sheriff, Ed …, glad to see you," Roger responded. "I can confirm these are all genuine greenbacks."

"Terrific," Ellsworth exclaimed. "I will run this money by the mayor so we can use it for payroll."

"I can't let you do that just yet," Roger cautioned. "I'll need Ron's authorization to do that."

Ellsworth looked at Roger for a moment before speaking, "Certainly, good point. I have a meeting with Ron in the morning. I'll put that money in safekeeping until then, thanks."

While Ellsworth was carrying the money sacks into his office, he nodded to Deputy Vickers to follow him in. Once the two were behind closed doors, Ellsworth motioned for Vickers to sit and the sheriff pulled up a chair next to him.

"Ted, Lester and I aren't sure about this new customs agent," Ellsworth began in a low voice. "I want you to put a tail on him and report to me tomorrow morning at the Panhandle diner. Lester and I will be having breakfast there."

"No problem, boss. Shall I look for anything in particular?"

"Just gather as much information as you can," Ellsworth said through clenched teeth. "It could mean the difference between life and death."

"Yes, sir," came the reply, and Vickers returned to his desk.

Roger decided to examine a few more bills with the magnifying glass to see if he could find any discrepancies. While doing so, he was disturbed by a scuffling sound coming from the room behind the locked door. He approached the door to it in his office and listened. Convinced someone was in the room, he tried again to open it but to no avail – the noise stopped.

Roger made a quick exit and crossed the main office to knock on Ellsworth's door. He entered to see the sheriff coming out of the back room and quickly closing the door behind him.

"Can I help you?" Ellsworth said, staring at Roger.

"Oh, sorry, Ed, I… ah, I was wondering if any more shipments of cash were expected today."

"Not that I know of, why?" Ellsworth asked.

"Oh, just curious, if it's okay I've got some errands to run," Roger answered.

"Sure, sure that's fine. Just go about your business," Ellsworth said, sliding into his chair behind the desk.

Roger closed his office door and left to ride back to Freedmen's Town and report his findings, unaware that Deputy Vickers was following him.

Meanwhile, Nik, Ambrose and Agent Mason were keeping a close watch on the locked warehouse just outside of Freedmen's Town. Before long, a buckboard wagon pulled around in back of the building. They saw the driver climb down from the wagon and unlock the chain securing the two, large back doors.

The doors swung open and two small individuals came out carrying large sacks. They placed the sacks in the back of the wagon and hurried back into the building. The wagon driver closed the doors behind them and refastened the chain. He boarded the wagon and then rolled out of the alley and headed in the direction of Houston.

"I recognize him," Ambrose said. "He was on the train with me when we made that silver shipment."

"You're right, Ambrose, he's one of Ellsworth's deputies," Nik replied. "Where do you suppose he's headed?"

"I would say either to the bank or wherever Roger is stationed," Sebastian said. "I do believe those two men who brought out the sacks were of Asian ancestry. Gentlemen, I believe it's time to investigate, won't you join me?"

Assuming only the two Asian men were in the warehouse, Mason produced an odd-shaped key. He placed the key into the lock and then looked down as he gently probed the padlock. Within a matter of seconds, the lock popped open. The agent signaled for Nik and Ambrose to draw their guns as he removed the chain and opened the two doors. What the lawmen saw were two frightened men huddled together in the middle of a dark room.

"As I feared," Sebastian said. "Lester has been keeping these men captive in order to do his dirty work."

"That's reason enough to arrest Lester, or at least arrest that deputy, don't you think?" Nik asked.

"Not yet," Mason responded. "Let me interrogate these two to see what they know. In the meantime, inspect what appears to a printing press to produce counterfeit bills. Just look at the reams of paper and containers of ink. This was quite an operation.

"Ambrose, why don't you make sure the front door is locked and remain there just in case Lester shows up," Nik instructed.

"And if he does?" Ambrose asked.

"Stay in the shadows and let him come through. Then block his escape and we'll arrest him. In the meantime, we'll collect evidence."

Fortunately, one of the Chinese laborers being questioned by the agent spoke some English. Nik began gathering uncut sheets of counterfeit bills and searched for the plates used to replicate the greenbacks. "Wait," Sebastian said. "Let's not disturb anything before we hear from Roger. If Lester finds out we've discovered this place, our cover is blown and perhaps even your brother's."

"What about these two?" Nik replied, looking at the two Chinese printers.

"From what I understand, no one is expected until tomorrow,"

Sebastian advised. "They say they're safer if they remain here. Their presence should assuage suspicion of our intrusion."

At that moment, Roger was passing by the warehouse when Ambrose spotted him and hailed him inside. They entered the back room.

"What have we here?" Roger called out, prefacing his question with a whistle. "It looks like you guys have broken this case wide open. However, I do have something that might interest you."

"Let's hear it, brother," Nik said, looking up from his search.

"Deputy McIntyre brought me a couple sacks of money from the bank…" Roger began.

"Those probably weren't from the bank, Roger. My guess is they were from here," Nik countered. "We watched him pick up the sacks and ride off in a buckboard."

"That explains why very few passed inspection, but here is the interesting part," Roger said. "When I told Ellsworth they were all good, he wanted to use the money for payroll."

"That means they're distributing this through the government," Sebastian cut in.

"Did you give all that money to Ellsworth?" Nik queried.

"Like Sebastian said, I found three bills that were genuine using his eyepiece," Roger added. "I told Ellsworth I couldn't release the cash until Lester authorized it."

"Wise thinking, we need Lester's approval of that money," Mason offered. "Why don't we meet tonight and devise a continuance strategy."

"Let's meet at Leathers' for dinner," Nik said, turning to his deputy. "Sound good to you, Ambrose?"

"Music to my hungry ears," Ambrose said, smiling.

Ambrose let Roger out the front door and locked it behind him. Vickers was positioned between two buildings across the street. He didn't get a good look at Ambrose, but assumed him to be the deputy marshal from Galveston. Vickers continued trailing Roger, while Nik, Ambrose, and Sebastian concluded their efforts before departing.

That evening, Rudy Leathers gave Nik, Roger, Sebastian and Ambrose a table in the back of the diner where they could talk undisturbed. Anticipating their efforts would be discovered, the four men devised a scheme to gather as much additional evidence as they could before making their move.

Roger relayed his plan of sneaking Nik and Sebastian into the room behind Ellsworth's office to eavesdrop on Lester's and the sheriff's conversation. Roger added that he could use his knowledge of the counterfeit money to gain their confidence in making "Brown" a part of their operation.

"Don't go too far," Nik advised. "If we have to come to the rescue we may never find out who killed Lenny and Letterman."

"It's risky, dear brother, but I think it's our best shot at busting up this ring and convicting those two."

"He's right," Sebastian said to Nik. "But we'll have to remain vigilant as to their intentions. My assumption is it will be a fine line between gaining their trust and falling prey to homicide."

"Your eloquence is frightening," Nik said, forcing a smile and reluctantly agreeing to the plan.

Early the next morning, the four men gathered behind the sheriff's office, well before anyone was scheduled to arrive. Sebastian used his utility key to unlock the back door, only to discover it was chained from the inside.

"There must be something of value in there to chain it like that," Nik said.

"Nik, if you and Sebastian can crawl through that window there's a door in my office that's adjacent to that room," Roger suggested. "It's locked, but I don't think it's chained because it's never used."

Nik went over to try the window. "The window is locked from the inside," he quietly announced.

"Let me try it," Sebastian offered. The treasury agent removed a glass-cutting tool along with a short dowel and some resin from a small pouch attached to his waist. After sticking the dowel to the window using the resin, Sebastian cut out the pane near the widow latch and used the dowel to pull it out, handing it to Roger. The agent reached in, unlocked the window and opened it. Ambrose provided the lift and soon both Sebastian and Nik were inside.

"We'll work on getting these doors open," Nik said, speaking through the window. "Roger, when the clerk arrives, enter that way. Ambrose, find a place to keep out of sight and be ready to lend a hand if anything goes wrong."

Nik then closed the window and stacked some boxes in front of it.

When Doberman arrived, he expressed surprise to see Roger waiting for him.

"Do you have urgent business, Agent Brown?" Doberman asked.

"Agent Lester arrives today and I want to have everything ready for him," Roger answered deadpan.

Doberman shrugged and unlocked the front door. Roger went straight to his office and closed the door behind him. Nik stepped out from behind the boxes and signaled to Roger. As Roger approached, he noticed the side door was already open and was shocked at what he saw inside.

"So, this is where they keep all the counterfeit money," Roger said in a whisper.

"Apparently so," Nik answered. "We have evidence against Ellsworth, now we have to connect Lester."

Sebastian and Nik positioned themselves inside the money room where they could hear any conversation taking place in Ellsworth's office.

Roger returned to his office and sat down to wait.

Vickers found Ellsworth and Lester seated at a table in the Panhandle eatery. He pulled up a chair next to the two men.

"Well, what have you got, Ted?" Ellsworth inquired, tossing his napkin on the table and turning to his deputy.

"I don't know if you're going to like this, boss, but I saw Brown go into the factory and come out again later. I think that giant deputy marshal from Galveston was at the door when he left," Vickers said.

"I was afraid of that," Lester growled. "I had hoped I wasn't spotted coming out of that place, but I had no idea Brinkman and his deputy were staying in Freedmen's Town. They must have gotten wise and broke in."

"That still doesn't implicate us," Ellsworth said. "There's nothing there to tie that place to us, and those Chinamen can barely speak English. Besides, they'll keep quiet if they know what's good for them."

"That's not all," Vickers continued. "I followed Brown back to Freemen's Town last night, where he had dinner with the Galveston marshal and his deputy."

"There's something strange going on between Brown and that marshal," Lester started. "Did I mention that it was Brinkman who introduced Brown to me? And, get this, Brown said the marshal checked him into the Globe House. I found that strange since the marshal and Brown were supposed to have just met. Who does something like that for a stranger?"

"The Good Samaritan," Vickers said, looking kind of embarrassed that he said it.

"What are you talking about? Ellsworth interjected, looking at his deputy.

"Sorry, boss, it's just something my Ma taught me a long time ago. I didn't mean nothin' by it," Vickers said, sheepishly. "But there is one more thing. There was this dapper dude, also a white guy, who ate with them."

"Dapper dude, what did he look like?" Lester said, taking a deeper interest in Vickers' report.

"Just some guy with them in a nice suit and wearing a derby hat," Vickers answered.

"Sebastian Mason," Lester hissed through his teeth. "He's the last person I wanted to see."

"Who is Sebastian Mason?" Ellsworth asked.

"He's a super-sleuth type who works for the Treasury Department. I think he was good friends with Foster Letterman," Lester said, pushing himself away from the table. "If that's who it is, we'd better get rid of Brown, and fast."

"How do you propose we do that?" Ellsworth said.

The men lowered their conversation, as they laid out a scheme to rescue their operation.

Roger was sitting behind his desk, innocently viewing greenbacks with his magnifying glass when Ellsworth and Lester walked into his office.

"Gentlemen, good morning," Roger greeted, receiving a grunt and nod in return. "I've kept out a couple bills for you, Ron. I believe they're both genuine greenbacks, but I told Ed your approval would be needed."

Roger handed Lester two bills from his desk drawer. Lester held the bills up and appeared to study them closely. He looked squarely at Roger for several seconds and said, "You're right, Rodney, these are genuine."

"Splendid," Ellsworth said. "I have the money in safekeeping and will report this to the mayor. We can use this money to meet payroll.

"Now, if you'll excuse us, Ron and I have some things to discuss," the sheriff added.

"Ah, gentlemen," Roger replied, before Lester could speak. "I would like to join you, if I may."

Lester bit his tongue, "What a coincidence, Rodney, I was going to suggest the very same thing. What do you say, Ed?"

"Sure, why not," Ellsworth answered. "Let's go into my office."

Vickers was at his desk with his head down when the three men passed by heading into Ellsworth's office. Vickers glanced over at McIntyre with a wry smile.

"What's on your mind, Agent Brown?" Ellsworth said, as the three men took a seat.

At the sound of Ellsworth's voice, Nik and Sebastian put their ears to the office wall.

"Gentlemen, I think you both know those greenbacks are counterfeit," Roger started. "Now, if you're willing to cut me in on this, I have a plan that can make us all rich."

"How do you know we weren't testing you by giving you those phony greenbacks?" Lester said.

"I couldn't be sure until you went along with what I said," Roger answered. "Otherwise you should have fired me on the spot, but you didn't. I even gave you a good bill and a bad one, which was a dead giveaway."

"Clever, Brown," Lester said. "What made you so sure about what you had found?"

"I didn't come here empty handed," Roger continued. "Before leaving Washington I was given precisely what I needed to destroy this operation."

"So, if you're so certain, why not turn your evidence over to the government?" Ellsworth queried.

"In case you haven't figured it out, I'm not in this to do a job, I'm in it for money. And thanks to what I've learned working for the government, I know how to get them to buy back these greenbacks in gold," Roger stated.

Nik and Sebastian looked at one another surprised by Roger's stealth.

"Gold, what makes you so sure you can do that?" Lester said.

"Oh, no, I'm too shrewd for that. I didn't escape hanging by being stupid. No, if I tell you my plan you'll do away with me like you did with those two in Galveston," Roger said.

"Whoa, wait a minute, what are you trying to accuse us of now?" Lester said, flashing an angry look at Roger.

"Let's cut to what's important here, gentlemen," Roger began. "It didn't take long to figure out the fish smuggling story was a hoax. And now that I've seen what's going on here, I thought this to be too good to be true. So, if you want me to keep quiet, you'd better cut me in."

"What's to keep us from killing you now? Lester growled. "Do you expect us to believe that story about the government buying this stuff?"

"Washington's on to you, Ron," Roger said, a little nervous that he may be taking his story a little too far. "If anything happens to me you're the one they're coming after."

"You're bluffing," Lester snarled.

"Let's hear him out," Ellsworth said, giving Lester a nod. "You've got nothing on me. What if I wanted to do away with you?"

"Ed, I'm sorry to say, you have been compromised as well," Roger countered. "We know about all the money you have in the back room. Have you been meeting payroll with that, too?"

Ellsworth lowered his head and turned his eyes up to look at Lester.

"How do we know we can trust you, Brown?" Lester said.

"You can't, really," Roger said. "Only by cutting me in can you be sure of my silence."

"I suggest we show Brown the 'factory,'" Lester said.

"Do you think that's wise?" Ellsworth responded.

"If we bring Brown in, then he's in. He might even be able to bring our plates back up to perfection."

"I'd like to see that factory, as you call it," Roger added, raising his voice to make sure Nik and Sebastian could hear.

"All right, the factory it is," Ellsworth said, rising from his chair and strapping on his gun belt. "I think you'll be pleasantly surprised, Agent Brown."

In the back room, Nik started to get up but Sebastian pulled him back down with his finger to his lips. "Hold on," he whispered, "they won't hurt Roger until they hear his scheme."

"But he doesn't have a scheme," Nik said, raising his whisper to its limit.

"When they leave, we'll lock up the two deputies and then head out for the 'factory' in all haste," Sebastian whispered. "We have the evidence we need, but not a full confession about those murders."

Nik looked as if he would burst, but held back until the three men vacated Ellsworth's office. Nik jumped to his feet to bolt for the door, but Sebastian restrained him, again holding his finger to his lips. Ellsworth could be heard talking in the main room.

"Lester, you go on ahead with Brown. I have something to discuss with my deputies."

Lester shook his head and motioned to Roger to follow.

When satisfied the three men had left, Mason swung the door open leading into Ellsworth's office. Nik marched across the office and burst into the main room.

"Gentlemen, you are all under arrest," Nik called out, his pistol in hand.

"What the…" Ellsworth blurted out, standing between Vickers and McIntyre.

"Sheriff, you're still here?" Nik said, surprised by Ellsworth's presence. "You make it too easy. I want you all to move into the jail room."

"Not so fast, Marshal," came a voice from behind Nik and Sebastian. Nik turned to see Doberman holding a shotgun.

Ellsworth and his deputies drew their guns.

"If you're smarter than you look, Marshal, I suggest you drop the gun and you and your dandy friend raise your hands," Ellsworth said with a broad smile.

Nik lowered his pistol to the floor. As he stood next to Mason, the two began to raise their hands. Suddenly, a derringer shot rang out and Vickers dropped to the floor. Both Nik and Sebastian dove behind a desk just as a shotgun blast was heard. McIntyre let out a groan as an errant shotgun slug ripped into his arm.

Nik grabbed his pistol, but held his position behind the desk between himself and Ellsworth. The sheriff was crouched behind McIntyre's desk.

"Marshal, you're right in my sights," Doberman said. "That desk only offers you protection from one side."

"Better listen to him, boy. Better taking your chances on a hangin' rather than being blown apart by a shotgun," Ellsworth called out.

Nik turned just in time to see Doberman flying across the room after being struck by a huge fist. Ambrose ducked behind the clerk's counter just as a bullet from Ellsworth's pistol hit the wall behind him.

Nik rose up firing in the direction of the sheriff, hitting him in the chest. Ellsworth staggered back as Nik fired a second time, sending the corrupt lawman to the floor.

"You can come out now, Ambrose," Nik called out, turning in his deputy's direction. Again, a bang sounded and the marshal wheeled around in time to see a hole in McIntyre's forehead as he slid from his desk followed by the pistol in his hand.

Mason stood up from the crouched position from which he had fired.

"My gratitude, Marshal, your brave actions gave me just enough time to reload my derringer," Sebastian said, smiling.

Ambrose had walked over and was helping Doberman to his feet, while holding the clerk's shotgun in his other hand.

"Let me check and make sure no one else is able to shoot," Nik said, cautiously inspecting the three downed lawmen. Two were dead, only Vickers was still alive.

Nik looked around satisfied, but realized the job wasn't done.

"Wait a minute," he exclaimed. "We need to go after Roger!"

Chapter 29
Wet and Wild

When Roger and Lester reached the end of Baker Street, Lester turned left, catching Roger by surprise.

"Where are you going, Brown?" Lester called out to Roger, who had turned his horse to the right.

Roger realized his error, since "Brown" would not have known in what direction the printing warehouse was located.

"I'm sorry, Ron, I just assumed we'd be headed in this way,"

"And, why would you think something like that?" Lester snarled.

Roger realized Lester had no intention of taking him to the "factory." It was now obvious that the customs agent and Ellsworth had no intention of taking him in as a partner in the counterfeiting operation.

"Just a stupid move on my part, Ron," Roger offered, knowing his situation was now grave.

"Don't think Ed and I don't know what you're up to, Brown," Lester said, throwing back his jacket to expose his holstered pistol. "Consider yourself on trial here. Its best you stick close to me or I will shoot you as if you were a prisoner trying to escape. And, Ed will back me up on that."

Roger now regretted that he had avoided wearing a gun, thinking being unarmed would help ensure his cover story.

"I don't understand, Ron. Aren't we partners in this thing?"

"Let me put it this way," Lester said. "What you do between now and where we're going could be the difference between you living or dying."

Roger thought it best to cooperate in hopes Nik and the others would not be far behind. However, he knew Lester wasn't taking him to the warehouse. He figured his best chance was to convince Lester he was a willing double agent.

"All right, I'll be straight with you," Roger began. "I was able to find out the location of your factory by sticking close to that lawman Nik Brinkman, like you asked. He told me where they believed the counterfeiting was being done. But that doesn't mean I don't want to be a part of what you and Ed have going."

"Play your cards right and that still might happen," Lester said. "Now follow me and don't try anything stupid."

Lester led Roger to a nearby livery stable where they dropped off their horses. From there, the two men boarded a trolley bound for the train station.

"The Galveston commuter train is due. I have our tickets to board," Lester instructed. "Stay in front of me and do as I say."

When boarding the train, the two men entered the last car and occupied seats across from each other near the back. Another couple was also seated near the front of the car, and when the conductor entered, Lester got up and approached him. Roger could see Lester was instructing the conductor and, when their conversation ended, the customs agent returned to his seat.

Roger noticed that the conductor leaned over to speak to the other two passengers, who left their seats and vacated the car. The conductor then nodded to Lester and also left.

"May I ask where we're going and why?" Roger queried.

"Isn't it obvious, we're on the train to Galveston," Lester said. "I have business to take care of there."

Roger wasn't sure he liked the sound of that and decided to probe a little further.

"What business might that be?"

"Not that it matters to you right now, but I'm expecting a telegram from Washington," Lester started. "I sent a telegram to a friend of mine back there giving him your information. He will either confirm or deny that you're telling the truth. That's your best bet right now."

Roger's hopes sank. Washington did provide his cover, but that didn't mean that everyone there was in the game. If Lester's contact was indeed a friend, he might well inform Lester that Rodney Eugene Brown is a fraud.

"That ought to clear me," Roger said, hoping for a positive response from his companion. "What did you say to the conductor, anyway?"

"I told him you were my prisoner and that if you tried and funny business I might have to shoot you," Lester said, turning and smiling at Roger. "That's why I had him clear out that other pair."

Realizing that Nik and the others would not be coming to his rescue, Roger closed his eyes and began to pray.

"You know, there is a way out of this."

The remark jolted Roger from his concentration. He opened his eyes to see the conductor in the seat in front of him. "What?" Roger asked.

"There is a way out of this, but you're going to have to be clever about it," the conductor said. "Without looking up, do you notice that cord that runs above the windows?"

Roger nodded.

"That's an emergency brake. If you can get to that and pull it, you may be able to get out of this situation alive," the conductor said.

"Thank you," Roger said in a whisper.

"What are you mumbling about over there?" Lester asked.

Roger looked over at Lester and then turned back to the conductor, who was no longer there.

"Ah, nothing," Roger said, turning again toward Lester. "I was just praying."

"Praying? Not a bad idea, but I'm surprised to hear that coming from you," Lester said. "Does praying work for a crook like you? That is, if you really are a crook."

Roger had been playing along with Lester in hopes of staying alive, but if what the agent said about that telegram to Washington was true, his cover would be blown. He now thought his best chance of survival was to get off this train. To do that, he would need to provoke Lester.

"Ron, I have to be honest with you," he said. "Marshal Brinkman is my brother."

"Marshal Brinkman is black," Lester said. "You did say you fought for the South, right?"

"Yes, I did," Roger replied.

"And now you want me to believe Nik Brinkman is your brother?" Lester said. "Look, if you're trying to save your hide, a confession like that isn't going to work in your favor."

"I'll come clean with you if you'll do the same for me," Roger offered.

"This ought to be good," Lester said, smiling. "Why don't you start?"

"Marshal Nik Brinkman really is my brother," Roger began. "My true identity is Roger Brinkman. I'm a minister."

Lester only stared for a moment. "A minister of what?" he asked.

"A minister of the Bible, I'm a preacher," Roger said.

"Those credentials from Washington said you were Customs Agent Rodney Brown," Lester responded. "If you're trying to pull something here then I'm not buying it. When that telegram arrives, your fate will be written on it."

"The Rodney Brown story was a complete fabrication," Roger blurted out. "It was cooked up so I could go undercover and find out what we could, like your alliance with Sheriff Ellsworth. Nik and Sebastian overheard everything."

"Sebastian, Sebastian who?" Lester queried.

"Treasury Agent Sebastian Mason, he knows you and set up this entire thing," Roger said.

At that moment, the conductor entered the car and said, "Five minutes until Galveston Bay, Agent." The conductor then made a quick exit.

"Mason, I should have guessed he would get involved," Lester said through clenched teeth. "I knew from the start that Letterman was a plant. I would like to do to Mason what I did to him."

"And what about the Galveston sheriff's deputy? You did the same to him too, right?" Roger quizzed.

"That punk, he was in over his head," Lester growled. "The captain... wait, why don't you shut up, Brown... Brinkman, whoever you are. Stand up!" Lester demanded, rising to his feet and drawing his pistol.

Roger pulled himself up using the seat in front of him. Looking through the window he could see the train had pulled onto the trestle crossing over Galveston Bay. He raised his hands as if in response to Lester holding his gun on him.

"You don't have to do..." before Lester could get the words out of his mouth, Roger slipped his hand under the emergency brake cord and pulled. The train's steel wheels screeched as the car lurched under the stress of the sudden brake. Lester pitched forward over the forward seat.

Roger was able to remain on his feet by holding onto the seat in front of him, hoping Lester would drop the gun. Although Lester fell awkwardly, he held onto his gun and shot wildly. Roger then burst through the rear door of the car and leaped from the landing area, whispering another prayer.

He splashed into the bay and remained underwater as bullets struck the surface leaving bubble trails behind them. Roger swam furiously in the direction of the trestle and did not come up for air until he was directly under it. He could hear the train chug as it again started down the tracks. Roger climbed on one of the piers that held the trestle aloft. He sat patiently until a nearby boat pulled up close enough to take him onboard.

Chapter 30
Promise Kept

United once again, Nik Brinkman took his brother, Roger, down to the beach to meet Abel Mosely. After catching up to the beachcomber, who served as the marshal's informant concerning the shipping operations that took place in Galveston Harbor, the men discussed Lester's whereabouts.

"He boarded one of those Sea Serpent ships named the Narwhale," Mosely said, concerning the last time Agent Ron Lester was seen. "He never came off that boat so he must be someplace where that ship sails."

"I do appreciate all your help, Abel," Nik stated. "I'm going to have a dinner in celebration of closing the counterfeiting case, despite the fact the criminal behind it has gotten away, for now."

"Much obliged, Marshal," Mosely said, "I would like that."

"We'll also celebrate the help my brother gave, and lived to tell about it," Nik added, smiling at Roger.

"I didn't mean to give you the anxious moments that I did," Roger said, laughing. "Good always triumphs over evil, but not always the way we would like."

After a brief farewell exchange, Nik and Roger left for the courthouse where they were to meet with Judge Jedediah Conklin. Ambrose waited for them in the marshal's office and then the three proceeded to the judge's quarters. When they entered, several people were there, including Sheriff Duke Atkins and his deputies, Senator Ashley Maxwell and Treasury Agent Sebastian Mason.

"Marshal Brinkman, thank you for coming," Judge Conklin said.

"I purposely did not tell you why I wanted to see you because I wanted this to be a surprise, if you will. With that, I will yield the floor over to Senator Maxwell."

Knowing Maxwell's feelings toward blacks were similar to those of former sheriff Ellsworth, Nik was a little puzzled why the senator was present.

"United States Marshal Brinkman, it is my pleasure to convey to you this certificate of appreciation for a job well done. It is signed by our president, Ulysses S. Grant and Secretary of the Treasury Lot M. Morrill. It is also signed by Edmund J. Davis, governor of the great state of Texas and of course by me, Senator Asley Maxwell, also of Texas.

"I must admit, Marshal, I was uncertain if a man of color could do the job," the senator continued, "but you have proven most capable, congratulations,"

"A round of applause, if you please," Maxwell said, scanning the room.

After the applause, Nik said, "Thank you senator, and may I also extend my deepest gratitude to Agent Sebastian Mason." All turned to acknowledge Sebastian. "And my brother, Roger Brinkman."

Maxwell immediately turned to Deputy Marshal Tucker, assuming him to be Nik's brother.

"I can see which one of you got most of the cornpone at the supper table," Maxwell said with a laugh, extending his hand to shake Ambrose's.

"No, senator, that is my deputy, Ambrose Tucker, who also deserves a vote of thanks. However, my brother is the man next to him," Nik said.

The senator froze, with an expression of bewildered embarrassment.

"Judge Conklin, would you explain what's going on here?" Maxwell requested.

"I think it best if Marshal Brinkman does that," Conklin said. "I've not met Nik's brother before."

"I am sorry about the confusion, senator, but you see I was raised by the Brinkman family," Nik started. "Although the law would not allow the Brinkmans to officially adopt me, they claimed me as their own anyway and Roger and I grew up together. The Brinkmans were Christian, and scolded me whenever I let prejudice and scorn get me down."

"Is this true, Mr.… Mr.?" the senator stammered, looking at Roger.

"Pastor, Senator, Pastor Roger Brinkman," Roger responded. "And yes, every word of it is true. In fact, we both fought in the war and he scolded me for fighting for the South. I'm ashamed to have to admit that, but Nik has forgiven me, right Nik?"

Nik gave Roger a wry look and then winked.

"Remarkable, truly remarkable," the senator muttered, shaking his head and turning to walk toward the group gathered in Judge Conklin's office.

"That is a remarkable and noble story," Conklin said. "And are you visiting, Pastor Brinkman?"

"I'm here to finish what our father could not," Roger answered, glancing over at Nik. "And that's to baptize my brother, right, Nik?"

"That happens today," Nik replied. "We will be gathering at Swan Lake on the mainland. There are some folks that will be meeting us there. Anyone wanting to witness is invited to attend. There will be food afterward," Nik concluded with a grin.

"Let me just say," Roger added, "God and the Brinkmans don't discriminate. So, anyone wanting to be baptized along with Nik, I'm offering it today for free, the way the Good Lord intended it to be."

Once again, there was a round of applause as the meeting broke up. Sebastian approached the Brinkmans and said, "I would love to witness. I just might indulge in the practice myself. Does it hurt?" he added with a laughing smile.

"Nothing in this world hurts less," Roger said, adding to the amusement.

After loading the necessary items into a buckboard rented from the livery stable in Galveston, Roger, Nik, Ambrose and Sebastian set out for the ferry. After crossing over to the mainland, they followed a crude trail leading to Swan Lake. Upon arrival, Esther

Boatman and her father were waiting, along with Madame Covington and Abel Mosely.

"Who do we have here?" Roger asked, as the four men climbed down from the buckboard.

"Roger, it is my great pleasure to introduce to you Madame Tillie Covington, Isaiah Boatman, and someone very dear to me, the lovely Esther Boatman."

Roger looked over at Nik, with a why-didn't-you-tell-me look.

"I had planned to tell you the moment you arrived in Galveston," Nik said, smiling broadly. "However, I didn't think we were going to meet in the middle of Galveston Bay. After what we went through, I didn't think it appropriate to lead with that, so I apologize for springing it on you this way.

"I hope you don't mind, because Esther and I would like to be baptized together."

"It is my sworn duty not to mind," Roger said, clasping Esther's hands in his, "but to baptize as many souls as Jesus presents to me."

After going in separate directions into a nearby stand of trees, Nik and Esther donned white robes, Nik with Ambrose's help and Esther with Tillie's assistance. They emerged together and joined hands as they approached Roger standing at the edge of the water.

"Thank you all for joining us today," Roger began, looking about at the small group of witnesses. He paused for a moment and said, "Where is Sebastian?"

"Wait for me," the agent said, stepping out of the trees wearing a long, white buttoned shirt that reached down to just above his knees. "You said I was welcome to join in this holiest of ceremonies."

"That you are," Roger said, chuckling at Sebastian's appearance. "But you will have to remove that Bowler Derby of yours."

After wading out into water up to their waists, Roger baptized each in turn and then presented them to those standing on shore and clapping. The four came out of the water and a picnic lunch was taken out of Covington's buggy and placed into the back of the buckboard. Four larger blankets were placed together on the ground where everyone sat except Nik and Esther, who both served those who were seated.

"So, Nik, what is going to happen to that pirate and his crew?" Roger asked.

"Depending on what they reveal, I think they'll eventually be sent back to Mexico to stand trial, which may or may not take place," Nik said, setting his plate aside and patting Esther on the arm in gratitude for the lunch. "I told Judge Conklin I would like to talk to Baudelaire and Paco before their release. There may be more to their story than we know.

"There's also the possibility of a manslaughter charge since the whereabouts of Casey Wyatt is still unknown."

"What about that Nelson character who jumped off the ship?" Roger asked.

"Ambrose, do you know what happened to him?" Nik inquired, turning to his deputy.

"Nelson was the seafaring gent deputized in Ellsworth's office, right?" Ambrose began and Nik nodded in the affirmative. "As far as I know, no one by that name came off the Navy vessel."

"Some things are not adding up," Nik said. "The only thing we've accomplished so far is to shut down the counterfeit operation and take out Sheriff Ellsworth and one of his men. Deputy Vickers will stand trial, but turning state's evidence could get him a light sentence.

"The silver shipment is gone to who-knows-where, as are Lester and Nelson. And we haven't heard from the captain of the barge who was fished out of the bay by the boat you were on, Roger."

"It sounds like you've still got your work cut out for you, Nik," Sebastian interjected. "If you need some help, I think I can get cleared to stay over for a while."

"We could definitely use the help," Nik said. "We still have a lot of greenbacks floating around, and we don't know what Lester worked out with the banks – if anything."

"Thankfully, Roger didn't lose my eyepiece during his little adventure," Sebastian remarked. "That will come in handy as far as clearing greenbacks for the banks."

"'Little adventure?'" Roger said with a chuckle. "My life was at stake. I wouldn't want to have to revoke that 'little' baptism, Sebastian."

All had a good laugh, as Nik chimed in.

"I don't suppose you would want to stay and help, Roger?" Nik asked, smiling broadly, which brought a laugh from the group. "We could sure use you."

"Not only as a marshal, but we need a good preacher in these parts, as well," Tillie chimed in. "Things kind of fell apart during the war and now we could use a church open to everybody."

"That's very tempting, Mrs. Covington, but I have a parish, so to speak, in the New Mexico Territory," Roger said. "Our purpose as saddle pastors is to help shepherd the flock scattered across the West."

"So, you're going to be leaving us now, Roger," Nik said. "We haven't had much of a reunion."

"Not right away, brother. Our visit got off to a rather 'western' start, so I intend to spend some peace time with you," Roger replied. "I'd like to get to know these folks you seem to have grown very close to," Roger concluded, smiling broadly at Esther, who blushed.

"We may need you in the not-too-distant future to perform another service now that we've done the baptisms," Nik said uttering a slight laugh. "I'd be pleased if you would get to know these folks better."

"Just promise me you won't ask me to be a deputy marshal again," Roger pleaded.

"I can't promise you that," Nik barked back. "The law isn't outside the realm of what you have now been called to do," Nik added with a straight face, surprising the others. "I know you preach salvation but the law is written on your heart. I see no reason why someone with your gifts can't help out now and again."

"Oh oh," Roger said, rekindling an even heartier laugh from all those present.

Roger spent the next week with Nik, as well as giving a deposition as to his findings during the investigation. The pastor decided to ride the rails as far as he could in returning to New Mexico. The brothers parted once again at a train depot.

"Well, brother, I guess we've come to the end of another adventure," Roger said, grasping Nik's hand. "Don't you go marrying that pretty Esther woman without me being here."

"The invitation will give you plenty of time to get here," Nik said. "And who knows, maybe the Marshals Service will have cause to send me out your way."

"For my sake, that would be great," Roger responded. "For your sake, I hope they don't."

The brothers hugged, said their goodbyes and Roger boarded the train.

As it rolled back over the bay, Roger was lost in thought. He watched the small breakers with a flood of memories going through his mind.

"Going far?" was heard from across the aisle.

"What?" Roger said, his thoughts interrupted.

"I was just asking if you were going far, señor," said a man sitting across from him.

The man was dressed in black with silver conchos running down the length of his pants. They also adorned the sleeves of his jacket and fastened the jacket in front. He had jet-black hair and a thin black mustache. A sombrero rested in his lap.

"Ah, the New Mexico Territory," Roger answered. "How about you?"

"A little farther south," the man said. "I am returning to Mexico. Have you ever visited there?"

"No, I've not been across the border," Roger replied, "Is Mexico nice?"

"Lovely, mi amigo," the man said. "For some reason, I do feel you will visit my country, and soon.

"Now, if you'll excuse me, I have some friends waiting for me in another car."

"Certainly, nice to meet you," he said, as the man made his way down the aisle and out of the car.

Roger sank back into his thoughts, when the conductor asked for his ticket.

Roger presented his ticket and asked, "Who is that Mexican gentleman dressed in black that was here a minute ago?"

"Sorry, sir, there's no one on this train that matches that description," the conductor answered, punching Roger's ticket. "Have a good trip, sir."

"I shall," Roger replied, looking up at the conductor with a puzzled look.

Roger sat back and thought about what the man had said: "I do feel you will visit my country, and soon."

Author's Note

I hope you enjoyed this book. Please consider giving it a 5-star rating and add a few words about your reading experience at your favorite online retailer.

The link below with a QR code will take you to the book's web page. From there, you can follow links to various online retailers.

Giving my book 5-stars and a short written review about why you enjoyed it will help me immensely.

Thank you!

Tim W. James

https://www.sastrugipress.com/iron-spike-press/counterfeit-justice/

Use your smart device to scan the QR code for the book's webpage.

Additional Books by Tim W. James

The Roger Brinkman Series

Blood Justice

Two brothers, one a preacher's son, the other
an adopted would-be slave, set out in opposite
directions to avenge their family's murder only
to cross paths in pursuit of the killer.

Counterfeit Justice

Preacher Roger Brinkman takes his crucifix
and his Colt to fulfill a promise and help his
lawman brother battle thieves, counterfeiters,
and murderers in the Old West.

Borderline Justice

Pursuing outlaws into Mexico, Preacher Rog-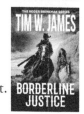
er Brinkman and his brother Nik team up to
recover a stolen U.S. Treasury silver shipment
only to find the truth they wanted was borderline at best.

Standalone Books

The Blind Man's Story

While on vacation, journalist Beau Larson
encounters a blind man high on a forested bluff.
This leads him to a brewing war between conservationists
and the timber industry, resulting in a mysterious murder.

About Tim W. James

Tim W. James has been a writer since grade school. When not writ-
ing, he continues his passion for athletics by playing golf and watching
his favorite sports teams. He and his family live in California.

Additional Iron Spike Press Books

Threads West (Large Print Edition)
Immigrants from Europe discover more than they bargained for when landing on the shores of America.

Maps of Fate (Large Print Edition)
The European settlers embark on their expedition west, only to discover their fates are inextricably linked to an unexpected map.

Uncompahgre (Large Print Edition)
The European immigrants are now wise to the ways of America but they soon find out what their knowledge is worth in the Rocky Mountains.

Moccasin Track (Large Print Edition)
A new generation of children finds that their parents' immigration to America created more than they bargained for.

Visit www.ironspikepress.com to learn more about these and other exciting titles. Thank you for your purchase!

Enjoy Additional Sastrugi Press Books

50 Florida Wildlife Hotspots by Moose Henderson Ph.D.

This is a definitive guide to finding where to photograph wildlife in Florida. Follow the guidance of a professional wildlife photographer as he takes you to some of the best places to see wildlife in the Sunshine State.

50 Wildlife Hotspots by Moose Henderson Ph.D.

Find out where to find animals and photograph them in Grand Teton National Park from a professional wildlife photographer. This unique guide shares the secret locations with the best chance at spotting wildlife.

Cache Creek by Susan Marsh
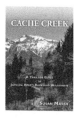
Cache Creek: A Natural Treasure in Jackson Hole's Backyard celebrates the wonders of nature in a way that is informative yet whimsical. This guide is a reference and keepsake for residents and tourists alike for the popular Jackson Hole area.

Journeys to the Edge by Randall Peeters, Ph.D.
What is it like to climb Mount Everest? Is it possible for you to actually make the ascent? It requires dreaming big and creating a personal vision to climb the mountains in your life. Randall Peeters shares his successes and failures and gives you some directly applicable guidelines on how you can create a vision for your life.

So I Said by Gerry Spence

Venture into the mind of America's most famous lawyer. He shares his thoughts on hope, love, oppression, power, and life. Gain insight from a man who has fought overwhelming power and won from small-town Wyoming.

The Burqa Cave by Dean Petersen

Still haunted by Iraq, Tim Ross finds solace teaching high school in Wyoming. That is, until freshman David Jenkins reveals the murder of a lost local girl. Will Tim be able to overcome his demons to stop the murderer?

The Diary of a Dude Wrangler by Struthers Burt

The dude ranch world of Struthers Burt was a romantic destination in the early twentieth century. He made Jackson Hole a tourist destination. These ranches were and still are popular destinations. Experience the origins of the modern old west.

Voices at Twilight by Lori Howe, Ph.D.

Lori Howe invites the reader into the in-between world of past and present in this collection of poems, historical essays, and photographs, all as hauntingly beautiful and austere as the Wyoming landscape they portray.

Use your smart device to scan the QR codes to visit website links.

Visit Sastrugi Press on the web at www.sastrugipress.com to purchase the above titles in bulk. They are also available from your local bookstore or online retailers in print, e-book, or audiobook form. Thank you for choosing Sastrugi Press.

www.sastrugipress.com
"Turn the Page Loose"

Use your smart device to scan the QR codes to learn more.
All titles available in print and ebook format.
Get your copies today!

Books by Sastrugi Press Polar Explorer Aaron Linsdau

2024 Total Eclipse Series
Sastrugi Press has published guides for the 2024 total eclipse crossing over the United States, Mexico, and Canada. Visit the Sastrugi Press website for the available 2024 total eclipse books: www.sastrugipress.com/eclipse.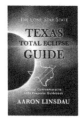

50 Jackson Hole Photography Hotspots
This guide reveals the best Jackson Hole photography spots. Learn what locals and insiders know to find the most impressive and iconic photography locations in the United States. This is an excellent companion guide to the *Jackson Hole Hiking Guide*.

Adventure Expedition One
by Aaron Linsdau M.S. & Terry Williams, M.D.
Create, finance, enjoy, and return safely from your first expedition. Learn the techniques explorers use to achieve their goals and have a good time doing it. Acquire the skills, find the equipment, and learn the planning necessary to pull off an expedition.

Antarctic Tears
Experience the honest story of solo polar exploration. This inspirational true book will make readers both cheer and cry. Coughing up blood and fighting skin-freezing temperatures were only a few of the perils Aaron Linsdau faced. Travel with him on a world-record expedition to the South Pole.

How to Keep Your Feet Warm in the Cold
Keep your feet warm in cold conditions on chilly ad- ventures with techniques described in this book. Packed with dozens and dozens of ideas, learn how to avoid having cold feet ever again in your outdoor pursuits.

Lost at Windy Corner

Windy Corner on Denali has claimed fingers, toes, and even lives. What would make someone brave lethal weather, crevasses, and avalanches to attempt to summit North America's highest mountain? Aaron Linsdau shares the experience of climbing Denali alone and how you can apply the lessons to your life.

The Most Crucial Knots to Know

Knot tying is a skill everyone can use in daily life. This book shows how to tie over 40 of the most practical knots for virtually any situation. This guide will equip readers with skills that are useful, fun to learn, and will make you look like a confident pro.

The Motivated Amateur's Guide to Winter Camping

Winter camping is one of the most satisfying ways to experience the wilderness. It is also the most challenging style of overnighting in the outdoors. Learn 100+ tips from a professional polar explorer on how to winter camp safely and be comfortable in the cold.

Use your smart device to scan the QR codes for website links.

Visit www.aaronlinsdau.com and join his email list. Receive updates when he releases new books and shows

Visit Sastrugi Press on the web at www.sastrugipress.com to purchase the above titles in bulk. They are available in print, e-book, or audiobook form.

Thank you for choosing Sastrugi Press.

"Turn the Page Loose"

About the Author

Aaron Linsdau is the second-only American to ski alone from the coast of Antarctica to the South Pole (730 miles / 1174 km). He set the world record for surviving the longest expedition ever for the Hercules Inlet to the South Pole route.

Aaron Linsdau at the South Pole.

Visit Aaron's YouTube channel: www.youtube.com/@alinsdau or scan the QR Code:

Made in the USA
Las Vegas, NV
20 September 2023

77860977R00198